ROAD TO OBLIVION
THE FOOTPATH BACK HOME

ROAD TO OBLIVION
THE FOOTPATH BACK HOME

A Novel of Discovery
Of Who We Are
And What Made Us The Way We Are
And Whether We Can Change Our Stories
And Be Who We Want To Be

ROB REIDER

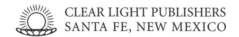
CLEAR LIGHT PUBLISHERS
SANTA FE, NEW MEXICO

To my wife, Barbara,
Who found me in the life I was in
And helped me
To the life I was meant to have,
And to my children, Kim, Michelle, and Heather,
And my dog, Brandee,
Who became a part of that life.

©2003 Rob Reider

Clear Light Publishers
823 Don Diego
Santa Fe, New Mexico 87505
www.clearlightbooks.com

First Edition
10 9 8 7 6 5 4 3 2 1

Library of Congress Cataloging-in-Publication Data

Reider, Rob, 1940-
   Road to oblivion : the footpath back home : a novel of discovery of who we are and what made us the way we are and whether we can change our stories and be who we want to be / Rob Reider -- 1st ed.
     p. cm.
  ISBN 1-57416-054-0
  1. Downsizing of organizations--Fiction. 2. Self-destructive behavior--Fiction. 3. Life change events--Fiction. 4. Businessmen--Fiction. I. Title.
  PS3618.E55 R63 2002
  813'.6--dc21

                               2002005213

PROLOGUE

William entered his office, possibly for the last time. What had once been his sanctuary, his escape from an ever-maddening world, was now steeped in pallor like a funeral home awaiting the deceased body. The body was his, no life left, a deflated shell and ego. He looked about the room—the room that had always given him great pleasure, the symbol of his success. The very things he had always secretly gloated over, now made him sad and depressed.

He looked down at his desk, an oversized, imported, genuine Philippine mahogany executive desk—the best that stockholders' money could buy. It had always impressed him, and he hoped it impressed others. The desk was a symbol of success that made him feel better than the others, the symbolic big "S" on his chest. He glanced at the papers strewn all about the desk and the floor— his overflow area. When anyone walked in his office, even when he was not present, the volume of work and debris would say to them, "This is a busy, important, indispensable man." Ha! Ha!

He looked back at his door that he had left open, which he had never left open before. As a way of saying good-bye to this life and, maybe, to any other, he read the name on his door. "William S. Bradford, III, Executive Vice President, Foods and Consumable Division." He thought to himself, "fucking big deal." William had never cursed, not even to himself. The room, which always brought in the sun and light, was now etched in gloom. "Holy shit," he continued to think, "it's downright dreary. I could grow mushrooms in the gloom of my desk, probably much more significant to humanity than the work lying there begging to be done."

William walked heavily over to his desk with his head seemingly down to his waist, his legs moving slowly like he was using a walker without wheels. He looked down at the work piled on his desk and began to laugh. All of those emergency projects and "ASAPs" were now dead ends. If they never got done it would be too soon. He picked up pile after pile and tossed them in the wastebasket. He might be angry and depressed, but he was still a neat guy. He felt he could still salvage little pieces of himself, whoever that was. Using the dragon-shaped cigarette lighter given to him by one of the company's Asian customers, he lit the pile of work in the wastebasket. He jumped like a kid in the air, clapped his hands and bitterly yelled "burn, baby, burn" as his lifework was cremated to ashes.

"Poetic justice," he was thinking. "You live by the sword, you die by the sword. I did what they told me, and they did it to me."

He sat in one of the eight leather high back visitor chairs. He had never done that before. They were always to be sparkling clean and ready for an important visitor. As Vice President, he had gotten plenty of visitors, but not any more. He put his feet up on another of the visitor's chairs, something he had never done before, and sat with his hands folded tightly against his chest. He could feel his heart beating against his shaking ribs while he looked out the floor-to-ceiling window wall. What had once been an impressive view of the entire downtown area was now a view of gluttony and greed; a world darkened by the death of the soul—in this case, his.

He sat in this depressed position for perhaps twenty minutes, which seemed like an eternity. He was a work of ice, a soft sculpture of a man no longer needed, a living corpse in repose. He became aware of someone behind him, someone talking loudly, perhaps yelling. It was his administrative assistant, Emily Bryson. She seemed to be yelling his name, but he couldn't recognize it. He looked over at Emily. He had never noticed how attractive she was and so young. In fact, he had never noticed anything about his assistants; they were just tools to him to get the job done. In fact, he had never realized she was there at all. His Assistant Vice President, Brad Myers, had hired her. People just weren't his thing. The nuts and bolts of work were his life; the people were only vehicles to get the work done. With his work gone, was he now one of those people?

"Mr. Bradford, Mr. Bradford, are you all right!" Emily kept yelling, directly in his ear. He turned around slowly, zombie like, and stared at her for what seemed like forever. My god, he thought, she really was attractive. But what did that matter to him? "Mr. Bradford, please say something." He started to speak, but nothing more than spittle came out of his mouth. He stuttered, and shut his mouth; it just wasn't working. "Mr. Bradford, can I get you something, some water, some medicine, some . . . ?" He nodded at the silver water pitcher on the desk. It was no longer his, but he could have some water, couldn't he? She walked over to get the water. He watched her walk away, swaying from one side to another. His thoughts strayed. "Son of a bitch, I should have noticed her before." She was more than merely attractive. "All work and no play makes William a dull boy. Ha! Ha!"

"Here, Mr. Bradford, drink this." She was holding a silver goblet in front of him. She was staring at him staring at her. She moved the goblet closer to his face and he automatically opened his mouth. He had become the baby, she the mother. He was scared. Just this morning he had the world by the *cajones*; now he didn't know if he had any himself. He sipped slowly at the water. He wasn't sure whether it was because he couldn't drink any faster or because he wanted to keep Emily there as long as possible, maybe forever. She was leaning over him and he could smell her perfume and feel the shape of her body. As she leaned closer, he could see the curve of her breasts rising from her bra. He had spent his adult life averting his eyes and keeping away from such temptations— he had work to do— and now he didn't know why he had. She finally pulled back. He was relieved, yet oddly at the same time displeased. He sat up and looked at her, as professionally as he could.

"What is it you wanted?" Even in depression, he could still function.

"Oh, Mr. Myers asked me to bring these reports to you. You know the ones you wanted on the new potato processing plant? This was my assignment."

He took the reports. He looked them over. They were very well done. She didn't know what had happened, but Brad probably did. Otherwise, he would never let an underling get credit for her work. He would have brought these reports to him under the guise that he had done them. This was Brad's way of playing the game and keeping threatening employees from undermining his position. What a prick, William thought, but he had been my prick—my hand-picked prick.

He looked as kindly as he could at Emily. It had always been an effort for him to be kind. "Miss Bryson, this looks like a thorough, competent job. Can you put the reports over there?"

She took the reports and started to place them on the top of the desk. She seemed surprised to find it empty. The few times she had been in his office, the desktop and the floor beside it were always overflowing with work. Everyone in the company knew that Mr. Bradford was the ultimate workaholic. He was unkindly known as WB, the Wicked Bastard.

"No, no, Miss Bryson, over there." He nodded at the wastebasket. "Over there."

She hesitated. She couldn't just throw the reports away. They represented over six months of work, mostly her own.

"Go ahead, it's okay. I'm the Executive Vice President," he laughed. "I'll make sure that you don't get into trouble." Hell, he thought, he wasn't sure if he would get in trouble, but, suddenly, he didn't care.

Reluctantly, she dropped the reports in the wastebasket. She noticed the ashes covering the bottom of the basket. She looked over at Mr. Bradford. Something was strange, he was strange, but she knew it was none of her business. She had no need to know. If WB wanted to burn his whole office down, so be it. She turned to go.

He looked up at her. He stuttered and sprayed spittle, hesitating like a kid at his first dance asking the most attractive girl to dance, when he knew he couldn't dance. "Thank you, eh, eh, Emily. I appreciate what you've done." It was the first time he had ever called one of his employees by their first name and it felt uncomfortably strange, but at the same time kind of good, like a successful kid at his first dance.

She looked at him. Maybe WB was human after all, she thought. He was kind of cute, in a professional way. Not affair material, but a potential friend in high places. She wasn't sure whether he was thanking her for the reports or for getting him the water. As if reading her thoughts, he wasn't sure either. He certainly didn't need those reports now. Who really gives a whirling fuck, not him. Probably, he realized, he was thanking her for getting close to him, he had never let anybody get close to him.

"Good night, Mr. Bradford." She moved to leave the room, shifting from side to side as she walked. He watched her intently as if he had recognized the difference in female walking for the first time—perhaps this was so.

As Emily left the office she was greeted by Miss Gregson, William's chief administrative assistant, the bulldog protecting the Vice Presidential gates. Her desk was right outside his office.

"How was old WB today, as nasty as ever?" Miss Gregson smiled knowingly.

"Surprisingly, he was really very nice. He even called me Emily. I think he may have been watching me walk out of the room. You know, like he was interested." Emily blushed ever so slightly.

"Yeah, he was interested in your ass all right. How much it cost the company and whether he could get rid of it. Don't let the wicked bastard fool you. They don't call him WB for nothing."

In her haste to leave, Emily hadn't closed his office door all the way and William overheard this conversation. This wasn't the first time he had heard himself referred to as WB, the Wicked Bastard. Now, however, maybe it would be the last time.

He continued looking out the window. He watched the people moving on the ground from his penthouse office thirty-three floors up. They looked like insects hurrying for the sake of hurrying. It was normal quitting time for most people and he watched them hurrying and scurrying to get as far from their workplaces as quickly as possible. This had never been his concern. He had nowhere to scurry to. Work at Apex Corporation had been his life for as long as he could remember. He arrived earlier and left later than anyone else. Today would be no different. Where would he go anyway? He would just sit and wait until it was time for him to leave, then he would go home as usual.

He sat and watched the people moving down below. Eventually it started to get dark, so that he could hardly make out the movements down below except when people passed by the lamp posts. His office became increasingly dark, but he stayed where he was. He sat and watched way past his regular leaving time of ten P.M. Finally, a little before midnight he started to go. He had no place to go and was in no hurry to get there. He left his office for the last time slowly. He took nothing with him—it was not his life anymore. He walked through the door, leaving it open. He took the elevator to the parking garage. It was a long drive to get home, but tonight he was in no hurry. No one really seemed to care whether he got home or not. His wife had moved into a separate bedroom and was living a separate life. He wondered whether she knew if he came home at all, tonight or any other night. He was always alone, but tonight he felt lonely.

His thoughts drifted to the thousands of sad and lonely souls he had laid off and downsized over the years. He had never known who they were; they were just names and cost savings on a piece of paper. He thought about his start with Apex, right out of college— twenty-two years old. He had worked for them ever since, over 30 years. He had always done his job diligently and obediently; the company had never seen a more obedient child.

His loyalty and hard work paid off in quick promotions through the management ranks. He was transferred from one division and location to another. At age 37, he was made the youngest Vice President in the company's history. Ten years ago, Diamond Industries, an international conglomerate that owned businesses producing goods from animal crackers to zoo cages, bought out Apex.

It became William's responsibility to close down or sell unprofitable businesses and to lay off, or downsize, thousands of employees. He was so successful at this that he was promoted to Executive Vice President of the Foods and Consumable Division where he was expected to do the same. Although he tried the same cost reducing tactics in this division, he had minimal success as sales decreased even faster than costs. Eventually, two years ago the division was sold to a leveraged buyout group, Consolidated Unlimited, and he remained as Executive Vice President.

Richard Sprague, who had a reputation for slicing up companies and selling the pieces, became the new CEO. William had always tried to keep the company intact and profitable through cost reductions not through unnecessary surgery, as he believed Mr. Sprague to be guilty of. Needless to say they clashed like peanut butter and ketchup. This afternoon Mr. Sprague had told William that he was being terminated under a cost reduction plan developed by Brad Myers. William was out and Brad was in. The downsizer had been downsized. Was it really poetic justice or repressed revenge? It was 1994, William was now 54 years old and it no longer mattered.

He drove home on deserted streets with the car in automatic pilot. He parked the car in the garage, went through the house in the dark, took off his clothes neatly, hung them up, put on his silk monogrammed pajamas, and got into his king-sized bed. He lay there, not sleeping, trying not to think, as moisture formed in his eyes. He hadn't remembered crying since he was eight years old and found out, in the middle of the night, that his father had a mistress and was leaving his mother. All this while his mother was out for the evening. One life had ended then and another life had ended now. William couldn't sleep; plenty of time for sleep later. Ha! Ha!

Buzzz! William heard the buzz and then voices in the room. He looked over at the clock on his night table. "Holy moley," he thought, "five o'clock." He still hadn't slept; he was still staring at nothing. Ordinarily, he would jump excitedly out of bed, looking forward to another day at work. Today, however, was the first day of the end of his life and he had nowhere to go and nothing to do. What he had to do he realized with terror in his crotch was to get out of the house before his wife woke up. He wasn't ready to admit to himself that this was the day when he was out of work, a condition totally foreign to him, so how could he admit it to his wife? If she smirked, or mildly smiled, his life would really be over.

Like a well-oiled machine, he went through his daily routine. He took off his silk monogrammed pajamas, hung them neatly in the closet, brushed and flossed his teeth, took a cold shower, shaved with a straight razor out of a shaving mug, applied aftershave and cologne. He then dressed in one of his standard three piece, pinstriped Italian imported silk suits with white on white monogrammed shirt, conservative striped tie, black knee length socks, and black finely polished, by hand by one of his assistants, wing tip shoes. He looked in the mirror. He might be out of work but he could still be into William.

He moved quickly down the deep, carpeted steps and directly out to the garage. He had developed the habit of never having breakfast at home, always at the office. He couldn't afford the time, and time was money. He sat in his black Mercedes luxury sedan with the key in his hand. His thoughts turned to suicide. It would be so easy to turn on the engine and wait for the fumes to get to him. In his vapor proof, totally sealed garage it wouldn't take long. Morbidly he thought he could test the garage door sealant guarantee. He had nowhere else to go, so he might as well wait here. He froze, unable to move, tears coming to his eyes. He fought to stop the tears, but they weren't to be denied. Was this to be his new life, crying alone in his garage never to be found?

After some time he thought he heard a noise from the house, possibly his wife moving around. This new fear far exceeded his present fear. Somehow his hand moved quickly to the ignition and the car was running, purring like the Mercedes, high-pressure guy had assured him. Thank God there were still some things left to trust in this world gone crazy. He always backed up slowly and cautiously, as he did everything, and this time it was even slower. This was fortunate as the garage door was still down, which became apparent as he heard the clash of the back fender against the door. "Shit, now what?" He pushed the automatic garage door control and the door slowly and quietly opened. Fucking A Ronald Reagan he was out. Now what to do? He had the day to himself, but nothing to do and nowhere to go.

He drove to the little shopping center he always passed on his way to work. He never stopped, as the center was located in the industrial part of town. He always noticed older pick up trucks and low-end cars and figured it was not a place for him and his Mercedes. They would strip his car to the bones within ten minutes. No, this had not been the place for him. Today, however, it was just the place to hide. He would hardly be recognized in this part of town. It was too early for any of the shops to be open. The parking lot was empty except for the night security truck. He pulled over to the remotest corner, which was hidden from view by a dumpster, and stopped the car.

He put his head in his hands and tried to push back the tears. It was a tough fight and he was losing it. He clutched the steering wheel as hard as he could to keep from crying. Finally, the tears cascaded down his face onto his white-on-white shirt, oblivious to his will to stop them. He closed his eyes as his face caressed the steering wheel. In the early morning quiet of the parking lot, his thoughts became loud within the solitude. He was all alone in the world, adrift and drowning in his own failures.

He thought of all the contacts he had made within, and outside of, the company: all the power breakfasts and lunches he attended each week, all the social events he was invited to, all the people who just wanted a minute of his time. There wasn't one he could think of that he could call from the company car phone. Without his job, he was without power. He was alone in the company Mercedes without a tow.

Time passes and the vision of his childhood appears in his mind. At least that is still working, he thought to himself. It is his first recollection: he is about three years old; his father holds him down at his feet as he sits in his favorite rocking chair. His father is humming an old German lullaby as he sings in his Germanic broken English:

"Ya, das is ein ugly child. Ya, das is ein ugly child."

He sings the song over and over again while William struggles to get free. He is crying, but no one hears him. This is William's first view of life, he remembers, alone in his torment.

Ultimately, his mother enters the scene to take him from his father. This scene has recurred to William many times over the years whenever he feels lonely, which is most of the time. His mother tries to yank him from his father, but his father won't let go. His mother and father pull him by the arms and his crying gets louder. Back in the present, he puts his hands over his ears as he sits in the Mercedes. The sound is crushing him.

His mother pleads. "Please Karl, let the boy go, Wilhelm needs to get his sleep. I can't fight with you like this over the boy every night. Here, let me have him. I will put him to bed, ya?"

Karl continues humming and saying again and again "Wilhelm (with a capital V), das is ein ugly child."

"Please, Karl, let me have him. You are hurting the boy. You need to show him more love, not less."

"Karen, not enough love is killing me. Why should I give him any?"

Karl gets up from the chair, throws the crying William at his mother, who drops him on the floor. He cries uncontrollably.

"Here, Karen, you deal with him. I don't raise crying babies."

Karl leaves the house abruptly, slamming the door behind him.

William's hands automatically cover his ears; this is part of the ritual dance.

His mother goes after his father. "Karl, don't do this. Every night, always the same. You upset the boy and then you run off, leaving me alone with him. I can't do it any more. Please, Karl, no more."

She picks him up harshly. "Come, I put you to bed. Always running off with him. Where does he go?"

William remembers crying for the first time when he recalls this scene.

The scene shifts, he is eight years old. The story always unfolds this way: His father is taking him to his first baseball game for his eighth birthday. It is supposed to be just the two of them, father and son bonding. They leave the house together hand in hand. It is one of the times that he is not crying. He loves the Yankees and they are playing a doubleheader with the Red Sox, his next favorite team. They are both smiling as his mother says good-bye as they leave. She also smiles, strange as he has never seen her smile in life. She warns his father. "Karl, make sure the boy doesn't eat too much junk. I don't need a sick child."

Karl nods, but ignores her as he usually does.

His father has gotten them box seats, directly behind first base. He has a hot dog and an ice cream in his hands as they wait for the game to begin. He is happy, possibly for the first time in his life. A lady sits down on the other side of his father. William watches him watch her. She is dressed for the theater, not a baseball game. Her makeup is thick. Her clothes are tight. His father touches her as she sits down. William realizes his father knows this woman.

His mother would call her a hussy, a loose woman. His mother never wears makeup and always wears a loose housedress, even when she leaves the house. His father doesn't care because she never goes out with him.

Karl turns to talk to the lady, leaving him alone. His father spends his time during the first game of the doubleheader with this woman. He allows William to buy whatever he wants—first the hot dog, next the ice cream, then Cracker Jacks, a large coke, another ice cream, peanuts, and so on. William is into the game, but he feels alone. The Yankees lose the first game 6–2. Karl leaves with the woman between the games and tells him to wait there. William is scared and starts to cry, but there is no one there who cares. He needs to pee, but cannot go by himself. He waits for his father to return, but he doesn't come back. He feels the urine going down his leg and can't stop himself. He sees his father returning as the second game is beginning. The woman is holding onto his arm. He stops crying and turns away. His father doesn't notice. He cries to himself the rest of the day. Happy birthday! He thinks to himself.

He sees his mother and father fighting and yelling at each other; this is how he always remembers them. They always argue over the same thing. Why his father is never home, why his mother has to raise Wilhelm on her own, and why his father bothers to come home at all, as he obviously doesn't want to be there. He hears the screaming even though his hands are held tightly over his ears. It is always the same, they argue and he cries. The fight always ends the same way, too. His father hits his mother until she falls to the floor, then he stalks out slamming the door behind him. His mother lies there looking at him.

She cries out. "If it wasn't for you, he'd stay here."

Wilhelm runs from the room and cries himself to sleep, once again.

He is lying in his bed, hiding from his father. It is late at night, but he can't sleep. He is afraid to fall asleep in this house. His mother can't touch him, and he wishes his father didn't touch him. If his mother loved him, then his father hated him. He just wants to be left alone. Why can't they leave him alone? When he grows up, he will leave everyone else alone. He screams in his head, "Alone, alone, just leave me alone!"

He hears his father in the hall. His mother is at her only friend Sophie's funeral. It's the first time that he remembers her out. He goes to his door and opens it a crack. He sees his father taking suitcases from the hall closet into his parents' bedroom. His father is throwing clothes into the suitcases. He is in a hurry. He turns to pass William's room, William closes the door and hides, and he is scared to move. His father hurries out of the house, slamming the front door. He hurries to his window and sees his father getting into a cab with the painted lady from the ball game. William cries into the morning.

He never saw his father or counted on anyone else again. He never cried again until yesterday. He was alone and was much better off. Who needed him, or her?

He presses harder with his hands around the steering wheel. His head falls hard onto the steering wheel. His tears are uncontrollable now. He doesn't mind the crying so much, in a way it is a relief, but why can't his head stop thinking? He just wants to be by himself for the rest of his life; hopefully it will be short. He presses his head harder against the steering wheel. Maybe if it hurts enough, he can think about the hurt, and not his life. He presses and presses, but his head won't leave him alone. He cries out, "Fucking head, leave me alone, just leave me alone! Goddamn fucking head never leaves me alone!"

PART ONE
GETTING THERE

1
GROWING UP

William was born Wilhelm Broadfort to Karl and Karen Broadfort of the Bronx. He would never cry again, internally but not externally, after the night his father moved out. His mother never cried on the outside either. He was alone, but he always remembered himself being alone. It had always been more desirable than being with either of his parents.

His mother started work at Rufkin and Son two days after Karl had left her. Bernard Rufkin, the owner, was her only friend Sophie's brother. He gave her a job in the office. She was 25 years old. She now had to take care of herself and a child alone, but she vowed that she and Wilhelm wouldn't starve. She would get his breakfast and prepare his lunch before she left for work. When she came home from work she would make his dinner. He would get himself dressed, have his breakfast, walk to school and back all by himself. His mother called him "her little man."

Mother and son spent very little time together. When Karen came home from work she was either too tired or had one of her frequent migraine headaches. She would prepare Wilhelm's dinner by herself and while he ate alone she would sit in Karl's old easy chair and stare out the window until it was time to sleep, but she never really slept. Such was their existence, day after day, as Wilhelm grew up.

Karen tried to provide everything that she thought Wilhelm needed, other than her, as that wasn't possible. Wilhelm was denied nothing, except books and religion, which were both forbidden in her house. His father never returned.

At eight years old, he was a pudgy boy with sandy hair and a rough complexion. He was not attractive, either physically or socially. The other kids had little to do with him. He walked to school alone behind the other kids from his block, ate his lunch alone in the library, and walked home from school alone, after the other kids had left for the day. While the other kids played games outside in the street after school, he sat in his room alone, sometimes looking out the window at the other kids playing. Wilhelm read books he snuck home from the school library. He especially liked books of literature and philosophy. He went days without speaking to anyone else. He didn't particularly enjoy his own company, but he had no other choice.

At recess time, he would sit alone by the fence reading one of his books. The other kids would tease him, calling him the "book Nazi." He was one of the smartest kids in his class. The teacher would always call on him when she wanted the right answer, usually after the other kids had all given the wrong answer. The other kids didn't like the little "Nazi smart ass."

One day at recess, while Wilhelm was sitting alone by the fence reading his book, a dodge ball came racing toward him and knocked his book down. Bobby Segal, one of the most popular and athletic boys although dumb, came racing after the ball. He stopped short when he saw the ball sitting by Wilhelm's feet. He didn't want to get too close to the "book Nazi."

Bobby called out to Wilhelm. "Hey, book Nazi, throw the ball over here."

Wilhelm continued reading his book, ignoring Bobby.

Bobby called to him again and again. "Hey book Nazi, what's the matter, you don't touch Jewish balls?"

Wilhelm continued to ignore him. He wanted to throw the ball back to him, but he didn't know how to either throw the ball or make contact with a kid his age. So, he just ignored the situation.

Before Wilhelm realized what was happening, Bobby grabbed him by the shirt and lifted him off his feet. His shirt ripped and he cried internally. He knew his mother would be mad as each shirt had to last at least a school term. They couldn't afford to replace his clothes, even those he had outgrown. His mother painstakingly ironed each of his shirts each day, and he always wore a dress shirt and dress pants—she would be mad.

He just stood there staring, and crying internally, as Bobby pummeled him about the face and body with his fists. Wilhelm was not violent, could never be, and passively took his beating. Bobby finally stopped, as there was no satisfaction in beating up someone who refused to fight. He was also feeling remorse, as Wilhelm had done nothing but exist. Bobby looked back to make sure he was being approved of by his peers. When they seemed to lose interest, so did he. After this Bobby and the other kids left him alone, at least physically. They still teased him. Bobby made sure none of the other kids touched Wilhelm, maybe out of remorse, maybe out of respect for taking a beating like a man. When Bobby saw him after this, he would call him "Killer". This became Wilhelm's nickname, and with a nickname from Bobby Segal he was left alone, but he was still alone.

He sat back down by the fence, picked up his book, and started to read again as tears fell uncontrollably inside his head. He was unhappy in his world, but knew no way out. He had to spend the rest of the day with a ripped shirt and dried blood on his face. The other kids in his class would look at him and laugh behind their hands. He learned his lessons obediently, but did not learn to like other people.

When he got home, he stitched his shirt as best he could and cleaned himself up. When his mother came home, he waited until his dinner was ready and she was sitting in her chair by the window. Only then did he come down for dinner. He avoided her for three days until his bruises had gone away. This was easy to do as neither one looked for contact from the other.

He lived like this all through elementary school. As time went by, he would have other kids to talk to, outcasts and misfits like him, but he had grown used to being alone. He didn't enjoy the things that other kids enjoyed. When they talked about baseball, he would get sick to his stomach thinking about his last baseball game with his father. He graduated from elementary school, but didn't look forward to junior high school. He was now eleven years old and still alone.

In the summers between school terms he would stay mainly in the house and read his books. Since his mother forbade books in the house, he had to sneak them in and hide them from her. Just like during school, his mother would prepare his breakfast and lunch before she went to work. He would wait in his room until she left. He would then come down, have his breakfast, and start to read. Before he knew it, his mother was returning from work. If he were downstairs, he would rush up to his room before his mother came into the house. She would prepare his dinner and go sit in her chair. This was the way it was and continued to be.

The junior high school was over a mile from his house. The other kids on his street walked together to school, and he wasn't asked to join them. Rather than walk alone, and risk being laughed at by the other kids, he would take a city bus. He used part of his lunch money, going without lunch some days or skipping milk, to pay for the bus. He didn't tell his mother or ask her for more money, he just couldn't.

There were other kids going to the junior high school on the bus, some from further distances, others like him with no one to walk with. One of these kids, Howie Eskin, who was in his grade, would sit next to him most days when the seat was open. They traveled like this for the first four weeks of school. Howie was in his algebra class. They were both loners, readers, and good students.

One day Howie spoke to him while he was reading Goethe on the bus. He was startled as he wasn't accustomed to being spoken to on the bus.

"I don't think you're a Nazi," said Howie as he looked away.

"I'm not a Nazi. I'm only eleven years old. How could I be a Nazi?"

"The other kids say you're a Nazi. They call you the book Nazi?"

"I can't help that. I've done nothing to any of them. I just want to be left alone."

"Me too," said Howie.

"They tease you too? I didn't know that. I thought I was the only one."

"So did I until you came to school. Now they leave me alone some times."

"What's the matter with you? Too smart, like me?"

"No, it's not that. My mother is not Jewish, my father is."

"So?" said Wilhelm, quite perplexed.

"You don't understand. I'm neither Jewish nor gentile. I don't fit in."

"I guess I don't either," said Wilhelm, but he didn't know why.

Wilhelm and Howie became friends of a sort. This was the first friend Wilhelm had allowed in since his father had left. They would sit on the bus together, to and from school, eat lunch together at a table with just the two of them, study together, but never at Wilhelm's house, and go to the library together. Outside of school, though, they rarely did things together. Wilhelm would never have anyone to his house, not with his mother. Howie never invited him to his house. In this manner, Wilhelm got through the seventh grade.

Wilhelm spent the summer between seventh and eighth grades much as he had his other summers. He got up late after his mother had left, read his books, ate a little lunch, read his books, ate his dinner after his mother had taken her seat by the window, and then went to his room to read as late as he could and slept very little. The year was 1952 and he was twelve years old. The other houses on their street all had televisions and the other kids and their families would gather around to watch their favorite television shows such as The Milton Berle Show, I Love Lucy and so on. His mother would have nothing to do with television as she considered it a tool of the Nazis to dumb their minds. She was convinced that she and Wilhelm were better off in their world. The days continued this way until the summer ended and it was time to return to school.

Back in school, Wilhelm and Howie returned to their routine. They weren't really friends, but they protected themselves from being alone and from the other kids. Their geometry teacher, Miss Evans, encouraged them to join the math club. Neither one of them had ever joined anything; they were never asked before. In the math club, they met other kids like themselves, social outcasts and misfits. They also found other kids with whom they shared interests in math and books. Four of the boys from the math club started to sit at Wilhelm and Howie's lunch table. They now had a full table and didn't need to feel so obviously rejected. While they still didn't socialize outside of school, the group was becoming closer. They even kidded among themselves. They joked with Wilhelm about not having a television — the only house left in the Bronx without a television and an antenna on the roof.

In the math club was a scholarly, mousey girl named Amantha. She would sit in the math club and look askance at Wilhelm. Howie mentioned this to Wilhelm but he denied it. He had been devoid of female contact, other than the little attention paid him by his mother, all of his life. He saw girls as another species, foreign to him. Wilhelm had never been interested in social contacts, particularly with girls.

While the other kids in school were going to parties and bar mitzvahs for Jewish boys becoming thirteen, Wilhelm was never invited and had no interest in such frivolous things. He preferred his books. Besides these other kids were only interested in wasting time. He was going to be somebody.

There was an eighth grade dance coming up in October to celebrate Halloween. Wilhelm had never celebrated Halloween in his house and he had never been out trick or treating with the other kids. Wilhelm's mother had called it frivolous Nazi nonsense. On Halloween night, they kept all the lights off and didn't answer the door if kids came. Wilhelm read in his room.

Wilhelm was sitting next to Howie in math club. Amantha got up to leave the room. As she went by Wilhelm's desk, she dropped a note on the top of it. He just let it sit there. Howie looked at him. Neither one of them had ever been approached by a girl before, even a mouse like Amantha. It was frightening.

"Aren't you going to look at it?" asked Howie.

"What for?" said Wilhelm. He went back to the math problem he was working on. He moved the note to the side.

Howie reached over and picked up the note. "You mind if I read it?"

"Go ahead, doesn't bother me." Wilhelm went on working.

Howie looked at the note. "Wow, look at this!"

Wilhelm half looked over, looking like he didn't care, yet somehow he did. He wasn't interested in girls and they weren't interested in him, yet, somehow, he was interested.

The note said, "I want to go to the Halloween dance with you. Please take me and I promise we'll do more than dancing. I think I love you. Amantha."

"Holy shit," said Howie, "you're a lucky stiff."

"She probably watches too much television," said Wilhelm. He continued working on the math problem. Wilhelm never responded to the note and Amantha switched her attention to another boy in the math club, Sheldon Bayfield. He would see the two of them holding hands in the halls, kissing behind their lockers, and so on. He was told they were lovers and he didn't care.

In the ninth grade, Wilhelm and Howie entered the district science fair and won first prize with their entry on automated robotics. They were sent to the state finals and again won first prize. Their science teacher, Mr. Brown, got them into an intern program for ninth graders whereby they would spend a half a day at the junior high and the other half a day at the high school.

Wilhelm and Howie became mini-celebrities. This was the first time either one of them had received positive attention by anyone, particularly their peer group. Some of the popular crowd started talking to them, asked them to help them with their studies or homework, and they were even invited to some parties. They both turned down these invitations. What would they do at a party with girls?

Mr. Brown asked Wilhelm if he would tutor Rick Robbins, one of the star athletes in the ninth grade. He resisted, but Mr. Brown impressed upon him how important it was to the school. Rick could throw a football, shoot a basketball, pitch a baseball, but couldn't diagram a sentence or solve a simple math problem — he was as dumb as a catcher's mitt. Wilhelm reluctantly agreed.

He started tutoring Rick. They would meet at the school library or at Rick's house after school or after Rick's sports practice. Wilhelm tried to teach

Rick the elements of good English and basic math principles. Rick was either too dense or really didn't care. During football, basketball, or baseball season Rick would toss the ball in the air, sometimes tossing it at Wilhelm who would usually drop it. Rick would laugh and taunt him about never getting anywhere in life without athletics. He was going to the big leagues, why waste time with meaningless academic shit. Wilhelm knew nothing about this world, his was a world of ideas. He would be the king of ideas.

He helped Rick on his homework assignments. Although Rick was obstinate against doing any of it and tried to persuade Wilhelm to do it for him, he refused. He didn't care if Rick did it or not, but his moral principles prevented him from doing it for him. Eventually, Rick started to get a little grasp of English and Math so that he could complete his homework assignments with Wilhelm's assistance. When tests were imminent, he would drill Rick on the related course materials, so that Rick began consistently earning C's and sometimes B's. At the first reporting period, Rick got a B in English, although he still couldn't put a sentence together or spell athletics, and a C in Math although he still couldn't add two double-digit numbers together in his head. The coach and Rick were ecstatic. The coach found Wilhelm other students, that is other athletes appearing to be students, to tutor on a paid basis, which provided sorely needed money for his clothes and food. This was the first time he had been paid and it was the beginning of his knowledge of his worth and value.

Rick had in mind a different kind of reward. Although he initially resented Wilhelm's authoritarian style of forcing him to learn, he was grateful for the results. After Wilhelm had been tutoring him for a while, he started bringing his girlfriend, Bonnie Barnes, to their tutoring sessions. Sometimes they even met at Bonnie's house. Although Wilhelm had little interest in girls, he liked Bonnie. She was, of course, a cheerleader at school, and the most desirable of all the girls. At least, that's what Wilhelm heard from the other boys in gym class. She was blond and blue-eyed, very well developed in the breast area, and had a rear end to die for. The regular guys called her Bonnie Buns. She was a "real piece of ass" — the quarterback's choice.

Rick and Bonnie would sit together and make out while Wilhelm tutored Rick. When Rick got something right, Bonnie would get excited and lean over and kiss Wilhelm on the cheek. Although this made him feel quite uncomfortable, as no one had ever touched him before, it felt good in some strange way. Wilhelm found himself wanting Rick to get the right answer, maybe even setting it up to happen.

On the day that Rick received his grades, he and Wilhelm had arranged to get together for a tutoring session at Bonnie's house. Wilhelm arrived a little early and Bonnie answered the door, as Rick wasn't there yet. Bonnie was wearing a tight halter-top and a short tight skirt. Such an outfit on such a body probably would have had any other boy overstimulated and salivating. On Wilhelm, however, it had minimal effect. His fear of girls was so intense, that seeing Bonnie dressed like that only increased his fears. He looked away as Bonnie bent down to open the door and exposed the tops of her breasts. He turned away and went into the den where they usually had their tutoring sessions. He sat in his usual place on the sofa. He was alone for a few minutes and took the time to get his materials together.

Bonnie entered the room and looked down at him and smiled. He turned his head away as girls smiling at him made him uncomfortable. She moved to the cocktail table where he had spread out his tutoring materials. She picked them up with one swoop of her hands and tossed them to the floor. She smiled down at him. "You won't need those today." He choked down the anxiety in his throat.

She sat on the cocktail table and began to massage his legs from the ankles to the thighs, stopping just short of his penis. He became clammy all over his body and his inner voice started to scream, as he was feeling sick and choking. As she continued doing this, his penis enlarged on its own. He tried to stop it, but he couldn't — he was getting sicker. He was aware of this scientific phenomenon and knew other boys stimulated themselves so as to ejaculate, but he never touched his penis, even when showering, as it was dirty and physical. Bonnie leaned over to touch and stroke his penis. As she did this, her top fell open and he could see her entire breasts — nipples and all. She had removed her bra for him. His anxiety increased, his inner voice screamed louder, and he quickly pulled away.

"You all right?" asked Bonnie. "Would you like to touch them? It's okay."

He had watched Rick fondling her breasts through her shirt, but never bare. He spoke clumsily. "No, it's okay. I'll wait for Rick." He got up to move away.

She held him in place. "You do like me, don't you?"

He was stuck. "Of course I like you. Just not like this."

"I know what you'll like."

She lifted herself up so that her thighs were directly in his face. He couldn't avoid looking directly into her vagina. She had no panties on and had positioned herself so that the lips of her vagina had parted exposing her pinkness.

"Rick said to reward you. Is this okay?"

He looked down, saw the exposed vagina, gasped and vomited all over the both of them. His body was clammy and his inner voice screamed for a quick death.

She jumped up disgusted, threw her soiled skirt at him, and ran from the room.

"Oh my God, that's gross," she said, as she ran.

He didn't even watch her bare ass leave the room. Any other boy would have given his virginity just for that sight. He used the clean part of her skirt to clean himself off as best he could. He placed his papers back on the table and waited for Rick. His inner voice was settling down, telling him all was right now.

A little while later, Rick arrived. He walked into the den smiling, male to male.

"So" he said, "how was your reward? Like it?"

Wilhelm said nothing. He just sat and stared at Rick.

Rick noticed smears on Wilhelm's usually clean slacks, but assumed it was the obvious joy juices.

Bonnie came to the door, this time clothed from neck to ankles, and motioned for Rick to come into the other room. They left Wilhelm sitting and waiting for perhaps ten minutes. His breath was slowly returning to normal.

Rick returned grinning. "Hey it's okay, stud. I probably should have just gotten you some book."

"Stud" became Wilhelm's new nickname at school and his fame spread.

Near the end of the ninth grade, Mr. Brown approached Wilhelm and Howie about applying for admission to the Science and Math high school. It would mean a bus and subway commute for each of them. While there was tuition to attend this school, Mr. Brown assured them that he could get them a full scholarship for all three years. Wilhelm saw this as a chance to get away from the type of kids who attended regular public school, those who liked sports, television, movies, and sex, and get fully into the world of academics and ideas. He told Mr. Brown he would have to talk to his mother to get her permission.

When his mother came home from work that night, he was waiting for her beside her regular chair by the window. Usually, he waited in his room until his mother prepared his dinner and had retired to her chair. They spoke very little to each other. Tonight would be different.

His mother looked surprised. Wilhelm had never done this before.

"Wilhelm," said his mother. "So what is this?"

He looked down at the rug, at the stains and where the threads were coming through. "I, I . . ." he stuttered, "need to talk to you."

Karen sat in her chair and looked up at him expectantly.

"Wilhelm, you know I'm always here. So, what is it? You in trouble?"

"No, no." Wilhelm took the application from his pocket. "I need your permission, to go to this school."

"What kind of school is it?" Karen took the papers from him. She looked them over, nodding to herself as she did. "So, you need me to tell you to go?"

"No, no, Momma."

"Then what, I don't understand."

"Momma, you need to sign the papers."

"Oh." Karen nodded her head from front to back—now she understood. "So, what kind of school is it?"

"Oh, Momma, it's the Science and Math school. Only the best are accepted."

"And you're the best?"

"I hope so, Momma."

"Only science and math. No literature, no philosophy?"

"No, Momma, only science and math."

"Good, I want you to be safe from the world of ideas."

He didn't quite know what she was talking about, but he knew from his mother that the world of ideas was bad.

"No, Momma, no world of ideas, just science and math."

"This is for nothing? I can't pay."

"I know, Momma. Mr. Brown will get me a scholarship. It will cost you nothing. And I'll work to pay for the subway and books and anything else. You'll see, Momma."

"And your clothes. Will you buy them and iron them and polish your shoes? You must look right at all times."

Karen had always dressed him in dress slacks and shirts and finely polished black leather shoes. She would buy him his clothes and shoes so that he always looked like her little gentleman. Each night she continued to iron his shirt and press his pants for the next day. She would also polish his shoes so that they shined. She did this as she sat in her chair staring out of the window at the world. Wilhelm owned no casual clothes or sneakers like the other boys for Karen was afraid he would become like them.

"Yes, Momma, I will buy my clothes. And iron and polish if I have to."

"Ya, Wilhelm, let me think about this. So, no literature, no philosophy?"

"Yes, Momma, just science and math."

"Ya, I think."

She sat in the chair holding onto the papers and staring out the window.

Wilhelm made his own dinner for the first time that night— peanut butter and ketchup sandwiches with potato chips. His mother wouldn't approve, but he didn't care. His mother sat in her chair for the entire night drifting in and out of sleep. The next morning he came downstairs. His mother had left already for work. The application was on the kitchen table, it was signed by his mother with a little note. "I do this for you Wilhelm. I hope it is right."

Wilhelm entered the Science and Math high school the following year. To this day, he still doesn't know if it was right.

He received his notice of graduation from junior high school with four tickets for guests. He knew no one else but his mother. Would she want to come to his graduation? Would he want her to be there? She never went out. She went to work, and she came home. She would go to the stores in the neighborhood for food, but would come right back. She was ashamed of her English, so she had Wilhelm write out shopping lists for the grocery, the butcher, and the produce store. She would hand each merchant the note and then stand in the corner while they filled her order. She would then go directly home. Each store was within two blocks of her house. She would talk to no one coming or going.

Wilhelm had never had any friends over to this house since he had never had any friends. Neither had his mother since Karl had left them. Even Sophie while she was living had not been to their house, Karen had always visited at Sophie's house. The neighbors and other children on the street and in the neighborhood called Karen "the German lady" but never spoke to her. How could he take his mother to his graduation, yet how could he not? He would be ashamed of her if she came and ashamed of himself if he did not ask her. He was to graduate with honors and was told that he might win one of the graduation prizes. Did he want his mother to witness this or not?

He waited for his mother to come home from work with the letter and the graduation invitation in his hand. He was clammy, but knew he had to do this. When she came in the door, she had a package in her hand. She held it out to him.

"Here, Mr. Rufkin made these special for your graduation."

He opened the package to find a pair of the latest slacks. Karen had always insisted that he wear the old country style. She was afraid that she and Wilhelm might become too American and forget their roots.

He was struck dumb. He just sat there with his jaw hanging.

"Well, Wilhelm, nothing to say?"

"Momma, are you sure. I can wear these?"

"I didn't drag them home so you couldn't wear. Ya?"

He looked down. "Thank you, Momma." He wanted to hug her or kiss her on the cheek, but he knew his mother wouldn't allow this.

He looked down in his hand. The slacks had made up his mind. "Here, Momma. I'm inviting you to my graduation, as my guest." He handed her the invitation.

"Here, you read it. I don't read English well."

He told her about the graduation, when and where it was, and that he wanted her to come.

"No, Wilhelm, I don't go."

"Why, Momma?"

"This is for American mothers, not for German mothers."

"No, Momma, this is for all mothers. I want you to be there, to be proud of me. Like the other mothers."

"I be proud of you from right here."

He tried to persuade his mother, but she was adamant. He would be prouder if she wasn't there. It was no place for "the German lady."

On the day of the graduation, Karen helped him dress. She pressed his new slacks, ironed his dress shirt, finely polished his shoes, and made sure he had new underwear. She felt proud of him, and he felt proud of her. She had only completed the second year of high school when she had to leave Germany. She had never graduated from anywhere. Now her Wilhelm was to graduate junior high school, this was something to live for.

When he was ready to leave, he stopped at the door. He wanted to hug or kiss her. He came forward, but she moved back. She took his hand in hers and looked into his eyes. He thought he saw tears forming in the corner of her eyes, but she pushed them back. This was as close to affection as his mother had ever come.

"Go, Wilhelm, you will be late."

He left the house and walked alone to the school. He looked back at the window and his mother was sitting in her chair watching out the window as he walked up the street. He swore he saw tears in her eyes.

The principal, Miss Padgett, was announcing the awards for the graduating class. Rick had won a number of athletic awards, and Bonnie had won a number of popularity awards, among others. They were announcing the scholastic awards, which always came last as the school considered them the least important. They had given out the dramatic and literature awards and were now coming to the math and science awards. Miss Padgett looked over to where Wilhelm and Howie were sitting. Wilhelm knew that Howie would win the awards, and Howie knew that Wilhelm would win the awards.

The math award was announced first and Wilhelm started to get clammy. What if he won? He couldn't get up in front of his classmates and the filled auditorium. There was no one there to clap for him.

Miss Padgett read the award for math excellence and stopped. She then read the name "Howard Eskin.". Wilhelm's inner voice said, "Thank you. God." As Wilhelm realized relief, Miss Padgett was announcing the science award and before Wilhelm could get in touch with his anxiety, he heard his name called. He froze. Howie grabbed him by the elbow and walked him over to Miss Padgett.

As he looked around the auditorium, he noticed a little lady in a shawl covering her head sitting in the back row. She had a broad smile on her face. It looked like his mother. This was the first time he had ever seen her smile.

After the graduation, Wilhelm went to look for his mother, but he could not find her. He wanted to walk home with her. Let the other kids make fun of her if they wanted to. It didn't matter, she was his mother and she came to his graduation. He walked home alone. When he got home, he found his mother sitting in her chair staring out the window in her housedress.

"So Wilhelm, it was all right?"

He nodded his head. He didn't mention his award or seeing her at the graduation, but he was sure that she knew that he knew. He slid the award under her bedroom door on his way upstairs. He never mentioned it, and neither did she.

Wilhelm knew that it was time that he had some money of his own. His mother made just enough money working in the office at Rufkin and Son to pay their bills. He knew it was rough for his mother to buy his clothes and the things he needed at school. She never complained and she rarely bought anything for herself. When he would get her a gift for her birthday or Mother's Day, she would say that was American foolishness and return the gift to the store for something for him. At home, she had worn the same two housedresses from the time that he could remember. She had three "old lady" outfits she alternated to wear to work. Each night she would wash and press the outfit for the next day. He was going to be fifteen in July and his mother was now thirty-three years of age. She was still a young woman physically, but psychologically, she was an old lady waiting for death to come.

The day after graduation, Wilhelm applied for a job at the new super-market six blocks away. The store manager offered him a job as a bag packer, but he would have to get his mother's permission as he was under sixteen. He asked his mother when she came home from work.

"A job, Wilhelm? You don't need a job. I take care of you."

"No, Momma, now I take care of you."

Karen was adamant. How would it look to the neighbors? He pressed the point that the neighbors hardly knew they existed. She finally relented, but he had to promise that he would always be honest and wouldn't get dirty. He promised.

Wilhelm left each morning for work in the clothes laid out by his mother —freshly washed and ironed. When he got to the supermarket, he would change into work clothes and shoes that he had bought on his own. When he left for the day, he would clean up and change back into his dress clothes. His mother was never the wiser and never would be. She had never been more than three blocks, the distance to Rufkin and Son, from their house.

Wilhelm found that he couldn't control his work ethic. While some of the other packers his age would goof off in the back or take an unearned break or have a soda from the refrigerator, he would work con-tinuously. Although the other packers had little to do with him, the store manager and the front-end manager loved him. When there was extra work or an extra shift to be given, they would pick Wilhelm. This meant extra money. Wilhelm was beginning to accumulate more money than he could spend, as he spent very little. He would get gifts for his mother, but she still would return them and get him something. He had little else to spend his money on. He soon realized that he liked working and accu-mulating money—and he wanted more of each.

Before the summer was over, the store manager promoted Wilhelm to cashier. He was the youngest cashier in the store, but one of the most efficient. The front-end manager would assign Wilhelm to the express aisle whenever he could. The person working this aisle had to be fast, accurate, courteous, and honest as this was the aisle with the most traffic. He loved the challenge and the opportunity to succeed. He found that he was liking the business world. By the time it came to start high school, he had saved over $1,000 working at $2.12 an hour.

Wilhelm, at fifteen, was starting to fill out. He had always been a flabby boy with little muscle tone. He detested physical activities, preferring instead to remain in his world of books. During the summer, however, his work sched-ule had hardened him. His body now had definition and his face was becom-ing more adult. As he was maturing, his features were becoming more like his father's. His mother started to recognize this and moved further away from him. It was difficult for her to look at him for too long now. It had always been difficult for her to touch him.

Wilhelm went each day to the Math and Science High School (known as MSHS), taking one bus and two subways. He would ride back and forth with

Howie. They were the only two boys from his junior high school who had been accepted by this high school. Their neighborhood wasn't known for its geniuses. After school and on weekends, he would go to work at the supermarket. He did his homework at school or on his breaks at work. He had no social life, but he didn't want one. What else would he do anyway? His school and his work were his life. With such a schedule he saw very little of his mother, which was fine for both of them.

Wilhelm and Howie continued working together on various science projects throughout high school, winning numerous awards. They both made the honor role every report period. They alternated each grade period as the top student in the class. They both flourished in such a high academic environment. The tensions they felt in junior high school were not present, such as social pressures and gym class.

In junior high, they felt the impending tension and pressure of a gym class the day before. To get dressed in their gym suits, they would hide in the back of the locker room so that none of the others would see their pale and flabby bodies and make fun of them. During gym class, they would never be picked to be on any of the teams. They were assigned to the "fat boys" squad where the gym teacher would make them run around the gym for the period at their own speed. After gym, they would never take a shower. They would watch the other boys flip towels at each other and make smart remarks particularly about the size and shape of their penises and the lack of pubic hair. They didn't care about this and the other boys didn't care about them. If they stayed alone, they were left alone. Once Rick was in their gym class and chose Wilhelm to be on his softball team, thinking Wilhelm would appreciate this. After trying to hit and field the ball unsuccessfully for one inning, as the other team laughed and called him the German mauler, Wilhelm went back to the fat boys squad. He was happier and, he was sure, so was Rick. Happily at MSHS, the gym requirement could be met through Chess, math or science lab, calculus and so on. There were no gym lockers or showers.

Although girls were eligible for admission to MSHS, very few applied and were accepted. This made it relatively easy for Wilhelm not to have to relate to girls. However, as he had started to fill out he was becoming somewhat attractive. He had always been broader than he was tall, but now he was growing. He was almost five foot ten in tenth grade, which was taller than most of the other boys. He had dirty blond curly hair and a rough complexion. His physique was starting to develop and you could sense the burgeoning of physical strength. If he didn't attend MSHS you might take him for an athlete, perhaps a wrestler. He, however, abhorred physical contact of any kind. He still lived in the world of his mind.

Wilhelm had successfully avoided any real social contact throughout the tenth grade and the following summer. He went to school and worked at the supermarket. He had little time for anything else. He saw very little of his mother and they co-existed peacefully on a parallel basis. This was the best year of Wilhelm's life thus far. He was accumulating more and more money and this made him very happy. He spent very little of what he earned.

When Wilhelm returned for the eleventh grade, he noticed that Gladys Smedley had changed quite a bit. Wilhelm and Howie had worked with Gladys on a number of math and science projects in the tenth grade. She had been an annoying, unattractive girl. She said very little but was always dedicated to the project. Howie had kidded Wilhelm that Gladys liked him, maybe was in love with him. Wilhelm ignored this, he had no time for it. For the most part, attractive girls were not attracted to MSHS.

Gladys was now blossoming. Over the summer, she had developed. She now had very noticeable breasts and a shapely body. She was wearing make-up and had her hair long and flowing. Her clothes were tight and short. Other than her mind, she looked like she belonged in the regular high school. Howie whispered to Wilhelm that she must have gotten laid over the summer. Wilhelm blushed and looked away from Gladys.

Gladys was in the science lab with Wilhelm. They were assigned together to the last lab table in the back of the room. They were to work on experiments together. Gladys would work closer to him than necessary. While it made him uneasy and gave him the clammy feeling, he wasn't comfortable saying anything. He just tried to move away as much as he could. Gladys would continuously ask Wilhelm to come over to her house after school to study together. He avoided this by having to work. Gladys started wearing nylon stockings and a garter belt under her short skirt. Before class she would hike up her skirt to fix her stockings, hoping Wilhelm would look and perhaps get excited. Wilhelm, however, would look away. He would then come late to class hoping to avoid Gladys. She would then fix her stockings during class while they worked on an experiment. He would get the clammy feeling and leave the room.

One day Wilhelm and Gladys had the lab room to themselves to complete an experiment. Gladys was working as close to him as she could. She would try to breath in his ear and rub gently on his arms. He would move away as best he could. They both wore lab coats over their regular clothes. He was engrossed in completing his part of the experiment and tried to pay little attention to her. He heard her say his name. He looked over while he continued to work. She had her lab coat open and she was bare breasted. He began to choke and breath heavily. He dropped the test tubes filled with ammonia. The room filled with ammonia and the alarm went off. Mr. Herbert, one of the science teachers, and Leroy Perkins, another student, ran into the room to find Gladys's breasts out. The rumor the next day was that Wilhelm and Gladys were screwing in the lab. He became somewhat of a campus hero, as most of the boys at MSHS had never seen a girl's breasts, while Gladys never returned to MSHS. Wilhelm was relieved.

Near the end of twelfth grade, the students were being advised as to which colleges to apply to. Wilhelm's counselor, Mr. Greenspan, had suggested a number of scientific oriented colleges to him, with the possibility of a pre-medical or medical research program. He really wasn't interested in medicine as he would have to deal with people. He had become a member of the school newspaper staff in eleventh grade and was now one of two editors. He thought he might want to pursue a career in journalism. He liked writing and the task of putting a newspaper together every week. This also enabled him to read material other than math and science. He found he enjoyed reading literature and philosophy. He knew his mother wouldn't like this course, so he put it out of his mind. When his counselor suggested Roget Institute, a prestigious institute of technology that applied math and scientific principles to business, he knew he had found the school.

Roget Institute was located in Massachusetts, which meant he would have to live on campus. It was also extremely expensive, appealing to the scions of wealth and industry. While Wilhelm had accumulated enough money for the first year's tuition and board, he would have to work during the school year and summers to be able to continue. The only way his counselor saw that he would be able to attend this school would be to get a full scholarship — tuition and board. As this was a heavily endowed school, there were numerous scholarships available. Mr. Greenspan said he would help him apply for these scholarships, but he would need a general scholarship form filled out by his mother. She would have to state her financial position and her inability to pay his tuition and board. If there was a need, there might be a way.

He knew his mother would never approve of his going to a school out of New York. He knew she wouldn't let him go into the "Nazi world." He had never lied or deceived his mother, but this was the only school he wanted to attend. If he told her the truth, she would forbid him from going and he knew that he couldn't go. If he lied to her and went anyway, he would probably kill the rest of his mother's soul.

He decided to fill out the application himself and forge his mother's name. This wasn't difficult as he normally wrote his mother's name on official documents. She was still ashamed of the way she wrote in English. He also applied to a number of other colleges within commuting distance specializing in the sciences. Doing it this way seemed to be all right with him. He probably wouldn't be accepted to Roget Institute anyway. This way he would know he tried and wouldn't feel he wasted Mr. Greenspan's time.

During the months of March and April, college acceptance letters were sent out to high school students. Wilhelm had been accepted to three local colleges, but he hadn't heard from Roget Institute. As Mr. Greenspan knew a trustee on the institute's board, the trustee contacted him directly to let him know that based on his recommendation and Wilhelm's records they were going to offer Wilhelm two scholarships that would pay his full tuition and board together with a work opportunity. They were quite impressed with Wilhelm's academic record in both math and science, but particularly impressed with his award winning writing ability for the school newspaper.

They considered this extraordinary for a science student and a future businessperson. Most science, math, and business students couldn't write worth a darn; Wilhelm could.

Mr. Greenspan tried to find Wilhelm but he had already left school. As it was after five in the evening, he assumed that Wilhelm would be at home. He arrived at Wilhelm's house close to six and knocked on the door. There were lights on in the house, so he assumed Wilhelm was home. He knew Wilhelm lived alone with his mother, but he knew nothing else about his home life or background since Wilhelm never spoke about his personal life. Mr. Greenspan was puzzled when there was no answer.

Mr. Greenspan was leaving the house and decided to tell Wilhelm in the morning. He would try to control his excitement until then. As he walked past the front of the house, he saw Karen sitting in the window staring out. She hadn't answered the door as no one ever came to the house and if they did they were sales people or Jehovah's witnesses. She had no time for either one. He waved to Karen and tried to get her attention, but she continued staring. He went to the window and tapped. She looked up. He tried to tell her who he was, but she didn't seem to understand. He had a report cover with the high school name on it in his briefcase. He held it up and said he was Wilhelm's teacher. She nodded her head, she understood, Wilhelm's teacher. For the first time since she had lived there, she opened the door and her world for a stranger.

Mr. Greenspan explained the good news to Karen that Wilhelm could go to the institute fully paid. He told her that they were impressed with Wilhelm's writing for the newspaper. As each fact was revealed, Karen would nod her head. She understood fully. He left her sitting in her chair with the application papers in her hand. When he left, she continued to stare out of the window. This was her only world, hers and Wilhelm's.

When Wilhelm came home, he found his mother with her head down sitting in her chair. He thought she was dead. He rushed over and she looked up. There were traces of tears in her eyes. She had the papers in her hands. All she said was, "The man knocked on our door. It's always a knock on the door."

He continued to work at the supermarket, trying to make as much money as he could until he had to leave for school. The store manager and the front-end manager were extremely proud of him. They knew only rich kids went to Roget, from expensive prestigious prep schools. Roget was a science finishing school for rich kids with smarts who would one day take over the family business. Wilhelm didn't even have a family. They posted signs all around the store with Wilhelm's photograph, taken candidly while he cashiered the express line, stating that their Wilhelm Broadfort was to attend Roget Institute on a fully paid scholarship. They were as proud that Wilhelm worked at their store as they were of Wilhelm.

They announced a scholarship fund for Wilhelm where they had persuaded the company to put up matching funds of up to $250. By the time he was ready to leave for school, the fund exceeded $300, which meant the company provided a scholarship of over $500. This was an extremely large amount of money for a poor boy in 1958. It was equal to almost a year's tuition at one of the city colleges. At the award ceremony in the store, where the managers, other employees, and over thirty customers attended, Wilhelm was quite embarrassed. As the two managers praised him, he looked at the floor and avoided all eye contact. It wasn't that he didn't think he deserved the money and the praise, he just wanted the money without the personal contact.

Wilhelm put the check for $587 in his pocket and smiled to himself. He liked to accumulate money. He already had more than enough money to get through his first two years of college. He didn't need this extra money, but it was his and it showed how he was valued.

Howie Eskin had also applied to Roget Institute and a number of city colleges. With his grades, he was accepted to all of them. However, he wasn't offered a scholarship at Roget. They only offered so many "low income hardship" scholarships and never to two students from the same high school. Fortunately, Wilhelm could write and Howie could not.

Howie's father, Bobbie, was a brilliant man, but without a college degree. Maybe he was too smart, for he had a horrible time getting along with people. He knew all the answers and let everyone know it — this was not acceptable diplomacy. He had gone from one job to another, losing each job in a fight with the boss. He was now working for his brother-in-law who owned a small women's wear manufacturing plant. Bobbie was a cart pusher within the New York garment district. This was typically an entry-level job, paying almost nothing. But, his brother-in-law paid him a little more as the price for continuing to live with his sister.

The Eskins couldn't live on what Bobbie brought home, net pay less his bookie expenses, so Bobbie's wife, Anne, had to go out to work. She didn't mind as she said, "What would I do home all day, play canasta?" However, being of the female persuasion, with only a general high school diploma and minimal skills, she could only get a job as a receptionist at a small somewhat grungy advertising agency. Her job was to answer the phone while being mauled by the so-called ad executives. They were paying her, so it was their privilege. For this, she got paid little. Between their take home pays, they could just barely survive in their low-income section of the Bronx. Many months the rent didn't get paid on time. They were always making up and never getting ahead.

Due to these circumstances, there was no way Howie could go to Roget Institute; that was out of the question. However, he was considering one of the city colleges, where tuition was about $400 per semester. He was willing to work his way through, if only he could come up with the first semester's tuition. His parents had nothing to give him and suggested he work a year and then go to college. Neither one of them had a college degree and didn't see the importance of going to college. Howie was also considering this option. He just didn't know.

Howie was afraid that if he didn't get his college degree he would wind up like his father, a smart guy who never had any money. He was at Wilhelm's scholarship ceremony at the supermarket. While this was the last thing he would ever want to do, he felt he had no choice, and he knew Wilhelm had enough money for college. He would ask Wilhelm to lend him the $587 he had just received from the supermarket.

He went over to congratulate Wilhelm. "Wilhelm, you have all the luck."

Wilhelm looked at his shoes. He felt bad for Howie. He was going to Roget and Howie was going to City College. Wilhelm finally spoke. "I'm sorry."

"What are you sorry for? You're going to Roget—lucky stiff.".

"And you're going to City College. I'm sorry. If it wasn't for me, you might have gotten the scholarship. Who knows?"

"I don't know, Wilhelm. I might not be going to City College either."

"Not going? You must go. Why?"

"I don't have the money. I have to work next year, maybe the following year."

Wilhelm fingered the $587 check in his right pants pocket. He thought for a brief moment. "You'll get there. You'll see."

Howie never asked Wilhelm for the loan. They walked away from each other. Howie took a job at his dad's employer in the accounting department. He never went to college. What a waste of a mind. Wilhelm heard years later that Howie was now the head bookkeeper — so be it.

Wilhelm never brought up the subject of Roget Institute with his mother again. He accepted the scholarship from the institute. He continued with school and the supermarket through the end of the term. He and his mother still said very little to each other. She knew she had lost him to the "Nazis," but said nothing. She went about her daily routine. She stayed in her chair staring out the window later into the night. She would never find what she was looking for, not anymore. He worked at the supermarket through the summer. He worked as many hours as he could get to accumulate as much money as he could to take to college.

Throughout the summer he received materials and literature from the institute. His mother would leave them on his bed. They said nothing to each other. When it came time for him to leave, he went to his room to pack his bags. His mother sat in her chair and stared out of the window. He brought his bags down and placed them by the door. A cab was to pick him up and take him to the train station. He waited while his mother stared.

"Momma, will you talk to me?" His mother stared out the window. "Please, Momma, I don't want to leave like this."

His mother stared out of the window. A tear formed in the corner of her right eye, the only eye that he could see from the side.

He went to his mother. He tried to get her to look at him. She continued to stare out the window. He tried to touch her. She moved away. "Please, Momma, talk to me. I can't leave you this way."

He continued to plead with his mother. She continued to stare out the window. The cabbie was honking the car horn outside for him. Still he pleaded. "Please, Momma, I'm your son. Talk to me."

She looked at him, inner tears streaming down her mind. She spoke slowly in her best broken English. "I have no son. He has become a Nazi."

He cried inside. "Please, Momma, don't do this."

She continued to stare out the window.

He picked up his bags and walked out of the door to the cab. He didn't look back then and never has, except he sees this scene in his head every day of his life. His inner voice cries, he tries not to hear.

2

COLLEGE DAZE

Wilhelm took the cab from his house in the Bronx to the Greyhound bus terminal in Manhattan. He arrived two hours early to make sure that he got his ticket with the best connections to Boston and the Roget Institute, which was about 20 miles north of Boston. He was leaving nothing to chance. He had also left for college a week ahead of time. He wanted to arrive early so that he had sufficient time to orient himself to his new surroundings. He had always lived in the little house in the Bronx and had never slept anywhere but in his own bed. He also wanted to get out of that house as soon as he could. His mother's staring and not talking had created more tension than he could handle.

He would also be the only student attending Roget Institute to arrive on a bus. He didn't want anyone to know of his arrival in this manner. The other students would arrive in chauffeured limousines, large cars or in their own sports cars. He would arrive early and be there when they arrived. There would be no issue as to how he arrived. As a freshman that no one knew, they wouldn't care if he didn't arrive and no one would know the difference.

At the bus terminal, he was informed that he could take a bus directly to Boston with two rest stops. He could then take another bus from the Boston bus terminal right to the institute. The bus stopped in front of the institute's administration building. He would only have to carry his luggage from there to his dorm room. This was the same bus that the local employees used to go to and from work. He didn't want to be seen on the same bus. He decided to take the bus to the nearest town and then take a limousine, if available, or a fancy cab direct to his dormitory. If he couldn't travel elegantly, he would arrive elegantly.

He had been in touch with Mr. Roberts, the dean of students at the institute. Mr. Roberts had cleared it so that he could arrive a week early and stay in his dorm room. As he was on a full scholarship for tuition and room and board, Mr. Roberts obtained permission from the scholarship source to pay the additional costs for this week. While this was a minor fund for the source, it would have been substantial for Wilhelm. Mr. Roberts had even arranged a work-study job for him with Dr. Selzer, a professor in the economics department. If he liked the job and Dr. Selzer, he could continue on the job throughout the academic year. While many of the students at the institute took on such work-study projects, they usually did not get paid. Paying these students would be like giving a handout to a Rockefeller. In his case, Mr. Roberts arranged that he be paid surreptitiously at a more than adequate hourly rate, almost double what he had been earning at the supermarket.

When he arrived at the bus terminal in the little town near the institute, it was late afternoon and there were no cabs, or limousines. He found out later that primarily the low-income population, domestics, janitors, kitchen help and so on, used buses and there was very rarely a cab at the bus terminal, and certainly not a limousine. He went to the phone booth outside of the terminal, which was in its final stage of deterioration. He opened the phone book cover and found that the phone book had been stolen. He tried dialing information and found that the phone had been pulled out from its connection.

He started walking toward the institute hauling his two large suitcases and placing a smaller one on his back. The institute was approximately three miles away on a two-lane winding road. He estimated that it would take him two hours walking at such a slow pace with numerous stops, but what choice did he have. As he walked he thought of reasons why he would be entering the campus on foot — his sports car broke down, his limousine had an accident, he stopped at the nearby inn, and so on. It was now close to six o'clock in the evening and for this time in late August the sun set around seven thirty. He estimated that he would arrive at the institute after the sun had set, but before total darkness had settled in. There would be enough light for him to find his way to his dorm building, but hopefully not enough light for him to be seen by others.

He struggled along the road, taking about ten steps and then stopping, taking another ten steps and then stopping. Progress was much more tedious than he had figured. With each step the suitcases got heavier. The small bag on his back started to cut into his shoulder blades and his back ached with each step. He had gone about one hour and a quarter and calculated that he had gone less than one mile. The sun was starting to set and the sky was darkening. The moon would not be out for some time. Very shortly he would be walking in darkness. While there wasn't much traffic on the road at that time of night on a Sunday evening, there was enough to scare him each time a car passed. Most times the passing car startled him so that the bag on his back fell to the ground and the two large suitcases pulled him onto the road or into a ditch. Progress was slow and he was wondering why he was doing this. If it weren't for his poor boy's pride, he would have stayed on the bus until it stopped at the campus grounds and he would be lying on his bed in his dorm room right now.

A large sedan sped past him around a curve in the road and forced him into a ditch with all three bags flying from his back and hands. As he stumbled into the ditch to avoid the car, he twisted his ankle. He sat by the side of the road using the largest suitcase as a chair while he massaged his ankle and bemoaned his fate — an inauspicious start to his career at Roget. He sat there wondering what he should do, trudge on in spite of the ankle or just sit and wait for possible help. This wasn't the kind of neighborhood where you would expect anyone to stop and help, particularly at night. They might stop and rob you in the Bronx, but in suburban high end Massachusetts they would expect to be robbed. The change in geography and the change in incomes made all the difference in the world.

As he waited and contemplated, a large black Cadillac sped past him striking the suitcase sitting closest to the road. The thrust of the car toppled the suitcase back into the ditch. As he went into the ditch to retrieve the suitcase, the Cadillac stopped and backed up to where he was. The window across from the driver automatically came down. A voice from the car called out to him.

"Are you OK? Sorry about that." It was a workingman's voice, gruff and guttural.

Before he could respond the window went back up and the car started going forward — so much for being rescued by a big black Cadillac. He sat back on his suitcase. He looked up to see the Cadillac backing up again. This time the rear window came automatically down and a more cultured male voice spoke.

"Can we help you, young man?"

He didn't know what to say, so he said nothing.

"Are you in trouble?" purred the cultured voice.

He fumbled and stumbled and still said nothing.

"Where are you going?"

Wilhelm somehow got out of his mouth "Roget Institute."

"We are going right past there. Can we offer you our humble transportation?"

In his haste to move toward the car Wilhelm stumbled with his bags

"Please, let Timothy help you."

The driver's side opened and an enormous man wearing a driver's cap came out. The trunk opened automatically as he left the car. Timothy picked the three suitcases up as if they were newspapers and with one quick toss threw them into the enormous trunk. To Wilhelm the trunk looked larger than his small room in his house in the Bronx. His suitcases, which were such a burden for him to carry, filled one small corner of the trunk.

The door to the passenger's side in the back automatically opened and a voice said, "Please, come in and join me."

Wilhelm hesitantly entered the car to find two large seats facing each other. Sitting in the very back seat which faced forward was an elegantly dressed older gentleman — surely one of Massachusetts's multi-millionaires. He wasn't sure whether he should sit next to the man or across from him. As he hesitated, the man motioned for him to sit across from him. It seemed that there was at least six feet between the two seats that faced each other. Surely enough room to prevent him from contaminating the elderly gentleman, thought Wilhelm.

The elegant man spoke slowly as Timothy drove off from a signal by the man. "So, you are going to Roget. May I inquire as to your purpose?"

Wilhelm had never met anyone who spoke or carried themselves in such an elegant manner. He was certainly different from anyone he'd known in the Bronx, and a much improved role model.

"I'm a student there—or I'm going to be one," he stammered.

"Quite marvelous," said the man. "My grandson is also a student there. Perhaps you know him."

"Oh no, I'm just starting there."

"Aha, a new student. So, what brings you walking along our road?"

Wilhelm didn't know what to say. Should he admit the truth or make something up? His mind came quickly to his rescue. "My car broke down."

"Would that be the blue sports car we passed along the way?"

He remembered walking past the car on the side of the road. It was an MG with a soft top. He noticed that it had Connecticut license plates. "Oh, you saw my MG. Was the top OK? I always worry that someone will slice it."

The man nodded his head but didn't respond. He put out his hand. "I am Lewellyn T. Blanchard III."

Wilhelm stammered and took the hand limply. "I'm, I'm—Stanford (he had applied there) R. Yale (he had applied there as well) the fourth (the fourth had to be better than the third)—from Connecticut." That should keep him safe. Connecticut should be far enough away.

Mr. Blanchard nodded his head again. "Of the Westport Yales perhaps?"

Oh, boy! Wilhelm knew only one city in Connecticut, which was New Haven as that was the home of Yale University. He didn't know if this was a prestigious address or not, but he didn't want Mr. Blanchard to ask him any more about the Westport Yales. "Oh no, I'm from New Haven."

Mr. Blanchard seemed to accept this. "What do they call you? Is it Stan?"

"Oh, no. It's always been Stanford. Sometimes the fourth, but never Stan."

"I see. So, Stanford, what will you be studying at Roget?"

Now this was a question he could answer. He went on about his plans to use mathematical models in the conducting of businesses. Mr. Blanchard listened intently; this was something he was interested in.

The car was pulling onto the campus grounds. Timothy had stopped the car right inside the entrance gate. "So, Mr. B, where to?"

Mr. Blanchard looked at Wilhelm. "May we take you to your room? Timothy can help you with your luggage."

Wilhelm gasped; he had to stop this. If they took him to his room, they would know he had been lying. This was hardly a noble way for his initial entrance into the upper class.

"Oh no, no, I have to check in with the dean of students. He knows my dorm assignment."

"Very well. Timothy, take him to Kenneth Roberts' quarters."

Oh my God, thought Wilhelm. He knows Mr. Roberts. I hope he doesn't want to come in to say something to Mr. Roberts. It would only substantiate their opinion of the lying, cheating lower class.

The car stopped in front of, to Wilhelm, a very impressive residence. It was made of stone and completely ivy-covered with large trees all around.

For a man his size, Timothy quickly got out of the car, removed Wilhelm's bags from the trunk, and placed them in front of Mr. Roberts' residence.

"Will this be adequate, sir?"

Wilhelm quickly responded. "Fine, just fine."

Mr. Blanchard laughed without any sound. "Oh, no, Stanford. Timothy was addressing me. He doesn't talk to anyone else." To Timothy, "Yes, this should be just fine." He nodded to Wilhelm and actually winked.

As he rushed to get out of the car Mr. Blanchard put out his hand. Wilhelm took his hand and found a business card in his palm. "Please advise me of your progress. Perhaps I can be of assistance—to one of the Yales of New Haven." He winked again. "Please contact my grandson, once you have settled in. His name is Ingersoll B. Blanchard, Junior. He's in his third year. Perhaps he may be of assistance as well."

Wilhelm stammered a thank you and put the card in his jacket pocket. It was his good fortune that his mother had taught him to always travel in a business suit. As he got out of the car, he noticed the street sign. It read Blanchard Boulevard and was the main road running through the campus. Wilhelm later learned that Mr. Lewellyn T. Blanchard III was the chairman of the institute's board of trustees and the chairman of the board of Blanchard Industries. Wilhelm's first real contact with the upper class and he couldn't use it. His grandson, Ingersoll, spent the first semester trying to locate a freshman named Stanford R. Yale IV on his grandfather's request. He was, of course, unsuccessful. Wilhelm, on the other hand, was successful in concealing his identity until Ingersoll graduated the following year. The mystery of Stanford R. Yale IV was never solved. Somehow he never appeared at Mr. Roberts' residence that night and was never heard from again. Mr. Blanchard endowed a scholarship in the name of Stanford R. Yale as gratitude for their conversation in the car that night, thus beginning the legend of Stanford R. Yale at Roget Institute. The scholarship became known as the "tome of the unknown student."

Wilhelm slept in his clothes the first night. He was too tired and achey to unpack. He slept well and long. He awoke around nine in the morning the next day. He had an eleven o'clock meeting with Mr. Roberts, the dean of students.

Mr. Roberts wanted to orientate Wilhelm personally as the school admitted only two students with financial scholarships each year. This was the trustees' way of providing opportunities to the less fortunate, enough but not too much. Mr. Roberts came from a middle class background. His father was a headmaster at one of New England's more prestigious prep schools and not a captain of industry, so he knew first hand what it was like to be economically deprived. It was a special interest of his to make sure the so-called "less fortunate" students did well. He would take special interest with Wilhelm as the first student from anywhere with a name like the Bronx.

This gave Wilhelm sufficient time to put his things away, clean himself up, and get dressed in a clean suit, tie, and shirt. He had fallen on the first bed in the room when he arrived the night before. He now noticed that there was another similar bed in the room. The other bed was closer to the shared bathroom, closet, and bureau. He assumed this was the more favorable bed. He hesitated as to whether to select this bed instead of the one he had fallen onto. He debated as to whether the first to arrive or the first in wealth should have their choice. He ultimately decided that wealth always wins out anyway so he kept the bed he started with. He was sure that his roommate would have to be wealthier than he; even if it was another scholarship student he would have to be. In truth, half the room and half the bathroom were more than twice what he had had at home in the Bronx.

Wilhelm also took what he thought to be the second best bathroom position to place his toilet articles. This was the cabinet furthest from the door with the smaller mirror and no window on the side. He took a long shower as he always did to make sure he was absolutely clean. He used his own scented soap and shampoo rather than the institute issue. He also used his own towel, which he had brought from home.

Wilhelm had been taught to be fastidious about his cleanliness and dress by his mother and he was always a good and obedient student. He dressed in his new silk blend suit and imported white cotton shirt with a 100% silk neck tie. These items were purchased from the money given to him by the supermarket. When he had pampered and fretted sufficiently, mindful of making the right impression with Mr. Roberts, he left the dormitory. As he hadn't been given a meal ticket yet, and he didn't want to spend any more than he had to, he skipped breakfast in the student cafeteria.

He arrived at approximately a quarter to eleven at Mr. Roberts' office. He was greeted by a rather schoolmarmish-looking elderly lady who informed him that Mr. Roberts would be right with him. He looked around the handsomely appointed office with its rich paneled walls and furniture and thought to himself, "This is where I belong. I will never return to that other life." He picked up the most recent copy of the alumni news. It read like a Who's Who in American business and industry. He was quite impressed and looked forward to the day when his name would appear. He was half way through ogling the names, with their accomplishments, when the door opened and Mr. Roberts appeared. He was dressed and groomed impeccably, making Wilhelm feel inferior in his clothes that were more than the best his money could buy. Wilhelm had another role model and now knew what it meant to dress your part.

"Welcome to our little institute. I hope everything is to your liking."

"And more so." What else could he say?

Mr. Roberts led him into his office and went over what he felt needed to be known to be successful at Roget. Things like dormitory hours and privileges. He gave Wilhelm his meal ticket for the semester that included three meals plus two snacks — tomorrow he would have a full breakfast. He told him about specific facilities such as the library, student center, cafeteria and snack bars, and so on. He also went over the terms of Wilhelm's scholarship as to how to register for classes, buy his books and supplies, purchase his meals and other essentials without bringing notice to his status. As far as Mr. Roberts and the board of trustees were concerned, Wilhelm was just another student. Their role was to make him as successful a graduate as possible, as this was how the institute continued to attract rich and successful students.

In the course of orientation, Mr. Roberts passed over a form to him that asked by what name he wished to be addressed while at Roget. He asked what his choices were. Mr. Roberts replied that he was free to select any name he wished. This was to be his Roget name. Legally he could have any other name. He asked whether he could have a Roget name and the same name legally if he wished. Mr. Roberts thought a moment and then told him he didn't see why not.

"Do you have a name in mind or do you want to think about it? Typically, this form is used for students' nicknames. We seem to have a number of Biffs, Chips, Cliffs, Juniors, and the like. You might want to use a nickname as well."

"I don't know. I've never really had a nickname."

"What name would you like? Wilhelm isn't a typical upper class name, is it?"

"No, it probably isn't. Would William be okay?"

Mr. Roberts stroked his chin for a bit. "We have had a few Williams. I think that would be fine. How about a last name? You want to stay with Broadfort? Again, this is not good upper class. You have to think about your future."

He thought for a minute. "Would Bradford be all right? It's pretty close to Broadfort and I saw a number of Bradfords listed in the alumni news."

"Umm, quite right. There's the Bradfords from Bradford Industries, all alumni. Now, how about a middle name? A good middle name always helps."

"My middle name is Siegfried. He was a good friend of my mother's parents. Would it be all right to keep it?"

"I'm sure it would be, if that's what you want, but it is a mite Germanic, wouldn't you say?"

"That's not good?"

"Not really acceptable upper class. Not in today's times. Can we do something with that?"

"I noticed a number of alumni use just a middle initial. Would that be all right?"

"Hmmm, William S. Bradford, a good upper class Protestant name. Sounds fine to me. Has success written all over it. Would you also want a suffix?"

"Suffix, what's that?"

Mr. Roberts laughed without making a sound. Wilhelm would have to practice that. "Wilhelm, I mean William, a suffix is your generation designation. You know, like Junior, the second, or the third."

Wilhelm nodded affirmatively. "Oh yes, a suffix. I like being a third."

"So be it. I dub you William S. Bradford III." He tapped Wilhelm on both lapels with his ruler as he said this. He handed Wilhelm a form.

"What is this?"

"That is the legal form in Massachusetts to have your name changed."

"You mean I can be William S. Bradford III legally."

"Certainly, if you would like. Fill out this form, have your mother sign it as you are under the age of 21, and return it to me. I will have our attorneys take care of the legal work. No charge to the student, just part of student services. You won't be the first student to have been born in this office."

"But I don't live in Massachusetts."

"You do now, as of yesterday."

Wilhelm filled out the form, forged his mother's signature as usual, and returned the form to Mr. Roberts a few days later. In a few weeks he was notified that he was now legally William S. Bradford III of Massachusetts. That was the day that William was born and Wilhelm died.

William started working with Dr. Selzer the following day. She was the only female full professor at Roget (there were two others—one an instructor and another an associate professor). It had taken her almost double the time to make full professor than her male counterparts. She was resented by most of the other faculty for being female, pushing her way into the institute, and mostly for being Jewish or by others for being German and Jewish. She was also more renowned than the other professors, more sought after for speeches and articles, and known as a genius in the field of economic and business models.

Ruth Selzer (then Ruth Teitelbaum) left Germany in 1935 after she had completed the university with a bachelor's degree in economics. She was then 20 years old and loved her life in Berlin and the university. She came to America on a scholarship to be part of a special master's degree program at the Harvard Business School, the first to combine business, economics, and the sciences. She was one of eight core students from around the world. The students in this experimental program developed the main thinking for many of the business and economic models still used today. Each of the eight students was offered an additional scholarship by Harvard to continue their studies leading toward a doctoral degree in economics. Ruth had spent almost three years at Harvard and wanted to go home to Berlin. However, this was the same time that the Nazis were making it difficult for Jews to remain in Germany.

Her parents in Berlin urged her to stay at Harvard and become an American citizen. They would join her as soon as they could. Ruth accepted the doctoral scholarship to Harvard, became an American citizen, and within a year was able to bring her parents to America. She was one of the lucky ones, however. She left the prejudice of Germany for the prejudice of America.

In 1958, when William started working with her, Ruth had been in the country for 23 years and was now 43 years old. Both of her parents still lived in the Boston area. They talked on the phone or saw each other every day. They were still not sure that they were safe, even in America. Ruth still had a slight German accent, but only if you listened closely, or you wanted to place her as a German—you heard what you wanted. Ruth married Herman Selzer, another one of the Harvard doctoral students in economics, when she was 22 years old and he was 24. They had recently celebrated their twentieth wedding anniversary. They had a good marriage, both socially and professionally, and held on to each other for dear life.

They had wanted to have children when they married but after three years of trying and four miscarriages they felt that something must be wrong. Upon extensive examination, it was determined that Ruth had irreparable damage to her reproductive system. The doctors estimated that the damage occurred during Ruth's puberty, prior to her losing her virginity. Ruth could only remember a study that she took part in while at the university when she was 17 or 18 that was required of all Jewish females. She was told that it was to determine whether there was a gene that made Jewish females more intelligent than their gentile counterparts. They were asked to ingest a yellowish liquid and then were gynecologically examined. Ruth figured this must have been when the damage was done. The Nazis were systematically ensuring that the brightest Jewish females would not reproduce. The bastards, she thought, if they didn't kill you, they would make sure your children didn't live or were even born. Ruth and Herman accepted their fate; they still had each other. She never forgave the Germans, and the rest of the world who let it happen. She loved people, but she hated small minds.

When Ruth and Herman graduated from the Harvard doctoral program, they both applied for faculty positions. They had agreed that they would like to work together as university professors and economics researchers. Ruth, as first in her class, assumed she would have little difficulty in being accepted at Harvard, so she did not apply anywhere else. At that time, there were no females in the economics department, although there was female faculty in the other departments as a token minority. Herman placed in the middle of the graduating class and to hedge his bets applied to a number of other leading universities with reputable economics departments. It was agreed that as the man it was more important for Herman to have employment than Ruth. She could find part time work wherever they wound up.

Ironically, Herman was offered a faculty position in the economics department at Harvard, while Ruth wasn't even granted an interview. She was furious. This was her alma mater; they had no business treating her that way. Herman was offered two other positions in the midwest and offered to take one of those jobs if this would be better for Ruth. She had only known Berlin and Boston and didn't want to start somewhere else. She would talk to the head of the economics department. There must be some mistake.

Ruth went to see Dr. Roy Aikman, the chair of the economics department at Harvard. He was most cordial, in a pompous way, to her as she was a recent doctoral graduate and the top in the class. She bluntly asked him why she wasn't granted at least an interview for employment. Dr. Aikman hemmed and hawed, shuffled his feet and said nothing. There was nothing to say.

Ruth started to fume. "Come on, Aikman. What's going on here? I was your best student. You owed me at least an interview."

Aikman postured and stroked his chin and his little obscene Vandyke beard. He pulled and pulled, saying nothing.

"Listen, Aikman, you tell me what's what or I go to the President."

Dr. Aikman knew she would do that. "Ruth, yes, you were our best student, maybe the best ever."

"So, this is how you treat your best. I'd hate to be your worst."

Aikman played with his fingers—he had these long tapering fingers, always meticulously manicured—the man was indeed a dandy and an expert university politician. He didn't teach or lecture anymore, he didn't do the necessary administrative work; he postured and politicked. This was what was expected of a department chair and this was how the successful ones survived and continued to get very nice annual salary increases. As their reputations grew, so did their compensation.

"Okay, Ruth, let me explain."

"So, I'm stopping you?"

"No, no, I didn't mean that. It's just very difficult."

"The truth always is."

"Ruth, please trust me. I tried to do what I could."

She was trying to control herself. She felt like a Jew trapped by a Nazi, and maybe she was. "And what was that? Ignore me and hope I disappear. Well we don't disappear."

He postured. Oh, could that man posture. "Look I fought for you, as hard as I could. The other department members weren't ready for a woman."

She began to fume. "And you, you are ready, for some real competition?"

"Please, Ruth, I did what I could. They wouldn't accept you, so I got them to accept Herman. It was the best I could do. Please try to understand."

"What I understand is that you are all a bunch of academic bastards, protecting each other. You know Herm won't give you any trouble, but you're afraid of a competent woman. Shame on all of you Nazi bastards!"

Dr. Aikman was taken aback. No one talked to him like this, not if they wanted to keep their jobs. We made the right decision, he thought.

"Look, Ruth, I know you are angry. What can I do for you? I know the system doesn't always work right. Tell me what I can do?" Aikman was pleading. He wanted her out of his office; he would tell her anything.

"You can make it right. You know what you have to do."

"Offer you a faculty position in the department, is that you want?"

"That would make it right. It is the only honorable thing you can do."

"Ruth, why do you always make things so hard? Even as a student always challenging, always challenging." Aikman shook his head.

"So you don't do that?"

"Ruth, please. I can't, my hands are tied."

"Always, blaming the others. Why should this be different?"

"All right, Ruth, this is what I can do. I'll get you at least two adjunct classes a semester, maybe more, to teach and a research position on one of our grants. That's probably the best I can do. If other crumbs come along, I'll throw them your way. You are an excellent economist."

"Crumbs, you throw crumbs to an excellent economist."

"Please, Ruth, I thought you wanted a job. I'm trying to help you."

"I don't want a job, I want my job. The one I earned."

"I'm afraid that is impossible."

"Yes, it always is, isn't it?"

Dr. Aikman said nothing. He fidgeted, hoping the meeting was over.

Ruth stared up at him. Another Nazi bastard justifying himself, she thought. She got up abruptly and walked confidently from the room—back straight, head up—leaving the office door open.

He called after her. "Let me know if you want the adjunct position."

He hoped to never hear from her again—he got his wish.

After a great deal of discussion between Herman and Ruth, they decided that Herman should take the faculty position at Harvard. They wanted to stay in the Boston area. Ruth could find adjunct and research work elsewhere. She would have nothing to do with her alma mater; she would show them who was excellent. Ruth began her career at Roget Institute, at age 28, teaching adjunct and working on outside research projects. She did this for four years. During that time, Roget hired five additional faculty members in the field of economics — all men. Ruth applied for each opening. In the meantime, Ruth had three books published, all extremely respected in the field of economics. She was becoming nationally known and sought after. When the next faculty position opened at Roget, they could no longer ignore her. They offered her a full time faculty position at less than a male's starting salary and she surprised them by accepting the position. That was twelve years ago and the faculty boys still resented her. She was the best liked and respected teacher by the students. She brought in many grants worth thousands of dollars on her name alone. Students came to the school just for the chance to work with her. Her salary was still less than the other male faculty in similar positions. Once she earned the position of full professor, it took two years longer than normal to be granted tenure. She was much sought after nationally and her books continued to sell well — to hell with all of those Nazi bastards.

When William met Dr. Selzer in her office the following morning, she was waiting for him with coffee and a Bundt cake she had baked herself. She was on the short side; a little over five feet tall, and over the years had spread out considerably. She was the epitome of a Jewish mother, except she wasn't one. Although she had no children of her own, she practiced on everyone else's.

William didn't drink coffee, but he sure could eat cake— he had three large pieces. He was happy and so was Ruth—she liked to see a boy eat well.

"So, Wilhelm, you want to be an economist. Why is this so?"

He thought of his own mother, whom he missed in his own way, with the size, the appearance, and the voice of Dr. Selzer. "Please, I'm now William."

"Another victim of Mr. Roberts, eh? He's out to make Protestants of us all. What Hitler couldn't do, Mr. Roberts do, eh?" She looked at the form in her hand. "So, it's now William Siegfried Broadfort?" She looked up at William.

He hesitated. "Oh no, it's William S. Bradford III."

Dr. Selzer laughed to herself, just the way his mother did. "The gentile bastard is thorough, eh?"

"Oh no, this was my idea. I didn't want to be the book Nazi here too."

Dr. Selzer nodded her head. "So the kids made fun of your being German, and being Jewish too?"

He was quick to correct. "Oh, I'm not Jewish!"

She looked him over. She was never wrong. There was a Jew lurking in William S. Bradford III, even if he didn't know it— she knew it. "Don't be so sure."

This was the first time William thought about the possibility. His mother had kept him away from all religious affiliations. True she always crossed the street to avoid passing in front of a Jewish temple, but she did the same for Catholic and Protestant churches. True Sophie was her friend and Jewish, and she worked for Sophie's brother Mr. Rufkin. True she really didn't have any gentile friends, but she really didn't have any friends. Karl, his father, could be Jewish, but he really didn't know and he really didn't want to know. He said nothing.

She stared at him for a long uncomfortable period. "Ah, ha! So, let's get to work."

When Ruth got home that evening she couldn't wait to tell Herman about Wilhelm or William. Herman was working in his study when she got home. She didn't like to interrupt him, they had an agreement not to do this to each other, but she had to tell him about William. She knocked softly on his doorjamb, as the door was open. Herman was greatly absorbed when he worked; she always thought this was so cute.

Herman looked up. "So, Ruthie, what is it that can't wait?" Herman actually liked to be interrupted by Ruth; she was his life. It was Ruth who didn't want to be interrupted by Herman; he was not her life.

"Herm, you won't believe this. The most extraordinary young man came into my office this morning. He's going to be my new work-study. His name is Wilhelm Broadfort!"

"German, Ruthie?"

"Not only that, but I think Jewish."

"Ruthie, you are always making everybody Jewish. He might just as well be Nazi."

"I don't think so. He wears a suit, neatly dressed, and well spoken".

"So, Ruthie, that makes him Jewish?"

"No, no, Herm, I have my instincts."

"OK, but don't get too close. You remember what happened with Charles. How devastated you were when he decided not to accept your offer to be your research assistant."

"Ya, Herm, I remember, but this one is different. I just know he is."

"OK, but don't get overly involved. You can't be everyone's mother."

"I know, but this time it will be different. You'll see."

"I hope so. I don't want you to be hurt again."

Herman looked at Ruth with much love. "I love you, Ruthie." He continued to stare at her.

She said nothing and slowly moved away.

Herman went back to his work. Ruth went into the kitchen to prepare dinner. Tonight it would be Herman's favorite, lamb chops and mashed potatoes with maybe a little red wine, or maybe a lot. She would see.

William worked with Dr. Selzer the remainder of the week. The more they worked together, the more they liked each other. She was the mother he had never had and he was the son she never had. This was when William started to miss his own mother and wrote her twice a week to no avail — each letter returned unopened. On Friday afternoon, Dr. Selzer called William into her office. He stood at the front of her desk, smoothing down his suit jacket. He always worked with his suit jacket on and it got ruffled as he got into the task. Dr. Selzer had her head down in her work; she always worked like that. When she worked, nothing disturbed her.

William coughed for effect. "Dr. Selzer, you wanted to see me?"

Ruth looked up. "Ah, Wilhelm. I mean William. I was wondering. You have plans for tonight, no? Your first Friday here?"

"Plans, no I have no plans. I was finishing the study I was working on."

"On your own time. Oh, no. That won't do. You come to our house. Friday night, you should be with family."

He saw no greater significance to be with family on Friday night than any other night. He didn't want to be with family on any night.

She handed him a note. "Here. Our address. You will be there at seven, no?"

Just like his mother, he thought. He took the note.

The Selzers' house was within a mile of the Roget campus, a distance that William could easily walk. He left his room around six o'clock so that he could walk leisurely. It was the end of August and still fairly warm and humid. He didn't want to be too sweaty when he arrived at the Selzers'. He was wearing another one of the new suits he had bought with the supermarket bonus money. He wanted to look good for the Selzers, not only for Ruth Selzer but also for her husband whom he hadn't met yet. To William, Herman was a legend in the field of economics. He had authored and co-authored many groundbreaking journal articles and was considered one of the top economics professors in the country.

On the way to the Selzers' house, he came upon a beautiful patch of wildflowers along the side of the road. Since they belonged to no one, he saw no harm in picking a bouquet. He couldn't afford to bring anything else. He wrapped the bouquet in his handkerchief to make it look more presentable. He was sure Dr. Selzer would like it. She always had fresh flowers on her desk next to the picture of Herman. As he was picking the flowers, a large black Cadillac limousine passed by him scaring him so that he almost tumbled into the bushes. As the limousine passed by, the driver honked the car horn at him. He looked up quickly and thought he saw Mr. Blanchard sitting in the back. He couldn't be sure as the tinted window was all the way up and visibility into the car was poor.

As he continued his walk to the Selzers', a large blue convertible filled with six college kids passed him by almost knocking him to the ground. He was holding the bouquet way out in front of him, so as to not soil his clothes. William always walked erect with his head up. He looked like the Frankenstein monster on the way to a funeral. As the blue convertible passed him it slowed down and the kid sitting next to the driver leaned back and yelled at him.

"You walk like that, you're going to hurt the pansy."

He looked back at the car. What dummies, he thought, didn't know a peony from a pansy. William called back at them, as he couldn't tolerate stupidity.

"It's not a pansy, it's a peony." He kept on walking.

The kid in the car yelled back at him. "I was talking to the peony."

The six kids laughed at him, gave him the middle finger and sped off.

This was why he preferred to be alone, especially not with people his age.

When he arrived at the Selzers' door, he stopped to fix himself and the bouquet. He hesitated and then rang the bell. The Selzers lived in a very neat and clean Cape Cod house in the middle of an elegant formal garden. He was sure that Ruth must care for the garden; however, he found out later that it was Herman. Both Ruth and Herman came to the door. Ruth tried to hug William, but he pulled away. He placed the bouquet between himself and the Selzers for protection. Ruth took the bouquet and Herman settled for a handshake. Thus began William's relationship with the Selzers. It was to last the four years that he attended Roget.

Although William was always uncomfortable with people, that first Friday night at the Selzers' went very well. The Selzers spoke mostly about the Roget curriculum and the field of economics. William was surprised that he had anything to contribute and the Selzers seemed pleased talking to him. After dinner, Herman took him into his study to show him his library and the projects he was working on. Herman offered William the use of his library and the freedom to borrow any of the books he wished. William was quite flattered. He liked Herman's easy manner and the way in which he respected his input and opinion. Herman and Ruth seemed to share this ability.

As both Ruth and Herman were doctors of economics, it was proper to address them as such. William would continue to address each of them as Doctor Selzer and they would answer him at the same time. It quickly became a joke between them. Ruth, as she was laughing, told William that it would be quite all right to call her Ruth and her husband Herm in their home, as long as she was Dr. Selzer at school.

After the first visit, he would find a note each Friday morning inviting him to the Selzers' house for dinner. This became a standard joke between them. Ruth would ask him what he was doing on Friday night and William would respond that he had been invited to dinner. This was the one time in the week that Ruth was sure that William ate well. He always arrived at the door dressed in one of his suits and ties holding a bouquet of flowers picked from the side of the road—this too became a tradition. Ruth always gave him a bag of leftovers when he left to make sure that William had some good food for the rest of the week.

As the term went on, William would be invited over to the Selzers' for Tuesday dinner under the guise of working late on his project and then for Sunday brunch so that the Selzers could review the work on his projects. Ruth was using William on a number of grant projects other than the original work-study project, as many projects as William could handle. William turned none of them down. Each project was different, challenging, and new learning. When Ruth had exhausted her projects and William was still eager for more challenging work, Herman found a couple of grant projects in his department at Harvard that William could work on.

He was paid for his work out of the grant money, and he felt he needed every dollar that he could earn. While working closely with both of the Selzers and now coming to their house at least three times a week, William and the Selzers had become close allies. Ruth had her Jewish son, William had parents he could turn to, and Herman had a friend and colleague he could trust.

After a few months of this routine, William arrived one Friday night to find a strange girl around his age standing with the Selzers at their door. William offered his bouquet to Ruth as she tried to hug him (this also had become a standing joke), but this time she passed the bouquet on to the strange girl. William stood there uncomfortably shuffling his feet.

Ruth looked at him fondly, wanting to pinch his cheek, but not daring to. "What a boychik," she thought to herself. He'll make some nice Jewish girl a wonderful husband. Ruth would make certain of that.

Ruth pushed the girl to the front. She was as shy as William. "William, this is Carla Gladstone. She's the daughter of one of Herm's colleagues. Her parents are out for the evening and we thought tonight we make it a foursome. Maybe play Scrabble as teams. Ya?"

William spent his first uncomfortable evening with the Selzers. Neither he nor Carla said much. He tried to talk economics with the Selzers, but they kept bringing the conversation back to personal issues related to him and Carla. At the door, when William was leaving, Ruth somehow worked it so that William would walk Carla home, as it was "right on his way." As it turned out, it was a mile and a half out of his way. Neither of them said anything as they walked along — they both felt uncomfortable with the situation. As Carla would move closer to him, he would feel the clammy feeling coming on and would move farther away. At Carla's house, she said a quick good bye and ran for her door. Her mother opened the door; she ran into her arms and disappeared into the house.

William never said anything to the Selzers. He knew they meant well. They wanted him to have a social life and a girl. While he felt he didn't need their help, he would get his own girl if and when he was ready, he couldn't bring himself to tell this to the Selzers. They had been too good to him.

As William said nothing, the line of unexpected girls his age continued on his visits to the Selzers. He couldn't remember all of them, but there was Natalie, Linda, Carol, two Bonnies, three Susans, Sharon, and Sonia, each of them as shy and colorless as he was — a perfect match in the eyes of Ruth Selzer. He would have avoided these "dates" if he could, but he didn't know how to without hurting Ruth. So he came each time, had an uncomfortable dinner, and an after dinner walk home. The evenings when such a mystery guest appeared at the Selzers, the evenings ended earlier and earlier.

On one of these evenings, a girl unlike the others greeted William at the door. She came to the door by herself and automatically took William's bouquet and placed it on the table beside the door.

"Hi, I'm Becky Goodman. You must be William Bradford. Ruth and Herm have told me so much about you. I can't wait to hear what you think about Herm's new supply theory."

She took William's arm and led him into the kitchen where Ruth and Herm were preparing dinner together. They looked up casually. Ruth winked at him. William had started to get the clammy feeling, but somehow he let Becky take him by the arm. She seemed to be a different kind of girl, actually more like a man.

Ruth continued tossing the salad. "So, you've met our Becky, ya, William?" William nodded. Becky smiled.

Becky was on the dark side— dark hair, deep olive complexion, and dark brown eyes. She was on the large side, but not fat— meatier. She was wearing a tight short skirt and a tight sweater. She had large solid thighs, much too large for a short skirt, and large solid breasts much too large for a tight sweater. This was the kind of girl who had always intimidated William, but somehow he didn't feel that way with Becky. She didn't seem like she wanted him physically, but more intellectually. As long as William could avert his eyes from looking at her breasts, he felt that they could get along.

The four of them had a wonderful evening together talking about economics and the politics of their respective institutions. Becky was attending Jones College, an exclusive girls school for very wealthy elite Protestant heiresses of proper upbringing. Her father was on the faculty of its brother institution, which had a reciprocal agreement for free tuition at the other's school. Becky was the first Jewish girl to insist on admittance to Jones College under this agreement. There had never been a problem as Becky's father was the first Jewish faculty member, hired at Herm's insistence, at either school. No one at Jones College would have expected Becky to want to go, as there were plenty of other good colleges for her kind. This was the very reason Becky insisted on admittance to Jones.

The four of them became a regular Friday night team. They talked through the night with none of them wishing for the night to end including William. Becky (William called her Rebecca) would drive him home in her two-door Plymouth at the end of the evening, as it was late and usually quite dark outside. He would sit rigidly against the side of his door, as far from her as he could get. Regardless of the lightness of the discussion at the Selzers', he would grow silent on the ride home. Becky would drive and look at him slyly out of the corner of her eye. He felt her laughing internally at him, but he said nothing. He didn't want to get any closer to her, but he didn't want her to stop coming on Friday nights.

William shared his dorm room with Chandler Harrington (either the sixth or seventh), a rather pretentious rich kid that he found intimidating. He made William feel cheap, dirty, and unworthy of sharing space with someone of such stature. He tried to spend as little time as possible in his room, coming in late from working with Dr. Selzer and leaving early to have breakfast on his own. He avoided all of the "Chandler Harringtons" on the campus as best as he could.

Saturday was the most difficult day for him. Dr. Selzer's office was closed, so that he couldn't work on his projects if he wanted to. Chandler would usually have some of his chums meet him on Saturday, most times in their room, to spend the day together—at a polo match, a cricket game, a horse and hound hunt or some other such activity. William was never invited along; it was made quite clear he wouldn't be welcome; such activities were not for his kind. This didn't bother him as he found Chandler and his chums quite boring. He was forced, however, to leave his room quite early on Saturday mornings to avoid the whole Chandler scene.

For the first few months of the semester he would leave his room on Saturdays usually by six in the morning. His roommate was a late and deep sleeper. If he was careful and quiet, he could avoid Chandler for the entire week. For William, it was just like living alone in his room at home. He would walk into town, timing himself so that he arrived around seven o'clock when the local diner opened. He would always order the same thing — whole-wheat toast, dry, two poached eggs, and a small orange juice, with water on the side. He would sit at the counter by himself talking to no one. The counter waitress, who was about his age and semi-attractive, tried to get friendly, but William cut her off. She thought it strange that someone her age would be dressed in a suit and tie on a Saturday with apparently nowhere to go. She nicknamed him "the tie."

After his breakfast, which he prolonged until after eight, he would get to the library as it opened. He would then spend the mornings reading the books that Ruth and Herman, and sometimes Becky, had mentioned the previous Friday evening. Most of these books were classic literature or philosophy. This entire subject area was completely new to him and he enjoyed reading and then discussing these books with the Selzers. This was the extent of his liberal education. Becky, on the other hand, was in a liberal arts program and enjoyed talking about economics, as she had no formal education in this area. When he became hungry, he would go to the park and eat his lunch. In bad weather he ended up at the library cafeteria. His lunch usually consisted of leftovers from Friday night's dinner at the Selzers'. He would take a book from the library with him to lunch— he had a deal with the librarian. After lunch, he would walk around the town never going into any of the stores or acknowledging anyone he passed on the street. When he was done for the day, he would return the book to the library (he never checked out a book) and walk back to his room. He would arrive late in the afternoon, always after four o'clock when he was sure Chandler would be gone for the rest of the day and night. Once Chandler left on Saturday, he was either gone until early the next morning or late Sunday night. William didn't care where he went; only that he was gone. He was becoming addicted to his Saturday routine as much as he had been addicted to his daily routines at home. He was content with his routine, but not happy. He started to look for work on Saturdays so that he could fill his time more productively. So far, he had no success, other than wait person or delivery type jobs.

One Friday night in November, Becky mentioned that she had two tickets to an art opening at a museum in Boston. She made eye contact with William, but he said nothing. Ruth, always the matchmaker, suggested, somewhat strongly, that maybe William could go with her. Becky raised her eyebrows at him. Ruth looked at him sternly. William looked down. "Sure, that might be nice."

Becky smiled. "Great, I'll pick you up at your room at nine."

He shook his head. "No, no, meet me at the diner."

William had never been to an art museum before. Becky knew all about art and the lives of the artists. For William it was like a whole new education. However, he would turn away from the nude female pictures. Becky noticed this and tried to steer clear from this form of art. He was much relieved. After the first night at the Selzers', when Becky had noticed his discomfort looking at her large breasts, she had worn loose fitting tops that de-emphasized her breast size. Today, however, as it was a Saturday, she had worn one of her tight fitting sweaters. William had successfully looked away. Most other male visitors to the museum couldn't take their eyes off her breasts; some stared unabashedly at her chest. She didn't seem to notice or care, but he felt quite uncomfortable. A number of the males winked knowingly or gave William the okay sign as if he owned those breasts.

William and Becky began to plan their Saturdays together, to other art shows and museums, a theater production, a concert and so on. They enjoyed sharing and talking about these things, but stopped short of really becoming closer. They were merely sharing their loneliness together. William was very much alone at Roget with the rich kids, while Becky was very much alone at Jones College as the only Jew with the rich, gentile kids. Both schools had restriction policies, Roget as to Jews, no more than four at a time and only upper class, and poor kids, Jones College as to no Jews and poor kids. In this regard, the two schools were quite similar. Both of them suffered from not meeting their school's entrance criteria as to family background.

Often times during one of their discussions on a Saturday, Becky would feel particularly close to William and reach over to touch his arm or take his hand. He would quickly pull away and retreat into himself. She would nod and accept this. She didn't quite understand it, but she accepted it. Other guys were always trying to grab at her breasts, but he had no interest at all in her breasts or in her as a female. This intrigued her and somehow made him more attractive. It also allowed her to be completely at ease with a male, making it unnecessary to work at being more attractive or sexually alluring. This was a relief to her. They had an exclusive world on Friday nights and Saturday days, but never Saturday nights. They made no contact at all during the week. It was an arrangement that worked well for each of them.

William felt he couldn't go home with the way he had deceived his mother and that his mother wouldn't welcome him. So he stayed at school on the weekends. Becky didn't want to go home to face her father. He was quite against her pushing her way into Jones College, a place where she and her kind were not welcome.

It was embarrassing to him as the only Jewish instructor at his school. He had always kept a low profile, as a person and a Jew. He was content with his subservient role within a dominant society that did not include him. His daughter, against his wishes, had pierced his veil of invisibility. He could not forgive her for this, and Becky could not forgive his acceptance of oppression by a dominant society.

William was lying on his bed one Wednesday night reading his economic modeling homework assignment. His mind wasn't focusing as sharply as it normally did, and he found that he had to read each section over a number of times before it became clear to him. This was particularly frustrating to him as he was used to grasping everything the first time. He was trying to understand a difficult section on exponential smoothing of modeling results when there was an abrupt knock at his door. His body shook. No one had ever knocked on his door before, at least not looking for him. This was Wednesday and everyone in the dorm knew that Chandler spent Wednesday evenings with his family at the Harrington Manor. That was why William studied in his room on Wednesday evenings. He went back to his studies. It must be a mistake. The knock came again, this time with a voice.

"Bradford, put your suit on. Call for you. It sounds female. Better put your tie on too."

He heard footsteps move away from his door. Whoever it was, he was just doing his duty. He didn't care if William answered the phone or not. It was just another chance to poke fun at the "outsider." He moved slowly to the phone downstairs in the hall. He had no idea who would be calling him. He had instructed the Selzers not to call him here. The only other female he could think of was his mother, but she didn't have a telephone. As he approached the phone, there were two other students waiting to use the phone. One of them called out to him.

"Hey, Bradford, move your poor ass. We have important calls to make."

He picked up the phone. "Hello." He sounded there, but not there.

"William, is that you?" It was Becky.

"Becky, you called me here. Why?"

"Why not, this is where you live."

"But, how did you get this number?"

"You're a registered student there, aren't you?"

"Yeah, I guess so. So, what do you want?" He didn't like this at all.

"Really glad to hear from me. Is that it?"

"No, it's okay. It's just that I like to keep this part of my life private."

"William, you like to keep all parts of your life private. I'm sorry I penetrated your privacy shield."

"No, it's all right. It's just that I'll see you on Friday. Couldn't it wait?"

"No, not really. It's about Saturday."

"Becky, I know. We're going to the new exhibit on dinosaurs at the museum of natural history."

"Yeah, right. This is about Saturday night."

"Saturday night? We never see each other on Saturday night. I thought we agreed to that."

"Yeah, we did. But this is something special, very special. I need your help."

"Okay, Becky. I'll help if I can. So?"

"So, it's a mixer."

"What's a mixer?"

"A social. Kind of a get together with boys and girls, sort of a dance, you know a mixer."

"A dance? I can't dance."

"Don't worry, you won't have to dance if you don't want to. I just want you to come and bring some friends, if you want."

"I don't have any friends here. Remember, I'm the poor boy."

"Look, can you come?"

"I'm not sure. Why is it so important?"

"Oh, boy." She was getting frustrated. "Because these rich bitches are such shits. Is that what you want to hear?"

He always felt uncomfortable when he heard off-color words. He didn't know what to say.

"William, are you still there? I'm sorry, rich girls. Is that better? Listen. Once a month the school has these freshman, ah, woman mixers and invites boys from all the neighborhood colleges. It's part of Jones' program to get their students married before they become sophomores. They believe that's best for future contributions. The college department of MRS sends out flyers to male colleges to post on the bulletin boards."

"I've never seen any here at Roget."

"That's because the administration here doesn't consider Roget boys as proper husband material. Rich enough, but too smart for a Jones girl."

"I see. So how would my coming to the—mixer—help you?"

"I'm the middle class Jewish girl here. The gentile boys dance with me to get close to my—uh—upper body, but they are forbidden by the code of the elite to date me. William, please, I'm all alone here. I need a friend. Please come—alone, or with some others. I'll pick you up. Please, just come. Say you will."

There was silence on the phone.

"William, are you there?"

"Yeah, I'll come. But, stay close to me. These things really scare me."

"I know, William. I'll stay as close as you'll let me."

This was William's first real Saturday night date, or any real date for that matter. He waited with trepidation for Saturday night to come. He didn't want to go alone. However, he had told the truth to Becky; he really didn't have any friends at Roget. He didn't know what to do. He had the clammy feeling all the next day and couldn't sleep at night. He kept dreaming of exposure to female body parts. At night he woke up drenched in sweat with his mouth dry. He had agreed to go and now he felt stuck. He wanted to bring some others as a buffer, but from whom? He searched his mind as to who he could ask without being put down or laughed at. The only one he could come up with was Gaylord Dalton. He wasn't exactly the best choice for a dance with females, but he was safe to ask. Gaylord was the scion of Robert Dalton, the founder of Dalton Industries, who had made a vast fortune in the weapons business, inventors of the automatic pistol and rifle. Gaylord, called Gay, was a small unassuming boy, frail of body with horn-rimmed glasses. He was studious and a loner, like William. Gay and William had worked on a number of class projects together, as others avoided them. Sometimes they sat together in the library absorbed in their individual studies. Gay wasn't perfect, but he was William's only real choice. There was a rumor that Gay engaged in sexual activities with the more popular upper classmen; the term used was that he "blew their whistles."

He asked Gay the next day in math class. Gay blinked his eyes in disbelief. Even another male had never asked him to a mixer with girls before.

"A Jonesey freshman mixer," Gay muttered, "this Saturday night?"

"That's right. I'm invited and I can bring some others. You wanna go?"

"Sure," said Gay quickly. "You want me to go with you. Right?"

"Go with me, sure, but not as my date."

"I know that. Can I get Lawrence to drive us?"

"Lawrence? Does he go here?"

"No, silly, he's the family chauffeur. We can take the Jaguar or the Rolls. What do you think?"

William didn't know what to say. His frame of reference was a Ford or a Chevrolet, used.

"Can we drive ourselves?"

"I can't drive. I've never needed to."

"Neither can I and I don't have a car." William was down again.

"I know," said Gay. "I'll see if Buck wants to go. He has his own MG convertible." Buck was Barrows Morgan, another rich studious classmate. "Is that okay? Buck can come?"

"I was asked to bring some others. I'm sure it's all right."

"Good, then let's bring Clifford too."

Clifford was Clifford Drysdale IV, another studious one.

So that is how the "fearless foursome" got to go to the Jones College freshwoman mixer together— an unholy alliance at best. They were all scared to death of females, but there was safety in numbers.

On the night of the mixer, Gay, Buck, and Cliff arrived at William's room before six o'clock. The mixer was to start at eight and Jones College was about twenty minutes away. While the "fab three" were ready, William was at his desk working on a class paper. The three of them were dressed in casual clothes, dress slacks and silk shirts. William was expecting to wear his best silk blend suit to make the best impression. He explained this to the three of them and suggested that they go back and change to suits and ties. They did as they were told.

They returned to William's room at seven o'clock and left by seven fifteen. On the ride to Jones College, Buck insisted on riding with the convertible top down. They were four cool cats out on a Saturday night. They arrived at Jones College at a quarter to eight and found the commons building quite easily. When they went in, the room for the mixer was still being readied. William didn't want to be embarrassed, so he hustled them back to the car. They pulled off a distance from the commons building and waited impatiently in the car. Gay kept asking William when they could go in. Buck and Cliff sat nervously in the front seat. Cliff kept asking them whether they thought he looked all right. All three kept saying yes and shut up. At eight fifteen, when William couldn't stand to stay in the car with them any longer, he gave them permission to drive back. Buck put the MG in gear and sped out on the gravel road—four real cool cats.

When they arrived at the dance, it was now getting into full swing. There were at least twice as many girls as boys. As they entered the room, most of the girls looked over— hope springing eternal for the arrival of "Mr. Right." Some of the girls giggled behind their hands while others laughed outright. They were a scene: Three scrawny guys with short hair and horn-rimmed glasses dressed in suits that appeared too large for them, and a brawny guy dressed like their fathers. The boys already at the dance were all dressed in casual clothes, mostly khaki pants, tee shirts, and penny loafers— so much for making an impression.

William ignored the giggles; he had heard them all his life. The other three cringed uncomfortably. William looked around the room for Becky. He found her on the dance floor. It was a slow dance and she was dancing with a classic preppy type. He was trying to get closer to her and she was trying to push him away. She was wearing a tight skirt and sweater, the size and shape of her breasts were quite visible, as they had nowhere to hide. While the preppy was trying to get as close to her breasts as possible, his right arm kept sliding down her lower back towards her buttocks. She kept pushing it back up. It didn't look like much fun for Becky. William waited until the dance was over and Becky went to stand with three other girls, supposedly for the three boys with William.

William pulled the other three away from ogling the girls who had turned away from them. Becky looked up to see them approaching. The other girls looked up as well and started primping — checking their lipstick, combing their hair, straightening their skirts, and so on. Becky moved out in front to greet William.

"William, am I glad to see you. I thought that last one was stuck to my sweater."

William smiled in spite of himself. "I saw. It must be awful."

"You don't know the half of it. These are the desirable rich kids. You should see the undesirable."

"I can imagine," said William. He stood there awkwardly.

A tall thin blond girl nudged Becky in the ribs.

Becky looked around. The girl whispered in Becky's ear.

"Oh, William, this is Katherine." Katherine blushed and turned away.

"And this is Cissy (a ferret looking girl with an acne condition), and Binky (an extremely short girl, about four feet eight inches tall, who looked ten years old)."

Katherine looked exactly as Becky had described the "rich bitches." From the look of her clothes and hair she must be worth plenty. From the looks of them, Cissy and Binky must have been the other two middle-class freshmen that Becky had mentioned. He looked around the room. A few of the other girls were dressed up like Katherine, but the rest of them just looked like typical rich, preppy girls trying to look like regular girls and live down their coming out parties. They dressed in flair skirts, loose sweaters, penny loafers with white angora socks and a string of pearls around their necks. They were mostly blonde and blue-eyed. Not one of them looked, dressed like, or had breasts like Becky. She was a black beauty among the blonde princesses of rich society. No wonder they resented her in their midst.

Gay nudged William sharply in the ribs. He wanted to meet these girls.

William hesitated. "Uh, uh, this is Gay." Gay moved closer to Katherine. She moved closer to William. The other two moved closer in. "Oh, yeah, and this is Buck and this is Cliff." Buck moved quickly to Cissy's side. This left Cliff with Binky. Cliff didn't seem to mind.

The band was playing a fast jitterbug tune. Becky asked William to dance. He refused, as he couldn't dance, certainly not a fast dance.

"Come on, William. I'll teach you to jitterbug."

Buck saw his opportunity. "I'll dance with you." Obviously the other three had all had dance lessons. William was the outcast once again. William stood in his spot. Gay asked Katherine to dance but she refused, so he danced with Cissy. Cliff automatically danced with Binky.

William stood and watched them dance. Becky was a terrific dancer and so was Buck; it scared him. The others were excellent dancers as well. It was astounding what the ability to pay for things could accomplish.

Far and away, Binky was the best dancer; she was all over the floor, and Cliff. He appeared to be enjoying it immensely. It was apparent that all of them had been practicing for quite some time for this moment.

"So, you're William, Becky's friend?" Katherine was talking to him from his back.

William barely heard her. He turned around. She looked nervous, maybe more than he was. "I'm sorry. Were you talking to me?"

Katherine blushed and looked down at her shoes.

William saved her. "You're Katherine, right?"

"Uh, huh. Katherine Angel."

"And I'm William Bradford."

"Yeah, I know. Becky talks a lot about you."

"Really?" He didn't know what else to say.

Katherine put out her hand. They stood facing each other awkwardly. Neither one was comfortable talking to the opposite sex. They would both rather be back in their rooms studying. He finally took her hand and shook it meekly. He looked at her. She was extremely tall for a girl, almost his height of five foot ten, and extremely thin with no body definition. She appeared to have no breasts and no rear end — just straight up and down. She held herself upright which exaggerated her height. She was elegantly dressed in a silk dress that covered her from neck to feet. Her face was drawn and elongated, ending in a drooping jaw. Her hair was quite long (down to her lower back) and the color of a bright blond sun. She looked at William quite intently as if she had known him before. She moved closer to him and stood watching the dancers. He didn't move away.

"So, you don't dance?" asked Katherine.

From almost anyone else he would have felt uneasy. Somehow with this girl, the question seemed quite natural.

"No, I don't. Not really. And you, you don't dance either?"

"Oh, no. I'm a good dancer."

"How come you didn't dance with Gay?"

"I'm too tall. I feel awkward enough. I don't need to be made more fun of."

"You too, eh?"

"They make fun of you too? What for? You're very handsome, you know."

William had never been called handsome before or any other form of physical compliment.

"Oh no, it's not physical. It's my manner. I'm considered stuffy."

"Really! I don't think you're stuffy. Maybe you'll dance with me."

He didn't know what to say. "That would be nice."

"Don't forget."

They continued to watch the dancers. When the dance ended, Buck tried to take Becky by the arm but she tactfully pushed him away. She came over and took William by the arm. He was uncomfortable, but he didn't move away. Somehow he found it important to stake out his turf from Buck and Katherine.

The next dance was a slow dance and Becky quickly moved William to the dance floor before he could get away. He just stood there and Becky put him in her arms in the dance position. She tried to pull him closer, but he would pull away. He kept looking at her breasts closing in on him. She helped him move around the dance floor. He wasn't graceful, but he managed not to step on her feet. He endured, but it wasn't fun. As they danced, she looked him in the eyes. He wished he was feeling something, but he wasn't. He just wished he hadn't agreed to come.

"So," said Becky, "you were talking to Katherine. You like her?"

"I don't know. She seems kind of strange."

"Katherine is extremely intelligent. She's number two in our class. But she's very awkward with boys because of her size and thinness. She's afraid of getting fat so she never eats."

He hadn't found her awkward at all, just a bit strange. "That long face doesn't help either, I guess."

"Oh, that. The boys call her Hoss, like the big brother from the Bonanza show."

William thought. "Horse, I don't think I know that one." He had never really watched much television.

"Not horse, Hoss, with two esses".

"Oh, it must be rough for her." He thought of all the teasing and cruel jokes he had suffered with in his life. He empathized with Katherine—two misfits alone in the world.

Becky changed the subject before he got too interested in Katherine. "So, I thought you didn't have any friends at Roget. Who are those three guys?"

"Oh, them, they're not my friends. They're just three of the most undesirable guys at Roget. I thought I would be safer with them."

"And are you?"

"Until I saw Buck dancing with you."

"Jealous?" He had never been jealous of anything in his life; unhappy with his lot, but not jealous.

"I don't know." He nodded at the three other girls watching them dance. "They're your friends?"

Becky laughed. "Oh, no. As the only Jewish girl at this place, I have to befriend anyone I can. They are the other three social outcasts in the freshman class. We are a conspiracy of misanthropes."

"I think I can join that club."

They danced silently and then stood on the sidelines away from the others. As they stood there, a rather good-looking, blond boy approached them. It was another slow dance.

"Rebecca, could I please have this dance?" The blond boy bowed at Becky.

"I'm sorry, I was talking to William."

"So, this is the elusive William. I finally get to meet him. Are you going to introduce me?"

"Sure, why not. William, this is Archibald Magiver . . . the fourth or the fifth."

"It's the third." Archibald put out his hand and William took it softly. Archibald squeezed down on William's hand. It hurt, but William said nothing. "Charmed, I'm sure." Archibald let go of William's hand and looked him in the eye. He tried to pull Becky away from William. She pulled back closer to William.

"You think your father can protect you. Hiding behind pussies."

"Look, Archie-balls, why don't you leave us alone."

"Okay with me. But when you're looking for a real man later, I might not be available."

"I should only be so lucky."

Archibald stared at Becky and William and stalked off. William had the feeling that Archibald Magiver wasn't refused too often.

"Nice guys you know, Rebecca."

"I don't really know him. He comes to all of these dances and tries to dance the slow dances with me. Pushes himself against me as if I should be appreciative because of his family's money. Just another rich prick."

William blushed at the word.

"They all want to dance just the slow ones with me. But they can't jitter-bug with the Jewish girl or ask her out. Ugh, like I would go out with them. They think their money can buy anyone. Now you know why I wanted you to come tonight." She looked lovingly at him.

He pulled away. "I'm glad I came. It's nice to see you on the outside."

She blushed. "Why, William, that's the nicest thing you've ever said to me."

He danced a number of slow dances with Becky. He was still awkward, but it was becoming easier. He also felt that he should dance with Becky's friends. So he danced with Binky, which was really awkward, but she was an excellent dancer so it made it easier for him. He danced with Cissy who just kept gushing and giggling. He saved the next to last dance for Katherine. He didn't know why he was avoiding it. Somehow Katherine was the most grace-ful dancer of them all. She flowed around the dance floor. Other couples turned to look. It was obvious that they were as surprised as William. Katherine was considered a wallflower or, by the mean, rich boys, a dog. William not only felt quite natural holding Katherine, but she was the only girl in his life who didn't cause him to have that clammy feeling.

He danced the last dance with Becky. It was a slow dance with the lights turned low. She leaned closer to him, careful to put her head on his chest without touching him with her breasts. He started to sweat almost immedi-ately. He knew it was important for Becky to do this in front of the rich kids. His suffering for once might be less than the other persons'.

As they walked back to join the others, Becky asked William if she could drive him back to his room. She had something important to tell him. He was so relieved that he didn't have to ride back with Buck in his MG with the top down that he quickly agreed.

As William waited for Becky to get her car, Katherine came over to him.

She said very softly, "I hope I see you again, William." She emphasized his name. "You remember my name?"

"Sure, you're the angel, right?"

"That's right, a guardian angel and I'll be looking out for you." Katherine moved away as Becky returned.

The ride back to his room was silent for the first few minutes. He wasn't sure what Becky wanted, but somehow he felt uncomfortable unlike other nights she had driven him to his room.

Becky cleared her throat. "William, I just wanted to thank you for coming tonight. I appreciated your standing up to Archie-balls for me. He's been trying to grab my tits since the beginning of the term. He's frightened off the other boys who tried to protect me from him. He's just a fucking rich prick."

"Rebecca, I didn't do anything but stand there. I was scared he would get physical. You know I can't stand violence of any kind. I was really shaking."

"Yeah, I know, but you stood your ground. Most of the other boys run off after Archie's handshake trick. You showed no emotion."

"Rebecca, I never show any emotion."

"I know, but thanks for being there, and for bringing those other guys. It was good for Cissy and Binky. They don't normally dance."

"How about the rich girl?"

"The rich girl?"

"You know, the tall, thin blonde. Katherine the angel."

She laughed. "She's not the rich girl. She's poorer than me. She just wants to be like the rich girls. I think that's why she came to Jones."

He said nothing.

"The other two, Cissy and Binky, they're the rich girls, but socially unacceptable. But they'll marry some rich guy. Money always finds money. It will be a merger not a marriage, but they won't care."

"I think I'm liking Katherine better."

"She certainly seemed to like you. Couldn't keep her eyes off of you."

"Jealous, Rebecca?"

She hesitated. "Yeah, a little. You're a strange one, but Ruth says you're a real boychik, a mensch. Maybe she's right."

They stopped in front of William's room. Becky reached across the seat to get her handbag in the back of the car. As she did so, her breasts rubbed across his arm. He automatically moved quickly to the other side of the car against the door. Becky sensed the sudden movement. She knew how afraid he was of females and their anatomy.

"I'm sorry, William, I was just reaching for my handbag. It's not easy having these things." She pointed to her breasts and shook her head. "I didn't mean to make you uncomfortable."

He didn't say anything.

"Here, I was just getting the direct phone number to my room. Please call me when you'd like." She placed a small card in his hand. He took it and stumbled from the car. She watched him quickly walk to his dormitory. She sat there as he disappeared behind the door. "What a strange boy," she thought. "But I like him."

That was the end of William's first Saturday night date.

As it turned out, Gay had attached himself to Cissy and Buck had done the same with Binky. This made Cliff and Katherine the odd ones out. They were both used to this.

Buck and Gay started to visit Cissy and Binky at Jones College as often as they could. They would ask William if he wanted to go along with them to see Becky. Sometimes during the week when he knew they had to get back early he would go with them. Becky was always surprised, but enjoyed talking with William. It was good to see him away from the Selzers.

William went to see Becky, but when he dreamed, he dreamt of Katherine. He didn't know why, but he couldn't stop it. While it was nice talking with Becky, there was something inside him that yearned to see Katherine again. He would ask about her every so often and Becky would always look at him funny. One time Katherine was studying with Becky in the library at Jones College when he met them. Becky, to be polite to Katherine, suggested that the three of them go to the campus coffee shop. Katherine readily accepted. William noticed the excitement on Katherine's face and alarmingly his inner excitement as well. They walked together, with William in the middle. The two girls chatted to each other over William— he felt good. Becky had always made him feel clammy when she got close to him, but Katherine had the opposite effect— he felt nothing. As his visits to Jones College came more often, so did the incidents of the three of them doing things together. It was Becky and Katherine with William in the middle. It was as close to real friends as William had ever come. He was still closed, but he wasn't as alone.

Ruth Selzer intensified her efforts to get William and Becky closer together. She assumed that as normal kids their age they had more going than just two people meeting at the Selzers' on a Friday night. William was feeling more pressured and tried to get out of as many of these Friday night get-togethers as he could. He sensed that Becky was doing the same.

He was one of the only students at Roget who had nowhere to go on the holiday breaks. The first real holiday to arrive was Thanksgiving, a four-day weekend. He would be quite alone on campus. The only other students who stayed on campus were those whose family would rather not have them come home. Most of the other students either went home to the family estates or went with their families to a plush vacation spot. Ruth offered William to stay with them over the holiday so he wouldn't have to be alone. He refused, but asked permission to work on his grant projects in Ruth's office and said that he would come for Thanksgiving dinner.

Ruth started treating William and Becky as if they were a romantic couple, even though neither one displayed any outward romantic affection for the other. They could have been two college colleagues. In Ruth's mind, she was already planning the wedding. She glowed in her matchmaking skills. Herman advised her not to put too much pressure on William and Becky as the more she would push, the more they would pull away. For Ruth, it was like planning the marriage of her favorite son and daughter.

Holiday dinners, Jewish and gentile, became a tradition for William and Becky at the Selzers'. Ruth was creating her own instant family. Herm admonished her not to do this; she would only get hurt again. Ruth pushed ahead regardless.

When William stayed on campus during holidays and school breaks, he would work on grant projects for both Ruth and Herman. The Selzers would then have him to dinner on Tuesdays and Fridays with Becky and for Sunday brunch, with or without Becky. On Saturdays, William would spend the day with Becky and Katherine. Sometimes Katherine would go home to visit her parents in Newport, Rhode Island, but these visits became less frequent as she became part of the threesome. William looked forward to Saturdays for the first time in his life. Very infrequently did their Saturday get togethers extend into the evening though. Saturday night still held a special male-female significance to William, and he wasn't ready for this type of commitment.

This pattern of school and work, the Selzers, Becky and Katherine extended throughout William's first year at Roget. He felt most comfortable with predictable behaviors and events. He felt safe and secure for the first time in his life. He wanted this feeling to last. At the end of the first year, official grade point averages and class rankings were posted for both Roget Institute and Jones College. William had a grade point average of 3.78, which placed him third in his class, Katherine had a grade point average of 3.89, which placed her second in her class, and Becky, whom they considered the smartest of the three, had a grade point average of 3.46, which placed her twelfth in her class. Becky had all As in her classes with the exception of a couple Bs and Cs. William suggested that there might be some prejudice lurking at Jones by the two instructors involved. Becky said it wasn't worth fighting as she was used to this. William told her that it still wasn't right. Becky shrugged her shoulders. She couldn't change the world.

William needed to make plans for the summer. He still hadn't heard from his mother. He had stopped writing to her, but still expected some response from her. The way he saw his relationship with his mother, he couldn't return home. Herm Selzer suggested that William spend the summer in Boston. He could work with him on some ongoing grants, which would more than pay for his expenses and allow him to save some money for next year. Herm had a friend who rented out rooms to students during the school year. He knew that his friend would rent William one of these rooms during the summer, as they remained vacant anyway. William was able to get a room for nothing in exchange for helping with some maintenance and renovation work. William moved into his room the day after school was over. The Selzers helped him pack up and move. Ruth helped clean and decorate the room so that it didn't look so gloomy.

Becky was panicked as to how she was going to spend the summer. She wasn't ready to return to her parents' house, but she didn't know where else to go. When William told her about his plans, she knew she would do the same. She talked it over with the Selzers. While Herm was not sure that they should encourage her, Ruth seized the opportunity. She convinced their friends in Boston to let Becky have another room in exchange for cleaning and persuaded a professional colleague to engage Becky as an editorial assistant on a book he was writing. He would pay Becky enough to survive in Boston for the summer. She jumped at the deal.

William and Becky spent that summer and the others between school years in this fashion. They would both work during the day and then spend the nights together either walking around Boston or just talking in one of their rooms. The Selzers' friends, David and Emma Friedman, were gone most of the summer, so they basically had the house to themselves. While they were living close together, they were not living together. William saw Becky as his first close friend, but not as a girl friend. When he perceived her as a female, the clammy feeling would return. As they got more familiar, Becky had started to get dressed and change her clothes in front of William. As he would catch glimpses of her thighs, underwear, brassiere, or breasts, he would choke up and get red in the face. He never said anything to Becky, but somehow she became more careful as to what she did in front of him. He had never been so happy as during those summers in Boston. He had work to do, responsibilities, no money worries, and a good friend — and a surrogate mother.

When William returned for his second year of college at Roget, he moved into a room of his own. Ruth helped him get a single student apartment next to her office building. She gave him a key to her building and her office, so that he could come and go as he pleased. She trusted him to do the required work on the grant projects and to submit the hours he worked. This arrangement allowed William to do what he wanted when he wanted. He was used to being alone and responsible. His work ethic and self-responsibility were unquestioned. He wouldn't miss his roommate Chandler, and Chandler wouldn't miss him.

For the next three years, Becky and William became even closer. They shared what they were doing in school, he in economics and her in literature and philosophy. They both now spent Tuesday and Friday nights and Sunday mornings with the Selzers. This was the first real family for all of them. Ruth only assumed that it would be like this for the rest of their lives. Her life was now Herm, then William, and then Becky.

William and Becky still spent Saturdays together, many times with Katherine. Katherine looked at William with yearning; William looked away. Katherine was starting to fill out, but was still far from a beauty. She was looking less like a "hoss," and so the nickname became less of a problem. When the three of them were together, Katherine absolutely glowed and bubbled. Becky said that she was still just the opposite when they weren't together.

Eventually, graduation was upon each of them. Most of the other students planned to go right into the family business at somewhat high, but not too challenging, positions. William, however, had to find his own job. He had gone to a few interviews that the school had arranged with some of their alumni, but none of them appealed to him. The jobs appeared to be tokenism to a Roget graduate, to avoid embarrassment, with no recognition of his achievements. He finished third in his class with four years of experience working with the Selzers, which was ignored as working for "those Jews."

During his process of looking for the right job, he was called into the office of Roget's president. As this had never happened to him before, he was quite interested. As a low-income student, the administration allowed him to attend classes, but otherwise ignored his existence. There was little likelihood that he would bring prestige, and future contributions, back to the school like one of the extremely wealthy students. When William entered the President's office he didn't find the President seated behind his desk, but Mr. Blanchard. William was startled. He didn't think Mr. Blanchard had even remembered him; at least he hoped he hadn't. It was one of the only times in his life that he had lied.

Mr. Blanchard nodded. "Please sit down. Stanford R. Yale, isn't it?"

William stumbled. "So, you know."

Mr. Blanchard looked up at William. "Oh, I knew the first thing the next morning. It only took Timothy one call to Mr. Rogers. What a web you weave, when you first start to deceive."

William started to apology.

Mr. Blanchard held up his hand. "Please, William, no need. I would have done the same thing in your position. I've done a lot worse, believe me. Please sit down."

He sat across the desk from Mr. Blanchard and crossed his arms and legs.

Mr. Blanchard looked up. "I see you got your suit cleaned." William was wearing the same suit as the night he was picked up on the road to Roget.

"Yes, sir."

Mr. Blanchard removed a folder from his briefcase on the floor. It had William's name on it in big, bold letters. "I've been watching you since that night. You're quite an engaging young man, and you've done quite well at Roget. The Yales . . . uh Bradfords should be quite proud of you."

"There are no Bradfords, sir. I'm the one and only."

"I know, William. Timothy is very thorough."

"And a good driver."

Mr. Blanchard laughed. "Yes, that too." He glanced down at the folder. "I see you've worked for four years with the Selzers; wonderful people, well respected. Blanchard Industries could never hire them, but we've used both of them as consultants. Highly intelligent those people. Helped us immensely. They both think the world of you. Herman recommended you, unconditionally. Ruth was a little more reluctant, something about a Jew in a gentile world. She thinks you are her Jewish son."

"I know, even after four years."

"Hmm, well, regardless. Blanchard Industries would like to offer you a position. One where you can use the talents you've exhibited here at Roget and with the Selzers. Not one of those token alumni offers I know you've received. I was waiting to see if you would turn them down—and you did. Good for you. What we have in mind is for you to start as Assistant Plant Manager at our Kalamazoo location. We have a real production flow problem there and I would like to have you tackle it. Consider it as an internal consultant. The same kind of thing you worked on with the Selzers on paper, now this would be real life. I will of course follow your progress. If you do well and I'm confident you will, I would consider you for a headquarters trouble shooter-type role here in Boston. So, how does that sound to you?"

William was quite flattered. This was a dream job offer, particularly for an outsider. "Can I think about it? This is so abrupt."

"Of course, William. Take some time. Let's say by tomorrow evening."

Mr. Blanchard started to put the folder away. He looked at one last item.

"Oh, by the way, we would expect that you don't marry that Rebecca Goodman person. She's just not Blanchard Industry corporate wife material. It would be unfair to her to subject her to this life. I'm sure you understand."

William wasn't sure that he did. He looked away.

Mr. Blanchard got up from the desk and came over to shake William's hand. William took it. At that moment the door opened as if by magic and Timothy entered. He went over to William and extended his hand.

"Good to see you once again, Mr. Yale. Need any help with your suitcases?" He winked at William.

Timothy helped Mr. Blanchard leave and carried his briefcase for him. Mr. Blanchard placed a card in William's hand as he left. "You may have lost the first one."

"Don't forget, let me know by tomorrow evening. I hope the answer will be yes. Opportunities like this don't knock more than once in a lifetime."

William sat stunned. "I know, Sir, thank you."

"Good bye, William. I hope this isn't our final good bye."

Timothy winked at him again as they left.

William discussed Mr. Blanchard's offer with the Selzers that evening. Herman thought it was the offer of a lifetime and encouraged William to strongly consider taking it. Ruth, on the other hand, called them "Nazi anti-Semitic bastards," and encouraged him to run for his life. He would be doomed to a life of corporate oppression and servitude. He didn't tell them of the condition that he not marry Rebecca.

Ruth made some calls the next day and lined William up with a number of interviews with good liberal organizations that had no trouble hiring the best employees regardless of their backgrounds. She knew this would be a much better world for her William.

He went to three of Ruth's interviews the following day and was offered a fairly attractive position with a defense contractor outside Boston. He now had an alternative to Mr. Blanchard's offer. He spent the remainder of the day considering what he should do. Professionally he couldn't beat Blanchard Industries; personally he might be better with the Boston company. In the end he turned them both down. He would find his own job. He always had.

Two weeks before school ended, William heard from a second tier industrial fastener manufacturer, Apex Industries, whom he had contacted on his own. He read about them in one of Herm's professional economics journals and how they were effectively using mathematical models for such things as maximizing production throughput, plant locations, inventory minimization and so on. These were just the things that William was most interested in. They more or less offered him carte blanche to apply some of the techniques he had developed working with the Selzers as a company troubleshooter. This was exactly what he had been looking for. The only condition was that he needed to be there within a month after graduation and that his first assignment would be at their Alabama plant location. They offered him twelve thousand dollars a year, which was quite an attractive starting salary in 1962. It was just a little less than the Blanchard starting salary, but he would be his own man. William readily accepted.

When he told the Selzers of his decision that night, Herman was quite supportive. Ruth, on the other hand, didn't like it at all. Taking a job with a gentile organization and working in the anti-Semitic south, that was no place for her William. And to go there alone, leaving their family, when would Ruth see him again?

William thought about what Ruth had said to him. He had never been away from home except for his four years at Roget. He was fortunate to have met the Selzers his first day at Roget and to have had them, and Rebecca, as his friends for his four years at Roget. Otherwise, he would have been alone at Roget. He had made no real contacts with his classmates. They were as foreign to him as he was to them. He didn't want to be entirely alone again, especially in a new place with a new company. Ruth had made the south sound threatening, Jewish or not. All that night he thought about what to do. He had accepted the job, he wanted the job, but he was scared.

In the morning, he knew what he had to do. He got Buck to take him to Jones College. He went to Katherine's room, but she wasn't there. He hadn't called ahead because he wanted to surprise her. He found her sitting alone in the student union building. She was reading a book and sipping on a soda. She looked just lovely. He sat down beside her. She looked up surprised. It wasn't like William to just show up.

"William, what a pleasant surprise. And it's not even Saturday."

William explained about the job with Apex Industries and his going to Alabama alone. He stopped talking and stared at her.

She was becoming very uncomfortable. She didn't know what William wanted from her. "William, that sounds great for you." She hesitated. "I'm going to miss you."

William looked down at the table and talked into it. "I'll miss you too."

"Oh, William, don't look so sad. We can still keep in touch. You won't be that far away. You can come visit us, can't you?"

"I guess. I'm just not good at keeping in touch. I get too consumed with my work."

"Yes, William, I know."

They laughed and then stopped and stared at each other. She didn't know what else to say. William knew what he wanted to say, but he just couldn't. Why were social interactions so difficult for him? He had known her for almost four years and he still couldn't say what he wanted to her.

She couldn't stand sitting and staring at each other any longer. William, she knew, could stare at her forever, but she crumbled.

"William, would it help if I came down with you, you know, just to help you get settled in, maybe for a couple of days." She quickly added. "I'd stay somewhere else, get myself a room."

He continued staring.

"William, please say something. This isn't easy for me."

He started to speak but his voice froze. Frog-like sounds came out.

She pushed her soda over to him. "Here, drink some of this."

He ordinarily wouldn't drink from anyone else's glass. In this instance, he grabbed the glass and rinsed his mouth with soda. This seemed to calm him down some. He started to speak again. This time his voice didn't fail him.

"I'd like you to come with me, yes."

She was relieved. She didn't want to lose William, but the decision was out of her control. She really hated to be out of control. "When would you be leaving? I'll have to make arrangements to get away for a few days."

"No, no, I want you to go with me. Not a few days, go with me."

She didn't quite understand. He had never asked her to go anywhere with him. "William, what are you trying to say? Please, I'm confused."

He talked very softly. "Come with me, stay with me. Please."

"What are you talking about? Move in with you, become your mother?"

He looked struck. "No, not my mother, my wife."

She said nothing. While she had dreamed about this, she hadn't given it much of a chance.

He started to get up. "I'm sorry, I just thought . . ." He didn't know what else to say. He started to move away. She grabbed his arm.

"Please, William. I'd love to be your wife." She had dreamt of this for four years, almost from the first time she had met him. But, she never thought it would happen. She was afraid she had answered too quickly. So she added, "You would have to meet my family first. Is that okay?"

She had no need for him to meet her family. She knew they wouldn't like him, and he wouldn't like them. She was just grasping for time.

He sat back down. What had he done? A wife was one thing; an entire family was another. He just never thought of others as having a family.

She touched him gently on the arm. This time he didn't try to pull away. She looked at him tenderly with small tears in her eyes.

"William, it will be all right. I'll be with you."

He left Jones College a happy man. She would make him a perfect corporate wife. He now had the right job and he would have the right wife. Also, a wife would keep him from being drafted into the service, particularly with action increasing in Vietnam. The military would kill him, his soul and his body. Now he would be safe, for the rest of his life. Yes, Katherine would be the perfect wife for him; she would take care of him just like his mother. He couldn't wait to tell Ruth and Rebecca. They would be glad that he wouldn't be alone.

He tried to find Rebecca while he was at Jones College, but she wasn't there. No one knew where she was. He left a note for her to contact him, that he had something important to tell her. Then he left to tell Ruth and Herman. He knew they would be as happy as he was.

3

COURTSHIP & MARRIAGE

Wᵢᵢᵢᵢₐₘ's life was coming together. He had the job he wanted. It
would allow him to apply what he had learned at Roget Institute
and working on grant studies with the Selzers. His main interest was to apply
mathematical business models to real life manufacturing situations. He
enjoyed solving business problems from a theoretical standpoint. Now he
would have the chance to apply these techniques in the real world with a real
business and real people. He was looking forward to the opportunity with the
fear of excitement.

He also felt that he had the future wife that he needed. Katherine would
be the perfect corporate wife. She was attractive without being demonstrative,
with a real patrician look. Her height and thinness always brought attention
to her. This would be good for him. She was also well educated as a Jones
College graduate. She would be able to hold her own in a discussion with the
other male workers as well as with their wives. She would definitely be an
asset in his career. There was little chance she would ever embarrass him. She
would not be sexually demanding, he was sure of that. Yes, Katherine would
be the perfect wife.

William had not had many joyful moments in his life, but this was one of
them, as he approached the Selzers' house to tell them the good news. He was
sure they would be pleased. He wouldn't be alone in Alabama now. He knew
they would like Katherine as well; she was perfect. He was smiling to himself
as he rang the Selzers' doorbell. "Mother" Ruth would be proud of him; he just
knew it. Ruth answered the door and was drying her hands on an apron. There
was a pleasant look on her face. She was preparing one of Herman's favorite
dinners: stuffed veal. The look on her face suddenly went sour as she saw
William at her door. She was still plenty mad at him for leaving them to work
for a gentile company in the anti-Semitic south. "UGH!" thought Ruth, a fate
much worse than death. He had a dumb smile on his face—the idiot son
returns. She looked at him sadly. "So, William. You want to break my heart
again." Ruth turned back into the house. William followed her uninvited.

"Ruth, please. Can I talk to you?" He had followed her into the kitchen.
She had gone back to preparing dinner. She ignored him. "So, talk."

He hesitated. She wasn't going to make this easy for him.

"I know you're not happy with my job decision."

She interrupted him. "Not happy. That's an understatement!"

"Okay, but I need to do what I want to do. Apex will let me do that."

"Yeah and strip your soul. Damn anti-Semitic Nazi gentile bastards. William, they will own you. Please trust me. Run for your life. Yes?"

"Please try to understand. I was hoping that you and Herm would help me."

"Help you enrich those anti-Semitic bastards, never! What, so they can oppress more Jews?" She turned away. She had tears in her eyes.

"Ruth, please, they don't oppress anyone."

"So, how many Jews they have working for them? And how many Jewish firms do they buy from? And how many Jewish customers do they have? And do they get the best terms? You know so much, so you tell me. Ya?"

"Ruth I don't know."

"That's right. You don't know. Well, I know. I do studies on these things. Apex Industries subtly practices ethnic cleansing their own way. No Jews, Catholics, Italians, Irish, or colored. Only white Protestants. Welcome to your new family."

"Ruth, it's only a job. If it's as you say, I can leave."

"We'll see." She turned away again.

"I came with more news. Can I tell you?"

"So, tell. After Apex Industries, this better be good."

He beamed as Ruth turned around to look at him. He could see the dried tears in the corners of her eyes. "I'm going to get married. I won't be alone in Alabama."

Ruth had received a message at her office that afternoon that Becky had called. She didn't leave a number for Ruth to return her call. The receptionist said that Becky sounded excited. Ruth sensed a real mitzvah in the works. Oh my God, William and Becky were going to be married. Ruth's mind raced forward to the plans for the wedding. William was talking but she couldn't hear him.

He was shouting. "Her name is Katherine. Katherine Angel."

"Whose name is Katherine? Who is this Katherine?"

"Katherine. I've been trying to tell you that is who I'm going to marry."

Ruth had to sit down at the table. She put her head in her hands. This was the end for her. "And Becky. You're not marrying Becky?"

"No, Ruth. I'm marrying Katherine. I thought you would be pleased."

"Pleased. Becky spends four years with you; a good, Jewish girl. And you, you want to marry someone else, some white Protestant named Katherine. I was wrong. You are not Jewish. You are a goy, with a goy job and now a goy wife."

William persisted. "I wanted to bring Katherine with me to dinner this Tuesday, so that you and Herman could meet her. I'm sure you'll like her."

Ruth shook her head and forced her tears back. "So, you told Becky. She's happy about this? You want her to come to dinner too?" Ruth turned away.

"I tried to tell Rebecca. I thought she would be happy for me. I couldn't find her at her school, so I left her a note."

"A note. After four years, you leave her a note. A goy, a real goy."

"Ruth, please, I'd like you and Herman to approve, and come to the wedding, as the matron of honor and the best man."

"Approve? Never. You do what you want. All of you always do."

He didn't know what else to say. He expected Ruth to be happy for him.

Ruth sat at the table with her head in her hands. The tears were streaming down her cheeks. She could hardly speak.

She said softly through her tears. "Please, William, leave my house."

He tried to speak but he couldn't think of anything else to say. He turned slowly and left the Selzers' house for the last time.

He invited the Selzers' to the wedding, but they didn't come. He didn't expect them to come, but he had hoped they would. He left Boston without hearing from them again. For William this was another set of parents lost.

He tried to contact Rebecca a number of times, but she wasn't at the college. Eventually, Katherine told him that Becky had called. She was in New York interviewing for jobs with the major publishing houses as a fiction editor. Ruth had recommended her to a number of non-fiction editors she knew. These editors, in turn, recommended Becky to fiction editors in their firms. Becky had called Katherine to tell her the good news; she had two offers and was going to accept the offer from Doubleday. As a Jew, she felt more comfortable there. She was starting work the following Monday and wouldn't be returning to Jones. She wanted Katherine to send her things to New York. She wouldn't be attending graduation. If she never saw Jones again it would be fine with her. She told Katherine that she had tried to contact William, but she couldn't reach him at his place. She had called a number of times, but he was never there. She asked Katherine to give William her telephone number in New York.

Katherine was excited about Becky getting the job that she wanted, but she was bursting with her own excitement. She told her about William asking her to marry him. Becky was knocked over and said nothing. She expected William to call her. He had left a number of messages for her and probably wanted to tell her himself. She would wait for his call. Katherine told William about Becky's phone call, but being scared to lose him to Becky she neglected to give him Becky's phone number in New York. William waited for Becky to call him, but of course she never did. He invited Becky to the wedding, but Katherine never mailed the invitation. Becky didn't come to the wedding. He didn't quite understand. Katherine said that maybe she felt jilted and couldn't face him. He thought this might be so. This was the first time he felt that his actions had made someone feel badly. He couldn't and wouldn't contact Rebecca, he just couldn't. He would miss her. He felt abandoned once again, but this time it would be different as he had Katherine.

Katherine had borrowed her father's Ford station wagon to bring her college possessions back home. She had originally planned to take some time off before she either looked for a job or went to graduate school. Most of the other girls graduating Jones College with her, particularly the rich girls, had either been married and left school or were engaged to be married soon. Even Cissy and Binky were engaged, to Gay and Cliff. Katherine and Becky had remained the outcasts until the end. The goal of Jones College, as stated in their recruitment bulletin, was to help girls of breeding, i.e., upper class elite, prepare for a life with the proper husband, i.e., upper class elite. They were very successful at this. Over 80% of the girls who had started with Katherine at Jones as freshmen were either married or engaged. Most of the others were sent abroad for a period after college by their parents in shame. They would return when either they had landed a husband abroad or the family had found them one at home. Should a girl of such breeding still be single after 25 she might as well be condemned to a life of spinsterhood. The upper class charities were full of such women as volunteers. The Jones College graduation ceremonies were usually poorly attended. For the family, it meant that their daughter was still available; it was not a proud moment. Discretion dictated a quiet absence.

Katherine and Becky had planned to attend the graduation as a statement of their independence. They were both planning careers, Becky in publishing and Katherine in the arts, possibly museum work. They believed that they were graduates to be proud of, not those rich girls who would tend to their husband and his estate. Now that Becky wasn't going to attend, Katherine wasn't sure what she should do. She was now, she thought, engaged to William. This put her on the side of the graduating enemy. The graduation was scheduled for this coming weekend. Her parents and three brothers had planned to attend and they were to celebrate afterwards. When Katherine had told her family about William they were ecstatic. Her mother had dreamed of the day when Katherine would marry wealthy and leave the middle class life that she had been doomed to. Her father was glad that someone else would be taking over Katherine's expenses. He was already planning what to do with the extra money. They, of course, wanted to meet William. Her mother was already practicing her new name, Katherine Bradford the third, simply elegant. Her father was questioning what kind of fellow would have a name like that. They all decided that Katherine and William should spend the weekend with them in Newport. They would plan the wedding together; the hell with the graduation. Katherine had graduated with her Mrs. as her mother had planned, to a third no less.

Katherine and William left early that Saturday morning for Newport and the Angels, taking all of their possessions with them. There was no need for either of them to return to their schools and they had no one to say good-bye to. They planned to move to Alabama right after the wedding. William had pictured the two of them getting married quietly, a Justice of the Peace, the Selzers, and Rebecca. That was his family. Katherine's parents had expected a large wedding with all of their friends and relatives. Katherine's mother had put her wedding money away for years; this would be some event. William never realized other people had families like this. Why did life always have to be so complicated? He just wanted to live his life alone and now he had a family he didn't want.

Katherine's mother had asked her about William, but she had successfully avoided too many details other than his name and that he was an honors graduate of Roget Institute. This impressed Katherine's mother, a graduate of Roget Institute, the science school for rich kids. She was already visioning her visits to the Bradford III estate. Katherine's mother had asked her about the engagement ring; the size, the color, the details. There was, of course, no engagement ring. William not only knew nothing about such things, but he could not have afforded much of a ring. He only wanted to get married and be safe. Why was that so difficult? Katherine had bought a ring at a local jewelry store. It wasn't diamonds, but it looked like it was. The store manager told her that they sold many of these rings to the rich boys. They used them to seduce less affluent girls who thought they had snared a rich guy, but the girls didn't get the ring, they only got screwed. Now Katherine had one of these fake diamond rings. She hoped she wouldn't just be screwed. She knew William was different. She trusted him.

Katherine's parents lived in a middle class neighborhood of Newport, Rhode Island, made up of primarily old row homes. The Angels' house was on the corner so that they had a side yard as well as one in back. Katherine's father, Augustus (Guy), of Italian-American extraction, was proud of this. At the time he bought the house in 1955, a corner house cost $2,000 more than a middle house. Katherine's mother, Anne, of English extraction, hated her middle class existence, corner house or not. Guy made sure that his first two sons, Roberto (Bobby) and Alphonse (Alley), as good Italian-Americans, went to the parish parochial school and Catholic high school. The nuns would give them a good education. They both turned out much like Guy, tough Italian kids who knew everything. Each of them attended the state college for one year. They partied as hard as they could and each in turn flunked out. You can't pass a class if you don't go to the class. While Anne was disappointed, Guy was happy to have them in the family business, Angel's Boat Heaven, now home for the three Goombas. Their third son, Guiseppi (Joey), turned out to be fair skinned and sensitive just like Anne. Guy left Joey to his mother; he had his two Italian stallions. Their next child was finally a daughter for Anne, whom Anne named Katherine, after the great, and they called her Cassie. Katherine was fair of skin and hair just like her mother, definitely an English Episcopalian.

Anne made sure that Joey and Katherine went to the best private schools. Guy complained that they didn't have money for that and insisted the parish educate them. Anne persisted anyway and somehow Guy found the money. Anne joined the Episcopal Church in the adjoining neighborhood and attended Sunday services with Joey and Katherine. Guy countered by taking Bobby and Alley to Catholic mass on Sunday. Joey was smart enough to get into one of New England's top prep high schools and then into a top engineering school. He graduated with honors and moved to New York City. He was now 24 years old and a junior engineer for United Construction Engineers, builders of large chemical plants. Katherine spent her high school years at an upper class, all-girl, prep boarding school which prepared young ladies for the cotillion circuit and the best female colleges. Katherine placed in the upper 3% of her graduating class. It was no problem for a girl like Katherine to get accepted to Jones College. Anne helped her fill out the application. For income, Anne filled in Guy's gross not his net, and for religion she filled in Episcopalian. By the time Anne was done with the application, Jones College would believe that they were getting an extremely wealthy Episcopalian debutante from Newport, Rhode Island. Anne was confident that Katherine would meet and marry a rich husband with similar credentials, and now it was coming true.

Katherine pulled the station wagon into the driveway of her parents' house. William didn't know much about Katherine's family other than that they were more middle class than upper class, they were Episcopalian, and she had three brothers. Katherine, to him, always acted upper class and he expected her family to be the same. Their home was not impressive, but it was more impressive than where he had lived in the Bronx. Joey, Katherine's youngest brother, was waiting for them on the front porch. He rushed down when he saw Katherine get out of the car, hugged her, and swung her around.

"Congratulations, Miss Cassie, on your graduation and your engagement."

She blushed and turned away. William got out of the car and stood next to her.

Joey looked over at William. They sized each other up. Joey was nodding approvingly. "So," said Joey.

"Oh, this is William." William noticed that she was now wearing a large diamond ring. It glared in the sun. There was no hiding from it. "This is my brother Joseph." They shook hands. He liked Joey immediately and Joey liked him. No one, but Joey, ever wore a suit in their house. Joey was taller than William and much slimmer, a male version of Katherine. He was fair and pretty like Katherine, not handsome. William, Joey, and Katherine walked up to the house together.

"Cassie's here," yelled Joey as they entered the house.

"Down here," came the voice of Katherine's father from beneath them.

William looked befuddled. He didn't know why Katherine's father would be in the basement. In William's neighborhood in the Bronx the basement was used for either the coal bin or the oil burner. Otherwise the basement was to be avoided.

"Oh, they're downstairs watching the baseball game, the Red Sox and the Yankees," Joey said not quite sure. William cringed. It was always the Red Sox and the Yankees. Just like the last time his father took him to a baseball game and that woman appeared. He sensed another disaster.

The three of them walked through the front room, which was kind of an indoor-outdoor porch. It was furnished with outdoor patio-type furniture, the large wicker type variety. Joey thought he sensed William making a face at the decor.

"Really yucky, isn't it? It's dad's room, not much of an interior decorator."

William said nothing. The wicker furniture, although distasteful, was of better quality than anything in his old Bronx home.

They walked past the living room. It was roped off with a velvet sash. Inside the room was plush wall-to-wall carpeting, a luxurious sofa and side chairs, a crushed velvet love seat, a number of gold gilded floor and table lamps, an immense wrought iron coffee table with glass top, and two well-polished side tables. All of the upholstered furniture was covered with see through plastic slipcovers. The room looked like it had never been used, a living room that wasn't lived in. William stopped to stare, making sure he stayed on his side of the sash. Joey went over to him and they both stared. "This is Mom's room. She decorated it herself. We can look at it, but we can't use it. It's her shrine to old English elegance."

William was intrigued. He would be extremely pleased to have furniture like this some day. If and when he did, he wouldn't hide it behind a velvet sash. He saw no other room where the family could get together. He could see in the back of the house there was a dining room with a rather used large dining room table and chairs and a small kitchen with little room to sit down.

"Where do you all get together?" asked a perplexed William.

"Aha!" said Joey. "Hence the basement."

"The basement," William repeated as he shook his head.

There was a small ornate and mirrored door off of the dining room. Joey opened the door and a set of stairs was revealed that led down into the basement. Joey led the way for William and Katherine. The basement was furnished as a man's room, in early sports bar decor. There was a heavy overbearing deep plush red leather sofa with three matching side chairs. Evidently the sofa was for her father, Guy, as he was presently lying across it, and the side chairs were for the three sons as the other two sons, Bobby and Alley, were sitting in theirs. Joey's chair was empty and looked like it hadn't had much use. In fact, Bobby and Alley were using it as a footrest. The three of them were short, stocky, and swarthy, with black wavy hair and heavy body hair.

The room was paneled in an oppressive dark wood. The paneled walls were covered with various sports teams' pennants so that there was very little wall remaining. In the back of the room was a wet bar with refrigerator. Behind the bar was a full bathroom with toilet, sink, and shower. The bathroom door was open so they could use the toilet and at the same time watch the television. In the center of the room was the largest screen television that William had ever seen. Father and sons had their eyes glued to the screen. In front of the television was an enormous coffee table upon which were three bottles of beer, each one in front of one of them—and many empty bottles. William had the idea that the three of them could live in this room alone, and he was right, as many times they did just that.

Joey coughed. "Dad, Cassie is here."

"I heard you before." He kind of waved. "Hold on, the inning's almost over. Yaz is up, two runners on, two outs." He went back to watching the game.

Katherine, William, and Joey waited for the inning to end, none of them too concerned as to what was happening on the television. William looked at the father and two sons. They were all dressed in faded oil-encrusted cut off jeans with grimy sports tee shirts and no shoes, only dirty feet. William found this to be extremely disrespectful to Katherine. They were three barbarians with an elegant daughter and sister. Katherine and Joey must be adopted, thought William. He couldn't think what the mother would be like.

"Cassie, so you're home." Guy sat up on the sofa; the inning must be over. He made no motion for her to come over or recognition of either William or Joey.

Katherine moved closer to William. She made sure her ring finger was on display. "Hello, father."

Her father nodded. "How about a beer? For you or them." He nodded toward William and Joey.

Katherine was obviously embarrassed by her father. He hadn't even bothered to zip up his shorts. You could plainly see his colored boxer shorts and the top of his pubic hair spread across his middle.

Her father burped, but said nothing. Bobby and Alley did the same. They had not changed their positions on their chairs. They were all looking side-eyed at William, as if a monster had entered their den.

"Daddy! This is William, my fiancé."

Guy looked over at William. "How about a beer, Willy?"

"That's William."

"Okay, William, How about a beer? There's plenty in the fridge."

"No, thanks, I don't drink." William was very uncomfortable with these people, he was getting that clammy feeling.

"And this"—Katherine pointed in their direction—"is my brother Robert and my brother Allen." The two brothers nodded at William while his father and two brothers ignored Joey.

"Nice to meet you." William walked over to shake their hands. They both turned back to the ball game as the next inning had started and ignored William's proffered hand. Guy lay back down on the sofa.

Katherine guided them back upstairs. As they ascended the staircase, William said, "Nice meeting you." All three nodded, as they were absorbed in the ball game.

Bobby mimicked his father. "How about a beer, Willy?"

Alley responded, "That's William."

Guy chimed in talking like a fairy, "No, thanks, I don't drink."

The three of them picked up their beer bottles and stroked the neck of the bottle in the jerk off sign, the thumb and other fingers encircling the neck of the bottle as their hands moved up and down. "Here's to you, Willy!" They chug-a-lugged the remainder of their bottles and went back to the ball game. Let Joey entertain Cassie and her fiancé, birds of a feather and so on.

As they went upstairs Katherine's mother, Anne, came out of the kitchen. She was dressed as elegantly as Katherine and Joey. She had on a simple, but expensive looking, black dress with well-shined black heels and a simple string of pearls. Her hair was done professionally. She was tall and slim like Katherine but there was a sexiness to her. William started to get clammy.

Anne came towards them with her hand outstretched. She came directly at William. "So, this is William. I'm so pleased to meet you."

William was not sure what to do so he grabbed her hand and shook it. He moved back before Anne had a chance to hug him and kiss his cheek.

It didn't matter as Anne's attention had refocused on the ring on Katherine's finger. "Oh, William, what a lovely ring." She said this as if it was William's ring.

William didn't know what to say, so he said nothing.

"Thank you, Mom," said Katherine to save William.

"So," said Anne, "let's go into the living room."

Katherine and Joey could not believe what they had heard. No one had ever been allowed to sit in the living room.

William sat with Katherine, Joey, and Anne in the living room. Anne acted as if she entertained in this room all the time; she even offered them drinks. Luckily for Anne, no one wanted any. They talked about college, literature, museums, art and so forth. Eventually, Guy came up from the basement; the ball game must be over. He peered into the living room, not believing his eyes, and looked at the three of them inquisitively.

"So, Anne, are we eating tonight?"

Anne looked at him as if a worm had come up from the carpeting. "I was talking to Katherine, Joseph, and Katherine's fiancé, William. Do you think you can wait? And zip your pants."

Guy looked down. His shorts were around his hips. He quickly pulled up his shorts and zipped up the fly. "Sure, we'll be in the back yard. The Sox won. We'll start happy hour."

Anne looked at him with disapproval. "Every hour is a happy hour with the three of you." She turned back to Katherine, Joey, and William. She addressed William directly. Looking at him the way she did made him uncomfortable—he looked toward Katherine for support. "My husband and *his sons* are Italian Catholics, not English Episcopalians like us. Please excuse them William." She reached over and placed her hand on his knee. He cringed but he held steady. He thought about what Apex Industries might think about this, Italian Catholic in-laws. He hoped they never found out. He would have to warn Katherine.

Dinner was served in the back yard. There was a large picnic table with four benches around each side. Next to the table was a barbecue grill that was caked with the grease of previous meals. Guy barbecued thick steaks for Bobby, Alley, and himself. They had been drinking beer non-stop all afternoon. They took turns watching the grill and running inside to the bathroom. William was hoping not to have to eat anything cooked on that grill.

Fortunately, Katherine's mother had prepared broiled salmon for the three of them, as both Katherine and Joey were not fond of steak. Guy, Bobby, and Alley sat on one side of the table talking about sports, while Anne, Katherine, Joey, and William sat on the other side continuing their discussion about Dostoyevsky and Chekhov.

When dinner was over, Katherine, Joey, and William helped Anne clear the dishes, take them into the kitchen, and clean them up. Guy, Bobby, and Alley stayed outside drinking more beer and continuing their discussion as to who was better, Yaz or the Mick.

Anne offered to serve tea and cakes to Katherine, Joey, and William in the living room. Katherine and Joey just looked at each other. When they were seated, Anne started the conversation.

"Can we talk about the wedding?" Anne looked over at Katherine and William. Katherine and William looked at each other. Joey sipped his tea. William looked at Katherine as if to say "what wedding?"

Katherine saved him before he said anything wrong. "Oh, Mom. I don't think we want a wedding. We thought a small ceremony before we drove to Alabama." She nodded at William.

"Nonsense, it's already planned. Just tell me when."

"We thought next Sunday, after services, in the minister's room."

"Uh huh. What about the celebration for family and friends?"

"No, Mom. No celebration. Just the wedding ceremony for family, no friends."

"Your father has already set up with Frederic Fauntleroy to use his grounds for the wedding party. He can't tell him no now. Frederic was a customer of Guy's and one of the richest men in Newport. His yacht was worth at least ten times the value of the Angels' house. Katherine knew how impressed her mother must be to have her wedding on the grounds of the Fauntleroy estate. She had saved all of her married life to give her daughter such a wedding, and to marry into the Bradford family was a well-advised investment.

Katherine looked at William. Her mother had trapped her and now William was trapped.

"Would that be okay, William? We can still have a quiet ceremony and then Mom can have her celebration. I know it means so much to her. We can leave whenever we are ready. Right, Mom?"

Anne nodded her head affirmatively.

William was silent. Things always seemed to get out of his control, never the way he planned them. Joey reached over and patted William gently, but uncomfortably, on the leg. What could he do? He agreed silently.

"So," said Anne, "that's settled. "So, William who would you like to invite? We've already invited over 80 people on our side. We thought you could invite a like amount."

William took out a piece of paper and a pen.

"No, William. You don't have to tell me now. Take some time to think about it. It's still ten days away." Anne was worried about all the arrangements she had to make in such a short time. She didn't need to worry about William's guest list too. Let him invite them directly.

William handed Anne the piece of paper. On it were written the name and address of Herman and Ruth Selzer, and the name of Rebecca Goodman. "Katherine can get you Rebecca's address."

Anne looked at the list. She didn't know what to say. There were only the three names on the list. "William, how about your parents and the other Bradfords?"

"There are no parents and no other Bradfords."

Anne was perplexed. "No Bradfords. What do you mean?"

Katherine intervened. "What William means is that he is an orphan. He has no living relatives."

"Oh, I see." Anne started to beam. "Then William is the Bradford heir."

"No, Mom. There is no heir, just William."

"No heir, no money?"

"That's right, Mom, no money, just William."

"Oh, I see. Then it will be a small wedding?"

"That's right, Mom, a small wedding."

Anne didn't tell Guy about the change in Katherine's fortunes. She wouldn't allow him to smirk at her and her daughter. She did, however, change her guest list from over 80 to about 25.

Katherine wanted William to stay with them until the wedding the following Sunday, but William insisted that he had to get back to Roget to finish the projects he was working on for the Selzers. He knew full well that Ruth had terminated any such projects. He just couldn't spend another minute more than he had to with these people. Luckily, Joey offered to drive William back, as this would give him a chance to visit a friend in Boston. On their way out they called down to the basement (William would never enter that den again) to say good-bye. A resounding "good bye, Willy" came back.

On the trip to Boston, William and Joey talked about their life goals. William shared his ideas about making a difference in the business world by applying mathematical models to business problems. Joey wanted to escalate the aesthetics of architectural design, particularly interior design. They joked about the Angels' inside porch and basement den. Joey said that he didn't know if he could improve upon such creativity in thought and design. By the time they got to Roget, the two of them had bonded. Joey offered to bring William back to Newport the following weekend for the nuptials and to meet the rest of the Angel family. Joey promised to stay close to William, as he would need a friend, other than Katherine, for protection. When William was getting out of the car, Joey told him how lucky he was to have Katherine. As he said this, he held William by the arm. William got the clammy feeling; he didn't know why.

William spent his week trying to reach Rebecca and Herman Selzer and sitting in his room reading. He went to Jones College three times looking for Rebecca, not finding her, and leaving three notes. She didn't respond. He knew he couldn't contact Herman at home as Ruth would hang up or make Herman hang up. So he tried to contact Herman at his office at Harvard. As school was out, there was no answer at Herman's office. Finally, on one of his calls, he made contact with a colleague of Herman's. The colleague agreed to give the message to Herman. Two days went by with no word from Rebecca or Herman. William had planned to have Herman as his best man and Rebecca as the maid of honor. On the third day, the phone in the dormitory rang while William was there. There were only two other students waiting for their tickets from abroad to arrive staying for the week, and they were usually not there. William rushed for the phone down the hall and reached it on its final ring. "Hello, hello," yelled William. There was silence on the other end, then a faint hello. "Hello, hello," William yelled again.

Finally, there was a voice on the other end. "William, is that you?" It was Herman.

"Herman. Thanks for calling back. I thought you had written me off too."

"Well, William, Ruth is very upset. It's difficult for me to even phone you. I'm on a pay phone at the drugstore around the corner from the house."

"I see. I wanted you and Ruth to come to the wedding. I don't know if that's possible now."

"Oh, William. You know I would if I could. I'll try to make Ruth see the light. Right now she's mourning the death of her Jewish son."

"Yes, I know."

There was a hesitation on both sides of the line.

"Look, William, I'll do what I can. Give me the address of your in-laws and the church. If possible, we'll be there. But don't count on it."

"Sure, Herman, I understand. You've been a good friend."

"Sure. I just wish I could be a better friend. Please, William, keep in touch. Let me know where you are. I'm sure things will change."

"Thanks, Herman." He could hear Herman ready to hang up. "Oh, you wouldn't happen to know where Rebecca is, would you?"

He caught himself before he hung up. "Rebecca, no. I know Ruth talked to her, but I don't know where she was calling. From what Ruth said, I wouldn't count on her coming to the wedding either. You understand, don't you?"

"Yes, thanks Herman." William put the receiver down gently. Well, he thought, so much for his best man and maid-of-honor. They would just have to improvise.

Katherine persuaded William to ask her brother Joey to be his back-up best man—Joey was delighted. Joey called William on Thursday to see if he needed a ride from Boston to Newport. Katherine wanted to come get him, but her mother had her so busy with wedding arrangements that Joey offered to pick up William. For Joey it was a welcome relief from having to spend time with the macho male members of his family. Joey would pick William up on Saturday afternoon and they would drive to Newport. The Angels had arranged rooms for out of town guests at a nearby mid-level motel in Newport. Joey had convinced his mother that he and William should have one of those rooms for Saturday night. This would keep William from seeing Katherine until the time of the wedding, a Protestant tradition well respected by Katherine's mother.

William and Joey picked up their conversation from the week before. This made for a pleasant trip to Newport. It was a glorious May day in New England. They stopped for lunch at a small inn on the way. Joey ordered white wine with his lunch and William didn't drink. On the trip after lunch, Joey became more talkative and personal. He asked William about his family, friends, and other relationships. William felt he was trying to pry into his and Katherine's relationship, particularly the sexual aspects. William remained silent. Joey moved back to less threatening territory—Faulkner versus Hemingway.

William spent an uneasy night in the room with Joey. William had never slept in the same room with anyone else, other than his freshman roommate who was rarely there, and felt extremely uncomfortable. They had dinner at the motel and then went up to their room. They both started reading a book in their respective beds. When it came time to change into their pajamas, William hesitated, so Joey moved first. Joey had no problem changing in front of William. As he changed into his pajamas, he faced William so that he could look at his state of nudity as he changed. William hadn't seen another nude male body since junior high school gym class. William turned his head. He was sure that Joey meant nothing by his behavior, but it still made him uncomfortable. William changed in the bathroom and slid quietly back into his bed. Something made him uncomfortable the rest of the night. He figured it had to be the wedding the next day.

Anne Angel had changed the wedding ceremony from the minister's office to the main chapel to accommodate the number of guests. She had pared her guest list, but Guy had increased it to sixty-two by inviting a number of his rich clients and drinking buddies. Since it was money that Anne had put away for Katherine's wedding over the years, he reasoned it was not coming out of his pocket, so why not invite some guests who could help his business and possibly give Katherine a good gift. He still couldn't believe that his future son-in-law had only three guests to invite, none of them Bradfords. Anne had told Guy that the Bradfords were out of the country and with such a surprise wedding they couldn't get back in time. She was certain that they would take care of William and Katherine when they got back. There was no way that Anne would admit to Guy that Katherine was marrying a penniless orphan rather than a rich New England society type— at least not until after the wedding. She didn't need Guy making one of his scenes.

The wedding ceremony had been called for two o'clock on Sunday afternoon. William had expected a simple ceremony with the minister and had planned to arrive at the church around one thirty. When he and Joey arrived at the church, Anne was frantic. They had rehearsed the wedding procession down the aisle with everyone but William and Joey. She had also rented tuxedos for the two of them. They had just enough time to change and take their positions at the altar. The tuxedos were in the minister's bathroom. William was unhappy with what was happening, but he didn't want to ruin this day for Katherine and her mother. He was used to subverting his needs for others.

William and Joey went to change. As would be expected by Anne, the tuxedos were marked "William" and "Joey." This was really unnecessary, as William was five foot ten and weighed 185 pounds and Joey was six foot four and weighed 160 pounds. It would have been quite easy to determine which tuxedo was for whom. William went into a corner of the bathroom with his back to Joey to change into the tuxedo. His body was his secret. Joey, on the other hand, stripped off his shirt and walked around the room exhibiting himself. William started to get the clammy feeling. He now knew what it was that bothered him about Joey. It was the same feeling he got when girls showed him their breasts. William dressed quickly and went to take his place in the chapel. He wanted to see if the Selzers or Rebecca had come to the wedding. He was still hoping; he had no other family.

William snuck into the chapel by the minister's back door. He looked out at the crowd. There was no separation as to the bride's side and the groom's side as there was no groom's side. This meant that William had to check the entire group. He ran his eyes from the front of the room to the back of the room. Neither the Selzers nor Rebecca were in the crowd. He recognized no one. They would all be strangers at his wedding. However, William was used to being alone in the world and this would be no different. He would continue looking for the Selzers and Rebecca throughout the day, but they would not show up. He saw Guy looking in from the opposite door and their eyes met. Guy looked at William with disdain as if he thought that if William didn't have bundles of money he wouldn't be good enough for his daughter. William left the room immediately. That man, and his two macho sons, scared him. He would rather be alone.

William waited with Joey for the minister to tell them where to stand for the ceremony. When they were in place before the minister the music started. The organist played and the choir sang "Unchained Melody," one of Katherine's favorite popular songs. Katherine had chosen it as the wedding song.

Katherine and her father started down the aisle. She looked beautiful in her mother's old wedding dress. With her high heels on she was taller than her father. Her height made her look even more elegant. William felt he made the right decision with Katherine, but not with her family. She was beaming as she walked down the aisle; Guy was scowling as if he would much prefer working in his boatyard. About halfway down the aisle, Guy stopped abruptly as Katherine pulled on him. Guy looked directly at William, and looked over at Katherine. Guy thought to himself, should he stop it now before Katherine got hurt with this pansy. Then he said to himself, "Nah, they deserve each other, birds of the feather and so on." He let Katherine pull him down the rest of the aisle.

When they had all gathered in front of the minister, the minister began the wedding ceremony. William saw Katherine smiling at him through her veil. She was a beautiful bride, but he was a lousy groom. William had never been in an Episcopal church, or any other church, before. The religious liturgy bored him and he quickly faded out. He heard the minister say something about "whoever believes that this couple should not be wed, please speak out now." There was silence in the room. He felt Katherine's father shuffle his feet and begin to speak, but Anne elbowed him and he said nothing. For an instant William felt urged to speak. He didn't know if Katherine knew what she was getting into by marrying him. He felt he should warn her, but he said nothing and the moment passed.

The minister continued while William faded out. Joey was nudging him in the ribs. He looked up. The minister repeated, "Do you William S. Bradford, III take Katherine Dorothy Angel to be your lawful wedded wife?" He hesitated. Joey whispered in his ear, "say I do." He hesitated. Joey poked him again. He said meekly, "I do." Joey handed him the wedding ring that he had picked out in Boston. Joey whispered to William, "Put it on Katherine's finger." Katherine was holding her third finger, left hand out toward William. He looked at Katherine and the ring fell to the floor with a loud bang. William and Joey searched on the floor for the ring—it was lodged under the minister's podium. They tried to dislodge the ring but it only went further under. Some in the audience started laughing.

William and Joey were on the floor on their hands and knees, Katherine was still standing with her hand out, and Guy was rolling his eyes and shooting the jerk off sign to his two sons in the front row. The minister continued without the ring, "You may kiss the bride." William was still on the floor. The minister repeated louder, "You can kiss the bride." Joey poked William to get him to stand up and then put him in front of Katherine. She lifted her veil; she was a beautiful bride. He began having the clammy feeling, as he had never seen her made up like this or kissed her before—with or without makeup. Joey moved William closer to Katherine. He stood there not knowing what to do. Katherine grabbed his face and kissed him on the lips. William just stood there. She kissed him harder with her tongue penetrating his mouth. He felt sick. The audience laughed and clapped. He felt sicker. He looked for the Selzers and Rebecca; they were not there. He was really alone now.

William wanted to leave immediately after the ceremony, but Katherine insisted that they stay at the reception for at least an hour. It would be respectful to her parents and the guests. He reluctantly agreed, as it was Katherine's wedding too. He stood stiffly in the receiving line as the guests came through to offer their congratulations. He was hoping that the Selzers or Rebecca would be there, but they were all strangers. Some of the guests gave William an envelope, which was evidently a wedding gift of money. He felt like a fraud taking their money; they didn't know him and he didn't know them—and he didn't want to know them. Joey stood on one side of him, Katherine on the other side. Bobby and Alley came through the line and looked at William menacingly as if to say that if he didn't treat their sister well they would break all the bones in his body. William shivered. Joey and Katherine squeezed his hand on both sides to reassure him. He wasn't sure what made him more afraid.

Frederic Fauntleroy had provided limousines to take the wedding party to his estate for the wedding reception. William and Katherine had a limousine to themselves. They sat in the back of the limousine; the driver seemed to be miles away. "Unchained Melody" was playing on the sound system. Katherine was sitting close to William. She held his hand and placed her head against his shoulder. William sat upright facing forward, staring into space. He was thinking about Rebecca and how he must have hurt her. It was too late now. Katherine didn't notice. She was a beautiful bride and had a handsome husband. Everything would be all right; she would make sure of that.

The Fauntleroys were one of the richest families in Newport and their estate was one of the largest. Frederic Fauntleroy had always liked Guy Angel. He spent a lot of time at Guy's boat yard, many times when his yacht wasn't being worked on. He enjoyed drinking, smoking cigars, and shooting the breeze with Guy and his two sons. He couldn't do that at home or at work, as he had to be the "proper aristocrat." Guy's boat yard was his escape from his world and his patrician wife, Elizabeth. Frederic was pleased that Guy had asked him, as he had always liked Katherine, even better than his two daughters. His daughters were, of course, debutantes and graspy bitches. He would rather spend his money on himself than leave it to those two. He hoped that by having Katherine's wedding party at his home, he would be able to spend some time kibitzing with Guy.

Frederic had set up a series of tents in the back of the main house. There was a tent for hors d'oeuvres, a tent for the bar, a tent for dancing, tents for sitting down and so on. Anne Angel would only have to pay for the cost of materials—booze, food, other drinks, and so on. William had never seen a house like this before; he had never seen a city like this before. Everything was the finest, from the tablecloths to the silver. He held onto Katherine and Joey so as not to lose his way. He still hoped that the Selzers and Rebecca would show up; he continued to look for them in the crowd. Joey seemed to be looking for someone as well.

Katherine's mother asked to speak to William alone. Katherine and Joey went off to dance. Anne took William's hand. He didn't move, but he didn't like it. She moved them over to a quiet corner of the property, under an enormous evergreen tree. William didn't know anything could grow that tall and wide. He was looking up at the tree. Anne started to talk.

"William, I just wanted to thank you for marrying Katherine. She seems to love you very much. Please be good to her."

He never knew what to say in these situations. He didn't want to be unkind. "I intend to be." Anne noticed that he couldn't say, "I love her, too."

She handed him an envelope. "This is from Guy and me." William knew better. Guy would give him nothing but advice to run.

He took the envelope and started to put it in his inside coat pocket with the others. Anne touched him on his arm. "Please, William, open it."

He hesitated, as he was uncomfortable. He didn't like acknowledging presents; he had gotten so few in his life. Anne took the envelope and opened it for him. Inside was a card. She handed him the card.

He took the card and read the message; Anne Angel evidently handwrote it. It said, "To my beautiful daughter and her husband on their wedding day. May they remember this day fondly for the rest of their days, as I will. Today is the start of your life together. May it last long and be good for both of you."

"Please, open the card." Anne was smiling and had moved closer to him. He moved back a little. He opened the card. Inside was a check. He expected maybe a few hundred dollars to get them to Alabama. The check was for six thousand four hundred and thirty eight dollars. He gasped. He hadn't seen this much money in his entire life. Anne was still smiling and looking flirtatiously at him.

"I'll never forgive you for not being rich. This is what I didn't spend for the wedding. If you were rich I would have spent it all. It's better you and Katherine use it than Guy and the boys."

All William heard was that it was a sin not to be rich. He would make sure that didn't happen again. If that was what Katherine wanted.

William went to look for Katherine. She and Joey were talking to a group of guests—none of whom he knew. Katherine held onto William's arm as she introduced him. He nodded his head as each one was introduced. He would remember none of them. While they were standing there Joey looked over and found the person he had been waiting for. He excused himself, but no one seemed to notice. William saw him hug the person and then move away from the crowd. One of the guests, a Mr. Redmond, asked William if he could dance with his wife. William at first didn't know whom he was talking to, or about. Then he realized it was he. Katherine went off to dance with Mr. Redmond and William wandered about the grounds. The guests nodded to him as he walked about or shook his hand to congratulate him. He noticed neither.

He found the Fauntleroys' dog Muffy eating out of a garbage can at the side of one of the tents. He got her some fresh food in the tent and bribed her with the plate in front of him to go on the other side of the large bushes. He put the plate down for Muffy to eat. Why shouldn't she enjoy the wedding too. He was standing by the side of a beautiful, blue pond stocked with large goldfish. The sun was just starting to set over the water. It was a lovely place of solitude. On the side of the lake there was an open gazebo with benches on each side for sitting. William noticed a couple sitting on one of the benches holding hands looking at the sun. With the sun in his eyes, he couldn't quite make out the people.

As the sun set, the couple stood up and embraced each other. They looked into each other's eyes and kissed deeply and passionately. They stood like this with the sun going down. He looked away; he was uncomfortable. The couple started to walk toward him. He took the plate from Muffy and moved it to the other side of the bush, so that the couple would not see him.

He hoped that they would walk around him. He didn't need to know who they were. As he hid behind the bush, the couple walked right toward him. He turned away so as not to see or be seen. As the couple passed him, he heard Joey's voice say, "I love you" and then another man's voice say, "I love you too." They walked away holding hands. William said "Oh my God" to himself. He never told anyone about this, not even Katherine.

William had spent his hour and was ready to leave. Katherine wanted to have one dance with her husband. He consented. The band played "Unchained Melody." That song would never be his favorite song. Katherine got close to him and kissed him on the cheek. He recoiled automatically. She looked up at him knowingly. She held him a little looser. She would never encroach upon his freedom. She would be a good wife.

As they were ready to leave, Guy Angel stopped them. He hadn't said much, other than congratulations, to either of them. He had spent his time in the drinking tent with his two macho sons and Freddy Fauntleroy; the rest of the family hadn't missed him. William had hoped to avoid him, Bobby, and Alley—a polite congratulation was sufficient from each of them. He had no plans to see them ever again. Guy appeared to be drunk.

Guy held Katherine in his arms. He looked into her eyes. William could see what Anne might have been attracted to in Guy; there was an animal living there. Guy kissed Katherine on the lips, probably more than a fatherly kiss. "Cassie, be happy. I'll miss you." Guy was slobbering.

"I'll miss you too, Daddy." Katherine had started to cry

William wouldn't miss Guy and felt that would be best for Katherine as well. Guy approached William as if to hug him. He moved back. "Come over here. I won't hurt you. I wanted to give you and Katherine something."

William didn't mention the gift he had already gotten from Anne Angel.

Guy handed them an envelope. William looked at it. Katherine took it.

"Please, open it."

Katherine slit the envelope open with her long fingernail. Inside was a set of keys and a title to a new Buick station wagon. "Daddy, what is this?"

"It's your new car."

"But, Daddy, we have your old station wagon. It's loaded for the drive to Alabama."

"Not any more. We moved all of your stuff into the new car, Bobby, Alley, and me. This is from all three of us. We couldn't let you go to Alabama in the old wagon. It wouldn't look good for a Yankee. This way you can come home and visit without your mother worrying."

Katherine might come home to visit, but without William, new car or not. Guy, and Anne, wanted to make sure that they got to Alabama safely; the new car would insure it. He already had the contractor ready to turn Katherine's old bedroom into a billiard room. They had put all of her things in the new car. The furniture would be donated to Goodwill.

Katherine hugged her father and kissed him on the cheek. He kissed her on the lips again. "Thank you, Daddy."

Katherine tried to pull away but Guy held her back. Guy looked over at William.

Guy put out his hand to William, who took it begrudgingly.

"Well, good bye, Willy. Treat my little girl right."

William said nothing. He thought good-bye — forever. He wasn't sure what Guy would do if he didn't treat his little girl right. He didn't ask.

Frederic Fauntleroy had provided a limousine to take Katherine and William to their hotel for their wedding night. Another one of Guy's rich customers owned the largest hotel in Newport and had made the honeymoon suite available to them at no charge. As they were walking toward the limousine, William saw Joey and his friend walking up ahead. Katherine saw them as well at the same time.

"William, there's Joey and his roommate Steven. Can we say good bye?"

William wasn't ready to see Joey as yet, but he couldn't tell Katherine why. "They look like they're in a hurry. I'd like to get to our room."

Katherine looked up at William and smiled. She took him by the arm. This time he stayed still. They walked on toward the limousine. William looked back at Joey. He and Steven were holding hands. He hoped Katherine didn't see them. He would never tell Katherine what he saw.

When they arrived at their room they were dumbfounded. There were flowers and balloons all over the suite. The suite was immense, really three or four different rooms. In the main room were two king sized beds with satin sheets and down covers. On one bed was a negligee obviously for Katherine, and on the other bed were silk pajamas with the monogram WSB III on the pocket, obviously for William. The closets, his and hers, were open and inside were new clothes for Katherine and William. The next room was a sitting room, larger than William's living room in the Bronx, with a double chaise lounge looking out at the gardens.

The third room contained a hot tub spa and massage table with all of the lotions for a lifetime. The fourth room was a master bath, with a whirlpool tub, a shower for two (or three or four), a sink with makeup lights for two, a pedestal toilet and bidet. There was a telephone in the bathroom. Neither one had seen a phone in the bathroom before. Katherine wanted to call her mother to use the phone, but William stopped her. There were soaps and lotions galore to amuse her.

Anne Angel had thought of everything to make her only daughter's honeymoon night the best. This was the honeymoon she had never had, on her wedding night or any night thereafter. Anne wasn't sure whether Katherine was a virgin or not as they never talked about those things— it wasn't ladylike. She wasn't even sure whether William was a virgin or not. He was a good-looking and well-built boy, but extremely shy. She hoped one of them knew what they were doing. She wanted a grandchild and Katherine was her only hope at present.

Katherine was excited as she walked around the suite. She smelled all the flowers and tried all the lotions. She looked out of each window for a different view of the gardens. She turned on the television and the sound system. "Unchained Melody" filled the room; Anne had thought of everything. She plopped on the bed and used the remote to change the channels. William sat on the other bed and watched her. He was entranced. He had never seen Katherine so alive before. She was happy; he was apprehensive. Someday maybe he would be happy too, but he didn't think so. Katherine started to get undressed, but William motioned her into the bathroom. She was excited thinking that he wanted to be surprised. She took her negligee with her into the bathroom. He lay back on his bed and looked up at the ceiling. He resolved to get through this night somehow. He wanted a wife, not these barbaric rituals.

He heard Katherine splashing around in the bathroom. She was enjoying herself. He would try not to spoil it. He heard her on the telephone talking to her mother; he would let it be. He heard the swoosh of the bidet and water spurting all over. He was sure Katherine was sitting on it the wrong way. He heard her on the toilet. He had never heard a woman on the toilet before. He hadn't thought how intimate marriage would be. He didn't have to like it, but he would survive, he always had.

Katherine came out of the bathroom wearing the sheer negligee. William could see her entire body. He looked away. Katherine came over and lay beside him on his bed. He jumped up and ran to the bathroom with the silk pajamas. William quickly changed and looked at the monogram in the mirror, he liked what he saw. He sat on the toilet with the lid down and put his head in his hands. He was clammy and had a headache in the front of his forehead. He could sit like that forever, but he knew he couldn't.

Katherine called from the other room. She knew that William was strange around girls, but she didn't know how strange. "William, are you coming out? I don't want to have my honeymoon night alone." Katherine, due to her height, thinness and drawn looks, hadn't been with many boys. Mostly she had been fixed up by her girl friends—charity dates. Some of these boys had tried things with her, but she had rejected them. She wasn't really interested in sex as she was quite embarrassed by her lack of breasts. She didn't want boys to know, although they knew anyway. With William she felt that it didn't matter. He always seemed to be threatened by female breasts, particularly Rebecca's. Her lack of breasts might be a plus with William. She was a virgin, but didn't want to be. With William it would be all right, she was sure of it.

William heard Katherine, but he made like he didn't. He wanted to go out there, after all Katherine was now his wife, but he couldn't move. He was stuck on the toilet seat, maybe forever. William had little experience with girls and sex as he had always rejected it. It made him sick and clammy. He didn't know why. He liked that Katherine had no breasts, although he saw enlarged nipples through her nightgown. He hoped he could cope with that; he still wasn't sure. Katherine's body was still boyish, but it was a naked body. He hoped he could cope with that. He had looked at Katherine and saw her pubic hair through the negligee. It was light colored, which was good, but it was still pubic hair.

He hoped he didn't have to touch that and the thing beneath it. Thinking about it immobilized him. He just sat. He was a virgin, but didn't want to be any different.

Katherine called out again, this time sweetly and seductively from the other side of the bathroom door. She knew it would be embarrassing to go through with this, but it would be even more embarrassing not to. This was their wedding night. This was what they were supposed to do. Before she left the wedding reception her mother had whispered to her "make me a grandchild."

Katherine went back to her bed and lay down on her side seductively. She knew for a tall thin girl she had an attractive ass. Maybe that would entice William and make him romantic. William finally got his courage together and came into the bedroom. He noticed her and wanted to be able to caress her and make love to her, as he knew he was supposed to, but he was scared and clammy. He lay down on the other bed and pulled the covers over him. She looked over at him with sympathy in her heart. She would have left him be, but she couldn't. She went over to his bed and lay down beside him. She stroked him gently. She loved him emotionally, but she wanted to love him in all ways. She slowly removed the covers from him. They both noticed that his penis was erect. It was the first time the grown up Katherine had seen an erect male penis. It looked gigantic. She couldn't imagine it being inside of her, but somehow she wanted it to be.

William saw her looking at his penis and turned over. She tried to put his hands on her, anywhere, but he pulled away. She slid the negligee off of her body. She lay naked next to him, the first time she was naked with a boy. She felt strange, but good. She slowly removed his pajama bottoms. He didn't fight her. She stroked him until he was ready to turn over. Katherine thought he had an enormous penis, but she really didn't know, as she had no other men to compare. She rubbed her body against him. It felt good to her, and she hoped to him.

He cried inside, but tried to hide it. He would do it for Katherine; maybe that was love. Katherine sat up on him and rubbed his penis against her body and that thing. She was getting moist; he was getting scared. Suddenly, she placed his penis into the opening of her vagina. It was too big to penetrate. It was hurting her and it was hurting him. She pushed harder, through the hurt, until it finally penetrated. She screamed in pain. William screamed inside as he came. Katherine rolled off of him. William turned to the side. This was the first time that they made love. It wouldn't get much better, but it would be all right.

Katherine suggested that they spend the night together on the other bed. William turned from Katherine and said that he felt better in his own bed—he had never slept with anyone in the same bed. He wouldn't be able to sleep. She reluctantly went to the other bed. He sighed relief. He couldn't tell Katherine now, maybe never, why he was afraid to have anyone else in his bed. Girls or sex had never particularly aroused William. At the age that most other boys became acquainted with their puberty and the ability to ejaculate, he was more interested in work. While other boys were playing with their newfound penises and

jerking off alone or in groups, he was ignoring his own penis. He felt dirty looking at either male or female bodies, particularly his own. When he first met
Rebecca he was repulsed by the size of her breasts and her dark femaleness. She
became his friend as long as he didn't see her sexually.

When he met Katherine he felt safe. She was female but she had no
breasts, was thin and boyish with no female curves, with a light complexion.
Somehow, she didn't threaten him as a female and he felt safe with her.
However, shortly after he met Katherine he started to dream about her. At
first, it was just the two of them doing things together at the library, the
museum, the theater and so on. After a while, Katherine became sensual in his
dreams. She would have no clothes on and she would move toward him; however, he saw no breasts, no pubic hair, and no vagina. As he felt her getting
closer, he felt his penis enlarging. As she sat on him, as she did tonight, he
would feel himself slowly ejaculating. He knew it was just a dream, but when
he woke up his penis was sticky and the sheets were wet. He spent the next
day, sometimes two or three, in his clammy, sweaty, and headachey state. He
tried not to have this dream, but it returned repeatedly against his will, particularly when he had something important to do the next day like a test, a
project due, and so forth. He hoped that by marrying Katherine and having
her do the same things in reality his dreams would end. He would see, but he
didn't want her to know about his nocturnal emissions. So, he slept apart
from her.

During the night, Katherine felt alone. She went over to William's bed
and got under the covers with him. She was nude; William was wearing his
pajamas. She pulled off his pajama bottoms without waking him. She lay
down beside him and automatically her hand went around his penis. She
remembered other times when she was a young child. She would come into
her parents' room and get in bed with them. Somehow it was always on her
father's side of the bed. He would hold her until she went to sleep. Sometimes
she would wake up sore where she peed.

She remembered one time her mother screaming at her father, "If you
ever touch her again or have her touch you I'll kill you in your sleep. Do you
understand me?" Her father didn't answer. After that her mother and father
slept in separate beds. They had no more children. They locked their bedroom door and Katherine wasn't allowed in their bedroom anymore. She was
alone for a lot of years.

She kissed William softly on his cheek. She put his arms around her and
she fell asleep like that. She felt safe again after so long. She thought she felt
him come again while she slept. She remembered this happening before, in
her past, but she wasn't sure; her sweet William.

William wasn't aware of Katherine coming into his bed. He was dreaming of Rebecca. In his dream, Rebecca came into his room similar to
Katherine emerging from the bathroom. She was nude, but she had no breasts
or pubic hair. She was light, rather than her natural dark complexion. She
walked slowly toward him as if in slow motion. As she moved slowly toward

him, he felt his penis enlarging and he tried to stop it. He reached down for his penis but someone else's hand was already there. He didn't understand. Rebecca came closer and slowly lay on top of him. He could feel her body on his and her hair in his face. He sensed her breasts growing and pressing down upon him, they were all over his face suffocating him. As he gasped for breath, he slowly ejaculated and it seemed to drain him. He screamed in his dream and he thought it to be real. Then he went to sleep, a deep sleep. He dreamt of his mother for the first time in months. He pulled Katherine closer to him, he held on for his life. He slept like a baby.

The next morning William woke early as usual, about six, and found himself curled in a ball clutching the extra pillow between his legs. His pajama bottoms were off. He thought it strange. He looked over at Katherine's bed. She was sleeping nude, in the fetal position, with her back toward his bed. He stared at her ass and the glimpse of vagina between her cheeks. There was a tinge of excitement, but the feeling of disgust and the fear of suffocation were too strong. He shivered and turned away. He went over and placed the covers over her. He kissed her gently on the top of the head.

His bed was wet and bloody. He didn't know if he had come with Katherine or Rebecca; he would never know. He was sweaty and clammy and his head was clogged. He showered long as he always did on mornings like this. He hoped to clean himself off, but it never seemed to work. He dressed in a fresh silk suit, white dress shirt, and blue striped tie. He polished his shoes with the shoe rag provided by the hotel. He then went down to the restaurant for breakfast. He was better alone at these times. He let Katherine sleep, his little angel. He was safe and she was safe. It would be a good life together.

When he returned to the room, she was dressed in her travel suit. She had everything packed and ready to put in the car. Bobby and Alley had left the car at the hotel and the keys at the desk. They had filled the tank. They wanted to make sure that Katherine really left and that she took Willy with her. They left the hotel by seven o'clock. They didn't talk, and never did, about the night before.

She drove and he slept or read a book on economic models in manufacturing to get ready for the job. William had never driven a car and didn't have a driver's license, as he had never needed to. He would have to learn and Katherine would teach him. They stopped at a roadside stand for lunch. Katherine had a tuna fish sandwich and tea; William had a double cheeseburger with a large order of French fries and a large soda. William had never learned to eat well. He was strong, but flabby with little muscle tone. He would have to learn and Katherine would teach him.

They expected the trip from Newport to Alabama to take the good part of two days. They had planned to drive the bulk of the miles the first day. However, Katherine found her vagina sore; this made sitting in the driver's seat for long periods extremely uncomfortable. She also found that she needed to urinate quite often. This necessitated more stops than they had planned. This was all right with William as he still felt clammy, sweaty, and headachey, and it was hard for him to keep his eyes open. They talked very little, which was fine for both of them. Katherine would look over at William every so often, see him drifting in and out of sleep, and smile to herself — her sweet William and his little angel. They were both safe now.

When Katherine felt she couldn't drive any more that day they stopped at a roadside motel, nothing fancy but nothing shabby. William went in to get a room while Katherine parked the car. He met Katherine outside and they walked to the room. There were two beds in the room with a television and a night table, nothing exceptional but clean. Katherine looked at the two beds and then at William. She nodded affirmatively to herself. If it was okay with William, it was okay for her. William went out to bring all of the suitcases into the room. They weren't going to leave anything in the car. This was all they had in the world.

They were both exhausted from the night before and the long day's drive. They ate a light dinner at the motel restaurant. The food wasn't exceptional, but above college cafeteria standards. They weren't too disappointed. Back in the room, she started to undress in front of him. He forced himself to watch, but when she started to unfasten her stockings from her garter belt he could see she wore no underwear. The glimpse of vagina started him sweating even more. He thought he would be sick. He cupped his hand over his mouth and ran to the bathroom. She could hear him rasping in the bathroom. She felt sorry for her sweet William.

He came back to the bedroom with his pajamas already on, buttoned up to the top. He was sweaty but cold. Katherine was wearing a sheer black negligee. Her mother had really hedged no bets with her trousseau. He could see her entire body through the material; her protruding nipples, her belly button, her thin but curvy hips, the outline of her vagina iced with blond pubic hair, and the smooth curve of her buttocks. Another man, any other man, would have succumbed. William only became sicker. Katherine was expecting William to come over and hug and kiss her. Instead, he turned away and got into the other bed. He pulled the covers up to his chin and turned to the other side. In moments, he was asleep.

Katherine went to the other bed and lay on her back looking up at the dirt and cobwebs on the ceiling. Tears came slowly to her eyes. The tears trickled down her cheeks and she let them go. She cried uncontrollably like that for what seemed like hours to her. She fell asleep still crying. In the middle of the night, she went nude over to William's bed and removed his pajama bottoms. She got into bed with him and automatically grabbed his penis. It was already hard. She put his arms around her and went back to sleep. William dreamt once again of Rebecca and screamed to himself as he came slowly and gently. Katherine felt the moisture forming in her hand and smiled as she slept. In the morning she was back in her bed as the morning before—sleeping nude and hugging her legs with her back to him. He put the covers over her once again and kissed her gently on the head. He nodded to himself. This would be all right, for both of them.

The following evening they arrived after nine in the little town of Hereford, Alabama. Apex Industries had rented a furnished apartment for William and Katherine for the first three months at the company's cost. After that, he would have to take care of their living arrangements. William still didn't understand what Ruth Selzer had against Apex; so far they were treating them just fine. After some driving around and asking directions from Americans whom they couldn't understand, who spoke English but not their English, they finally found their apartment. It was in a new garden apartment complex and everything looked fresh and new. Their apartment was on the second floor. It took William, with a little help from Katherine, another hour or so to bring everything up to the apartment such as luggage, wedding presents, loose clothes, and so on.

William and Katherine were tired from being on the road so long. Katherine still had some vaginal pain and the need to urinate frequently. William was even more clammy, sweaty, and headachey than the day before and he could hardly keep his eyes open. They were tired, but they weren't sleepy. They decided to open their wedding presents and put away those that they could. They started with the wedding envelopes. Katherine opened each one, wrote down the amount and the giver, and handed the check or money to William. As he received each one, he would add the amount to his tally. As the last check was added in, he announced the grand total of eight thousand six hundred and forty three dollars. Katherine said that was impossible. He showed her the tally. She asked where the six thousand dollar check came from. When he told her from her mother, she was amazed. Her mother had bought her a lot of things, including her college tuition, but had never given her money, as that was sacred. They looked at each other; they were richer than they had ever expected to be. She started to hug him and hesitated. He looked at her and nodded, it would be okay. She hugged him and kissed him softly on the cheek. He turned away.

They had the wrapped presents thrown in the middle of the living room. They each took one in turn and ripped the wrapping and announced the gift and the recipient. She recorded each one to send back thank you cards. They laughed as they found duplicates and triplicates of the same thing, salad bowls, sugar and cream sets, salt and pepper shakers, bedding, and so on. Katherine was holding up a rather different looking gift. "Here's one we don't have, I'm not sure what it is, but I know we don't have one." She passed it over to William with the card. William gasped. It was a bagel and lox server from the Selzers. It was exactly like the one the Selzers used for all of those Sunday brunches with Becky.

The card said, "Something you always admired for someone we always admired. We hope you both get as much use out of it as we do." The card was signed simply "Ruth and Herman Selzer." He recognized the writing as Herman's. He was sure Ruth knew nothing about this. He felt sad. He wrapped the gift up and put it back in the box. He never used it, but he carried it from place to place as they moved around. They finished unwrapping the gifts, placing those they could use, putting aside the duplicates, and separating those they probably would never use. These they could give to others as gifts. They laughed about that. William kept looking, but there was no gift from Rebecca. He thought it would probably come later, a combination wedding and house warming gift, but it never did.

They entered the main bedroom for the first time. The first thing she noticed was the two double beds. She resolved to herself that this was the way it was going to be. Tonight it would be cotton pajamas; the nights of negligees were over. She started to change in the bedroom; he went to the bathroom to change. She got into her bed, he into his. In the middle of the night, Katherine nude got into William's bed, took off his pajama bottoms, and curled in beside him with her hand circling his penis and it was hard again. They slept soundly like this. William dreamt of Rebecca. He held Katherine closer. They both smiled as they slept. In the morning, Katherine was in her bed in her familiar morning position. William smiled to himself, covered her up, and went to the bathroom to clean up. This was to become their wedding dance, their anniversary waltz, their dance of love. The honeymoon was over; their life together had begun.

PART TWO
ROAD TO OBLIVION

4

CORPORATE MAN /
FAMILY MAN

William woke up early, around five o'clock, the next morning. He found his penis and the sheet around it damp. He didn't remember Katherine coming into his bed, but he had a recollection of dreaming about Rebecca and his mother. His body felt clammy and his head was fogged. This was a regular occurrence when he had something important the next day, in this case his first day at the Apex plant. He took his usual long shower to make sure that he was completely clean. It helped somewhat, but he would never feel completely clean. He dressed, in the bathroom, in one of his silk suits, silk tie, finely polished black wing tip shoes, and one of the French cuff mono-grammed (WSB III) shirts that Katherine had given him as a graduation/wedding present. He wore the gold cuff links that had come from Katherine with the six shirts. He had given Katherine neither a graduation nor a wedding present. He didn't know what to get a woman, particularly Katherine— she seemed to have everything. He would get her something special, when he knew what that was. He had wished that Katherine were up so that she could approve of his dress for his first day at work. When his head was like this he couldn't think straight. It made him work harder to concentrate on important things, but he couldn't deal with the simple things. This was to be his curse. He decided that it was better for Katherine to sleep the first day, after all the driving she had done the previous two days. There would always be tomorrow. They would develop their routines, just like he had with his mother.

The apartment was about two miles from the Apex plant location. They had arrived late at night when the temperature was somewhat cool for early June. The apartment was centrally air-conditioned which allowed them to sleep comfortably and for William to feel comfortable even in his clammy, foggy state. Hereford wasn't too big a town. William thought it would give him a chance to see the town by walking to work and to clear his head. He was sure that not too much, if anything, would be open at this time of the morning. This would give him a chance to see the town, without the town seeing him. He left the apartment around six o'clock. There was no one around the apartment complex as he left. This was not an early morning town. He saw one man in his pajamas walking his hound dog as he left the complex. The man nodded to him, he nodded to the man. He walked on, the man looked at his rear as he walked past. "Another silly Yankee newcomer," thought the man, "dressed in a heavy northern suit, carrying a heavy briefcase, in the southern clime. He would learn about southern heat and humidity soon enough." The man gave him less than three months before he returned north.

William walked through the downtown area of Hereford, Alabama. It was less a downtown than the central quad at Roget Institute. Downtown Hereford consisted of a diner, a gas station, and a convenience grocery store. The post office was in the convenience store. There was nothing else necessary for basic survival. Nothing was open and there was not a soul to be found. The Apex plant was within another mile of the downtown. In early June, the sun rose just after six. As he walked, the temperature increased and the humidity set in.

He started to sweat almost immediately through his shirt and into the armpits of his suit jacket. He felt his curly hair going limp and hangy. He would have liked to have stopped at the diner to freshen up. The sweat increased his clamminess and foggy head. He would have to adjust. By the time he arrived at the plant, he was soaked through and the dust from the road had covered his shoes and suit pants. His clothes were sticking to him, but he wouldn't remove his jacket or loosen his tie as appearance was everything. His undershorts were caught around his legs and pinching his genitals, but he wouldn't pull them loose lest he be seen. His hands were sticking to the handle on his briefcase. He would repeatedly shift the briefcase from one hand to another, but very quickly the sweat formed again. He now knew why there was no one else walking on the road.

The Apex plant was a small one-story building of modular construction. Its purpose was to produce components for the Apex industrial fasteners division. Apex management had calculated that it was much less expensive to produce the component parts at the Hereford plant and then ship them to Connecticut for assembly into fasteners for automobile and airplane manufacturers. The decision was based on the difference between higher union rates in Connecticut and lower non-union rates in Alabama. It was also expected that productivity would greatly increase at the Hereford plant without the need to deal with union imposed constraints. After operating the Hereford plant for five years, Apex management realized that productivity wasn't being achieved. With raw material and finished goods' shipping charges, combined with lower than expected productivity, the costs of the component parts were exceeding expected costs of manufacturing in Connecticut. William's assignment was to see if costs could be decreased and productivity increased at the Hereford plant to make it viable once again.

Otherwise, Apex management was considering closing the plant. William was to determine if his mathematical models could save the plant and reduce Apex's overall costs. This was just the type of problem that he wanted to work on; this was his golden opportunity. If he succeeded, Apex management had promised him challenging assignments at their other locations. William looked upon this as a temporary assignment. He wouldn't want to stay here any longer than necessary, and he had just gotten here. The three-month rental at company cost should work out just fine. William would make sure of that; perhaps it would be less.

He walked to the front door of the Apex plant. It seemed odd to him that there were no cars in the parking lot. It was now a little after seven o'clock. Surely the plant would be open by now. When he had talked to the plant manager, Donald Severance, he was told that "yes indeedy, they started early and ended late." This was just the way William liked it. He tried the front door, but it was locked. There was no sign as to the plant's hours. He cursed himself, "silly fool," for not asking Mr. Severance as to the specific hours. If the plant or office wasn't open at seven, the earliest would have to be eight o'clock, almost an hour later. He sat on the step under the overhang to get out of the sun for a while. In his foggy and clammy state, he found it difficult to think straight as to what to do. Times like this were when he preferred to simply immerse himself in work letting the details take over his mind.

When most of the sweat had evaporated, he decided that rather than wait at the plant it would be better to wait at the diner. He could get something to eat and clean himself up. He wasn't sure if this was the best course, but it was the best he could come up with. By the time he walked the fifteen minutes back to the diner, he was drenched again and thought he would have been better off waiting at the plant. He was never sure of his decisions in this state. Luckily, the diner was now open. There were a number of customers sitting at the Formica top tables and booths and at the counter. It seemed that they all turned to look at William as he entered the diner. Damn Yankee, doesn't know how to dress and when to come in from the sun. He felt them laughing behind their hands as he looked for the men's room. As he was entering the kitchen, the waitress behind the counter motioned for him to go to his far left. He found the little door with the picture of a male southerner on it, a farmer in overalls and a large straw hat chewing on a piece of hay. He washed himself down as best he could without having to take his jacket off or opening his trousers. He felt somewhat better — still clammy and foggy, but not as sweaty. The diner was only slightly more comfortable than being outside. The shades were drawn to protect the inside from the sun and the two overhead fans were running at full speed. This was the best it was going to get.

He looked around. The tables and booths were for four persons. Although most of them were empty, he decided he would be less conspicuous at the counter. As he sat down, the same waitress came over to give him a menu. She had a large name pin on her shirt. The name on the pin was Carey Sue. She appeared to be young, around William's age of 22, with a robust figure that seemed to be coming out of her uniform. Either she was too big or the uniform was too small. Her breasts were pushing the shirt away from her body, so that the buttons opened and he could see the bra and her cleavage underneath. He took the menu and looked away. He studied the menu with his face down.

"So, what will it be?"

He was startled. His hands and body convulsed from fright.

Carey Sue laughed. "I'm really sorry. I didn't mean to scare you."

He looked up. From the other side of the counter, Carey Sue was looking down at him. Her breasts were directly at his eye level. While the other men who came to the diner would probably find this sight quite enhancing, he felt uncomfortable and the clammy feeling intensified. He averted his eyes from looking directly at Carey Sue. She noticed his discomfort and chuckled to herself as she pushed her chest out farther. She looked down at him with her order pad and pencil in her hand, while she chewed gum to the juke box music of "Your Cheatin' Heart."

"So, what will it be?" Carey Sue said again.

He looked at the menu. He couldn't concentrate on the writing so he improvised. "Can I get two eggs, poached, on whole wheat toast with hash brown potatoes on the side? Oh, and an orange juice, fresh squeezed. Ice water on the side."

She looked sadly at him. "You must be visiting. We don't poach eggs, have whole wheat bread, hash brown potatoes, or fresh squeezed orange juice. What I can do is have Cookie soft boil some eggs, put them on white bread toast, with grits on the side, and concentrated orange juice. How's that?" She said all this while she chewed her gum. He had never seen this done before. He was amazed; his head entered another world.

"Not what I had in mind, but you make it sound good. That is, all except the grits. Just what are grits?"

She laughed. "New in town, huh?"

"Yesterday. Starting work at Apex Industries this morning."

She looked at him inquisitively. "Apex who?"

"The building down the road." He pointed in the direction of the plant.

"You mean the parts plant. That's what we know it as. Apex Industries, eh?"

He nodded his head affirmatively. "Yeah, the parts plant."

"Where are you from?" She could detect the northern accent as he could detect her southern drawl. But, in Hereford, Alabama, Carey Sue talked like everyone else; he was the outsider once again.

"Massachusetts."

She tried to repeat it back, but stumbled over the word.

William helped her out. "Boston," he said.

That she could handle. She repeated "Boston." She stood there chewing her gum with her chest out and nodding her head. She said it again—"Boston."

"I'm here to help the parts plant. To do things better."

Her face lit up with recognition. A 25-watt bulb went on over her head. "You must be the hot shot from headquarters. The one who's going to straighten things up, make everyone more money and work less hours. Well, welcome to Hereford. Let me get you some coffee on the house." She poured him a mug of coffee as he held his hands up to stop her. She walked away talking to herself. "Geez, he doesn't look any older than I am. I thought he would be older and taller."

He pushed the coffee away. The smell itself was making him sick. He realized he never found out what grits were. He would take his chances.

When Carey Sue brought his breakfast she looked down upon him with much greater respect. She carefully placed the plate of eggs, toast, and grits down in front of him. She went back to get his orange juice and a refill for his coffee. She carefully placed the orange juice down and started to pour more coffee. William put his hand up to stop her, but she automatically filled the cup anyway. He hadn't, and wouldn't, drink the coffee.

He tried the eggs on the toast. The soft-boiled eggs were more hard-boiled and the toast was burnt around the edges, but it would be okay. He tried the orange juice and it was indeed concentrated, more concentrate and water than orange juice, but it would be okay. Carey Sue didn't bring the ice water, but he would chance that another day. He tried what he thought was some kind of watery, buttery oatmeal mush. This had to be the grits, and this wasn't okay. He gagged and had to spit the grits back on his plate. He heard some snickering behind him. He didn't want to be insulting to southern hospitality on his first day by not eating the grits, but he just couldn't. He decided to wrap the grits as best as he could in a number of paper napkins. He could think of nothing better to do. He looked around for a discreet place to toss them, but he found none. So, he put the soggy mess quickly in his briefcase. He would get rid of it later. He would avoid anything he didn't know in the south from now on. When he was finished, he ate what he could. He motioned for Carey Sue to bring him the check by writing in the air. She looked perplexed, but came over anyway.

"Anything else, hotshot?"

He looked up at her, but to the side. "You can call me William."

"Okay, hotshot William." She smiled down at him with her chest out pushing her name tag closer to him. He turned away. "You can call me Carey Sue."

He flustered. "I need the check. I don't want to be late on my first day."

"Oh, the boss said this one is on the house, for the Yankee hotshot. He's expecting you to take care of the family."

"The family?"

Carey Sue smiled. "The family is the town. We're all more or less related. Almost every family has someone who works at the parts plant. My daddy, my uncles, my brothers, everybody."

He nodded. "Thank you, Carey Sue, and thank the boss. I'll do what I can to help." He got up to go.

"You don't need to hurry. The parts plant don't open for another hour. Have some more coffee, it's on the house." Carey Sue went to get more coffee. William poured his coffee into his juice glass.

He thought to himself, "Another hour, that would make it nine o'clock." No wonder the plant is in trouble. He had the first factor in his mathematical model. He also had his first taste of southern hospitality, and he liked Carey Sue.

He arrived back at the plant ten minutes after nine, stuck to his suit, shirt, and underwear. He was sweaty, clammy, foggy and caked with dust. As he walked down the dirt road from the diner to the plant, the dust would kick up on his shoes and trousers and as each vehicle (mostly older looking pick up trucks) passed him by, the dust thrown off by their back tires would encase him in dirt. On his initial journey to the plant there were no vehicles. Now there was a steady stream of vehicles, hurrying to get to work on time or not to be too late. They did not slow down when they saw him walking. Seeing a strange man in a suit on the road to the plant may have even caused them to speed up and maximize the dirt back draft. He tried to clean himself up before entering the plant, but he only succeeded in moving the dirt around his clothes and from his clothes onto his hands.

He entered the front door of the plant and was greeted with a blast of frozen air conditioning. The contrast to the steamy and humid outside was shattering. He got chills all through his clammy body. Inside the door were a waiting room and a receptionist window. Behind the window was an older woman with her hair pinned up with a tortoise shell comb in the back and matching eyeglasses. As he went over to the window, she looked down at him over her eyeglasses that were attached to her neck by a gold chain eyeglass holder. To William, she looked like Minnie Pearl, without the hat. All south-ern ladies over thirty looked like Minnie Pearl to William, as that was the only southern lady over thirty he had ever seen.

"Yes, can I help you?" sounded like what she said to him, but he wasn't sure. He would have to work on his southern style English. The North and the South were two parts of the same country divided by the same language. In front of her was a name plaque that read "Mary Lou Rogers, Receptionist." Mary Lou had long heavily painted fingernails in a dark purple hue and a heavily painted face, almost a mask. He had to move back from the heavy, strong perfumed odor.

"Pardon me," he said.

She said the same thing again. He gave up. "Is Donald Severance in?"

"Pardon me," she said.

He spoke louder. "Donald Severance!"

"Oh, sure. The duck. Who should I say is here?" Mary Lou was speaking slower, but not much clearer.

"William Bradford."

"Oh, the hotshot from HQ. I thought you would be older and taller." She turned in her seat toward the back. He could see she was wearing dirty jeans and boots. She called to the back. "Tell Duck the hotshot's here, ya'll hear!"

He wanted to ask her about a restroom so that he could clean up first, but before he could ask, the side door opened and a tall slender man wearing jeans and an open shirt appeared. He walked toward William, with a slight limp. He extended his hand. "Hi, I'm Donald Severance, the plant manager. You can call me Donnie."

Thank God he spoke northern English, thought William, even if it was with a slight southern drawl. He took Donald's hand to shake. "William Bradford," he said and he hoped he didn't feel too clammy.

Donald looked at William's hand; it was covered with dust. He looked at William, covered with dust. "What'd ya'll do, walk from Connecticut?"

"No, no. Just from home."

"And where is that again, Massachusetts?"

"Oh no, I mean home here. You know, the apartments down the road."

Donnie looked at him. "That's close to two miles away. Ya'll don't walk like that down here. You're liable to get boiled in road dust. It looks like ya'll were dragged. And those fancy clothes too." He shook his head back and forth.

Donnie took William back to his office. He tried to explain the way things worked here. Most of the employees were full time farmers, dairy, livestock, vegetables, nuts and so on, and part time factory workers. Mary Lou and her husband, Billy Ray, operated the largest pecan farm in the area. However, they needed their jobs at the plant to pay their bills, but their first love was the farm. This was the same for most of the other employees. Apex management wanted the workers to start at eight o'clock in the morning and end at six o'clock at night, a full nine-hour shift. Headquarters was depending on the Hereford plant to provide sufficient components on time and at high quality to support their production schedule in Connecticut. The Hereford plant was always way behind in meeting these requirements, which was costing the parent company greatly. William was there to correct the situation. Donnie had been sent down from Connecticut over four years before to increase efficiency and ensure that all production requirements were met. Donnie was originally from Hackensack, New Jersey. Unfortunately, instead of Donnie changing the Hereford mentality, they had changed his. The hours of operation were now officially nine or so, (some came later as their farm requirements dictated) until five or so (some left earlier). Donnie explained how the hours had to be compromised as the workers had their farms and there was only a limited population in the Hereford area, with even fewer who were interested in plant work.

To get anything done, Donnie had to compromise with the employees. He wanted William to understand this. As Donnie said, "You can only put so much bullshit into a five pound bag." He was trying, but he was up against it. William would see for himself.

Donnie took William for a tour of the plant. The workers seemed to be primarily socializing and secondarily working in the plant. As Carey Sue had said, everyone in town was either related or knew each other. They had lived in the Hereford area all of their lives with many of the families going back five or six generations. They didn't want to be the factory workers Apex Industries wanted them to be. The plant facility was chaotic at best. William was unable to determine where one work center started and the next ended or even if there were organized work centers. This would be a lot different from the desk projects he had worked on. Why did real life always have to be scarier than theory?

As they walked through the plant, the workers would slap Don on the back and take time to talk with him. William watched the informality of the relationship. It was as if Don was one of them and not the boss. William wondered what the effect of such informality was on productivity; he would find out. Most of the employees, almost entirely all males on the factory floor, called Don "Duck," "Duckie," or "the Duck." William thought it was because of the way he walked, but he found out later it was due to Donald Duck the cartoon character. William had no knowledge of such things. He was relieved that the employees weren't being insensitive to the northern guy, only insensitive to the cartoon character.

Don had set William up in an office as far from the plant floor as possible all by itself outside of the purchasing area. He settled in there to store his things and secure his papers, but he couldn't conduct his study from there. He had Billy Ray Stewart, the head maintenance man, set up a table in the middle of the factory floor. He kept himself socially isolated from the other employees, including Donnie. He took no breaks, bought his lunch in the company cafeteria and brought it back to his desk to eat it alone, and he worked as he ate. This procedure worked fine for William, particularly in his clammy and foggy condition. He was used to being alone. The workers complained to "the Duck" that William was spying on them, but William held fast. Donald could call his superiors at headquarters if he wanted to; that was all right with William. Donald never made the call.

William found that almost all of the employees went by two names, such as Carey Sue, Mary Lou, Billy Ray, Bobby Joe or Bobbi Jo, Laura Jean, Billy Bob, Stevey Ray and so on. Most of the employees also shared common last names, some with different spelling such as Rogers and Rodgers, Stewart and Stuart, Odum and Odem, Harper and Harpor, etc. The employees called William "Billy Brad.". This made him feel less of an outsider, but it also made him nervous.

He finished his first day of observing factory operations and locked his papers in his office. His personal notes he would take home in his briefcase. When he opened his briefcase he found grits all over the inside. He had forgotten the grits from his breakfast at the diner; it seemed so long ago. Some of the employees caught William cleaning out his briefcase from the wet grits, trying not to get his suit or shirt dirty.

He would continue to dress for work regardless of the lax dress code at the plant; however, the story got around that William used his briefcase to carry grits — dumb Yankee knew no better. The employees had a good laugh at his expense. Some were bold enough to ask him if he had any grits from time to time. They made him an honorary southerner. He wondered whether the laughter would ever stop.

Plant operations seemed to start about nine thirty in the morning and end at four thirty in the afternoon, with both a morning and afternoon break of close to a half hour each and a lunch break of about one hour. Based on William's first day of observation, he estimated that actual hours for production were less than a total of five hours, a far cry from headquarters expectations of nine hours per day. The scarcity of hours combined with the lackadaisical work atmosphere and absence of any meaningful production scheduling control resulted in daily production well below realistic expectations. In addition, the practice of scheduling production by headquarters' work order rather than by part number resulted in inefficient production and the inability to ship finished parts until the entire work order was completed. William already felt that he had a pretty good fix on what some of the plant operations problems were by the end of his first day.

No wonder headquarters was concerned about Hereford plant operations. The plant was being operated for the benefit of the employees and their families and not the company. William would try to save the plant if he could, but he had strong doubts. He was used to working late. He would have liked to write up his rough notes after the employees had left for the day, but Donald's policy was to lock up and go home after the last employee had left. This was usually around five fifteen. William had no choice but to leave with Donald. Donald had refused to give William his own key to the building, as it would be a breach of security. William would talk to headquarters about this the following morning, and he would get his own key and the permission to come in early and leave late.

Donald offered to drive him to his apartment, but he refused. He would rather walk. It was cooler now and the walk would refresh him, possibly relieve the clamminess and foggy feeling after being inside all day. He didn't want Donald to become his friend. He didn't need another friend; he had Katherine.

Katherine woke about ten in the morning. After tossing and turning for the longest time while agonizing over whether she had made the right decision, she had finally fallen asleep some time in the early morning. The last thing she remembered before falling asleep was William covering her with a blanket and kissing her lightly on the side of her head. She half noticed him looking fondly down at her in his silk suit and monogrammed shirt—her sweet William. Tomorrow she would get up with him, make him a good breakfast, and drive him to work. She would be a good and obedient wife.

Katherine woke up hungry, but there was nothing to eat in the apartment. She would do the food shopping today. She slowly showered and got dressed. She would always apply full make-up and dress up as if she was going into downtown Boston, even if it was downtown Hereford. By the time she was ready, there was no mistaking that this was a fancy lady from the big city.

She drove toward the downtown area. However, she was on the dirt road outside of town, in the direction of the plant, before she realized she had already passed through the two block long downtown. She had seen the diner driving through the town and had rejected it as a place she would want to eat. Yet coming back to the diner and realizing it was the only place, it now looked like a fine place to eat. She went in and sat at the counter. Carey Sue came over immediately and greeted her. There was little business in the diner between breakfast and lunch.

"Good afternoon, Mrs. Bradford. What can I get for ya'll?"

Katherine was surprised. "You know who I am?"

"Oh, no, ma'am. I just figured you couldn't be anyone else."

"And why is that?"

"Your husband, Hotshot William, was in here this morning. I haven't seen clothes like y'alls in all my born days. You got to go together, there's no other way."

Katherine nodded her head. This girl was no dummy. "Well, thank you, miss, I guess."

"Oh, you can call me Carey Sue. Hotshot William already does."

"Oh, he does, does he?" She looked Carey Sue over. Nope, she was not William's type — too much breast and not enough brain. She liked Carey Sue.

Before she could order, Carey Sue offered to take care of her. She noticed Katherine having trouble with the menu. Katherine didn't know what to do about barbeque, black-eyed peas, collard and mustard greens, grits, ham hocks, and so forth. Carey Sue brought her a plain hamburger on a bun with potatoes and a Coke on the side. After the last two days of eating on the road, it tasted wonderful. She knew then that she and Carey Sue would become friends. Before she left the diner, she got all the directions she needed from Carey Sue: where to shop for this and that, the post office, the dry cleaners, which bank to use, and so on.

Carey Sue told Katherine about a small library in one of the rooms of the regional elementary school about seven miles east of town. Katherine couldn't wait to see it for herself. She found the school in the direction that Carey Sue had said. It wasn't difficult as there was nothing else on this road. Finding the library proved to be more difficult. It was as if no one at the school knew there was a library there. Finally, after wandering around for some time, she found a small room with a hand-lettered sign outside the door that read "Hereford County Regional Library." She went inside and found a small, elderly lady wearing horn-rimmed eyeglasses with a string holder, her hair pulled back in a bun. The nameplate in front of the lady read "Ethel Biddle, County Librarian."

Katherine walked around the small library and was appalled at the sparse number of books and their quality. She shook her head negatively as she walked around. Ethel watched Katherine as she examined each bookshelf. It was obvious by the way she looked and was dressed that she wasn't the typical visitor to the library. In fact there were very few visitors to the library, as most of the county residents didn't even know of its existence. Katherine appeared to be ready to leave the library. She saw no purpose in talking to this seemingly backward, southern lady.

"Can I help you, dear?" Miss Biddle was talking to her, and it was in English,. Was she a northerner?

"Oh, no, Miss Biddle. I just wanted to see what kind of library you had."

Ethel looked relieved. "I thought so. Another Yankee. Thank God. Someone to talk to. Where are you from? Sounds like New York."

"Close. Rhode Island—Newport."

"I'm Ethel Biddle, from Newark, New Jersey. Please call me Ethel."

"Okay, Miss Biddle."

"That's Ethel." She looked sternly at Katherine. "And it's Mrs."

"And I'm Katherine Angel, that is Bradford. And it's also Mrs." She held out her hand to show Ethel her engagement and wedding rings.

"Just married?" Ethel looked up into her eyes.

"Three days ago. William, that's my husband, is here to work at the Apex plant."

"Oh, yeah, the parts plant. He must be the hotshot from headquarters. The one who is going to save the plant."

"That's him, Hotshot William." They both laughed.

They talked about the state, or lack thereof, of the regional library. Ethel explained that her husband John was the Apex plant engineer, sent down from headquarters three years ago to straighten things out. However, since John had been there, the situation had only gotten worse and he felt helpless. It was John who had requested that headquarters send someone down to look over the situation. Headquarters was frustrated as to what to do and suggested that maybe William could figure it out using a mathematical model. They felt they had tried everything else. Ethel, as a northern outsider, was isolated in Hereford. She saw an advertisement in the local paper for a librarian. She knew nothing about library work, but becoming friends with books seemed better than trying to become friends with these people. John, as an old farm boy from the Midwest had less of a problem adjusting to the rural ways of Hereford people.

She took the job, which paid relatively nothing, over two years ago and had been fighting with county officials ever since for additional funding. They told her that the federal government required them to have a regional library or sacrifice other funding; otherwise they saw no use for a library. It was rarely used and the most recent book was over five years old. As the county commission told her, they "needed a county library like a steer needed balls."

Before Katherine left, Ethel asked her if she would like to help her build up the library. There would be no pay, just good company and something to do to keep her from going crazy. She was excited, but told Ethel she would have to make sure that it was all right with William. Ethel told her John was the same way; he didn't want her to get too friendly with the locals. Katherine assured her it wasn't anything like that. She just wanted William to be comfortable with what she was doing.

Ethel shook her head. "Newlyweds," she said. "I understand, dear. You must be living at the Apex apartments."

"How did you know?"

"There's no other place to live. Apex built the apartments for plant visitors to stay. The only other place to stay in town is Odum's Rooms. You probably saw it when you drove through town. The only nice thing about the place is the sign out front. Old man Odum is so proud of it, the only sign in town that lights up at night. It draws the roaches from the rooms."

"Yeah, I noticed it. I thought it was a chicken coop."

They both laughed at the expense of southern hospitality.

"Now that you two are at the apartments, that makes three of us. The other nine apartments stay empty for visitors. But there are fewer and fewer visitors to the plant."

"So you and your husband live at the Apex? And who else?

"Jerry Babcock, the plant equipment repairman. Also sent down by head-quarters from Rutherford, in New Jersey. It gives us something to talk about together. We have Jerry over to dinner at least once a week to keep him from going southern crazy. He's a bachelor. He doesn't seem too interested in girls, particularly southern girls, so he keeps to himself. I think you'll like him."

Katherine left excited. She had only been in Hereford one day and already she had made two friends, Carey Sue and Ethel, and the possibility of a job although non-paying with Ethel. Her Jones College degree was already paying off. Ha, ha! She finished shopping and rushed home to put things away and prepare and dress for dinner. William would be proud of her, she was sure.

Katherine expected William home about eight o'clock based on his propensity to work late. She knew he wouldn't telephone to let her know he was on his way. She would just have to estimate. This was the first real meal she had prepared for the two of them and she wanted it to be perfect. Unfortunately, Jones College had not prepared her for meal preparation, just for ordering. The food selection in Hereford wasn't great, as most of the residents were farmers and either raised their own food or bartered with other farmers. What the convenience grocery store had was what you got. The next nearest food market was over thirty miles away in Bear Creek. Katherine arrived back at the apartment around five thirty. She figured she had enough time to take a short nap, shower the southern heat and grime off her body, remake her face, and dress appropriately for their first dinner together. She had bought the nicest bouquet of flowers she could find in Hereford and had arranged them in a vase as the centerpiece for the table. She would set the table and place the candlesticks when she had cleaned up, the silver candle-sticks and lavender candles that were among the wedding presents. It would be just right for her sweet William.

Katherine was coming out of the shower nude into the bedroom when she walked right into William. Her body stiffened from fright; he had scared her. He was almost nude himself, in the process of taking off his last garment, his under shorts. She stood there looking at him. Her nipples automatically hardened and stood upright. He turned abruptly away and quickly pulled his under shorts back up. He went around her and into the bathroom. She heard the shower go on. She stood frozen. She wanted William to see and enjoy her body; she wanted to enjoy his. Maybe someday this would happen. It would be all right for now.

With William home early, her dinner plans would have to be revised. She knew that he liked to have his dinner as soon as he came home. He expected it to be on the table just like when he was growing up. Katherine hurried to prepare everything. She had purchased a chicken, sweet potatoes, and fresh string beans with William's favorite ice cream flavor, Cherry Vanilla, for dessert. She unwrapped the chicken and was surprised that the feather stubs were still on the chicken. She didn't know whether she should cook it like that or not, so she waited for William. Maybe he would know. She stood there looking at the chicken until he came out of the bedroom dressed in another suit, shirt, and tie. He didn't know what to do with a half plucked chicken either, so they both just stared at the chicken. Katherine sat down at the table and started to cry into her hands.

William tried to pluck out the feather stubs with little success. He brought the finished product over to Katherine. She looked at it and cried more intensely.

"Oh, William, I wanted our first dinner together to be so perfect."

He patted her on the back of the head. He never knew what to do in these situations. "It'll be okay. Let's see what else you got. Maybe something quick."

He rummaged through the refrigerator and the shelves. "Here, this will do. You sit there and I'll take care of dinner."

She cried more intensely.

He opened some cans and put the contents on the stove to cook. When he was done, he spooned some of each of them onto two plates. He brought the plates over to the table and placed one in front of Katherine. He had prepared a plate of canned corn, macaroni, and corned beef hash. She cried until she started to laugh. William laughed with her even though he didn't know what was so funny. Through her laughter she was able to say, "William S. Bradford III, one of the great southern chefs." She laughed even harder and he laughed along with her.

"At least it's better than the Hereford diner. I can always get a job there."

They laughed and ate. Tomorrow night could be their first dinner and it would be all right.

Katherine told him about meeting Ethel Biddle and the non-paying job at the county library. He agreed that it would be good for Katherine as long as she could take him to work in the morning (his walking days were over), pick him up at night, and have dinner ready when he got home. If not, he threatened to cook again. He warned her to not get too friendly with the Biddles until he knew how his report would affect John Biddle. Their life together was emerging into proper routines. William liked that.

The routine became set. He would get up at five o'clock. Most of the time he would find Katherine lying nude across her bed with her legs pulled into her chest and her back to him. He would avoid looking between her legs as he covered her up. Sometimes he was aware that she had come into his bed the night before, cuddling and stroking his penis. Sometimes, in his sleep, he would become aware of her sitting on his penis. He wanted desperately to stop it, but he also desperately wanted it to continue. He would ejaculate almost immediately. She would smile at him and he would go back to sleep. Most of the time he was aware of dreaming about Rebecca suffocating him with her breasts and then cuddling with his mother. At that point, he would come slowly and fully. Katherine would feel him pull closer to her and his entire body would relax. This was the only time she ever felt him relax. She would hold his wet penis until she too fell asleep.

He would use the bathroom to take his long shower. He would use three kinds of soap, a shampoo, a hair conditioner, and a body gel. He still wouldn't feel clean or lose the clammy, foggy feeling on those mornings when he had emitted during the night. He would shave and dress in the bathroom. Katherine would prepare his clothes the night before and hang them in the bathroom when she was done. While he was getting dressed, she would get up and prepare breakfast in her "breakfast pajamas," as she and William called them. Breakfast was always the same thing: two poached eggs, whole wheat toast, fresh squeezed orange juice, with iced water on the side. Katherine would have a piece of toast and a cup of tea. She told William that she would have the rest of her breakfast later, but she never did.

Katherine would then drive William to the plant so that he arrived before six o'clock. She would wear her breakfast pajamas and a scarf over her hair. In her mind she looked terrible, but at that time in the morning in Hereford there was no one else to see her. He thought she looked cute, like a little old man going out to get the newspaper. He would let himself into the plant, as he now had his own key, turn on the lights, and perform mock production flow studies until the plant employees started work around nine thirty. He would then spend the day charting and graphing the actual production flow for the day using his mathematical model under various conditions. When the employees left for the day, William would run mock trials of the better production combinations to test out his calculated results. His job would have been easier had he been able to work with Donald and the production employees. But he was afraid to let them know what he was up to, as he didn't want to create fearful rumors. John Biddle offered to assist William in the morning or after work, but William turned him down, as he didn't know who could be trusted. He always worked better alone, and he always was alone. He would meet Katherine at the front door of the plant every evening at exactly eight o'clock. They both agreed that he should learn to drive, but he put it off. He felt awkward learning to drive and taking the driver's test with all of the teenagers. He was scared Katherine would stop driving him.

After dropping William at the plant in the morning, Katherine would go back to the apartment to clean up the dishes and her self. By seven thirty she was showered, made up, hair up, and dressed. Sometimes Ethel would come to her apartment for a cup of tea, and sometimes she would go to Ethel's apartment. They would talk, mainly about the sanity of the North versus the insanity of the South, until it was time to leave for the library. They would never talk about the plant. Katherine made it clear that William wouldn't like it. Sometimes Katherine would drive to the library and sometimes Ethel would drive. They were becoming good friends. Katherine liked that, even though the four of them couldn't be friends. Katherine always got back home in time to prepare dinner, take a shower, re-make herself, and pick William up at the plant at exactly eight o'clock. By the time they got back to the apartment, their dinner was ready. While he cleaned up, she put dinner on the table. They alternated between chicken (fully cleaned), steak, and hamburger, but no fish (William didn't like the taste) and never pasta (Katherine didn't want to be reminded). So the days went.

Katherine and Ethel had cleaned up the library. They had rearranged the shelves and brought the more current and popular books toward the front of the shelves. Katherine had started visiting the schools, elementary, middle, and high school, to conduct reading sessions with the students and get them to visit the library. The students thought Katherine talked and dressed funny, but they liked the funny northern lady; she was nice. Some of the teachers brought their classes to the library for story times and a discussion with Ethel as to how to use the library. Books started to go out and come back. They were building up a number of regular students from all grades. Ethel was no longer alone. Katherine and Ethel went to the county manager and presented their case for expanding the library. He was able to get them larger quarters in the elementary school and $10,000 to purchase additional books. Katherine and Ethel had a fine time spending the money, revisiting books that they both loved. Katherine was also soliciting funds from parents and local businesses. This was Katherine's first success.

Katherine would stop at the diner from time to time. Sometimes she had a cup of tea after dropping William off in the morning if she was properly dressed. Sometimes she would stop for lunch when she was soliciting funds for the library. She would always sit in Carey Sue's station, which was usually the entire diner. They were learning to understand each other's speech and were becoming close friends. Carey Sue would sometimes come out to the library on her day off and help Ethel and Katherine. Sometimes Katherine would take the same day off, and she and Carey Sue would go shopping in Bear Creek or hiking in the hills. Katherine was making a life for herself while William stayed isolated.

Every Wednesday evening she would phone her mother between six o'clock when she got home and eight o'clock when she had to pick up William. Wednesday evening was when her father had his card game with his two oldest sons and the boys at the boatyard. This gave Katherine and her mother time to talk. Since she was a young child, her father had also communicated to Katherine through her mother. This kept them close and apart at the same time; however, it worked for both Katherine and her father. William didn't resent paying the phone bill for Katherine's weekly calls to her mother. It was better than his having to have contact with that family. Her brother Joey would call her at least weekly, and sometimes she would call him if there was good news to share. She tried to limit her calls to Joey, as she knew William resented paying for these calls. William had no one to call, and no one called him. He was happy.

William was in his second month at the parts plant. He had finalized his mathematical production model and had been desk checking it with daily production requirements for the last week. He had calculated that with production flow changes and increased productivity by each employee, present daily plant productivity could be increased by at least forty percent. Such an increase would bring plant productivity to a level that would slightly exceed headquarters expectations. William believed that these production increases could be achieved with thirty-two plant production employees working an effective seven hours a day, rather than the present forty-six employees working less than an effective five hour day. For the last week, these numbers came out consistently day by day.

He was confident of his calculations and that such productivity increases could be achieved while at the same time increasing quality and drastically cutting costs. He was not so sure that these increases could be achieved under Donald's supervision or with the present complement of employees. He would have to be careful how he expressed this to headquarters management in his report. While he had been reporting weekly to Daniel Flynn, Apex Vice President of Operations, he had not shared his final conclusions as yet. He was saving that for the final report. How to increase productivity with greater efficiency, increased quality and on-time deliveries at less cost was his responsibility; what to do with the people was headquarters'. William didn't deal with people, just numbers.

Donald had been trying to learn what he was finding out. During the second week of William's study, William had come in one morning and turned the key to the office and swore that it was already open. He couldn't determine, however, if anything had been touched or taken. After this incident he was more careful. He would take anything of value with him onto the factory floor and then home with him in his briefcase. He would work alone in the plant on Saturdays; this was when he did his simulation modeling. John Biddle had offered to help him, but William refused, as he didn't want to get John in trouble. William was already generally feared and despised by plant management and employees. His secrecy and work ethic scared them; they didn't want to lose a good thing. If William blew the whistle, they might all lose their jobs. They would have to go back to being poor farmers and it was always hard to go back.

He was alone one Saturday working in the plant when he thought he heard a car parking quietly on the gravel outside. He had thoughtlessly left his office open. He had all of the vital papers with him, but someone else wouldn't know this. He heard faint footsteps in the office area. Someone was walking on tiptoes, probably wearing sneakers, around the office area. He gathered up his papers, locked them in his briefcase, and went quickly to his office. He stopped ten feet away. He could see a shadow through the frosted glass of the upper part of his office. He watched for a moment. The shadow was going through his desk and file cabinet drawers accumulating a number of papers on his desk. He saw the shadow move toward the office door,. He moved away. He watched Donald Severance take the papers to the copy machine. He knew there was nothing of significance in the pile of papers or anything that Donald would understand, so he did nothing. He went back to work in the plant. The following Monday he mentioned that he thought he noticed Donald's car in the parking lot on Saturday. Donald admitted that he had come in to get his softball glove for an employee game that afternoon. He hoped he hadn't disturbed him. He knew William preferred to work alone quietly. He assured Donald that he hadn't bothered him. William wasn't bothered again on a Saturday, and he didn't leave his office open again either.

There were two men's rest rooms in the Apex plant, one in the office area with four stalls and four urinals and one in the plant area with six stalls and eight urinals. William would use the rest room in the office area. It was cleaner and usually less crowded. There were only twelve male office employees compared to forty-six male plant employees. William preferred being in the men's room with office employees rather than plant employees. He tried to go into the rest room when he thought it was empty. He was sitting in one of the stalls late in the day, about a half hour before plant quitting time, working on some of his calculations. He always took his briefcase with him into the rest room and did some work while sitting on the toilet. Time was valuable and William never wasted it. While he was sitting there he heard sets of footsteps entering the men's room. He automatically raised his feet and pressed them against the door so that they couldn't be seen beneath the door. He heard a pair of footsteps come toward his door. He froze in his awkward position, as he didn't want to get caught looking like this. The figure bent down and looked under the door. William could see the front of his face, but he couldn't see William. The figure did the same thing with the other stalls. William's arms and legs filled with fear. They shook against the stall walls and he tried to quiet them. William heard a voice. It was Jimmy Ray Torgenson, the plant accountant.

"All clear."

There was a little space between the stall door and the doorjamb. If he looked a certain way he could see through. He concentrated on this space and was able to see three figures with their backs to him, each one standing at a urinal. He could hear them urinating. It was Jimmy Ray, Jerry Lee Nickels, the production control manager, and Joe Don Looney, the personnel manager. They were known as the "three J's" and were always seen together, in and out of the plant.

Jerry Lee was speaking. "If you get the papers, I'll try to decipher them as they relate to production."

"And I'll look at the personnel impact," said Joe Don.

"You're expecting me to get his papers? Come on, the little Yankee shit never lets them out of his sight. The Duck told me he even takes a shit with them. I wouldn't be surprised if he's working on our destruction as he takes his shit." Jimmy Ray laughed at his own joke.

"Okay, okay," said Jerry Lee. "Let's figure this out before the Yankee turd figures us out. I don't want to go back to farming. Shit, I hate that shit."

One of them farted. "You speak well for a Yankee." It was Jimmy Ray speaking to Joe Don.

"Oh, shit," said Joe Don. "I just fudged myself. Now I have to take a Bradford."

William saw Joe Don moving toward his stall. He froze. What if he tried to open his stall?

Joe Don veered at the last second and went into the stall next to William. As Joe Don sat down, William hoped he couldn't hear his heart racing or that his bowels started talking. He remained motionless. Joe Don made bowel noises, and William heard something drop into the toilet water. Joe Don called out to the other two. "There's Bradford number one. Number two coming up. Stick around, guys."

Jerry Lee made a sniffing noise and put his thumb and forefinger on his nose.

"Geez, Joe Don, you even smell like a Bradford. We'll catch you later. Don't worry, we'll get the Yankee shit."

William heard the urinals flush and Jimmy Ray and Jerry Lee leave the room. He only had to wait out Joe Don. He was taking his time, making a lot of noises and plops. Joe Don was whistling "Dixie" to himself and shuffling his shoes. He was dancing, probably on William's grave. After what seemed like hours, Joe Don finally got up and flushed. He left the rest room without washing. William wouldn't shake his hand again. He now knew where he stood at the plant; it was him against them.

Less than a week later, William had to use the rest room again. It was an emergency. The chicken barbeque sandwich he had for lunch was doing the Alabama Hoedown in his stomach. The office rest room was occupied, so he had to use the plant rest room. Luckily it was break time, and the rest room was empty. None of the plant employees would waste their break going to the bathroom. They would save their bathroom breaks for when they were on the clock and being paid. William just made it into the stalls, this would be a long one. He removed the latest plant layout and production flow together with his calculations. He would be able to finalize his calculations in here without worrying about someone looking over his shoulder. He was well into his work when the rest room door abruptly opened. It was Wee Willy Whitcomb, the head material handler. Wee Willy was anything but wee. He was six feet six inches tall and weighed close to three hundred pounds. He was a former defensive lineman for the University of Alabama. Unfortunately, his body far surpassed the size of his brain, and he never got through his freshman year.

Willy went directly to the stall William was in. He had his feet up as usual. However, they had fixed the door to show that someone was in there. They had also made sure that William would use the plant rest room and that no one else would be in there. They probably drugged his barbeque sandwich as well. Willy grabbed the sides of the door and pulled it abruptly off its hinges. There was now nothing between William and Wee Willy. There was hardly enough room in the stall for Wee Willy and William. He tried to get the papers in his hand into the briefcase, but Wee Willy had the briefcase between his leg and the stall wall. He clutched the papers against his chest; he would protect them short of his life. Wee Willy looked down and quickly yanked the papers from his hands.

The sides of the papers ripped off in his hands. Wee Willie looked at the papers, wrinkled his brow in confusion, and threw them down on the floor. He bent down and picked William up by his lapels. He was hanging in the air with his underwear and trousers hanging from his legs. His genitals and rectum were completely exposed. Wee Willy held him up by one hand and reached the other hand under his balls and squeezed. At the same time all of the air went out of him and he screamed silently. Wee Willy's middle finger went up his asshole. The pain was excruciating, but he couldn't make a sound. He remembered how the kids in elementary school had mocked him about this procedure being German toilet paper. Wee Willy lifted him against the back of the stall so that his shoes dangled into the toilet. As he held him in this position, Wee Willy started to speak.

"This is a message from all the boys." He spoke as if he had been well rehearsed. "They want you out of town by the end of the month. Leave your report behind."

William said nothing. He dared not move. Wee Willy pinched his balls harder and ran his finger farther up his ass. He could hardly breathe, let alone talk. Wee Willy grunted, "You understand," as he increased the pressure. William managed to say an okay. Wee Willy let him down hard on the toilet seat. Wee Willy wasn't smart enough to take the papers or briefcase, and he hadn't been told to. William gathered his papers, waited a sufficient time, and went back to nurse himself in his office. He resolved to finish his report and get out of there quickly.

Donnie sensed that William wouldn't be scared off short of killing him, and that had been considered. He knew by the sly smile on William's face, what the good old boys called an SEG (shit eating grin), that he was finalizing his report. The Duck knew it wouldn't be favorable to him. The boys came up with the ultimate weapon.

William, as usual, was working late on a Wednesday night. He had been overheard talking to Katherine in the parking lot when she dropped him off in the morning. He had reminded her that he would be working until nine that night and to pick him up at that time. He had just finished a turkey sandwich for dinner. He was throwing the wrappings away and preparing to get back to work. He was in his office. As far as he knew, no one else was in the plant. Most of them didn't want to be in the plant during work hours. As he was putting the papers that he was working with back on his desk he heard the soft staccato of a woman's high heels. He stopped what he was doing and listened. It wasn't Katherine's sound; he could hear that sound in his sleep and sometimes he did. The soft staccato came closer. It stopped in front of his door. There was a soft tap on the door, almost like velvet. The hairs on the back of William's neck went up. "Who is it?" He expected another trick by the boys.

A voice like southern comfort purred back. "It's only little old me, Bonnie Jean. I think I'm locked out of my car. You're the only one here. Can you help me?"

Bonnie Jean Cameron was the secretary/office helper in the quality control department. This was one of the departments recommended for elimination. He believed that with the quality control recommendations he was proposing and his concept of employee self-responsibility a formal quality control department was no longer needed. He was sure, however, that no one else knew about this.

Bonnie Jean was tall and shapely. She came to work in tight skirts and sweaters with high spike heels. It was a miracle that she could even move, but could she move. When she walked through the plant floor all work stopped. William could always sense when Bonnie Jean was walking through the plant. The workers got quiet except for the whistlers. The male workers would grab their penises and say in unison, "Here pussy, here pussy."

Bonnie Jean would smile and walk on through. Usually one of the plant workers, Lee Dean Rodgers, the plant comedian, would follow Bonnie Jean through the plant walking closely behind her. He would try to walk exactly like Bonnie Jean with her exaggerated swinging of her hips and the pulsating dimples on each side of her ass. He would put parts shaped like cones in his shirt to simulate Bonnie Jean's size 36 C cup breasts. When Bonnie Jean would stop and lean over, the entire plant would lean over with her.

Lee Dean would lean over next to her and look over at her. This would always break her up. When she laughed, her entire body shook, and everything shook with it. The boys in the plant would applaud and whistle loudly. When Bonnie Jean left the plant, it would take another fifteen minutes of howling and talking for the boys to get back to work. There was a rumor that she was Joe Don Looney's mistress. That would explain how she got the job. The quality control department didn't need a secretary, but the plant needed Bonnie Jean. It was said that Joe Don, as a form of employee morale, planned her walks through the plant. William was the only one who didn't look up when Bonnie Jean walked through the plant. He had work to do.

Lately Bonnie Jean had been briefly stopping in front of William's table on the plant floor as she walked through the plant. She would stop, look down at William, smile softly, wink her right eye, breath in and heave her breast, and then turn and walk slinkily away. William continued working, but he noticed her. She scared him more than Wee Willy.

He opened the door for Bonnie Jean and then went quickly back behind his desk. Bonnie Jean was an imposing figure standing in front of the desk while he sat behind it. She placed her hands on her hips, undulated her body clockwise and then counter clockwise, and then looked down at him and ran her tongue slowly across her lips. She leaned over the desk so that her breasts fell forward. He looked up quickly and saw that she wore no bra and that her breasts were hanging loosely inside her sweater. Her nipples were larger than Katherine's entire breast. She shimmied her shoulders so that her breasts danced inside her sweater. He thought of Rebecca and his throat constricted, and he felt like he has suffocating. He automatically looked away. He was more interested in his work.

She hiked up her tight skirt so that her thighs showed up to her hips. She adjusted her stockings as she smoothed them across her legs. He paid no attention to her. She sat down on William's side chair with her skirt hiked up to reveal her legs. William quickly removed the papers that were on the chair before she sat on them. Her hips and ass caressed his hands as he did this. He pulled his hands back quickly as the clammy feeling consumed his body. He sat back limply in his chair. Bonnie Jean stared at him. He looked away and went back to his work.

"So, big bad hotshot, can you help me? You know, get in … my car." She breathed slowly as her breasts went up and down. He tried to work. He said nothing.

She did everything she knew to get him interested, but he continued working. Bonnie Jean licked her lips, breathed slowly, pulled her skirt up further to show her bikini underpants with more than a hint of strawberry blond pubic hair, and stared at William, lips pouting. He only got clammier and turned further away. William heard footsteps in the hallway, loud male footsteps. This was evidently a signal for Bonnie Jean. When she heard the footsteps, she got up and sat on William's desk on top of his papers with her legs parted as far as they could go with her tight skirt. She reached over to grab hold of William, to pull him to her. He jumped up and moved to the other side of the desk.

When Joe Don came through the door of William's office, he found Bonnie Jean sitting astride William's desk fingering her vagina. William was standing inside the door on the other side of the desk. Joe Don had the company camera around his shoulders ready to snap a picture, hopefully of Bonnie Jean and William in the midst of something. When Bonnie Jean saw Joe Don she turned abruptly toward William and pulled her underpants aside with her other hand as she continued to finger her vagina. William was forced to see her pubic hair, the lips of her vagina with the finger penetrating, and the moisture escaping. William gasped and held his hand over his mouth; he was going to be sick. He turned his back abruptly from Bonnie Jean. He thought of his papers under all that. How would he be able to touch them again after this?

When Joe Don looked over the situation and saw Bonnie Jean on the desk and William with his back turned on the other side of the room, he realized there was no reason to take the picture. He already had better pictures of Bonnie Jean in better poses, and he didn't need a picture of William.

When Bonnie Jean saw Joe Don and realized that he wasn't going to take the picture, she jumped from the desk and into his arms. As she did so, she wiped her wet finger on the papers. William cringed in the corner. "Oh, Joe Don you saved me."

Joe Don looked at her. "Save it, baby, this one isn't human."

That was exactly what William was thinking, that they weren't human, only interested in body parts. Joe Don and Bonnie Jean walked from his office, Bonnie Jean swinging her hips and ass. She looked back at William and licked her lips. She blew him a soft kiss. That was the last time they tried to compromise him.

The following day William notified headquarters that his report was ready, over a month ahead of time. He sent Daniel Flynn a copy and scheduled to have him and the three production vice presidents come to the plant the following Tuesday for a final oral report and presentation. He notified Donald Severance to get the plant ready. William went home that night with Katherine and didn't return to the plant until the following Tuesday for the meeting. He spent the remainder of the week in the apartment finalizing his oral presentation and packing for their next move. His next assignment was to do what he had accomplished here at the Apex Columbus, Ohio, parts plant, this time a Midwest higher cost facility.

She was resistant to another move. She had just settled in and had made two good friends in Carey Sue and Ethel and she would miss them. The library was just beginning to shape up. Traffic flow in the library had increased, and she was in demand in the classrooms. Contributions had also started to come in. She hated to leave Ethel to handle these things alone, even with Carey Sue's help. William told her that it was better that they leave town. This was no place for a couple of Yankee hotshots. If this was important for him, how could she deny him?

William met John Biddle alone in his apartment. He went over the highlights of his report with John. William felt that he owed him that much so that John could prepare for what might happen. If the company agreed with his recommendations, William had recommended that John be made responsible for implementing the recommendations. If the company decided to close the plant, John would be forewarned so that he could protect himself. William felt the company would go along with his recommendations. John was sure the company would close the plant.

Daniel Flynn and the three production vice presidents picked William up at his apartment in the company limousine the following Tuesday morning. Katherine had sat on his penis the night before while he slept. She wanted to celebrate with William on his impending success. He came in spite of himself. He woke up clammy, sweaty, and foggy headed. He took his long shower but still didn't feel clean. Katherine had set out his best silk suit, monogrammed shirt which she had laboriously ironed and starched, most expensive silk tie, and finely polished black wing tip shoes.

She hoped that William looked even better than the three vice presidents. He certainly would be more handsome. While he was still in the bathroom getting dressed, Katherine got herself ready. She did her hair, her makeup, and her nails. She dressed in the outfit that William seemed to prefer the most. When she was done she looked in the floor length mirror. She looked stunning, if she must say so herself, since William would never say so. This was what a future vice president of Apex Industries and his wife should look like. If they came into the apartment, they would see so themselves.

As William was finishing up, there was a knock at the door. Katherine opened it to a chauffeur in uniform and cap. She looked around him to see the limousine sitting in front. She couldn't see in, but she went out on the steps and waved to them and gave them the two-minute signal. If they weren't going to meet her, at least they could see her. Katherine thought this might help William.

On the drive to the plant, Daniel Flynn and the three vice presidents told William how pleased they were with his report. They agreed with almost all of his recommendations, particularly having John Biddle in charge of the implementation. They agreed that it was best to get William out of town so that the implementation had a chance of success. The Columbus assignment would be good for his career. They also mentioned what an attractive wife he had; sorry that they didn't have time to meet her, but there would be plenty of other times. William beamed; he had done a good job.

When Daniel Flynn and the three vice presidents saw the present state of the plant and met the employees, their minds started to have doubts. They sat quietly through William's presentation, nodding their heads affirmatively as he made each point. They went to lunch with William and John Biddle. John affirmed that he was in complete agreement with William's findings and recommendations and that he believed they were implementable. The vice presidents nodded in agreement. They excused William at the plant; the chauffeur would take him back to his apartment. The company moving truck would be there to take him and Katherine to Columbus.

William went home feeling good. He had helped these people in spite of themselves, their threats, and tries at blackmail. They would remember the Yankee hotshot fondly. When he arrived home, Katherine was ready to go and the truck was almost packed. They were going to follow the truck in their station wagon.

She had wanted to stop at her parents' house in Newport on the way to Ohio, but William had told her that it was too far out of the way and he had to be in Columbus by Monday. The company had given William a $2,000 bonus and two additional weeks of vacation to be taken now or later. He would save them for later. He didn't need a vacation; he needed to work. He didn't tell Katherine. She agreed that if William said so, then this would be best. She could visit her parents some other time. William had no need to ever visit them. They were ready to leave their first home. They would always remember these two months in Hereford, Alabama, William's first success. Ethel and Carey Sue had both given Katherine a going away present. She held them closely in her arms; she wouldn't put them in the trunk. She would hold them all the way to Columbus. As they were closing the door, Katherine took William's hand. As he tried to pull away, she looked back at the apartment. Tears appeared at the corners of her eyes. She looked over at William. "Our baby shouldn't be born in Alabama." She walked out and slowly closed the door behind them.

William was to be a father. It had no emotional effect on him. He saw no reason to bring another human being into this world; his mother was right about that. But if it was good for Katherine, so be it. He had his work to do; she would have her work to do with the baby.

When John was invited to lunch with the vice presidents and William, he knew that something was going to happen. He didn't expect that William would be leaving and that he would stay behind to implement the recommendations. When he came home to tell Ethel what the decision had been, she already knew. She had just said good-bye to Katherine and William. They both said that they would keep in touch and would never forget what she and John had done for them. Ethel doubted it. The Williams of the world always took, never gave. She and John would plod along together; it was their destiny.

"So," John said, "you heard?"

"Yeah, I just said goodbye to Katherine. I'm going to miss her."

"And William?"

"I don't think I'll miss him. I don't trust people with no personalities."

John nodded his head. "I'll miss him."

Ethel said, "You would. You're so alike."

"And what does that mean?"

"Oh, nothing," said Ethel. She thought a moment and then added, "It's just that you both put work above all else."

"What else is there?" asked John.

"How about people?"

John pondered a bit. "I don't like people, do I?"

Ethel held his hand. "No, father, you don't. But, it's okay. I like you."

They went into the bedroom. If they had to stay longer in Hereford, they still had each other.

They would make the best of it.

John tried to get Don Severance and the rest of the employees to work with William's recommendations. He tried to make it clear that if this didn't work it was possible that headquarters would close the plant. They gloated that they had gotten rid of William the hot shot and that John was next. Apex couldn't run this plant without them, and they both knew it. John would send in his weekly report with nothing encouraging in it. After five weeks of continuing decline (production rose a little, but the costs of implementation far outweighed any gains), Daniel Flynn and headquarters decided it was best to cut their losses and close the plant. They told John of their decision on a Wednesday that the plant would be closed that Friday. Donald Severance would be notified late Thursday night. It would be best for John to be ready to leave early Saturday morning. They were transferring him back to the Stamford plant as a group manager in industrial engineering. John sighed the biggest sigh of relief of his life. When John told Ethel, a strange sadness overcame her. She would miss Hereford in a strange way: the library, Carey Sue and the diner, their routine, the solitude of just them. She felt she needed more time. She wasn't ready to share John with the world again. She was indeed selfish when it came to her and John.

Late that Thursday night, around four in the morning, there was loud knocking and yelling at their door. Both John and Ethel were exhausted. They had been packing boxes all night until after midnight. When they had finished, they had taken a shower together as had become another one of their customs. Ethel had started making love to John in the shower. If she couldn't give him any babies, she could give him her body. John, as a Wisconsin farm boy, could make love all the time; he seemed to be inexhaustible when it came to sex. John couldn't get enough of Ethel. They carried their love making into the bed. They screwed until Ethel couldn't take any more. She fell off of him and lay exhausted holding him close. It seemed that they both had just fallen asleep when the knocking started. John pried himself loose from Ethel, trying not to wake her. She said, "Father, don't leave me" as he got out of bed. This was what she always said when he got up in the night to go to the bathroom.

John went to the door and looked through the peephole. He was surprised (and yet he wasn't) to see Donald Severance at the door. With him was Wee Willy Whitcomb (the Neanderthal who had terrorized William in the men's room) and Willy's brother Jesse Reese. Jesse was even bigger than Wee Willy. Jesse worked part time at the plant when they needed an extra man for receiving or shipping. When Jesse worked, he didn't need a forklift; he picked the largest crates up in his bare hands. Jesse never played football like Wee Willy; he spent his time in jail for demolishing a bar and its patrons all on his own. Someone had called him a liberal for buying a whore a drink.

John had put on his robe; he had nothing on underneath it. As he looked out the door, his penis shriveled and his bowels contracted. He remembered what Wee Willy had done to William. Compared to Jesse Reese, Wee Willy was a pansy. John called through the door.

"Don, what are you doing here?" Don Severance had never visited John before.

"You know why I'm here, you Yankee son of a bitch. You and that little shit William had the plant closed on us, didn't you? Didn't like us southern boys?" (Don was from Massachusetts but he had forgotten) "have some fun, did ya?" Don had been drinking. He could barely speak clearly.

John didn't scare easy, and he was scared, especially with Ethel in the apartment. She had a habit of getting up half asleep and walking around in the nude to the bathroom or to the kitchen. This wasn't the time for that now. John didn't know what these three would do. They were pounding on his door and cursing him. He didn't need the neighbors upset. He thought of calling the police, but he knew they would do nothing. Possibly join the Whitcomb brothers in raping Ethel. They were all related somehow in this town. Against his better judgment, John decided the best thing to do was let them in and hope that Ethel wouldn't wake up before he could get rid of them.

When he opened the door, the three of them fell into the apartment. They had been leaning on the door as they pounded. Don, who was evidently the spokesperson and probably the only one who could still speak, spit at John as he cursed.

"God damn Yankees. Always ruinin' our fun." Don pulled himself up by grabbing onto John's robe. As he did so, the robe fell open exposing John's penis.

"Well, lookee here. A Yankee dingus." Don tried to grab onto it, but John had pulled away.

John tried to close his robe, but Jesse had already grabbed him. He held John's balls tightly in his hand. John gasped. He lost the power of speech. He could feel his eyes popping out from his head.

Jesse looked over at Don as if to ask what he should do with the Yankee piece of shit.

"Hold onto him Jess, while I think what to do."

Jesse Reese nodded. Wee Willy had John by the head, squeezing him together by the ears. John had never been in such pain.

While Don was thinking, he wasn't a fast thinker, Ethel must have entered the living room. John couldn't see her, but he heard her voice. He hoped she had some clothing on. She had on her robe. He didn't want these goons seeing her naked. His mind could only grapple at what they might do. To them, every female was a whore and just asking for it. It would be a favor for them to share their southern dicks with a white northern pussy. John had heard it all at the plant.

"John!" yelled Ethel. "What's going on here?"

Ethel expected an answer, but John couldn't speak. She noticed Donald Severance cowering by the door. At the sight of Ethel, his bravery started to leave him. Bravery was easier in the mind than in reality.

"Donald Severance, is that you?" Ethel screamed. "How dare you come into our home and put your hands on my husband. You get out of here this instant!"

Donald stammered. "Yes, ma'am."

Jesse was still holding John by the balls and Willy was holding him by the head. Donald opened the door.

"That means you two!" Ethel was screaming at the Whitcomb brothers, a risky thing to do. She moved towards them. "I said let him go! Go ahead! Get out of here!"

Nobody talked to the Whitcomb brothers like that. They let go of John. They turned to leave. As they did, Jesse pulled the drawstring on Ethel's robe and it fell open. They gaped at her nakedness, Don at her tits, Willy and Jesse at her vagina (they knew what they liked). Ethel didn't care. She let it hang open. "Just get out of here—now!!!" She was screaming.

Don's mouth had fallen open. He couldn't avert his eyes from Ethel's tits. They weren't anything spectacular, but they were tits. He couldn't help himself from staring.

He stammered. "I'm real sorry, ma'am." He kept staring.

They ran from the apartment—never taking their eyes off Ethel's nude body. When they had left, she double bolted the door. She took John back to the bedroom. She massaged him where he hurt until they both fell back to sleep. John didn't go back to the plant. He couldn't face the people he knew would be out of work by the end of the day, or Don and the Whitcomb brothers.

William found out later that Apex closed the Hereford plant. They tried to implement his recommendations, but the remaining employees fought John Biddle every step of the way. The company had no choice. They closed the plant on a Friday and told the employees not to return on Monday. John was transferred to the Stamford, Connecticut, plant. He had been right after all. Ethel would miss the county library, but she would get over it. She wrote Katherine to tell her the good news and congratulate her on the coming baby. Katherine never heard from Carey Sue after the plant closed. William was remembered in Hereford all right, but not too fondly. The Hereford plant was closed for good, but William S. Bradford III was on his way to success. They had lost some more friends, but Katherine still had William—and William was still alone. They were happy.

5

HELLO COLUMBUS

The Columbus plant was over four times the size of the Hereford plant. It was only slightly smaller than the Stamford, Connecticut plant—the largest of the Apex parts plants. The Columbus plant was one of the most sophisticated factory operations in the country. William was assigned as a staff person or internal consultant to the plant manager, Raymond Fogerty. Raymond, as he preferred to be called, was just the opposite of Donald Severance. He was polished, professional, and ran the plant based on sophisticated inventory and production control techniques—and he wore a suit at all times and kept his jacket on. William would get along with him just fine. Raymond asked William to review all of their production methods to determine if he could identify more efficient and less costly ways of manufacturing within high quality limits while meeting their delivery schedules. This was the kind of challenge William was looking for.

The company moved William and Katherine into a furnished, one bedroom apartment in a suburban area within three miles of the plant, close enough to get there quickly but not close enough to walk. As at Hereford, the company would take care of the first three months rent, and then they could continue renting the same apartment or make their own arrangements. Katherine would have to take him to work and pick him up. She was now about two months pregnant, the baby was due the following March, and this would be all right for now. As her pregnancy progressed she would reach a point where driving him would not be practical.

One of William's fears had become a reality; he would have to learn to drive. Katherine wanted to start teaching him to drive. He kept putting it off. She finally persuaded him that they would need a larger apartment when the baby came. She would prefer an apartment further from the city in a more rural setting. It wouldn't be practical for her to drive him back and forth from there, particularly with a new baby. William saw the baby already getting in his way, but he knew she was right. When he at last decided it would be best for him to drive, he went out with Katherine a few times, learned the Ohio driving laws, and took and passed the driver's test within a three week period. Now that he could legally drive, he still insisted that she drive him back and forth to work. When she couldn't anymore, then he would drive.

While they lived in Hereford, William was able to save most of his money. They had no rent and they spent very little. Of course William controlled the money. They had started with over $9,000 from their wedding. With the money they had saved, plus the $2,000 bonus, they now had over $12,000. With that amount of money and William's paycheck, Katherine felt they could afford a nice, two-bedroom apartment in the country. William nodded his head but said nothing,

William quickly got back into his work routine. He arrived at work by six o'clock in the morning and left work at eight o'clock in the evening. For the most part, he was the first one in and the last to leave. Sometimes Raymond beat him in and left after him, but not very often. Katherine would drive him in the morning, then return to the apartment and lie down for a while as she was starting to get morning sickness. Some days she could do no more until it was time to pick William up. Other days she would stay around the apartment and read. Some days she never got around to making herself up, doing her hair, and dressing up. This was traumatic for her as looking good was her life.

William would find her still wearing her pajamas at the end of the day. He felt sorry for her, but there was nothing he could do. She was resistant to pursuing new friends, after what had happened in Hereford and she didn't know if this time it would be for more than the three-month period. She didn't want to move again until the baby was born. She was depressed.

One Sunday, William suggested that they take a drive into the country. Katherine was curious, as he had never done that before. As she drove, he directed her. The further they drove, the nicer the country became. She became calmer, more relaxed, as they drove. He was talking more than he ever did, asking her how she liked this area and look at that house— what did she think? Katherine liked it all. They drove past a new development of houses. There was a sign on the road to come see their open house. He asked her if she would like to see the open house. She was feeling so good she would have looked at any house in this area. As William would say, "It doesn't cost to look."

William walked nonchalantly around the open house as if he was just passing some time on a Sunday. Katherine ran through the house excited. Every room she would go into she would yell at William "look at this, look at this." This was the house she had always dreamed of, a two story single home in the country. When she had gone around the house three times, she found William sitting in the sales office talking to a rather attractive woman — with large breasts no less. This was something William never would do. Katherine was concerned; she walked quickly to his side. He looked up at her and smiled. This was not like him.

She held onto the back of his chair. He looked at her and the sales lady. "Miss Harkins, this is my wife, Katherine. I think she likes the house."

Miss Harkins put out her hand to shake with Katherine. As she did this she said, "Is that right, dear?"

"Oh yes, I love this house. If only we could afford it. The sign said it cost $17,990."

Miss Harkins looked at Katherine. "That's right including all settlement costs. Your husband just signed a contract to purchase this same house. He said he was buying it for you. A belated wedding present."

She looked at the two of them. They were smiling at her. "Oh, William. I knew I made the right choice." She kissed him on the side of the cheek.

"This is the third time your husband has been here. He signed an agreement on Thursday based on your liking the house. You only need to sign the agreement and pick out the lot you want. The house should be ready way before the baby." Miss Harkins was smiling.

When they left the open house she was walking on air. She ran to the passenger's side of the car to open the door for him. He stepped aside to let her in.

"I'll drive from here. You look for your lot."

This was the beginning of his driving. From now on Katherine would rest.

They picked out a corner lot of two and a half acres with as many trees as they could find. They would make sure that all of the trees would stay. Katherine saw her child swinging from the large tree on the side of the house. William saw the side room as his office.

On the way home while he drove and she rested, she asked him how they could afford such a house. He explained that their mortgage would be less than rent on a two-bedroom apartment. He couldn't afford not to buy. He wanted her to have what she wanted. This would be a place where she could take care of the baby while he worked. They both had their work to do.

Katherine kept repeating herself as he drove home. He drove well. Anything he attempted he did well. If not, he didn't attempt it. "We really own the house, William. It's ours?" she kept saying.

He would answer her, "in thirty years, once we get the mortgage."

She would ask him like a little girl, "Does that mean we'll be here for awhile? I won't have to move again? I can have my own room?" and so on.

They looked like any other young couple out for a Sunday drive. Except that William was dressed in a suit and Katherine was dressed to go out somewhere fancy for the evening. He pulled into the parking lot of a restaurant that Katherine had always talked about going to. The neighbors had told her that this was "the place" in that part of Columbus.

"William, why are you stopping?"

"I'm taking my wife to dinner." He parked the car next to the restaurant. He got out of the car and went to her side to open the door for her. She sat motionless.

"Katherine, are you coming? I don't want to eat alone."

"But, William, I have a roast defrosting."

"So we'll have it tomorrow."

"William, you know so little about these things. It's defrosting today. I have to cook it today."

"So, you'll cook it today. We'll eat it tomorrow."

Katherine got out of the car and walked to the restaurant holding onto William's arm. He didn't pull away; today he was proud. They would be homeowners; it was the American way— to hell with the roast.

William's reputation had preceded him to the Columbus plant. The Hereford plant had been the joke of the Apex empire. Top management had given up on the plant and they were stuck as to what to do with it. They had opened the plant in the south persuaded by the cheap cost of labor. They had been warned about the lack of eastern or northern work ethic and the lack of a large trainable work force. The workers would take your money, but not necessarily return a fair day's work. They had assigned a good plant manager, Donald Severance, to ensure that operations were conducted efficiently. Donald had tried, but in the end he had sunk to the level of the work force— he had become inefficient. In exasperation, they sent John Biddle, one of their best plant engineers, to appraise the situation. John recognized the deteriorating situation, but believed there was nothing of a standard nature that could be done. He recommended that they send down a troubleshooter to pinpoint the causes and remedies for the problems.

They were going to send one of the vice presidents of production or hire an outside consultant to go to Hereford. When William contacted them for a position this presented a viable option, particularly with Herman Selzer's recommendation that William would be able to objectively identify the causes of the problems and develop implementable solutions. They were ready to close the Hereford plant but were resistant to do so as this would be the first failure in Apex's history. Either William would identify how to solve the problem, would recommend closing the plant and they would have a company scapegoat, or William would succumb to the charms of Hereford. Either way the cost to find out, at William's starting salary, would be minimal. The company couldn't lose. They would either have a solution to their problem, an employee to be reckoned with, or both. The company won. They eliminated their problem children, the Hereford plant and Donald Severance, and identified a rising star, William S. Bradford III.

William became an instant legend at Apex Industries. He became known as "the hero of Hereford." He had solved the unsolvable. His report on how to operate a parts plant most efficiently by maximizing productivity at the least possible cost became a classic case study for the entire Apex empire. A copy of William's report was sent to all twenty-four Apex plant locations around the world. All of the plant managers wanted William to perform a similar study for their plant. He couldn't be in all of these locations at the same time. Raymond Fogerty prevailed by suggesting that William use the Columbus plant as a model.

The Columbus plant was the best Apex operated facility, and if he could help improve upon already good standards, these standards could become best practice benchmarks for all of the other locations. Apex top management agreed. They wanted to get the best from William while his work ethic was still intact. There was a tendency for employee productivity to decline as their length of service and salary increased. William was a bargain as to low cost and high results. Raymond Fogerty would be a good mentor for William to keep his work ethic intact. Raymond was self-disciplined and expected the same from his employees. He believed that compensation should be related to results not just to time in. He and William were like two peas in a pod, a marriage made in corporate heaven.

On William's first day, Raymond met him at the door of the plant, quite unlike William's first day at Hereford. Raymond looked at him and liked what he saw. William was well dressed in a silk suit, a well-ironed, white, monogrammed shirt with gold cuff links, and a new matching silk tie—almost as well dressed as he was. Raymond put out his hand to shake and looked him in the eye. "Welcome, son," he said. William shook his hand; it was firm, friendly, and not sweaty at all. He was going to like working with this man. William looked back at him. "Thank you," he said. "I feel welcome already." They nodded affirmatively to each other.

Raymond took him on a tour of the plant operations. William was astounded. Each employee knew what he was doing and did it well without any apparent watching by supervisory personnel. The plant, on the surface, appeared to be a textbook example of how a manufacturing plant should be operated. Raymond respected each employee, getting out of their way to let them do their job. Each employee seemed to be properly trained in their job as well as that of others.

There appeared to be an atmosphere of cooperation, a striving to do their best job, and a concern for quality and customer service. William was perplexed as to what he could do to make plant operations any better. The Columbus facilities seemed to be the other side of the mountain from the Hereford plant. William thought, "How could two such plants belong to the same company?" Raymond expressed his confidence that William could help them do things better. He couldn't identify any specific concerns or problems, operations were running smoothly, but he knew that William could make them even better. He needed a fresh eye to look at what he had created; he couldn't objectively critique his own creation —William would be those eyes. Some of the employees started to call William "little Raymond." William had found his mentor, and father.

Raymond asked William to look at the production flow for Product D, the highest volume product in the Apex line. Over 40% of the entire Columbus plant facility was dedicated to product D. The systems improvements identified for Product D could then be replicated for the other products. William was assigned an office and a spot on the production floor directly in the Product D production area. He was to work directly with the Product D industrial engineers and production employees; they were to be a team. They expected William to help them do a better job through increasing productivity with less work. Such was William's reputation, "the hero of Hereford." With increased productivity would come increased compensation, a win-win for everyone. The Columbus employees expected nothing less than excellence from the company, William, and themselves. William had found a new home, maybe his first real home.

William spent his first three months working with each individual to understand his or her job and related systems and procedures. The team would have periodic brainstorming sessions to discuss each function and come up with cumulative suggestions for improvements. The individual involved would implement each suggestion. William would be the objective observer — a helping agent and a catalyst. There was no resistance on either side. William was an accepted member of a team for the first time in his life and he liked it. The company was giving him quarterly bonuses as positive reports came in from Raymond Fogerty.

Through this process, productivity was increased by over 40% and costs were decreased over 30%. The workers felt they were working better and simpler. The company increased the employee's compensation, based on William's recommendation to Raymond, according to a formula developed by William which accounted for increased productivity, reduced costs, and contribution to profits and increased customer service. The production employees were encouraged to develop additional improvements on their own. This process became a model for other plants to follow. William's legend grew within the Apex empire; he became known as "William the conqueror."

As William became more and more a part of the Columbus plant family, he spent more time at work and less time at home. He would get to work by six in the morning and not leave work until after nine in the evening. At the same time, Katherine was starting to show and less able to do things. She was still very much attached to her thinness and in her condition was reluctant to go out on her own.

William had started to drive himself to and from work. Katherine would stay in the apartment to read and rest, as she wanted her baby to be healthy. She made more phone calls to her mother, brother Joey, and Ethel Biddle, but William didn't care. The cost was little compared to Katherine and the baby. And it was better than him being home. The combination of William's family at work and Katherine's condition had resulted in the lessening of occurrences of William's nocturnal emissions. He would either dream about a particular problem situation at work and how to solve it or his new baby son, no more dreams of Rebecca or his mother. Such dreams would appear infrequently out of nowhere, possibly as a physical release for his built up testosterone level. Katherine had stopped visiting his bed at night as well. While he missed the comfort of her at night, he had become more attached to his work.

Katherine was starting to get depressed being alone so much of the time. She couldn't get up for breakfast anymore with William. He had started to eat breakfast with the Product D team prior to starting work, which gave them an opportunity to discuss current issues and increase their bonding. Although

William had no real friends in the group, he was considered one of them. He was also coming home too late from work to have dinner together with Katherine. He would get his dinner in the plant cafeteria with some of the Product D team, and sometimes Raymond Fogerty would join them.

Katherine would make something light for herself. She couldn't tolerate the smell of most things cooking and wanted to keep her weight down as much as possible. She didn't want to stay heavy after the baby was born. She wasn't treating herself healthily, but William wasn't around to see it. When he got home from work, she would already be in bed sound asleep. He would kiss her on the top of the head, undress in the bathroom, and quietly get into his own bed.

He would awake in the morning, dress in the bathroom—she still put his clothes out the day before—kiss Katherine on the top of the head, and leave for work by five thirty. Katherine would normally get up around ten o'clock and stay in her pajamas and robe for the remainder of the day. She would make herself some tea with crackers for breakfast. Most days this was all she ate until a dinner of soup and crackers or a salad with crackers. She hoped the baby was worth all of this.

On those days when Katherine had to see the doctor, William would get a ride with one of the members of the Product D team, usually Stephen Linderman, one of the plant engineers. Stephen lived close by and was glad to take William. He respected William's professional talent and wanted to become better friends, but William maintained his aloofness. Stephen believed that it enhanced his stature at the plant to drive William back and forth to work. Katherine would then be able to take the car and drive herself to the doctor's.

Somewhere between the sixth and seventh months of her pregnancy as she was driving herself to the doctor's', she started to bleed. She was just able to get into the doctor's office before there was blood all over her. The doctor examined her, gave her some medication to stop the bleeding, and advised her not to drive anymore. She didn't want to bother William at work. She knew how he hated this, so she drove herself home. She never told him about the bleeding.

Two weeks later, while Katherine was lifting William's suit onto the hook in the bathroom, she started to bleed again. She called the doctor, who called William, who came immediately to take her to the doctor. He chastised Katherine for not telling him sooner. She cried through her depression; she was alone and hated it. He insisted that he take her to the doctor's from now on and anywhere else she had to go. Her due date was now less than two months away and he was concerned about her. That night he called Katherine's mother Anne for the first time since the wedding. He asked her if she could come out to stay with Katherine until the baby was born. It would be good company for Katherine and would allow him to work the way he had to. The house would also be ready soon and they wanted to move before the baby was born. He offered to pay Anne's way, but she said that wouldn't be necessary.

Anne was glad to get away from her house. With Katherine and Joey gone from the house, she felt very much alone. Guy, Bobby, and Alley had their own lives that didn't include her. Anne was never one to have girlfriends; her friends had always been Joey and Katherine. Anne couldn't come immediately. She had to prepare enough meals for Guy to put in the freezer while she was gone. She knew if she didn't, Guy would only eat crap: pizzas, hamburgers, steak sandwiches, and those awful French fries and potato chips. She would come the following week. This was fine with William, as it would give him enough time to prepare for Anne. She would be good for Katherine, but not for him. He had to "Anne proof" the apartment for himself.

Anne arrived the following Sunday. William had planned to go with Katherine to the airport to pick her up, but Katherine didn't feel up to it. William, playing the dutiful son-in-law, met Anne at the gate. She tried to hug him, but he pulled away, carried her suitcases from baggage claim — she must be moving in permanently — to the car, and brought the car around for Anne. He had thought about securing the Apex limousine for this trip to impress Anne, her rich son-in-law, but his more professional senses prevailed. On the ride back to the apartment, he said very little. Anne asked him all kinds of questions, about Katherine's pregnancy, his sexual preference for the baby, their new house, and so on, but he only answered yes or no. He didn't know what to do with a mother-in-law. He had married Katherine, but Anne came with her.

When Katherine saw her mother, she ran right into her arms and hugged her as if this woman had just given her life. William left them to put Anne's things in the second bedroom. When he came back, Katherine was lying on the sofa with her head in her mother's lap. Anne was massaging her head softly and repeating, "Everything will be all right now, you'll see." Katherine's eyes were closed and she was smiling; her depression was leaving in a puff of closeness. Anne, as a mother, could do what William would never be able to do for Katherine. It would be all right. It would allow William to do what he needed to do, while Katherine was taken care of by her mother.

The settlement on the house was three weeks away. There would be no problem as Apex was lending the mortgage money, at one percentage point less than the market without any additional points or settlement charges. They wanted to make sure William stayed employed with them. They also agreed to pay for the move, since the apartment was only a necessary temporary move from Hereford. They would take care of all of the packing, moving, and unpacking. In Katherine's condition, this was a godsend. Anne could help Katherine organize things. With Anne's assistance, William and Katherine had also picked out furniture for the house and the baby's room, to be delivered on moving day. Katherine was due two weeks after their moving day. Anne would help keep Katherine rested. William would be in the way, but would gladly get out of the way.

The move went as smooth as possible. Anne and Katherine got involved immediately in decorating the house and the nursery, placing furniture, hanging pictures, putting things in drawers and cabinets and so on. William did as he was instructed, moving furniture and rugs back and forth, lifting heavy things, and running errands to purchase all of the little things they had forgotten. Within a week the house looked like they had been living there all their lives. Thank God for mothers-in-law, even Anne Angel.

The new house was isolated from things. You needed a car to get anywhere. For the first week in the new house, he took the station wagon back and forth to work. Stephen Linderman had offered to come out and pick him up, but it was over 20 minutes out of his way. William wouldn't allow him to do it. After the first week of seclusion in the house with her mother, Katherine pleaded with him to find a way for Anne to get out. She loved her mother, but she had never been able to live with her. That night he came home early, about eight o'clock, with a small sedan following him. He had bought a small Chevrolet for himself, so that she and her mother could use the station wagon. They would also need a larger car when Katherine was ready to go to the hospital. Sometimes her sweet William could be so wonderful. William had purchased his freedom back.

The following week William got an emergency call from Anne. She had never called him at work or anywhere else before. He was in a brainstorming meeting with the Product D team and had asked not to be disturbed. He couldn't ask the others to do this, without his agreeing to it as well. No one had ever called for him during one of these meetings before. The secretary who received the message didn't know what she should do, so she held the message until the meeting was over about two hours later. When William received the message, he called home immediately but there was no answer. He went back to work. Three hours later Anne called him at the office. It was now after seven at night. Katherine's water had broken and she had to rush her to the hospital. She had left a message for William but he had never called. Katherine kept asking for him at the hospital. Anne told him that it was lucky that she was there; what would they do when she had to go back home? "Kids," she said, "Do they ever grow up?"

William said that he would come right over as he wanted to be with Katherine while she was in labor. Anne said that wouldn't be necessary, Katherine had just given birth to a healthy baby boy and was sleeping; they would both be all right. Anne said she would stay at the hospital through the night and there was no need for him to be there. That seemed right to William. He went back to work; he had a lot to do. He went home around ten o'clock. This was the first night he had spent in the house alone, the first night he had been entirely alone since his wedding. He was tired. He undressed in the bathroom—habits are habits—and noticed his clothes for the next day hanging on the hook. He smiled, as only Katherine would think of that on her way to the hospital. He slept in Katherine's bed that night. He tried to dream of Katherine and his new son, but as he slept Rebecca crept into his dreams and as her breasts encircled his face he ejaculated slowly and thoroughly. He put his hand on his penis and it was drenched. He fell back asleep in his mother's arms. With the baby, he felt secure that now there was no way in the world he would be drafted into the military. He held his mother tighter.

The next morning he showered long and hard, but he still felt dirty. He changed the sheets on Katherine's bed. He dressed in the clothes set out for him. It made him feel closer to her. He had called work and told them of the baby and that he wouldn't be in that day. This was the first day that he had missed work since he started with Apex. He felt he should go to work, but he knew Katherine, and Anne, would never forgive him. He went to the hospital. He brought flowers for Katherine; he knew how much she loved flowers. Anne took him to the nursery to see his son. He looked in the window as the nurse held up his son. He had no emotion. It could have been any baby. William didn't see his life changing greatly with a baby. Katherine would take care of the baby; he would take care of them by working. William named the son Richardson S., the family middle initial, Bradford. Katherine could name her daughters. William had no plans for any other children; Katherine would see about that.

A few days later, he went with Anne to pick up Katherine and the baby. When they arrived in her hospital room brother Joey was with her. He wasn't sure he wanted Joey too close to his son. He wasn't sure he wanted to be too close to his son. Guy couldn't leave the boatyard, as it was spring maintenance time for the big boats, his major customers. Anne said that at least the baby wasn't any more important than she was to Guy. She expected nothing from Guy and that was what she usually got. Joey was holding the baby as if it was his own. William didn't like it. He didn't want to hold the baby, but he didn't want Joey holding it.

When Katherine saw William, she came over and kissed him on the cheek. He blushed and turned away. She took the baby from Joey and brought him over to William. She smiled at William and the baby. "Look, he has your face and hair."

He looked down at the baby. He saw no resemblance to anyone.

She held the baby toward him. "Would you like to hold your son?"

"My son," thought William. It was really Katherine's son. He felt nothing.

Katherine was pushing the baby into him. So as not to embarrass her in front of her mother and brother, he took the baby in his arms. It was like holding nothing, certainly not a human life. He felt queasy and handed the baby quickly back to Katherine.

Anne and Joey stayed another week with them. Katherine had been tired when she first came home and spent most of the day in bed. The stitches in her vagina were also hurting her. It was a relief to have help with the baby. Anne or Joey would bring the baby to Katherine so that she could breastfeed. William didn't like looking at her breastfeeding. Her breasts and nipples had swelled to accommodate the milk. He couldn't look at them, but Joey could. William continued to leave early and come home late. He hoped that everyone would be sleeping when he got home. Most nights Joey would still be up. He said he enjoyed talking to William. To be polite, William would talk to Joey, but he didn't enjoy it. Anne didn't talk to William. She told Katherine that he was strange, to watch out, but that he would always be a good provider.

So as not to disturb William, Katherine and the baby slept in one of the guest rooms. This was fine with William. When Anne and Joey left, Katherine continued to sleep in the guest room. After three months, William found her one night sleeping in their room. He said nothing, but he was glad to have her back in the same room. She left the door open between the two rooms so that she could hear the baby cry. At night time feeding times, she would walk quietly to the next room so as not to disturb him. Slowly her nightly visits to William's bed resumed. Everything was now as it was before except now Katherine had a baby.

William saw the employees as one factor in his mathematical models. If the model worked, it didn't matter who the people were. Each person only had to do his or her job according to his calculations. If they didn't, they would exchange that person with someone who could do the job. It was the employee's responsibility to learn to do the job right. William stayed aloof from the employees and they stayed away from him; in fact, he scared them. He set up each process to run by the numbers; only the numbers were important. Since William had joined the Columbus plant, the numbers had grown considerably, over 30% in every category. Headquarters' management was quite pleased for they had plans for William.

William had gotten into a routine: up at five o'clock, into work by six for breakfast with Raymond, at work by seven, 20 minute lunch at noon with Raymond, work until nine at night, talk with Raymond on the way out, and home after ten. When he got home, Richardson was already in bed and so was Katherine. He would slip into his own bed and quickly fall asleep. His life was work and it was working. Sometimes Katherine would come into his bed and hold onto him. Sometimes, less and less frequently, she would sit on his penis and he would quickly come, slowly and fully. It was those times that he would still dream of Rebecca. He would fall back asleep holding his mother. At other times, the dreams of Rebecca had stopped. He would dream of solving problems at the plant. This had become his life.

On Sundays, when William was home, he would work on his latest project. He would have breakfast with Katherine and Richardson, criticizing each of them as he ate. He would then go into his office to work. As Richardson grew he would try to get into William's office to play with his daddy. William would yell for Katherine to come get her kid, as he couldn't work with him around.

The Fogertys had started to ask the Bradfords over to their house for a Friday or a Saturday evening. Raymond and Patricia, Raymond's wife, liked Katherine and she liked them. Patricia tolerated William, but she wasn't sure she liked him. Patricia wasn't even sure that she liked Raymond. After dinner, William and Raymond would go into his den to talk. Katherine and Patricia would do the dishes, then sit in the living room; they were becoming good friends. They would laugh at the two strange husbands they had.

It became a ritual that the Fogertys and the Bradfords would spend time together on the weekends.

Katherine had filled out after her pregnancy. Her face had rounded, there was no more trace of the "hoss," her hips had widened, her buttocks had rounded, and her legs had solidified. Also, her breasts had become breasts; there was now a little more than just nipples, but not much more. When she dressed up, which was whenever she left the house, she was an extremely attractive woman. Raymond enjoyed flirting with her as he could flirt without getting close, and so did many other men. She and Patricia laughed about having an affair, anything would be better than what they had, but Katherine wasn't interested. Sex was never her thing, security was.

Katherine kept busy with Richardson; he was really a full time job. She was able to meet Patricia for lunch a couple of times a week. She had also become part of a playgroup in the neighborhood so that Richardson had friends to play with. Sometimes Katherine would be involved with the playgroup and other times another mother so that Katherine could have time to herself. Sometimes Richardson would go play with the other children and sometimes other children would come to their house to play with Richardson. It was a full life. She had everything but a full husband, and Richardson had everything but a daddy.

When Richardson was about a year and a half, Katherine got pregnant again. This time there was no problem, and Katherine knew what to expect. As time got closer, the neighbors would take care of Richardson for her. William continued his work routine. He told Katherine that if she needed him to be home or anything else to let him know. She never did. She didn't want to get in his way. He loved his work so, and she loved her sweet William.

She didn't ask her mother to come and discouraged Joey. She knew how uncomfortable they both made William feel. William also seemed uncomfortable with Joey around Richardson; she didn't know why.

The week of her due date, Katherine had a bag ready at the front door. William had set up a sitter for Richardson whenever necessary. He had informed his office to contact him, wherever he was, when Katherine called. Everything was set for the trip to the hospital. This time they would be organized. When the time came Katherine calmly called William. He told her he would be right over and he would notify the hospital. On his way out of the plant, Raymond stopped him with an emergency, one only William could solve. He was caught between two lovers. Raymond convinced him to stay at the plant and he would send the company limousine for Katherine. He would call Patricia, and she would meet Katherine at the hospital. William hesitated for a second, but knew that this was better than his going. He would be more help here, and Patricia would be more help there. Katherine would love going to the hospital in a limousine; he was sure she would prefer that to him.

Katherine had another boy and William named him Jameson S., the family middle initial, Bradford. He was as uncomfortable with Jameson as he was with Richardson. But now Richardson would have a brother to play with so he could get his work done. He visited Katherine every day in the hospital. He would leave the room while she breastfed. He resisted holding the baby.

William had the company limousine bring Katherine home from the hospital with the baby. Again, Anne and Joey came to help Katherine when she came home. William kept Richardson away from Joey as much as he could. Joey seemed less concerned with Jameson, and William was relieved. Richardson would always be Joey's favorite. William went back to his work routine, and Anne and Joey left at the end of the week. He then brought someone in to be with Katherine and the baby and to watch Richardson. Katherine healed much faster this time. She was back on her feet in less than a week and William was back to his routine. He paid even less attention to Jameson. He thought they were both good kids as long as they left him alone and he left them alone.

William had now been at the Columbus plant for three years. He had studied every manufacturing process and had implemented improvements in every one of them. Production figures rose every month while cost figures decreased. He was making more money for the company and the company was paying him more. He was accumulating wealth, but wasn't living any differently—it didn't matter much to him. He and Katherine had everything they wanted or so he thought. He was becoming well known at Apex, a corporate legend. He was now making frequent trips to the Stamford headquarters, in the beginning with Raymond, now most times alone. William had really become an internal consultant to the company. Raymond was pleased and happy for him. They would be able to get together when Raymond was the Stamford plant manager.

William became more enmeshed in the company. Katherine could do whatever she pleased with the children, as long as it didn't include him. He made sure that the children had everything she said they should have. He did want them to have a better childhood than his. He would do what he could to ensure that, short of being a part of it. His life was work; her life was the children. This was the way it should be.

Raymond and William were becoming inseparable. Unofficially they had become co-plant managers. This allowed Raymond to concentrate less on the details and more on the people. William took care of the details and less of the people. It was a good marriage.

Raymond belonged to the most prestigious country club in the Columbus area. He and Patricia had taken William and Katherine there for dinner a number of times. Katherine had become extremely popular with most of the male members. She never wanted for a dance partner. William preferred to stay at the table and talk business with Raymond. He was glad that Katherine was enjoying herself. She turned down numerous propositions on the dance floor, mostly with wealthy married men. She pitied their wives. She had been asked to join a bridge club by the ladies but refused as she thought William wouldn't approve of that for a young mother. They both enjoyed going to the club with the Fogertys.

Raymond proposed William and Katherine for membership in the country club. He paid the application fee as a surprise. Nothing would please Raymond more than to have William join the club. When Raymond put the application on William's desk and William realized what it was, he was at first very grateful to Raymond. The company would pay the dues if William were accepted. There would be no cost to them and he and Raymond could go together.

As William thought about the implications of applying for membership, he began to be concerned. This was the most exclusive country club in the area, but it was restricted. They didn't allow Catholics, Blacks, or Jews to join. What if they found out about Katherine's Italian Catholic father and those brothers? He also thought about what Ruth Selzer had said about his being Jewish—could that be and could they find out? He felt lucky that Katherine had joined the local Episcopal Church and took the boys on Sunday. He would have to start going. His fears, of course, were unfounded. With Raymond's recommendation and Katherine's popularity they were unanimously elected to membership. William thought nothing about the character of the other members; it would be his and Raymond's club.

Raymond had been encouraged to become a golfer by the company a number of years ago. They felt that this would be a good marketing tool. Raymond could take present customers and meet potential customers on the golf course. Many a deal had been consummated on the "nineteenth" hole. Raymond had become a fair golfer, an eighteen handicap, and was much in demand to make up a foursome. He always had a joke and a good word for his partners. He carried his people performance over to the golf course and he closed many deals.

Raymond now encouraged William to become a golfer. They could go together. William wasn't too interested. He let Raymond know that he had never had much of an interest in athletics nor much of a skill. Raymond convinced William that this was just an extension of business and that headquarters would be pleased. This wasn't athletics. It was chasing a little white ball around in a golf cart. William agreed to take lessons from the pro at the club. If he couldn't master the game in three months, he would give it up and Raymond would stop hounding him. Raymond agreed.

William had filled out as he moved into his late twenties just as Katherine had. He had become powerfully built in spite of himself — genes will tell. The golf pro suggested some exercises along with the golf lessons. William had always lacked muscle tone; now his muscles were starting to firm up and he liked the feeling. Katherine noticed the difference and mentioned it to him. She was impressed and liked the new look. He started out like most golf beginners by missing the ball entirely. He couldn't believe that he couldn't hit a ball off of a tee.

William had always mastered anything that he tried, and he wasn't going to let this silly game beat him. He would use every spare moment for lessons and practice. Interesting that he found the time for this, but could never find the time for his family. But, as Raymond said, this is business. By the end of the second month, he was playing well enough, in the low 90s, to let Raymond convince him to join a foursome. Raymond made sure that everyone had a good time and kept William relaxed. William shot an 88, his best score ever. It was even better by four strokes than another member of the foursome. This encouraged him to go out again. He really disliked the golf part, but he enjoyed being with Raymond. They would go out regularly, every weekend and sometimes in the early evening. He continued to improve and the game became just another mathematical model for William to conquer. Eventually he was able to beat Raymond every so often. William now had something to do other than work, or was this work? It got him out of the house and he now had something to fill his Sundays.

William saw his life as complete, and he was now the complete corporate man. He also saw himself as the complete family man. He provided everything that Katherine and the children wanted, everything but himself. He never thought that anyone would want him, so he stayed away from the house. He saw himself as the perfect corporate man and the perfect family man. He thought he was doing an excellent job in both places.

Katherine had gotten used to being without William. When she really needed him, he was there and she knew how to contact him. He was always accessible. Katherine adjusted to being a housewife and mother. William had arranged to have a service clean the house once a week, more often if necessary, which allowed Katherine to have a life. When she wasn't obligated with the two boys, she spent her time with Patricia at the country club, shopping, getting together and so on. After her second pregnancy, Katherine had filled out even more. She looked exciting in her clothes, and even better without her clothes. William didn't notice. She enjoyed dressing up for the club and having the daytime available males swoon over her, particularly in the nice weather when she wore her skimpy two-piece bathing suit. Even Patricia swooned at that. Katherine was one of those women who was going to get more beautiful as she got older, while the other women got less attractive. For the time being, Katherine was secure. This was good for her. She was proud to be the wife of William S. Bradford.

Katherine was aware of how well her body had changed. When she dressed, she always looked back in the mirror to admire her long tapering solid legs and her now shapely rear. She liked what she saw and she liked that the men liked what they saw. She might have preferred to have larger breasts for the men to look at, but William liked small breasts, ideally none at all, and that was all right for her. She remembered the awful way boys had treated her while she was growing up and how terrible they had made her feel. With the power she now had over men, she would get her revenge. Men were such pricks.

The first time Patricia had taken Katherine to the country club, Katherine made sure she looked her best. With her newfound shape from the waist down, she had begun to dress in the tightest of skirts or dresses with spiked high heels to accentuate her long shapely legs. William couldn't understand how she could walk or move like that, but move she could. When she walked, she stopped men's hearts, all but William's. When she and Patricia entered the dining room at the club, the club geezers all turned to look at them. Attractive women were at a premium at the club; unattractive dowagers were more the norm. Patricia was a big-breasted woman and always showed her breasts to advantage, either wearing a low-cut or tight top. Today it was a low cut top with her cleavage showing down almost to her nipples. The men in the room were transfixed on Patricia's tits. Katherine felt jealous.

As they walked into the room, the men's eyes walked with them. Their eyes followed the two of them as they walked to the far back table, switching from Patricia's breasts to Katherine's ass. As Katherine walked by, she looked back and noticed one male jaw drop after another; she loved it. Some of the stuffy, male club members had to put their hands quickly over their mouths to keep from spitting out their food; others didn't quite succeed.

Patricia also liked the men looking at her. For her this was one benefit of membership at such a stodgy club, perhaps the only one. She had thought about an affair, even with one of the club geezers, but she wouldn't jeopardize her security with Raymond. Before they were married, he couldn't keep his hands off her, particularly her breasts. She was uncomfortable with such demanding physical attention. A tight top or bottom would drive him wild. After their first baby was born, he lost all interest in her. She would walk around the bedroom nude or topless, but it made no difference to him. He would look up from his work, nod, and then go back to his work. His work had become his wife and mistress. His penis wouldn't go up regardless of what she did. In the old days it went up no matter what she did.

Katherine had always wanted to be attractive to men, first for her father, then her brothers, and then all other males. This had never happened. She was always too tall, too thin, too gawky, and too horsey looking. She knew it wasn't physical attraction that William desired of her, but she still desired male attention. Now that she had finally filled out and had a desirable body and pretty face, she wanted to use it. She had been cheated of male attention when she was younger; it was now make up time. She had always admired the sensuality of Bebe "Bubbles" Broadman, one of the most popular girls at Jones College. Bubbles was thin and had a flat chest, like Katherine, but she could dress and walk seductively. She made walking and slinking in high heels an art form so that every boy desired her. She also screwed around a lot. The boys said "you hadn't had it until you burst the Bubble." Bubbles had become Katherine's secret idol. Now it was her turn to dress, walk, and flirt like Bubbles. She had no desire to screw like Bubbles. It made her sick even to have flirtatious men touch her. What she had with William was sufficient.

Katherine would practice in the nude walking in high heels like Bubbles. She would walk past the full length bedroom mirror looking back to make sure that she had just the right reaction in her ass, first the right side and then the left side. She would experiment with the way she picked up her feet and laid them down, the sway of her hips, and the movement of each side of her ass. She would watch the dimples form on the side of her cheeks as her ass moved up as she strode forward. Her ass convulsing just right as she brought her leg up and swished her cheek at the same time, her ass came back into place before the next step — swoosh to the left, swoosh to the right — intoxication. Ah, the look, and the power. When she felt she had Bubble's walk perfect, she would improvise to make it better. She would then put on her bikini thong panties and walk in the same way. She would feel the strings of the thongs caress her crack in the back and her clitoris in the front as she walked and looked at herself in the mirror. She did this until the strap of her panties became moist in the front and her eyes glazed over. She then knew she had the right motion.

It made her feel good, but she had to stop; old memories consumed her and brought shivers. She then put on her short, tight skirt and made sure that as she walked she still had the same motion. She practiced with her long blond hair hanging down right above the top of her ass to see the motion of her hair sway as she walked this way. Then she tried walking with her hair up to see the motion of her ass uninhibited by the flow of her hair. Either way, she liked looking at herself in the mirror; it was fun.

Sometimes William would come into the bedroom while she was practicing her walk in the nude or in her bikini panties. She would watch her body move in front of him and she got excited. She would fantasize about William slowly moving his hands and tongue on her body, gently grabbing her ass with each hand enclosing one of her cheeks, pulling her cheeks slightly apart so that her clitoris pushed forward and the lips of her vagina parted. She imagined he would then place his penis between her legs so that it gently rubbed against her clitoris and vagina. She just knew with her high heels on, his penis would fit perfectly in place. She saw herself riding his penis until they both came. She could feel the moisture starting to flow between her legs as she thought about this. In reality, William would put his head down and go quickly into the bathroom. So much for fantasies. She would stop for a moment to cool down and then continue practicing. When he returned from the bathroom, he would put his head back down and leave the room. He never said anything. He thought Katherine was practicing her dancing. Some dance.

Once Patricia came over to the house while she was practicing her walk in the nude. She asked Patricia to observe her walk to make sure it was right. Patricia sat on the bed while Katherine walked back and forth. She enjoyed displaying herself as she flexed her ass, her hips, and made her cheeks jump and come alive as she walked. Patricia started to glaze over in the eyes as she watched her. Patricia came over and touched her ass gently on both sides. Katherine couldn't help but experience a chill through her body and into her vagina. She stopped, didn't say anything, and put on her clothes. She didn't practice for Patricia again.

As Patricia and Katherine walked to their table, a young male waiter followed them. As he walked behind them, he couldn't keep his eyes off

Katherine's ass. As she walked, each cheek winked at him as if a hamster was running quickly around a wheel in her pants. It was a performance that had him mesmerized. When they stopped at the table, the waiter almost ran up Katherine's ass. He had to grab onto the back of a chair to stop himself. This was the same chair that Katherine was starting to sit down on. The waiter abruptly pulled the chair out for her as she sat down. The appearance of that ass coming towards him shorted his circuits — he froze holding the back of the chair. Katherine just barely made it onto the chair. The waiter quickly pushed the chair under her so that she bounced twice before she settled into the back of the chair. The waiter was in love. Patricia observed it all. Usually she was the one that the waiter pulled the chair out for as he looked down her top. She smiled to herself.

When they were both seated, the waiter introduced himself as he was trained to do. "Good afternoon, ladies, I'm Walter. I'll be your wait person today." He handed them each a menu. "Can I get you anything from the bar?" He kept his eyes on Katherine's face as he talked. Patricia had ceased to exist. They were both silent. Katherine was hiding in the menu.

Patricia finally spoke up. Walter was jolted; he had to move his stare. "A vodka martini for me."

Patricia had started to drink heavily the last few years. Two or three martinis before lunch and the same before dinner alone had become standard for her. She had begun to get chunky for the first time in her life. If Raymond wasn't interested, what did it matter?

Walter said "uh huh" and wrote it down. He turned back to Katherine. She hesitated. She hardly drank. William never drank, so neither did she. She had been raised with wine for dinner since the time she was sixteen. With her marriage to William, this had stopped, as had so many other things.

The waiter looked down at her longingly. He was in no hurry. He could look at Katherine forever if necessary.

Patricia spoke up. "Bring her the same."

Walter said "uh huh" and wrote it down. He still hadn't taken his eyes off Katherine. He didn't move, he couldn't.

Patricia cleared her throat. The waiter didn't move. "Walter, you can get our drinks now. Oh, and bring us some ice water with lemon on the side."

Walter continued staring at Katherine. She still hadn't spoken.

"And you, ma'am. Anything else for you?"

Katherine was still hiding in the menu. Patricia poked her in the elbow.

"Oh, no." Katherine kept her head in the menu. Walter walked away not taking his eyes off Katherine.

When Walter had left, Patricia leaned closer to Katherine.

"Are you in love?" she whispered to Katherine.

"I don't know. William is difficult to love."

"No, not William. Walter, our waiter."

Katherine smiled from behind the menu, but she said nothing. Her cheeks reddened and she lowered her eyes.

Patricia smiled. "You like attracting men. So do I, I always have."

"I never have. I never could."

"Well, you can now. You sure got the club geezers' attention. Some of them choked on their watercress. Holy shit, what a walk."

"Really," said Katherine coyly. "I didn't notice."

Patricia leaned closer. She whispered in Katherine's ear. "Bullshit."

Katherine smiled. "Yeah, it does feel good."

"You bet your ass it does."

"So how about you?" asked Katherine. "Are you in love?"

"I don't know. Walter hardly looked at me."

They laughed.

"No, not Walter. With Raymond?"

Patricia looked quizzically at her. "Who's Raymond?"

This became a standard joke between them. One would whisper in the other's ear "are you in love?" and they would both laugh.

The martinis were served. Patricia drank hers down in two gulps; she must have been thirsty. Katherine sipped hers. Walter watched. Patricia ordered two more and dismissed Walter with the flick of her hand. He wasn't funny anymore; he was becoming tedious. After the third martini, they were good friends. Patricia had to carry Katherine home. Katherine liked Patricia and the club. She couldn't wait to go again and become a member.

When the Bradfords became members, Patricia and Katherine would go frequently to the club. Katherine started to work out in the club's gym and Patricia had joined her. They were in competition for the attention of the club geezers: Patricia with her breasts, Katherine with her legs and ass. When they weren't working out, Patricia would wear a tight top and Katherine would wear a tight skirt and high heels. When they left the gym, there was no competition; all male eyes were on Katherine. She was having fun.

It was now the mid 1960s, and mini skirts and the braless look were in. Katherine started to wear tight mini skirts with no stockings. She made sure her legs were shaved and tan, and wearing no bra, with just enough shirt for the image of her nipples to be seen. Patricia's build didn't allow for mini skirts or no bra. In the nice weather, they would have their lunch outside on the terrace, sitting at a glass see-through table. As they sat down, they both knew that all male eyes were focused on them. Walter would invariably be their waiter. They would ask for his table or he would take their table; it was mutual admiration.

After the first, and sometimes the second or third, martini, Katherine would get courageous. She would pull her chair away from the table so that she could cross her legs, one leg over the other knee. She would do this so that her leg went high and slow toward the other knee. She looked straight ahead as if she didn't know what she was doing. She also knew that all male eyes were looking. As one leg rose, the entire other leg was exposed up to her bikini panties. If a male at another table was sitting in just the right position, he could see the entire leg up to her panties and the outline of her vagina.

Katherine had started shaving the sides of her pubic hair so that none showed out the sides of her panties.

It had become a playful contest between them for the attention of the men at the club. They would hear loud whispers from the other tables, "I saw it, I saw it." Katherine didn't quite understand what men saw in female body parts, but she was really enjoying the attention and the game. And, there was no way that Patricia could compete with her. Katherine really liked this club.

When they went to the pool, Patricia would wear a one-piece bathing suit displaying maximum cleavage. She would bend over often for her breasts to show. She would periodically dip herself in the pool so that her nipples appeared through the top of her suit. She would sun her back and lower the top of her bathing suit so that the sides of her breasts hung down against the cushion of the lounger. Male members, of all ages, would find reasons to walk by.

Katherine would wear the skimpiest of bikinis that showed the side of her legs and ass up to her hips. There was no way to hide the entire outline of her ass, which left little to the imagination. She would wear high heel sandals so that when she walked into the pool area she knew she had all male attention. She would find reasons to walk back and forth to the snack bar, to the locker room, and so on. The men would wait. She had her bikini tops especially supported so that what little breasts she had were pushed up to create a mirage of cleavage. The material was always just transparent enough for the shadow of her nipples to show through. She never unhooked her top even when sunning her back, which she did often to show off her legs and behind. She never went into the water; she didn't have to. This was all part of their game. Patricia and Katherine were enjoying the club more and more.

When the four of them went to the club for dinner and dancing, many of the other males would ask Patricia and Katherine to dance. Patricia always refused, as she knew Raymond hated to see her with other men. He told her that they just wanted to feel her tits against them. She sat at the table while Raymond and William talked business, she drank, they talked, she said nothing. Katherine danced with all the men who asked her; she could dance continuously if she wanted to. William was proud of her, how she looked and how popular she was. She never told him of the propositions she got, mostly from prestigious married men. It wouldn't matter to him. He would be glad for her, that she was having fun. Listening to him and Raymond would only bore her, as it was all business talk. He was happy that she was happy. This was also part of the game.

During William's fifth year at Apex Industries Katherine became pregnant again. This time it was easy and she had no problems. She even wore her bathing suit as long as she could. She was being swooned at way past her fifth month. Katherine continued her routines at home and at the club until the week of her due date. This time she ordered the Apex limousine to take her to the hospital. There was no reason to bother William. She understood the importance of his work. She called William from the hospital to tell him that he was the father of a daughter. Katherine had named her Elizabeth Anne Bradford. William came that night with flowers for Katherine. She wanted him to hold the baby, but holding a girl was even more of a problem to him than holding his baby sons. William couldn't do it and Katherine understood.

This time William hired a nurse to take care of Katherine, which she refused, and she was up on her own the next day. He told Katherine there was no need for her mother or Joey to come. She agreed, although she missed them both. Unknown to William, Katherine went back to visit her parents and Joey once a year. Her mother and Joey had not been to see them since Jameson's birth. Her father and her older brothers had never visited. None of this disappointed William.

With the birth of Elizabeth, the house was becoming too small. Eventually each of the children would need their own bedrooms; the three bedrooms wouldn't be enough. Katherine suggested that they move to a larger house, maybe in the same development as the Fogertys. William would be closer to Raymond and she would be closer to Patricia and the club. William still despised a show of wealth from his Roget days, so he suggested adding onto their present house. There would be no disruption to their lives or those of the children. Katherine could design the addition, which would consist of a master bedroom, bath, and sitting room for them and a recreation room for the children. She was disappointed, but if that was what William wanted she would make it work.

The next few months for Katherine were taken up designing and working with the contractors to build the new addition. She wouldn't let William see the plans or the construction in progress until it was all complete. She was happy and so was he. When the addition was finished, Katherine had a party for the opening. She invited the Fogertys, some other managers from Apex, and some friends (hers not necessarily William's) from the club and the neighborhood.

Katherine had kept the work site covered, so William had not seen it yet; no one in the family but Katherine had. They all gathered at the door as Katherine was about to open it. She asked that she and William go in first. When William entered he found an almost exact replica of their honeymoon suite in Newport, from the two king size beds to the whirlpool spa overlooking the gardens. This was the first time William felt like crying since he was eight years old, but this time out of joy. Katherine could see his joy without him speaking. She went to hug him, hesitated, but he let her in. As the others entered the room, William moved quickly away from Katherine. She noticed, but she was pleased. William had liked the addition.

The house was now full: Richardson was four years old, Jameson two years old, and baby Elizabeth. William was about to be twenty-eight years old and was now the father of three children. Sex was not something he or Katherine had ever talked about. He was all right with her infrequent night visits. He had never asked Katherine if she wanted more than that and she had never said. He didn't know how he was going to prevent a fourth child in two years. He didn't know how the first three had gotten there. Katherine never told him that she had her tubes tied after Elizabeth's birth and she never would. She thought now that she had her daughter, that was enough — and William had his sons. William saw Katherine as the mother of two boys and a girl. He was naturally the father, but he saw no place for him. His place was at Apex.

William had every production operation at the plant under control. He had developed a reporting system that allowed him to make necessary corrections and fine tuning as necessary. The system operated seamlessly. He no longer had problem solving situations or details to work on. He still spent the same amount of hours at the plant, but he felt he wasn't accomplishing as much— only maintaining the system he had designed. Headquarters was happy, numbers kept increasing positively including his pay, but he wasn't happy. He spent more time talking with Raymond and less time on actual work. Both Raymond and William recognized that William's job was really finished in Columbus, but neither one would admit to it. They wanted to stay together.

Raymond was on a company-wide team that reviewed the other plant sites around the country. The object was to incorporate the practices that William had implemented at Columbus to the other locations. If Raymond saw a better practice at one of the other plants, he would bring it back to Columbus. The review team was more than paying for itself. Raymond suggested that William join the team; he would see things that no one else would. He could go when Raymond couldn't make it or they could go together. Headquarters thought this was a fabulous idea. William appreciated Raymond's speaking on his behalf, but he wasn't sure he wanted to travel. He didn't want to disturb his routine.

William had never spent a night away from home and Katherine since their wedding. At first, he wasn't excited by the idea. Raymond convinced him to try a two-day plant visit and see how that went. Katherine encouraged him to go. When he was home he moped around the house and yelled at the kids. She was better off dealing with the house and the kids on her own — he only made it worse. If William traveled, it might be a vacation for both of them.

William went with Raymond to visit the St. Louis plant. In two days, William came up with more good ideas to improve plant operations than he had for the Columbus plant in the past years. He was invigorated. He hadn't felt this challenged in a long time. The team got together for dinner to discuss the day's findings. William hadn't been this excited in a conversation since his days working with the Selzers. They talked way past nine o'clock. The others wanted to go out for a couple of drinks; they all drank except William. William couldn't wait to call Katherine and tell her how exciting this was. He went back to his room.

In the morning William went to get Raymond in his room. They had agreed to meet there and then go down to breakfast. As William approached

Raymond's room, the door opened and the waitress from the night before came out. William turned the other way until she entered the elevator. He waited a few minutes and then went to Raymond's room. William didn't mention what he saw. It was really none of his business.

William started to travel more and more for longer periods of time. He was becoming an internal consultant and troubleshooter for the company. He enjoyed his work again, but his nights were lonely. He would eat alone, sometimes in the restaurant, but mostly in his room. Then he would call Katherine and tell her about his day. This was more than he had ever talked to her in all the years of their marriage. He would never talk to the kids, as they didn't seem to care. If they needed anything, they would talk through Katherine. He thought they were relieved that he wasn't there. He would work and then go to sleep. He was alone again, but now he was lonely.

The Columbus plant ran on its own now. The employees knew that William was still watching, so their production stayed up. He really didn't need to be there anymore, but this was his home. It gave him a place to go when he was in Columbus. He would review the reports since he had been there last and then spend the rest of the day talking with Raymond. This was a perfect fit.

Although initially Katherine resented William's traveling, she had become comfortable with it. She had the house and the kids to take care of. As they got older, she had more and more time for herself. She had gotten involved in a number of activities at the club and in the neighborhood. It was becoming more convenient to have him away than at home. When he was at home he only got in the way and yelled at the kids. She tried to keep them away from William, but wasn't always successful. The kids called him "Daddy Nazi."

6

STAMFORD BOUND

The position of plant manager at the Apex Stamford plant had opened up once again. This time Raymond believed that he was in line for the job. There was no one else in the company with his experience, over twenty years as plant manager in Columbus. Once he got the job, he would bring William along. Life was only going to get better. William saw this as his opportunity to have his own plant. If Raymond went to Stamford, he would surely be appointed plant manager at Columbus. This would give him the challenge he needed right here. He wouldn't have to travel anymore. He could be home every night. His loneliness would end.

The review process at headquarters for the Stamford plant managers job went on for a couple of months. One Tuesday afternoon, Daniel Flynn, the vice president of operations, called Raymond to inform him that he would be at the Columbus plant the next morning as there were important things to talk about. Raymond ran excitedly to William's office to tell him the good news. He was going to Stamford and William would run this plant. Raymond opened a bottle of whiskey for a toast. He finished the bottle with the help of two others, while William had bottled water. Raymond called Patricia and Katherine to tell them to be ready to celebrate; he was taking them all to the club for a celebration dinner.

William was happy for Raymond, but he would miss him. Raymond told him he could come to Stamford as often as he liked. He would make sure of that. Katherine and Patricia talked and talked to hide their sadness; they would miss each other. They went to the ladies' room together and held each other and cried into each other's make up. It was a sad passing. Katherine kept losing friends and William kept losing parents.

Daniel Flynn was in Raymond's office when Raymond and William came in the next morning. He was sitting behind Raymond's desk. He motioned for the two of them to sit down in the visitors' chairs. Daniel held his hands entwined and pushed them in front of him across his chest. They could hear his knuckles crack. Daniel repeated this a number of times while the two of them waited for him to make what they already knew official. He finally spoke in an authoritative tone lacking friendliness. Raymond's spirits dropped a notch.

"As you know, we want to do the best for the company. I'm sure both of you understand that. The review committee has been deliberating the Stamford plant manager opening for the past three months. It is our largest and most important plant site." He looked over his eyeglasses at Raymond and continued. "We've had three different plant managers in the past ten years. The committee believes we need to bring some stability to operations. Every time we make a change, production levels and morale decrease. We need to bring these back up. The committee has decided what they believe is the best course." He put two envelopes on the desk. "There is an envelope here for each of you. I'm going to step out of the office for a few minutes. I want each of you to read your letter. Discuss it between yourselves. When I return we'll talk about the course we're taking. I'll answer any questions you have." Daniel left the room and closed the door.

Raymond got up and sat behind his desk. He picked up the envelope with his name on it and handed the other one to William. They were silent as they read their letters. Raymond's face lost its luster and gladness; it was turning to stone. William's face became more and more confused; it was turning to jelly. The usually calm and controlled Raymond Fogerty brought his fist down hard on his desk. The water pitcher, penholder and pens, nameplate (which read "Raymond Fogerty: World's Best Plant Manager") given to him by his managers, assorted papers, and so on flew around the room.

"Fuck it," said Raymond as his fist came down hard again. William had never heard him curse before. He flinched and got off his chair to pick the stuff off the floor. He was picking up the nameplate when Raymond roared.

"Leave the piece of shit where it is. It's just another fiction in my life."

William let the nameplate drop back to the floor. Raymond dropkicked it against the wall.

Raymond paced about the floor, fuming. He stepped all over the stuff on the floor. He rubbed his heels into the papers. William had never seen him like this and was scared.

"God damn sons-of-bitches. How could they do this to me? I give them my life, they give me shit back." He looked down at William. "You get screwed too? Wouldn't surprise me— some fucking golden boys the two of us."

William looked up at Raymond. He couldn't speak; he didn't know what to say. He held his letter out to Raymond. Raymond snatched it angrily from his hand. He paced around the room reading William's letter and kicking at the debris. The door started to open, probably Daniel Flynn. Raymond pushed his weight against it and set the lock.

William looked at him. "Raymond, that was Daniel."

"Fuck him, and the whores he rode in on."

Raymond continued reading William's letter. As he read, he looked down at William, nodding his head up and down. Raymond stopped directly in front of and over William. He stared hard and then threw the letter down at William.

"So, you screwed me too. Goddamn little pissant. The fuckers want you to be the Stamford plant manager. Jesus Fucking Christ." He banged his fist against the wall over William's head. William was scared; he abhorred violence.

"I teach you everything about running one of their fucking plants and you turn around and screw me, and take my fucking job." Raymond turned away. "Just get the fuck out of my sight." William didn't move, he couldn't. "What'd you do, get down on old lady Ingersoll; or in your case, Iron shit Ingersoll himself." Raymond unlocked the door. He sat down at his desk and put his face in his hands. "Go ahead, get out."

William hadn't moved. He sat motionless with his letter in his hand. He choked and cleared his throat. "I'm sorry. I swear I didn't do anything. I didn't know."

"Yeah, I know. I'm sorry. I shouldn't have blown up at you. It's just easier to blame someone else. I'm good at that. You wouldn't know what to do, if you wanted to. It's those corporate bastards. I give them my life over and over again, and they keep fucking me. It's nothing new. Some day I'll learn. I'll get those little shits. Flynn will be the first."

William sat looking over at Raymond still with his face in his hands. "You all right? Look, I don't want this Stamford job. I'm happy in Columbus, Katherine's happy here, and the kids are happy here—this is their home. They would kill me if I tried to move them. We both hate the East Coast. It wasn't good for either of us, growing up there."

"I know, William, I hate it too. But I've spent my time here. They owe me the Stamford job and then a Vice Presidency in headquarters. I've paid my dues to those fuckers. I'm 52 years old. There won't be another chance." He looked sadly over at William. "William, I don't want to die here. This is all I've got."

William looked down at the floor. "I'll turn the job down. I'll tell them I want to stay here, that's true. If I don't take the job, they'll have to give it to you."

Raymond brought his fist down hard on the desk again. William cringed. "Like hell they will. We'll both die here. I know these corporate bastards. Remember I'm the people guy and you're the fucking numbers guy. Trust me, I know. They love fucking with your life. You watch out."

"So, what can we do? I don't need their job and I don't need their money." William was scrunching the letter in his hands.

Raymond took his hands from his face. His eyes were red and there were signs of wiped-away tears. He looked over paternally at William. "Look, take their fucking job. You won't get another opportunity. You turn the bastards down once and they don't talk to you again. That's how I got here. I'll die here. Don't you make the same mistake. Goddamn mother fucking bastards."

Raymond pounded the desk again and again, but there was nothing left to fly off; it was all on the floor.

"I can't take your job. I can't move to Stamford. They don't like it, I'll quit. I can get another job. We'll go together."

"No, William, I can't go anywhere else. Those bastards know that. I couldn't be a plant manager anywhere else. I'm a fraud just like that damn nameplate." He kicked the nameplate to the other side of the room. He looked down at William. He put his hands on William's shoulders.

"William, don't be a fucking fool. Take the job. You're a made man. This is a ticket to heaven. Be their damn Stamford plant manager for a few years. You'll be the youngest vice president in Apex history. What are you now, 28?"

William looked down at the floor. "I'll be 32."

"Big shit, you'll still be the youngest. They like to promote fogeys, after they've beat the life out of them. Keep you around until you're fifty years old. Then they tell you you're too old, technology has passed you by, take a hike."

He touched William's shoulders. "Do it for me. Take the job. Maybe one of us can screw these bastards from the inside."

William nodded and put his head down. He knew Raymond was right, but he didn't have to like it. He looked at Raymond. He felt sad for both of them. He got up and walked slowly out the door. He looked back and smiled at Raymond, who attempted to smile back, but it didn't quite work. Raymond was back at his desk with his face in his hands. He waved for William to go, he would be all right.

He ran into Dan Flynn on his way out of the office. Daniel had been pacing in front of the office door waiting for the opportunity to get back in. He still thought he had brought both of them good news. Apex was offering each of them large salary increases, sizable bonuses, increased perks, and so on. He wouldn't understand that it might not be the money. He had been alarmed at the crashing sounds coming from Raymond's office. As William came out of the office, Daniel tried to enter. William stood in his way. Daniel stared at him as if he could crush him.

"I wouldn't go in there right now." William stared back at him.

Daniel wasn't used to being talked to in that manner. He started to talk down to William, but stopped himself. Right now the company needed William. Raymond Fogerty could do what he wanted; he was dispensable. He looked at William as if this was the first time he saw him as a human being. "Maybe you're right."

William started to walk away. Daniel called after him. "What's your decision?"

"I'll have to let you know." He continued walking.

"Call me later. I'm at the Hyatt."

He nodded and continued walking away, out of the building, as fast as he could.

Dan Flynn couldn't leave town without knowing William's decision. He'd wait until tomorrow evening. He couldn't afford to screw up again. They might give William his job.

William rode around aimlessly for a while, maybe two hours. He had to think this through. If it hadn't been for Raymond, the decision would be easy. He was ready for a new challenge. His job at Columbus had been done for over two years. He stuck around because Raymond needed him and he needed Raymond. He was tired of traveling and being alone in strange hotel rooms at night. He really missed Katherine. He wanted a stationary location where he could start problem solving again. This was what really motivated him; it wasn't the money. But what was he going to do about Raymond? If he stayed here, would the company allow it? He knew he would be unhappy, though; he would die. If he took the job in Stamford, Raymond would be unhappy and he would die. William realized he hadn't eaten anything yet. He was getting hungry and light headed. He decided to go home and have lunch with Katherine. She would know what was best for him.

William arrived home a little after one o'clock. He called for Katherine, but didn't get a response. He went and sat in the dark den to wait for her. He forgot about his hunger; he didn't feel like making his own lunch. He waited in the dark and thought about Raymond, how like a father he had been to him. He didn't want to walk out on another parent. He sat like that for over two hours. Sometime after three he heard Katherine's footsteps coming towards the den. You couldn't mistake the way she walked in high heels. He smiled to himself.

She peeked into the den. She saw William. "William, is that you?" She was alarmed that something must have happened for him to be home at this time. "What are you doing here? It's only three o'clock in the afternoon." She had just come from the club. She had had drinks and lunch with Patricia while sensually teasing the club geezers. She was feeling good and hoped this wasn't bad news. William sure looked terrible.

William told her the whole story. Raymond's disappointment and anger and his job offer to be the Stamford plant manager, the job that Raymond was expecting. She didn't want to leave Columbus. This had become her and the kids' home for almost ten years. This would break their hearts.

She had only bad memories of the East Coast and the petty materialistic people there, her parents included. A move back could kill them all, she, William, and the kids. She looked at him. He seemed so sad. He wasn't built for decision-making, only obedience. She couldn't tell him to stay and she couldn't tell him to go. She sat down beside him on the arm of the chair. Normally, he wouldn't allow this. Her mini skirt rode up to the panty line of her bikini underpants. She put her hand on his arm. He didn't move away.

"William," she said, "I don't want to move again. Not to the East Coast."

He looked down at the floor. He picked at what looked like dog hair. He forbid dogs in the house, so it couldn't be. He rolled the lint between his fingertips. "I don't either. But, I'm not sure I can stay here at the plant. I would have to get another job."

He looked back down at the floor and she looked with him. She stroked the back of his neck. "You're a good man, William. You'd stay here if I wanted you to?"

William closed his eyes. "It would be easier, on you and the kids, and on Raymond."

"Raymond, Raymond, Raymond," she said. "Is that what's bothering you?"

"Somewhat. I'm worried about him. If I leave him and take the Stamford job, that would be the end of him. I just know it would."

"Ah, ha. So you'd get another job here so you wouldn't have to face that?"

"I guess that's right."

"William, please tell me, do you want this job? Please!"

He looked at her. She smiled and he crumbled.

"Yes, Katherine, I want this job. I'm not being useful here any more. I stayed the last two years because of Raymond."

"And what does Raymond say?"

"He says I should take the job, that he'll survive."

"Then take it. We'll all survive."

He put his head in her lap. "You'll tell the kids?"

She stroked his head. "Of course, they'll hate you, but they'll get over it."

William called Daniel Flynn and told him he would take the job. Daniel wanted him to start the next day, but William held out for the following Monday. He wanted a few days at the Columbus plant to make sure Raymond was all right. Daniel assured him he had already talked to Raymond and he fully understood the situation. Trust him, everything would be fine. He didn't tell William that Raymond didn't like the situation. In fact, he cursed him and the entire Apex organization. He would have to be watched.

Katherine told the kids when they got home from school. They wanted to talk to William in the den. She told them that their father was resting, maybe later. The three of them ran to their rooms. Richardson and Jameson slammed their doors, so Elizabeth did the same. The boys got mad. They were tired of obeying a father who gave them very little except criticism and orders. It was obedience without respect. Elizabeth, on the other hand, was excited to move. She had asked Katherine if she could she have a dog in their new house. William didn't allow dogs in this house, not with the white carpeting. Katherine had told her that they would see. This was enough for Elizabeth; she ran upstairs excited. The boys didn't talk to William. They never talked to William and he didn't notice any difference. Elizabeth came into the den to sit in William's lap and cheer him up. He rushed her out before she could get settled.

Saturday night the company had a celebration party for Raymond (some celebration) and a going away party for William. Raymond and Patricia didn't show. William called him and Patricia said everything was all right, Raymond just wasn't feeling good. Actually he was feeling lousy, terminally lousy. William and Katherine left early. Katherine didn't dance, and William didn't talk. The employees didn't seem to mind too much. The party went on without them. He was given a nameplate, "William S. Bradford III: The World's Best Plant Manager." Had another fiction started?

He left for Stamford on a Sunday afternoon flight in the middle of April. Katherine drove him to the airport and saw him off. He walked slowly, with stooped shoulders, onto the plane. Katherine cried all the way home. She sat in the garage crying; she couldn't go back into the house. The kids hadn't talked to William since the announcement of their moving and they were mad at her for not doing something. None of them wanted to go, it was too sad.

When William arrived at the airport in Stamford, there was a company chauffeur, Leroy, waiting for him at the gate. He was holding up a large professionally prepared sign that read "Welcome William S. Bradford III, the hero of Hereford, William the Conqueror." He had witnessed this type of scene for others as they arrived at the airport. He had always been envious, as they must have been someone important. Now it was his turn. He was quite impressed. He remembered Mr. Blanchard's chauffeur, Timothy. The feeling felt good, a real hero's welcome. As he identified himself, the chauffeur was already grabbing his carry-on bag. At baggage claim, the chauffeur took the other bags and led him to the stretch limousine. It was larger than he had ever seen, with a radio and television in the back, separate climate controls, and a fully stocked bar with drinks and snacks. The back seat was large enough for him to lie down and put his feet up. There was a choice of slippers to wear and various magazines and newspapers. It had all the comforts of home — a very expensive home. He wondered whether employees received the same treatment when they left the company.

Apex had set William up in a company-owned, three-bedroom condominium apartment that was almost the same square footage as his house in Columbus. They had offered him the same three-month free rental deal as before and expected his family to move immediately with him. William re-negotiated for six months so that the kids could finish the school year in Columbus and then move out to Stamford during the summer. In the meantime, Katherine alone or with the kids could visit him here and get to know the area. William hoped that this might make it easier on the entire family. He was also able to get Apex to agree to his going home every weekend, or Katherine could visit him at company cost, with three trips for the children as well during this period. This would give him time to find a suitable place to live that they could all agree on and transition time for Katherine and the kids.

Apex had also promised to provide transportation for him while he was living in his temporary quarters. He assumed that since Leroy picked him up at the airport, he would be his driver and that the limousine would be the method of transportation. William was impressed. When he arrived at his new apartment, Leroy carried all of his bags and placed them in the apartment. He also gave him a tour of the apartment, showing him how everything worked, such as the full entertainment center, the automatic stove and oven, the intercom system, the whirlpool tub, the lighting and sound systems, and so on. When Leroy was leaving, William thanked him and said that he would be ready at seven in the morning. Leroy nodded and left.

William settled into the apartment and then called Katherine to tell her how wonderful he was being treated by the company. His story of sugarplums and fairy castles fell on deaf ears; she couldn't stop crying. She knew this was for the best for him, but she wasn't sure if it was the best for her and the kids. They talked for over an hour. By the end of the conversation, she had stopped crying and was trying to make the best of a bad situation. When he finally hung up, he felt like crying. He slept in one of the king sized beds in the master bedroom. As he tried to get to sleep, he thought of how miserable Katherine and the kids must be. As he slept, Rebecca came into his dreams and moved towards him. As she got on top of him and her breasts covered his face, he came slowly and fully. He turned to the other side and held desperately onto his mother. He was safe for now.

He got himself ready the next morning and waited for the limousine to arrive. When it was a quarter after seven and the car hadn't arrived he started to panic. He called the plant to find out what had happened. He wanted to be there early on his first day, set an immediate good example as the new plant manager. He had called a meeting of the plant department managers for eight o'clock. He called the plant and George Henderson, the personnel manager, got on the phone. He suggested that William go downstairs and look in his garage. He said he would see William at the eight o'clock meeting, and then hung up.

William did as he was told. When he entered the garage and turned on the light, a recording of "Hail to the Chief" blared on. In the middle of the large, two car garage sat a large black Mercedes sedan wrapped in bright blue ribbons with a banner which said "Welcome William S. Bradford III." The license plate was WSB III. The keys were in the ignition. Again he was impressed. As he realized that this was his transportation and started to open the driver's side door, he suddenly remembered his mother's words "beware of anything German; the Nazis are always there." He hesitated, as he would rather not defy his mother, but then decided this once can't hurt anything. He got in and drove himself to work. He now realized what they meant by German craftsmanship. How could the Nazis have developed anything so fine?

As part of his contract with Apex, William had insisted that John Biddle become his assistant plant manager. William would emphasize production systems, processes, and results by the numbers, and John would be the people person. Just like he and Raymond at Columbus, except that John Biddle wasn't Raymond Fogerty. John was a well-respected plant engineer, having been with Apex for over twenty years. During that time, he had become the ultimate obedient child. Whatever was asked of him he could do well, but he couldn't identify the cause of a problem or offer a practical solution. John's job was developing production systems as instructed, in his office.

John spent very little time out on the production floor dealing with the workers. If there was a question as to the accuracy of a standard production time that he had established, he would merely adjust the standard to the will of the workers. John never expected to become more than a staff employee. However, when William requested that he become the assistant plant manager he was quite flattered. His initial reaction was to turn the job down and stay where he was; it felt well over his head. He felt he was safe until retirement in fifteen years. In fact, he was retired in place. His wife, Ethel, however, persuaded him to take the job. She convinced him that William was a rising star and that out of his friendship in Hereford he would take John on the rise with him. The additional money would make their life easier for now and result in a larger company retirement. The employees felt this was a bad decision and that John wasn't a people person.

For the first month, William reviewed the job responsibilities of each operating and staff department together with all operating procedures, particularly those in manufacturing. By the end of the month, he had developed his plan for revamping all operations. He had eliminated all functions that he considered unnecessary or duplicated elsewhere, either within the plant or by headquarters, and streamlined remaining processes. He had effectively reduced the labor force by over 35% while increasing manufacturing productivity by over 40% according to his calculations, which were never wrong. While he had met with each of the department managers individually to hear their stories, he had not met too many of the other employees. For the time being, the plant operated as usual; the new plant manager was still invisible. John Biddle had been mainly carrying out William's orders: getting him information, dealing with any day-to-day problems, and being the conduit between William and the others.

William went over his plan with John. John was amazed at what William had come up with. He had been at the Stamford plant for eight years and thought it couldn't be run any more efficiently, he was wrong. William had set up a meeting with all department managers for that afternoon. They were to be responsible for implementing the plan in their departments, John was to be responsible to make sure they did what was expected of them, and William would monitor the entire plan to ensure that it was most successful. Headquarters had already approved of the plan. If he could even realize half of what he promised, they would be more than satisfied. If William could accomplish this much in less than a month, what could he accomplish in the long term? It boggled their minds and the legend of William the Conqueror grew.

At the meeting, none of the department managers could refute what William was saying. They were also somewhat disturbed as the clear message was that William had identified inefficiencies, some major, in each of their departments in less than a month, which they had not been able to identify in years. The specter of job insecurity raised its head for the first time in their careers. Apex had always been a lifetime employer; now with William they weren't so sure. William had provided the blueprint by which positions were to be eliminated; now it was their job to implement. William had not named names to be eliminated; he didn't know any. His concern was that the managers retain the employees that could function under William's compensation for results concepts. If they couldn't, William would know soon enough.

William didn't mention what would happen to those managers that couldn't function under the new rules; he didn't have to. He also reduced each of their budgets to minimal operating levels to implement his plan. If any manager couldn't manage on those numbers, he would have to take it up with William. None of them did.

When the managers announced William's plan in each of their departments, the employees were shocked. Their jobs at Apex had always been secure. If they did basically what was expected, as little as they could get away with, they knew they had a job until retirement. Now they weren't so sure. Some of the marginal employees started looking for other jobs. Part of William's plan was to retain the lower paid employees who were presently producing at a higher level of productivity than their compensation. He wanted to weed out the older employees who were being paid more and more as their productivity became less and less. He worked closely with George Henderson, the Personnel Manager, to identify those employees in each category. He then went over the personnel lists submitted by each manager. He had John handle any incongruities. Of course, the employees were unhappy, but within three months his plan was in place. Over 100 employees had left the company or had been reassigned to other Apex locations. William didn't know any of them or their families. That wasn't part of his mathematical formulas; that was the company's concern. The Stamford plant was now not only the largest of Apex's plants, but was the most profitable. At headquarters he was still known as William the Conqueror, but at the Stamford plant he became known as WB, the Wicked Bastard.

William had gone back to Columbus for the first two weekends that he was at Stamford. Katherine was still upset and cried a lot, but tried not to let him see it. She wasn't very successful though, and it made him feel awful. The kids weren't talking to him except for Elizabeth, who talked about the dog she was going to get. William ignored her. William and Katherine would get together with Raymond and Patricia, but they were just as gloomy. It was apparent that Raymond wasn't happy, and his concern for his job had bottomed. William offered to have Raymond come visit the Stamford plant to see what he was doing. He did it in a manner that solicited Raymond's advice and expertise. Raymond didn't care; he didn't need to see the wonderful things that William was accomplishing. His days of accomplishment were over. When William left at the end of the weekend he felt sad and hopeless. He didn't know what he could do for Katherine and the kids and what he could do for Raymond. People weren't his business.

The next two weekends he didn't go back to Columbus; he just couldn't. He wanted Katherine to come to Stamford, but she said she wasn't ready yet. He still called her every evening and they talked for a long time, but they were no closer to resolving the issue. Katherine said she would try to make the best of the situation; that was all she could do. He called Raymond every other day to make sure he was all right; he still seemed so despondent. He continued to invite him to Stamford, hoping that might cheer him up, but it had the opposite effect.

During the fourth week that he was at Stamford, he was paged to return to his office at once. This had never happened before and William was worried. Was there a problem with Katherine, the children, or Raymond? When he got to his office, his secretary told him that a woman was on the line. She had said it was an emergency. He couldn't imagine who it could be. Unknown women never called him at work. He picked up the phone and Patricia said hello. His heart jumped. It must be something with Raymond. Just recently, headquarters had sent him a report showing the drop in productivity and the rise in costs at the Columbus plant since his departure. They wanted his opinion as to what might have happened and encouraged him to pay a visit. He hadn't responded as yet, hoping it would go away. He heard Patricia's voice on the phone as she said "Hello, William." While her voice had always been pleasant and seductive, now it had taken on a permanent sadness.

"Patricia," he said, "how nice to hear your voice."

"William, I know I shouldn't bother you at work, but I'm getting desperate. You seem to be the only friend that Raymond trusts. I thought you might be able to talk to him."

"Patricia, I've been talking to him at least every other day."

"I know, but only about business."

"He won't talk about anything else. He says everything is all right."

"All right! The SOB is back to drinking. He leaves in the morning and I don't know where he goes. I call him at work and he's never there anymore. He just doesn't care about the job or about his family. He won't talk to me. He raised his hand ready to hit me last night. William, Raymond has never hit me. I'm afraid for him and for me. I don't know what to do."

"How about your kids, Joan or Jean? I know he's not close to either of them, but maybe one of them could talk to him."

"Oh, William. They both hate him. He never had any time for them when they were growing up and now they have no time for him. They love him, I think, but they don't care much for him. I really can't blame them. He never wanted to be a father. It was all my fault. Please, William." She started to cry with deep sobs.

He offered to come the next day. He needed to visit the Columbus plant anyway. When he arrived at the Columbus plant the next morning around ten o'clock, Raymond was locked in his office. His secretary said that he spent most of his days like this. The plant was operating on its own. Without William there to watch, the employees had sunk back to their old ways and productivity had suffered. Raymond didn't much care. When William was announced, Raymond opened the door. He looked awful. The usually well-dressed Raymond Fogerty looked like a bum. His slacks were wrinkled, his shirt was pulling out from his waistband, and his jacket was thrown on the floor.

There was a bottle of bourbon and a large drinking glass sitting on his desk, nothing else. He offered William a drink but he refused. William tried to talk to Raymond but he got nowhere. He threatened him that he was going to lose his job and his wife, but he didn't seem to care. He just kept ranting about "those fucking bastards" and getting drunker. William made a tour of the plant and was shocked at what he saw. It was much worse than he had imagined. With no real plant manager, the employees had created their own party atmosphere. Work seemed to be the last thing on their minds. When he went back to Raymond's office to say good-bye, Raymond was even more drunk. He asked William to go to lunch and then they could both get laid by a couple of well-stacked waitresses he knew. He refused, said he was meeting Katherine, why didn't Raymond join them? Raymond said he couldn't, he had a lunch date. William could only imagine with whom.

When he was ready to leave the office, Raymond came over and hugged him hard, almost crushing him. Through tears forming in his eyes, he said softly to William. "I love you, son. Be good to Katherine and your kids and to yourself."

This was the first time anyone had said I love you to William. It was the first time Raymond had said I love you to anyone else.

He met Katherine and Patricia for lunch at the club. They were both dressed conservatively. Their game of sexually teasing the club geezers had ended with the changes for William and Raymond. In fact, Patricia and Katherine had stopped drinking entirely. They were both working out every day and looked healthy, but sad. They were waiting for him in anticipation that he would have good news about Raymond. Patricia was extremely distraught, wringing her napkin between her fingers. Katherine was biting on her lower lip. She had created a long horizontal gash across her lip and it looked awful. He tried not to notice.

When he joined them at their table, neither one was saying anything. They were both looking into space, bemoaning their fates. Patricia looked up at him hopefully. He kissed each of them on the cheek. Katherine held onto his hand and so did Patricia. He told them how he had found Raymond drinking in his office. Patricia confirmed that he drank all the time now. He left early and came home late; sometimes he didn't come home at all, like last night. When he was home, they hardly talked. He had moved his things to Joan's old bedroom. He would drink himself to sleep there. He told Patricia it was for the best; he wouldn't disturb her this way. Patricia tried to get close to Raymond, to help him, but the closer she got the more he moved away. They were all concerned, but they could do nothing.

William spent the afternoon with Katherine and Patricia. It was long and heavy. He took them both out to dinner trying to cheer them up, but it only made him sadder. He and Katherine went home after dropping Patricia off at her house. They offered to have her stay the night with them, but she thought she had better be home in case Raymond arrived. William didn't tell her about the other women. William and Katherine spent as pleasant a night as possible together under the circumstances. The kids had finally started to speak to him again, civilly if not exuberantly.

The school term was coming to an end and summer was getting closer, and they were warming to the idea of moving. It was becoming more of an adventure rather than a punishment. Katherine was softening as well. She loved Patricia and Raymond, but the last few weeks were much too heavy for her. She could stand getting away from here.

They stayed in the same bedroom, but separate beds, that night. She came to visit him during the night and played with his penis and then sat on it. His ejaculation was slow and pleasurable. He had really missed her. It was she that he dreamt of that night. In the morning, she was still cuddled in the bed with him. He didn't mind. He tried to convince her to come back to Stamford with him. She didn't want to leave Patricia quite yet, and she would have to get someone to stay with the kids. She said that it was too soon, but she would come on the weekend.

That weekend, they went to look at houses. The company had a number of houses in their inventory of employees who had been transferred. If they liked one of them, their cost would be reasonable with current market prices. William had already looked at these houses and knew the one that she would like. He saved that one for near the end of the day. If she agreed, their search would be over and he would take her to a fabulous dinner. The property he had in mind was completely gated, on over twelve, heavily wooded acres. It was twice the size of their present home, with a separate playhouse for the kids, a greenhouse, a separate office/studio, a master bedroom suite twice the size of their current one, a master bath with a whirlpool tub and a sauna, a workout room, four other large bedrooms, a den for them and one for the kids, a gourmet kitchen, formal dining room, a four car garage, and six bathrooms—it was a mini estate. The vice president of international operations lived in it last. It was not easily marketed on the outside. The company would love to have the Bradfords in the house, as it would ensure their keeping William.

She loved the property at first sight. She ran from tree to tree hugging each one. Once inside, she ran from room to room. This was the kind of house that her father had always talked about, that his rich customers lived in and he wanted to live in. It was bigger than the Fauntleroys house where they had been married. Guy would be impressed. Maybe he would like William now, his rich son-in-law.

She grabbed him in the master bedroom and pulled him down on the floor beside her. He pulled away and got up. She lay on the floor looking seductively up at him. She licked her lips. "Oh, William, do you think we can use the whirlpool?" She looked mischievous. She started to take off her clothes.

"Katherine, I'm the Stamford plant manager. I can't be found like that. But, when we move in."

"You mean we can buy this house?"

"Of course, that's why I saved this one for last."

She kissed him on the cheek. "My sweet William. I knew you would make it better."

The next weekend the kids joined them in Stamford. They loved the house as well. Each one picked a different bedroom. It looked like there were to be no conflicts in this house. On Monday, he told headquarters that they would be buying the house. He had them and they had him. They planned to move in the week after the kids stopped school in June. They were happy again. Katherine stopped crying and started planning.

Katherine spent the days upon her return from Stamford planning for the new house and taking care of Patricia. Raymond was getting increasingly despondent, drinking more and not coming home. Patricia had gotten each of the daughters to speak to Raymond on the phone, but neither one was willing to visit. Joan was living and working in Minneapolis, and Jean was in Indianapolis. While Raymond had cried after each daughter had called him, he continued on his path of destruction. Patricia was spending almost all of her time with Katherine, either at the club or at the Bradfords house. Many nights she would stay over. She couldn't stay in her house waiting for Raymond to come home and then not come home. One morning as she returned home, she found Raymond's car in the garage. The motor was still running. She cursed him; he was forgetting everything lately. She went to turn the motor off and found Raymond sitting in the driver's seat. He was dead, she did not know for how long. She blamed herself for not being home. Raymond had attached a piece of Apex PVC piping that appropriately said "Thank You For Using Apex" to his exhaust system. At least he had died peacefully. He clutched an envelope in his hand and it was addressed to William. Patricia grabbed the envelope and drove madly back to Katherine's.

Katherine called William immediately at his office in Stamford. She was hysterical, Patricia was hysterical, and now William was hysterical. He pounded his fist on his desk and tossed everything else off the desk. His secretary, Miss Miller, came in to see what was the matter. She had never seen him lose his control. She was scared.

"I'm sorry, Miss Miller, but my best friend just killed himself." It was all he could do to stop from crying. "Tell Mr. Flynn I'll be off for the next few days. I have to attend Raymond Fogerty's funeral in Columbus."

Everyone knew Raymond at Apex. Miss Miller knew him from his visits to the plant. He had flirted with her as he had all the other females in the office. And now he was dead, how horrible. As he rushed from his office, he heard Miss Miller say "Oh my God" and heard her crying.

He arrived in Columbus that night. Patricia was staying at their house. Her daughters, Joan and Jean, were due the next day. The funeral was the following day. The three of them sat for most of the night holding each other's hands. Katherine and Patricia cried throughout the night; he sat staring into space.

Daniel Flynn had called William in Columbus and offered to attend the funeral as the representative from Apex headquarters. He saw himself as a long time friend of Raymond's. He couldn't believe Raymond would bear him any ill will for being the messenger. William told him he thought it better if he didn't come; he didn't know how the family would feel about it. He knew how he felt about it, damn corporate bastards.

The funeral was well attended as Raymond had many acquaintances, if not many friends. There were people from the Apex plant, the country club, the neighborhood, and the various organizations that Raymond belonged to, who attended. William and Katherine were asked to give a eulogy. William was just able to finish his eulogy before succumbing to choking. He had to leave the chapel to catch his breath.

Katherine started to cry. Almost as soon as she started, she couldn't continue. This was the first person close to her that had died. She joined William outside and they stood there clinging to each other. His two daughters kneeled in front of his casket and held each other as they cried. They loved the man, but he had been an absent father; they didn't know the man. They cried for what could have been.

Patricia joined William and Katherine outside. They held her up as best they could. Even at her husband's funeral she looked beautiful, but she felt anything but beautiful. She took Raymond's letter from her purse. She looked at it with fondness; it was her husband's last correspondence. She handed it cautiously to William. He looked at the envelope. It had his name on it in Raymond's handwriting. He didn't know what to do with it. He held onto it and Katherine and Patricia.

"William," said Patricia, "it's all right, go ahead and open it."

He slowly opened the envelope. It was a handwritten letter to him from Raymond. Ironically, it was written on Apex stationery. He started to read it out aloud.

"Please, William, read it to yourself," said Patricia.

He read the letter and nodded his head, just like Raymond. "I think he would want you to hear it, Joan and Jean too. Is that all right?" He looked at Patricia.

She nodded affirmatively. She called her daughters over. All five of them held each other as William read the letter.

Dear William:

I am alone again. I have always been alone except for the time we spent together. God I miss you something awful. Taking you from me was the last desperate act those corporate bastards could do to get me. They succeeded. You were the son I never had or could have. I thank God for the time we had together.

Please tell Patricia how much I've loved her. I was never able to tell her myself. I've blamed her for all my troubles, but I now know that I'm the one to blame. If I couldn't love her in life the way she deserved, maybe I can love her this way by freeing her from my curse. I know she tried her best to love me, but I wouldn't let her. For this, I am eternally sorry. Please take care of her and keep her well. I know you will. You are too obedient not to.

I tried to love my daughters, Joan and Jean, but my hate for myself prevented me. I loved them the best I could. Please tell them that. I can only hope that they can understand.

I have made you the executor of my estate. Better you should rob the estate than some slimy lawyer. I know you won't. You've been my only true friend and I'm going to miss you. The will and a list of my assets are enclosed.

Until we meet again,

Your friend,

Raymond Fogerty, of unsound mind, the world's second best plant manager.

P.S. Please try to love Katherine and your children better. The job's not worth it. Watch out for the road to oblivion and always keep the footpath back home clear.

By the time he was finished reading the letter, all of them were crying loudly. It was just the kind of letter Raymond would write. It was as if he had come back from the dead to speak with them one last time.

William looked at the will and list of assets. Raymond was a very rich man, over three million dollars in assets. As Raymond said it wasn't the money, it was his life. He offered to give Patricia the letter, the will, and the list of assets. She pushed it back to him.

"No, William, you keep it. He wanted you to have it. I have his memories."

William left in a couple of days to return to Stamford. He vowed to make sure that Patricia and Raymond's daughters were well taken care of; he would take nothing for himself as the executor. Raymond was right to trust William. Katherine stayed with Patricia after her daughters had left. Both Joan and Jean offered for Patricia to come stay with them, but Patricia wasn't ready to give up her memories. She had lived with this man for over twenty-five years. She was 46 years old.

However, after living with Raymond's memories for two weeks, Patricia decided that she would move back to New York City. Katherine was pleased, as Patricia would be closer to them. She had lost another friend in Raymond, but she would hold onto Patricia. William, as the executor, arranged it so that Patricia could purchase whatever she wanted. She chose a cooperative apartment overlooking Central Park West. Katherine would visit her there often, and she would visit them in Stamford often. Every time William saw Patricia he would remember Raymond and want to cry. He would get furious at those corporate bastards. They had killed his best friend, and maybe the only real friend he was to have in life, but they wouldn't get him. He would screw them from the inside, for Raymond.

At the end of June, William moved his family into the Bradford estate outside of Stamford, Connecticut. He was now somebody— one of the Bradfords from Stamford. Wouldn't Mr. Blanchard be proud of him?

The kids all adapted well to the new surroundings. The boys took over the playhouse and the other den. Sometimes they would let Elizabeth into the playhouse. Elizabeth became custodian of the tree house, she and her dolls. She soon forgot that William refused to let her have a dog. Katherine became the conservative wife that was expected of the Stamford plant manager and future vice president of Apex Industries. She went back to wearing long unrevealing dresses, padded uplifting bras, and tops that went to the neck. As a gesture of surrender, she cut off her long hair and had it permed in the fashion of the day. This was the first time she had cut her hair since she was sixteen years old. She told William that hippie hair didn't go with the Stamford plant manager's wife. He said nothing. He assumed that she wanted to do this.

As part of William's position as Stamford plant manager, Apex provided him with a membership in the most desired country club in the area, where many of the Apex executives were members. It was expected that William be an active member and be available for golf foursomes as required. He thanked Raymond again for making him a golfer. He still hated the silly game, but this was business. Katherine would go to the club to work out and would meet Ethel Biddle for lunch there at least twice a week. They would conspire as to what they were going to do, but they never did anything. Katherine would also bring Patricia to the club whenever she visited to work out and lunch, but that was all they did. There was no fun left in teasing the club geezers. They had both matured quite a lot in the last year.

Members of the club were mainly from old, New England moneyed families. Only recently had the club allowed newcomers to money, such as William, to join. They still had restricted membership policies, although unwritten, which prevented minorities, that is Catholics, Jews, and Blacks, from joining. A few Catholics, but no Italians, Irish or Polish please, had joined but they all attended Protestant churches—so they were all right. William and Katherine were among the youngest members. Most of the members were in their fifties or older. Many of the very wealthy men had divorced their older wives and married younger, flashier women. They wore tight dresses and low cut tops; it was expected of them. But Katherine and Patricia did not. Katherine was becoming a woman of stature, but less fun.

Katherine said to Patricia, "The East Coast is all big tits and sharp elbows, the Midwest is long legs, smooth curves, and well-shaped asses." She hated this lifestyle. Connecticut was no place for mini skirts and no bra, not for a thirty-two year old mother of three and the wife of the Apex Stamford plant manager. She missed Columbus, the old Patricia, and the fun they had. Life had become too serious again, but she couldn't go back.

William settled down at the Stamford plant. His systems were taking hold. Month by month productivity increased as costs decreased. It was the Columbus story all over again. Those employees who had survived the initial revamping became increasingly loyal. They understood the system that rewarded them for increasing their productivity not for time in. It seemed fair to them. They had quickly forgotten those employees who were no longer employed at Apex; there was little survivors' guilt. While most of the employees feared William, they respected him. He knew none of them; he didn't want to. His main contact with the people was John Biddle. They would meet in the morning for breakfast, at noontime for lunch, and at eight o'clock before they went home. William maintained control while John maintained the peace. William and John were strictly business. He wouldn't make that mistake again.

William continued his routine of leaving the house early, before six o'clock, and returning late at night, after nine o'clock. He would have dinner with Katherine at that time and they would talk about their day and the kids. This was his only input into his children's lives. She would ask him what to do about one of the children and he would make the decision. She would then inform the son or daughter. He was interested in his children's lives, he wished them the best, but he just didn't want to be part of it. He had always hated childhood as something that had to be lived through. He looked on these family decisions just like he looked on plant decisions. What was most efficient at the least cost? Katherine became the matron of the manor. Her job was to make sure that the children were safe, no bikes, no football, no climbing trees and so on, and to support William.

William had just completed his fifth year as Stamford plant manager. Each month results kept improving. The legend of William the Conqueror grew within Apex Industries. He was spending more time working with headquarters vice presidents in mapping out corporate plans. His input was valued throughout the company. He was asked more frequently to visit other plant sites throughout the country. It had become a similar scenario to his last days at Columbus. This time Katherine was more prepared for his traveling. The kids were now older, 13, 11, and 9, and she was well established in the community. She had taken to motherhood and suburban matronly life quite nicely. She still tried to get into New York at least twice a week to see Patricia and others, and visit the museums that she loved. William still felt alone on the road, even more alone than at home.

One morning while he was out in the plant, there was an emergency call over the speaker system for him to return immediately to his office. When he got to his office, Miss Miller whispered to him, "It's Old Ironsides Ingersoll (the Apex CEO) himself, on the phone."

Mr. Ingersoll had never called him directly before. If he wanted something, he would always have someone else, such as Daniel Flynn, deliver the message. This was rare indeed. William was concerned. It was either the best of news or the worst of news. He entered his office, closed his door (the halls have ears), composed himself, and picked up the phone.

"Hello, William Bradford."

"Hold on a minute. It's Mr. Ingersoll calling." CEO's never placed calls themselves. "William, how are you? And your lovely wife?"

"Fine, sir. We're both fine."

"Listen, William, I was wondering if you could join us a little later, say three o'clock, this afternoon. That is if you can spare the time. I know how busy you always are." The message was clear; be there at three o'clock sharp.

"Sure, sir. Three it is."

"Thank you, William." Mr. Ingersoll hung up quietly.

William called in Miss Miller and had her rearrange his entire afternoon schedule. He was busy all right, up to his armpits. But what did that matter to Old Ironsides? William could come in this weekend to finish the work.

When he got to Mr. Ingersoll's office in the headquarters building, he was immediately sent into his office. Mr. Ingersoll and the twelve vice presidents were seated around the conference table. It was apparent from the ashtrays and coffee cups that they had been meeting for some time. Some of the faces looked friendly and nodded, some actually winked, to William. Others averted looking at him.

Mr. Ingersoll waved William to a seat near him. He looked at the group of vice presidents. "You all know William Bradford, our Stamford plant manager." They all nodded as if Ingersoll had a string attached to each of their necks and his hand, a real puppeteer. He looked at William.

"William, I have to admit we've been talking about you. Daniel Flynn, our executive vice president of operations had to leave us suddenly (read let go for reasons never to be known). We were discussing his replacement and your name came up (read Ingersoll's choice). We wanted to know whether you would consider such a position?"

William was flabbergasted. This was not totally unexpected, but not at this time. He had expected a promotion to vice president or assistant to a vice president initially, not a direct move to executive vice president. No wonder there were so many solemn faces. He would be their boss in one quick leap. How many felt the job was theirs, not for an upstart like William? He had hardly been there long enough to qualify for such a job. Yes, he had been quite successful in such a short time, but he still didn't have the time in. Frankly, he scared the shit out of most of them. Here was a man who actually knew what he was doing, and he had done it well.

William hesitated. "Well, sir, this is a complete surprise. Quite a jump from plant manager."

Ingersoll interrupted him. "Hogwash," he said, "you'll be just fine. You'll be teaching these guys how to do their jobs right in no time. Just tell me whether you would take the job. We'll take it from there."

William reddened; he was quite uncomfortable. All of these men were at least twenty years older than him and had been at Apex all their working lives. They had been his bosses since he started working at Apex. Now some of them would be working for him.

"Well, William, what's your answer? We need to vote on this before sundown."

"Yes, sir, I think I can do the job. If you want me, I'll accept the position. I'll give it my best."

Mr. Ingersoll patted William on the arm. "I know you will, William. Would you mind waiting in the outer office. It shouldn't be for too long."

William was ushered out of the conference room by Mrs. Roth, Ingersoll's executive assistant. They sat and looked at each other for what seemed like hours, although it was less than five minutes. The door opened and the vice presidents started to file out. Some nodded at him, others walked right past him without looking at him. Mr. Ingersoll buzzed for Mrs. Roth. William could hear over the intercom. "Please send Mr. Bradford in."

William went back into Mr. Ingersoll's office. He was alone with the two remaining executive vice presidents. Mr. Ingersoll got up from his chair and came over to William, with a broad smile all over his face.

"Well, William, congratulations. You are now the executive vice president of operations. Some of the boys (he actually snickered at the word) didn't think you were quite ready. Maybe when you're as old as they are, and they're long gone, but I think we need some young blood up here. I fought hard for you, don't let me down." He shook William's hand. He had a firm grip as a CEO should. The other two congratulated him as well. It was evident they didn't share Ingersoll's enthusiasm. He was Ingersoll's choice.

William knew that he was solid in the position as long as he helped them make more money. It was always the money, never the human being.

"Fuck them," he thought, "this is for Raymond Fogerty. You damn, old fogey corporate bastards."

William never cursed out loud, only to himself. He felt good. At the age of thirty-seven he was now the youngest vice president in the history of Apex Industries. He wondered if Raymond had done anything to get Daniel Flynn out of there, and, if so, what it was.

He called Katherine to have her and the kids meet him at the club for dinner. This was a rarity for him. When they arrived he introduced himself as the new executive vice president of operations for Apex Industries. The kids jumped up to hug him and kiss him on the cheek. They were proud of their father, no closer, but prouder. Katherine smiled at him. She would save her congratulatory surprise for him for later, in their bedroom. She now knew she had made the right decision in marrying him. It was nice to prove your parents wrong.

As they ate dinner, numerous couples, members of the club, would come over to their table to congratulate William. The club was really a small community; good news and bad traveled fast. The males would give him a hearty handshake and wish him well, all the time looking over at Katherine as if she had become a more valuable prize for conquest. You could almost hear them bragging as they looked at her covetously and thinking, "I screwed the wife of the executive vice president of operations at Apex Industries." The females congratulated both of them. After all, if it weren't for Katherine, William would never have gotten the promotion—not with his personality. As the females congratulated them, they would look William over; he had become much more desirable. The young trophy wives in particular would get close to William and turn their backs on Katherine as if she didn't matter. They would bend over close to him pushing their low cut tops in his face. They all had large breasts; it was a standard requirement. He recoiled as the cleavage down to the nipples closed in on him. He wasn't interested, but he was enjoying the power of his new position. His two sons were impressed.

When they left the club and were ready to get their cars, the valet parkers already had their cars waiting with the doors open. The two parkers both rushed to help William into his car as Katherine and the kids stood there. He was impressed; he really was somebody not just Katherine Bradford's husband. The three kids wanted to ride with their father; this had never happened before. Katherine felt it important that the boys get closer to their father—they had never been close, just the opposite—and encouraged them to go with him. Richardson ran to the front seat next to his father. Jameson sat in the back with his elbows on the front seat staring at his father all the way home. Richardson and Jameson talked incessantly to their father telling him how terrific his promotion was, for them not necessarily for William.

Katherine made Elizabeth ride with her. Elizabeth whined that "it wasn't fair," but she got in the car with her. She sulked all the way home. "Why did I have to be a girl? The boys have all the fun."

As they entered the house, the boys were still jabbering at their father. William was saying nothing. It was apparent that they were both proud of him. They both ran upstairs excited; they couldn't wait to tell their rich friends. They both went to private school where there were only rich kids. Now they didn't have to be ashamed of what their father did. He was equal to any of their fathers. Jesus, Executive Vice President of Operations at Apex Industries. Apex was one of the biggest employers in the Stamford area and every one of their friends knew Apex Industries. Some of their friends' fathers were only vice presidents at Apex or other places. Their father was an executive vice president. Holy shit!

William was exhausted. His exuberance had settled into tension in his neck and a growing headache in the front of his eyes. He was enjoying the attention and newfound adoration, but it was wearing on him. He just was not a people person. He went to his den to sit in his lounge chair in the quiet in the dark. Katherine would take care of the children. As he sat there, the realization of his new position was beginning to sink itself into his being. For the first time in his life he felt like somebody. It was a good feeling. Elizabeth came running into the den in her pajamas, the bear ones with the feet. She jumped up on William's lap and kissed him on the cheek. She hugged him around the neck. Tonight William was her hero. "I love you, Daddy," she said as she hugged him harder. She was nine years old and getting too big to be on his lap, and William thought he detected signs of her breasts developing. He thought of Rebecca for the first time in many months. It was either the thought of Elizabeth with breasts or his promotion, or a combination of each. He lifted her off his lap and put her on the floor. He said nothing. Katherine came to the door and picked Elizabeth up and took her upstairs to bed. She was too excited to sleep.

Katherine returned to the den. He sat quietly in his chair massaging the back of his head. She went over and stood behind him. She began to softly massage the back of his head. She had never done this for him before; it felt good, better than doing it himself. She worked on his head and his shoulders; the tension was leaving his body. She kissed him on the back of the neck, the side of the neck, the forehead, the eyes, the cheeks, and finally on the mouth. He didn't recoil. She took his hand and led him out of the room and upstairs to their bedroom.

She put him on his bed and removed his shoes. She continued to massage him around the head and shoulders. He started to relax and closed his eyes. She excused herself and went into the bathroom. She came back with nothing on but her underpants. She didn't know if he was ready for that as well; she would start with topless. He opened his eyes slightly and then closed them. She had brought a bottle of massage oil with her. She removed his shirt and threw it on the floor. William the plant manager would have never approved of this. She poured some massage oil on his chest—he was big chested and hairy, she liked that—and slowly massaged his upper body. As she finished his upper body, she unfastened his belt and removed his trousers. He offered no resistance. In fact, he helped her. As she pulled down his trousers, she also pulled down his underpants. He wore old-fashioned, loose boxer shorts and they came off easily. She slowly worked in the massage oil on his stomach, his hips, his legs, and his feet. With each touch on his body, his penis got harder; she had never seen it so long and hard and free. As she picked up his legs to massage his inner thighs and her hands caressed the top of his thighs he came all over himself, quickly and forcefully. His entire body pulsed, and she could sense him suppressing a scream. She worked the come into his body with the massage oil. He lay back and softly moaned. She easily turned him over, as he had become much lighter. She massaged the back of him, the shoulders and neck, the upper body, and the back of his legs. As she massaged his ass and the subtlety of his crack, she quickly reached under and grabbed his penis— it was hard again. He came again almost immediately. This time she thought she heard a bit of a scream leak out. It gave her pleasure to give him such pleasure. She left him lying on his back as she went into the bathroom. She came back and took his hand and led him slowly into the bathroom. He gave no resistance; he was like a little boy with his mother. She helped him into the whirlpool tub and then slowly dropped her underpants as he looked away, and got in with him. This was the first time, but not the last time, that they would whirlpool together. She washed him all over. Again, he showed no resistance. He let the whirlpool jets and her hands caress him. He kept his eyes closed. His penis had hardened again. She was excited and wanted to mount him right there, but he discouraged her from even touching it. It hurt and he was exhausted. She thought that maybe next time he would massage her in return.

Katherine and Patricia had begun getting massages at the club by the well-built male masseuses. This replaced their sexual, geezer teasing.

Katherine chose Lance as her masseuse; he reminded her of William, stocky, muscularly built, and reserved. Patricia used Burt, as he was gregarious like Raymond, although Raymond had never been gregarious with her. Katherine would take her clothes off while Lance waited outside. It excited her to be nude like this and then get onto the massage table with Lance just on the other side of the door.

Lance would slowly and methodically massage each part of her body. She liked being nude in front of a man with only a thin sheet covering her. This was the most sensual experience of her life. She thought of William doing this to her as Lance moved around her body. As he massaged her lower back and legs he was careful not to expose or touch her vagina — she wouldn't have cared. He would cover one side of her ass while he massaged the other side. He would move his hands slowly and gently working in the massage oil. As he moved from one side of her ass down the inside of her thigh, she would lose control and start to flow gently from inside her vagina. She could only think of the puddle she was creating on the bottom sheet.

If Lance noticed it, or told other club members, she would be absolutely mortified. She noticed that Lance gathered up the top and bottom sheets after each massage and threw them directly into the hamper. If he knew the effect he had on her, in the role of William, he never made it known. She wondered what effect massaging her body had on Lance. She thought she felt a more sensual touch as he massaged her ass and sometimes an almost audible moan as he touched her there. When Lance was done, he would leave the room to allow her to dress. She would liey on the table for a few minutes, hardly able to get off. When she did finally manage to move off the table, she didn't want to get dressed for the longest time; she wanted to enjoy the mellowness of her naked body. Her body shivered with sensual pleasures. She hoped someday William could make her feel like this.

Katherine had become addicted to her massages with Lance. She had bought the massage oil hoping that someday William would massage her in the same way. This had become her fantasy. She had never seen William so at peace. She let him float in the whirlpool while she got out. She slowly dried herself off, caressing her body; she liked feeling her body. She put on a new see-through negligee she had bought for just such an occasion. She never thought she would get to use it.

She helped William out of the whirlpool. She toweled him off slowly, caressing his body with the towel and her hands. She hoped he liked it. His eyes were still closed and he seemed to shiver as she touched him softly. She led him into the bedroom and into her bed. This was the first time that he had slept without his silk monogrammed pajamas. She put him under the covers and he moaned softly. She took off her negligee, he hadn't noticed it anyway, and got in beside him. He still offered no resistance. She held him tightly and he held her back. This was the first time that they had slept together for an entire night, particularly in the nude.

He slept soundly for the first time in a long time. He dreamt of Katherine, of her hands on his body. He pulled her closer to him. He wasn't aware of his penis entering her. She pulled closer to him so that she could feel his full length. He was able to stay longer than he had ever had. She felt signs of an orgasm, the first that she was aware of. She tried not to make a sound. He came slowly and fully for the third time that night. She opened her eyes to see a soft smile on his face. She hugged him closer and went back to sleep. He would dream often of this night, and so would she.

This wasn't about sex; it was about self-worth and power. William and Katherine had never felt worthy by their parents or their peers. They had both always felt inferior. They had both hid in their relationship; it was a safe and secure place. Now that he was the executive vice president of operations for Apex Industries he was finally somebody. He was now worthy and superior, in a position of power. He now felt worthy of Katherine and allowed her, but no one else, to touch him. His power and feeling of superiority came from his new position. How strange it felt. Katherine's power came from being the wife of the executive vice president of operations of Apex Industries. Men had already started looking at her differently, maybe even her father.

William bought her a Mercedes convertible when he was promoted to Executive Vice President. She loved the car, but she really wanted him. She settled for the car. It was bright yellow, the color of her hair. When she got out of the car, she knew she was being watched. She would make sure that her skirt or dress hiked up when she exited the car, hoping there were men (or boys) still watching her. There always were. She loved driving her car with the top down. She would hike her skirt up above her knees, so that passersby could see her legs. When a trucker pulled next to her, she would pull her skirt up even higher, so that the trucker could look down at her and whistle. She found the little fun that was left wherever she could; there wasn't much.

With William as Executive Vice President, she had to become more mature and matronly, the demure wife. She danced less, showed less leg, and flirted less —she was boring herself. She was invited to join more committees at the club and in the community. She was a respected member of the community. She had become Mrs. William Bradford III and the mother of his children—how awful.

Katherine spent considerable time with Patricia Fogerty and Ethel Biddle. With John's promotion to vice president, the Biddles had become company paid members of the country club. Ethel wasn't happy with all of John's traveling and she blamed William. She looked to Katherine for consolation; Katherine felt obligated. Katherine would spend many late nights with Ethel, sometimes at Ethel's house, sometimes at Katherine's. Katherine was accumulating women friends, but she was losing her male friend, William. Between Patricia and Ethel, Katherine was becoming a full time counselor.

It was about this time that Patricia first took a lover. Not really a lover, but a male partner. His name was Peter Scovill. He was an environmental lawyer in

Manhattan. Patricia had met him at a party in her condo building. She had not even considered another man since Raymond had committed suicide. She still hated him, and consequently all men, for doing that to her. Patricia and Peter started their relationship as concert and museum partners. He had been divorced for over twelve years with one married daughter and was sour on women of any kind. Patricia felt physically and sexually safe with him. They were able to have a good time without any sexual overtones. Patricia was 53 years old at the time and Peter was 57. They weren't kids anymore; they just felt like it.

Katherine urged Patricia to give love a try, but she wasn't ready yet. Raymond had been dead for over five years, and she hadn't been with a man in that time. Katherine and others had fixed her up on dates a number of times, but she never went out with any of them a second time. They all wanted to get close to her immediately and take her to bed. She was still a very attractive woman, with the body of a much younger woman.

Peter was pushing for more than a platonic relationship; Patricia was still happy being just friends. Katherine told her that it was impossible for a man and a woman to remain just friends; sex was always there. If Patricia didn't do something about it, she would lose him.

Katherine invited Patricia and Peter to her house for dinner one night when William was out of town. The children were all with friends. It was just the three of them. Katherine had a champagne cocktail hour, free flowing wine with dinner, after dinner aperitifs, and brandy cake for dessert. By the time dinner was over, they were all feeling mellow. They went into the den to listen to music and sip on brandies. Katherine took the single chair, which forced Peter and Patricia to sit together on the small love seat. Classical guitar played on the stereo.

As Peter held Patricia's hand and Patricia leaned her head on his shoulder, Katherine got up to go. She looked at the couple enviously. "Good night, you two. You don't need me anymore." Katherine started to leave the room.

"Oh, don't go," whispered Patricia. "Please."

Peter looked over at Katherine knowingly. They nodded to each other.

"I left your suitcases by your bedroom door. I'll see you both in the morning."

Patricia was confused. They had already put their suitcases in the bedroom each of them was going to sleep in. She let it pass. She probably just misunderstood.

When Peter and Patricia finally went upstairs after the fire burnt out, sure enough there were their suitcases sitting in front of the master bedroom door. Patricia picked up her suitcase and went to the bedroom in which she thought she was supposed to sleep. The door was locked and so were the others. She came back to Peter. She looked perplexed.

"Peter, the weirdest thing, all the doors are locked."

He understood. He picked her up and carried her over the threshold. He dropped her on the bed. He picked up a note with their names on it. He read it aloud.

"Hope you like the accommodations. Please enjoy. Love, Katherine. P.S. The whirlpool is ready."

Peter looked down at Patricia and she looked up at him. "So, what do you think?"

Patricia looked disturbed at Katherine, at Peter, at the situation.

"Oh, shit," she said. "Why not? Come on, I'll race you."

As they ran for the whirlpool, they each threw their clothes off. By the time Patricia got to the tub, she was naked. She jumped right in. Peter hesitated on the side in his underpants.

Patricia looked up at him. "Come on in, chicken." She made clucking noises.

Peter gave her a "what the hell" look. He slowly removed his under shorts like a stripper, trying to tease her by withholding the sight of his penis until he was ready to get in the tub.

Patricia gasped at the sight of his penis. She didn't remember how big and hard those things got. "Holy shit," she thought, "now what do I do."

She needn't have worried. He knew exactly what to do. He began by massaging her body, purposely staying away from her breasts and vagina. She had forgotten how nice a man's hands could feel. She closed her eyes and thought of Raymond; she hoped that he would forgive her. She opened her eyes and looked at Peter. It would be all right; she knew it would. She moved closer to him. There was no way she could avoid his penis. He tried to move back, but it was no use. The only way she could avoid it was by inserting it in her vagina. So she did. That was better; now she could massage him. They both came quickly; it had been a long time for each of them. They slept naked. He sat up in bed admiring her body; he was a lucky man. They made love off and on throughout the night. She cursed herself for waiting. But she could still see the son of a bitch watching her; Raymond wasn't letting go. She was only free when Peter's penis was inside of her; he would just have to continue doing that.

Katherine lay naked in Elizabeth's room down the hall thinking of Peter and Patricia making love. It made her itch all over. She thought that it should be her; she just wasn't sure whether she wanted it to be Peter or Patricia. She thought of Ethel Biddle telling her how John couldn't wait to get home and seduce her. He had her clothes off even before he had put his suitcase down. She thought about when William came home from work, in or out of town, and how he went right to work. They still slept in the same bedroom, but it was mainly sleep. The few times that she went to William's bed now it was just to feel close to another human being, but it usually didn't work. Rarely, when she would mount William's penis, it would be a maintenance fuck and she would try to get off on it. However, William would try to get to sleep. She thought of Patricia climaxing and her finger was in her vagina. She fell asleep masturbating; she hadn't masturbated since she was in college.

When they went back to New York, Peter moved into Patricia's apartment. He had a bachelor's efficiency, while Patricia had her large, two-bedroom condo. Peter was a working lawyer making a decent living, but his divorce had cost him dearly. It had, however, forced him to work less and enjoy life more. He had very few assets; Patricia was a wealthy woman. William had increased Raymond's estate by tenfold in five years. Patricia would never have to be concerned about money. She didn't care about Peter's lack of wealth; she had enough for both of them. Peter cared about his lack of wealth. She would make him forget. They wouldn't get married, neither one was ready for that. They would see how it went.

Katherine was happy for her friend Patricia, but it didn't make her feel any different. She wanted what Patricia had; she was jealous. She didn't want to wait until William died; she wanted it now. Patricia had been reborn while she was living a slow death. She was living someone else's life and waiting for her own to begin.

Katherine was 38 years old when Peter moved into Patricia's condo. She had always thought of herself as young, with everyone older than her. Now people, at the club and in the community, were younger. She saw 40 approaching and felt that her life would be over if she didn't do something about it. In the meantime, she would go on being a corporate wife; she actually did it very well.

She watched the children get older and agonized through each of their problems as they moved through their teenage years. She felt paralyzed to do anything for them. She was caught up in her own life. She had seen her dream come true, to be a rich socialite, and it hadn't made her happy, and now she had no dream. This was worse than having a dream unfulfilled.

As each of her children went on to college and moved out of the house, she became just a little lonelier. She was able to fill her time at the club, trips to New York, visits to the children, but it remained unfulfilled. She had resolved that this was to be her life. She was the wife of the Executive Vice President of Operations and she would always be Mrs. William Bradford III. Where had her life gone, when would her life really begin? She had fully become her mother and she didn't like it one bit.

William was working on acquisitions, mergers, restructuring and the like. She was working on keeping herself together. She spent more and more time looking at her naked body in front of the full-length mirror. She still liked what she saw. She was still thin; she had become fuller with age, and could still move her ass. But, what good was it doing her. She would walk around the room in the one pair of real high heels she had saved and looked at herself as she moved. She always hoped that William would come into the room at that time and make love to her. It never happened. He would merely pass through on the way to the bathroom.

She, and sometimes Patricia, was getting massaged more often at the club. She found herself lingering naked in the massage room before and after her massage, hoping that Lance the masseuse would catch her naked. She tried to move on the massage table so that Lance's hands would get close to her vagina. She knew there was something wrong with her life, but she didn't know what it was. She had a good husband, three healthy children, but all with problems, and a rich lifestyle—and a yellow Mercedes convertible. What was the matter with her? This was what her mother wanted all her life and now she had it. It just wasn't what she had wanted all her life; she just didn't know what that was.

She was getting more and more daring with the men at the country club. She had always gotten propositions from the men on and off the dance floor. She had never taken any of them seriously, although she knew some of the men were serious. They would have liked to screw her; that was all. The thought of another man in her had always been repulsive. Lately, the thought of William in her had become repulsive. She was seriously thinking of an affair. Even some of the slimier men had started to look good.

She tried to talk to Patricia, but she was too much in love with Peter. She told Katherine she needed to get laid, which was probably true, but Katherine didn't know how to go about it. She still wanted it to be William, but she wasn't sure that it ever could be. She couldn't be unfaithful to William, but being faithful to him was killing her. She would hold on for as long as she could. She wasn't sure how long that would be. For now, she would just let it be. She had been doing that ever since they had moved to Stamford.

PART THREE
TURNING POINTS & CORNERS

7

CHILDREN & OTHER STRANGERS

Richardson

Richardson was born in March 1963, when William and Katherine were both 23 years old. Many would say that this was much too young to start having children; others might say what were they waiting for. In this case, William was extremely mature, and adult like, from a work and professional standpoint. This was the world he hid in. However, from a social and emotional standpoint he was very immature. His problems relating to other people were damaging in his work and personal life and crossed over to his relationship with his wife. He really didn't relate, but possessed Katherine as a source of security and someone to take care of him. Katherine, on the other hand, may have been hiding from her own reality, that of an unattractive, unpopular child with her father and older brothers and her peer group. William may have become her hiding place that gave her security from an unfriendly world. These then were Richardson's young parents, maybe no more or less dysfunctional than other first time parents, with their own set of idiosyncrasies, which would have a profound effect on the baby Richardson. There were William and Katherine's genes, as well as their psychological and emotional patterns, that would help form Richardson.

Richardson was born a physically healthy baby at seven pounds and six ounces. Katherine's pregnancy was without major complications. She was thin and tried to stay thin during her pregnancy, which may or may not have had an effect on the baby. Richardson was a long, thin baby with wisps of blond hair. He had a long angular face with a fairly sharp chin. He was not cute and cuddly as might be said for other babies. Richardson looked just like his mother, the image of Katherine when she was a baby. He was Katherine's son.

When he was born, William was at work, which was not unusual. The first male to pick him up and cuddle him was not his father, but his Uncle

Joey. From the first time that Joey held him, Richardson felt safe and secure. It was instant bonding between adult male and baby. When William first came to the hospital and was given Richardson to hold, he held him tentatively and gave him back to his mother as quickly as he could. There was no bonding between father and son. From the first day, Richardson preferred his Uncle Joey to his natural father. The bonding between father and son remained a problem.

When Katherine held her first son it was like nurturing a baby version of herself. As the baby breastfed, she had the sensual feeling of arousing herself. While she had rather small breasts, she had fairly large nipples and a more than ample milk supply. She would flow almost continuously. She tried to get Richardson to feed as often as possible.

While she was still in the hospital, the nurses would confine feedings to normal feeding times, about once every four hours. At those times, Katherine would force the baby to feed for as long as possible. Not only did she think this was good for the baby, he looked so thin, but it also felt good for her. When she came home, her mother and Joey stayed with her. They would bring the baby to her for the entire day. He would sleep in the bed with her. She would have him sleep on her stomach with his mouth turned towards her nipples. As her breasts flowed, she would try to get the baby to suck the milk. Sometimes there was milk, other times he would merely suck. Either way it felt good to Katherine.

Joey would stay in the room with Katherine as much as he could. He would hold the baby to relieve Katherine and help her with her breastfeeding. She would lie in the bed with her small breasts exposed. When William came into the room she would cover up; she knew his discomfort with female breasts. At feeding times, when she had to expose her breasts, William would leave the room. Joey, and sometimes her mother, would stay to help. William, with what he knew about Joey, became instantly uncomfortable with this arrangement. He hastened their departure. This removed Richardson's male bonding to Joey or to any other male, as William remained unavailable to his son. Richardson's initial bonding with his Uncle Joey would remain throughout both of their lifetimes.

With her mother and her brother's departure, Katherine was now on her own with the baby. She had trouble calling a baby Richardson, but she had agreed with William that he would name the boys and she would name the girls. William had no family names to fall back on. He used the name of a few classmates at Roget. It was a name that he thought brought distinction, breeding, and upper class attachments. It would give his son an advantage when he entered the world of business and commerce later in his life. William was sure his son would want to follow in his footsteps. He didn't allow nicknames or shortened versions of names, so that the baby had to be called Richardson in his presence. Joey called the baby Ricky, and always would. William would cringe when he heard it. Katherine got into the habit of calling the baby Ricky as well. Her mother and Joey encouraged it. Her mother said to her, "What kind of name is Richardson for a baby?" So, what's in a name; only Richardson would know the suffering of such a name.

Katherine would be with the baby all the time. The baby slept a lot and she would sit in the room with him as he slept in his crib. As she watched and marveled at what she and William had created, her breasts would engorge with milk and the milk would start to flow from her nipples. She would try to let him sleep as long as he could, but when he made a sound or tried to roll over, she would pick him up. She would immediately place him on her nipple. Sometimes he would start sucking and feeding, pushing his gums and mouth around her nipples. Other times he would fall back asleep with her nipple in his mouth. If her nipple would fall out of his mouth, she would place it back in. She would sit like this for hours, with the baby on her nipple and a satisfying smile on her face.

When the baby needed changing, she would do it with pleasure. She liked looking at his little behind and his little penis. He was her little man and always would be. When William was home, she would bring the baby with her to greet him. She initially tried to breastfeed while William was there so that the three of them could be together, but William would leave the room. Eventually, she would breastfeed Richardson in his own room. If the baby needed changing, she would do it. If William found the baby wet or soiled, he would call Katherine. She was the mother.

While her mother and Joey were there the baby slept in William and Katherine's bedroom. This continued for a time after they left. However, as Richardson would wake up late at night or early in the morning, Katherine would get him from his crib and try to breastfeed him. Either the crying or the sounds of sucking would wake William up. He would look over and either find her changing the baby or breastfeeding. Both of these activities made him uncomfortable, he really didn't like babies or children including his own. He persuaded Katherine to have the baby sleep in the next room and for her to go in there to change and feed him. She agreed. As William left early in the morning and returned late at night, he needed whatever little sleep he could get. She didn't want him to hate his son for interfering with his career.

Richardson grew up as his mother's son. In the early years, she would take him with her everywhere she went. She trusted him with no one, including his father. When her mother or Joey came to visit, she would leave him with one of them for only short periods of time. Richardson would always be glad to be with his Uncle Joey though not as much with his grandmother, she was too fussy and strict. Uncle Joey was always fun. They both liked playing with each other. After the first six months or so, William got uncomfortable with his son getting too close to Joey. With Joey's homosexual leanings, he would be a bad influence on his son. It would be better to cut it off now than to have a larger problem later. He asked Katherine to discourage Joey from visiting. She thought it was just William's male jealousy, so she agreed. He never told her what his reason was and she never asked.

Richardson's earliest memories were being with his mother and Uncle
Joey. In his mind, this was his earliest family unit. William became the man
who forbade or stopped him from doing things. William wouldn't, and could-
n't, get close to his son. There was no hugging, kissing, or "I love you." He
expected Katherine to raise the son he wanted, someone like him, but he did-
n't see himself having any role in such raising. In his mind he wouldn't have
brought another child into this world. If Katherine wanted children, that was
fine with him as long as it didn't interfere with his work. Work would always
come first; life would be second.

William kept away from his son as much as possible. William designed
his life to have as little contact as possible with his son. When Richardson
wanted to be with his father, William would call for Katherine to come get
him. It wasn't that he wanted to be a bad father; he just believed that if he
tried to be a father that would be worse than not being a father.

Consequently, Richardson spent his first few years primarily with his
mother. There would be infrequent trips to visit his mother's parents and
brothers. He remembered his grandmother as more concerned that he
wouldn't make a mess in her house than about him. His grandfather would
hold him and make baby noises at him and say, "He definitely is Katherine's
son — looks just like her." He would put Richardson down quickly and
Katherine would just as quickly gather him up and rescue him from her
father. Katherine would tell him, "You are whoever you want to be." His
mother's older brothers, Robby and Alley, would try to rough house with him
to make him a real man. When Uncle Joey was there Richardson would go
directly to him and they would play on the floor for hours. His grandfather
and older sons would be relieved and go down to the basement.

The housing division in Columbus, Ohio, that they had moved into was a good
affordable community for middle class young families with small children. When
Katherine first started taking Richardson outside, first in a carriage and then in a
stroller, she would meet other young mothers walking their babies. She became
friendly with a neighbor on the next street over named Carol Cohn, who had a
son a month older than Richardson named Michael, but called Mickey.

Katherine and Carol would walk their babies twice a day and then get
together at one of their houses for coffee and tea while the two sons played
together on the floor. This was Richardson's first real playmate and friend.
Katherine told Carol and Mickey to call Richardson "Ricky." It would make life
much easier for Richardson, and William wouldn't have to know. Katherine
would make sure that Carol and Mickey were gone before William got home as
well as all signs of their visit. William was strict about no dirt around the white
carpets throughout the house. Katherine tried to get her and William together
with the Cohns, Carol and her husband Mort, who worked in his family's delicatessen, but William balked. William said that he was busy with work and
besides what would he have to talk about with a delicatessen owner. Katherine
knew better than to push it or try to find out what William's real reason was.

When Richardson was three, Katherine and Carol joined a neighborhood playgroup with other mothers with children the same age. This allowed both of them some free time. Sometimes Carol would take care of Richardson so Katherine could do things on her own, and sometimes Katherine would take care of Mickey. They were becoming good friends. Katherine liked Carol and would like to have the families grow closer, but William still wasn't interested. He was civil to Carol, but didn't encourage a relationship. She reminded him too much of Rebecca and he kept his distance. William didn't like to be reminded of the past. His real life had begun when he started work at Apex— so be it.

The following year, Carol was sending Mickey to a pre-school. She wanted Katherine to send Ricky as well. The two boys could stay friends and they could carpool and get together while the kids were at school. Katherine was excited at the prospect. Carol had given her the school's brochure to share with William. When Katherine presented the prospect to William, he was all for it. Education was important and you couldn't start too young. However, when he read the brochure, he wasn't so sure that this would be the best school for his son. At the end of the brochure was a statement that the school was housed at a Jewish temple but was not affiliated. Something about this statement made him uncomfortable.

He told her he would think about it. The next day he asked a number of managers at the Apex plant what was considered the best pre-school in the area. The consistent answer was "The Learning Center," a completely unaffiliated pre-school. Somehow this made him feel more comfortable. He talked to the people at the school and was assured that Richardson would learn rather than play and that the school prepared children to excel academically once they reached regular school. He stopped on his way home for a brochure and to see the school. He signed Richardson up tentatively, pending Katherine's approval. Katherine knew this was important to William so she reluctantly agreed. She would miss Carol and Mickey. The Learning Center was another eight miles further away, but Katherine would do it.

Richardson from birth was a tall thin child. He had been well nurtured as a baby through Katherine's breast feeding and ate well as a toddler. She tried to feed him the right nutritious foods, but he didn't seem to gain weight or get much heavier. He was destined to be tall and thin like Katherine, with the same type of long face. Katherine had always been overprotective due to his frail physical condition and sensitive nature. William was also concerned about him hurting himself, as he wasn't built for endurance in the real world. Physical activities were de-emphasized and academic endeavors were encouraged. The Learning Center would be perfect for him. William was already programming his career in business and upper middle class society. Richardson could play later; now he would learn.

Richardson, just like his mother, took to books and learning easily. Even at four years old he was learning to read, write, and solve math problems. William was proud of his son; he was going to be just like him. Katherine was concerned he was going to be just like her, too many books and not enough fun. She wanted her son to have a more normal childhood, maybe even to enjoy it. She would have to accomplish this in spite of William.

Katherine didn't object to Richardson's learning, but she felt that he needed more in his life. In spite of what she knew would be William's objections, she continued to have him play with Mickey and the other kids in the neighborhood after pre-school. Some of the other kids went to different pre-schools, some with Mickey, or none at all, but none of them went to The Learning Center. It was more expensive than the others and quite a distance away. Richardson was already becoming exclusive. William liked that, Katherine wasn't so sure.

Richardson excelled academically at The Learning Center and with that accrued popularity at school. While this was good for him, he really craved popularity with the neighborhood kids. This didn't come easy, as popularity in this group was based more on physical capabilities such as ball playing, swinging, running, skipping, and so on. He wasn't very good at these things and always stayed on the periphery. Mickey was good at these things, a natural athlete, and made sure that Ricky was included. Mickey and Ricky would remain friends, Ricky the student and Mickey the athlete, and they would help each other.

The following year Richardson was to start regular school. The public school that the children living in their area went to was only two years old. It was in a suburban school district that was considered the best in the Columbus area. Katherine thought it would be best for Richardson both academically and socially. William was looking into private schools that would ensure his son a spot in one of the best high school prep schools. He had Richardson graduating from Roget just like him, except he would be accepted legitimately, even before he finished pre-school. He found a private school, Edgemoor Academy, which boasted of many graduates who had gone on to impressive careers. Once again, William prevailed. Richardson, with his sensitive nature, would be much more comfortable in an academically oriented private school; kids in public school could be so cruel.

Richardson became even more alienated from the neighborhood children. He stayed friends with Mickey as Katherine and Carol stayed friends, but it wasn't the same as going to the same school. He was an outsider to the other kids, the rich private school kid. Mickey would try to protect him, but the other kids moved away from him. They started to call him names such as Sticks, Pole, Slats, Mantis, and yes, Hoss. Katherine heard her son being called such names and she felt for him, it was her childhood all over again.

Richardson would be the only kid in their development picked up by his private school bus. Some of the other kids, particularly the older kids, would taunt him as he got on the bus. Slowly, he made friends with some of the other kids at his school. They were more like him. Sometimes he would go home with them and sometimes they would come back with him. Katherine would try to make them comfortable. Many of the kids at Edgemoor came from the wealthiest and oldest families in Columbus. It made William beam when he heard the names of these children. Richardson tended to go to the other kids' homes, as they were much larger and richer. He was becoming ashamed of his own house and his mother who did everything. Most of the other kids had maids, butlers, and chauffeurs.

When Richardson was two years old, his brother Jameson was born in August 1965. At first Richardson was displaced as his mother's center of attention. When Jameson was born, his grandmother and Uncle Joey came to stay with his mother. While Uncle Joey paid attention to him, most of his time was spent with the new baby and his mother. Joey again assumed the role of mother's helper and assistant nurse maid while Anne took care of Richardson, as she wasn't really good with babies. Richardson found his grandmother too strict and started to resent the new baby. It seemed that his mother was always feeding the baby and he couldn't come into the room, even though Uncle Joey stayed there with her.

Soon, however, Katherine would take the two of them, Richardson and Jameson, with her when she went out. As they were fairly close in age, she really had two babies for a while. She would encourage Richardson to teach his brother things that he had learned. He enjoyed the role of big brother. It made him feel important in the family. He spent more time with his baby brother than his father did, but he didn't mind this. He would be Jameson's father.

When Richardson started school, he had to leave Jameson home alone. Jameson would wait by the window looking for Richardson's bus to bring him home from school. When he saw the bus, he would yell to Katherine, "Wicky, Wicky." When Richardson didn't go to school, go to friends' houses, or have someone over to his house, he would play with Jameson. He would try to teach Jameson to read, write, and do math problems. At the time, Jameson was going to The Learning Center pre-school. Two years later, Jameson started Edgemoor Academy and they would ride the bus together. Eventually, Jameson moved away from Richardson and made his own friends. Jameson was a stocky, bulky kid, much like William. He never took to academics the way that Richardson had; he was much more physical and athletic. Where Richardson would get together with friends to study or play intellectual games such as chess and bridge, Jameson would be outside playing. In time, while Richardson still remained the older brother, it was Jameson who protected him.

When Richardson was eight years old and in third grade, other kids started to tease him. At first it was about his mother driving and picking him up in a station wagon. Then they started to call him not so endearing nicknames, such as Rails, Lurch, Skeleton, Bones and, of course, Hoss. Richardson retreated with a few friends who also were the butt of the other kids' jibes. They formed an exclusive academic circle. He didn't particularly care for these kids, but they were the ones he was left with. He preferred to come home alone and read books and do homework by himself in his room.

Katherine insisted that he go to other kids' houses and that they come to their house. They stayed inside and read or played games. William was pleased and Katherine was quite concerned. They did nothing about it.

When Richardson was four years old, his sister Elizabeth was born in May 1967. He paid little attention to her, as did Jameson. His mother spent most of her time with Elizabeth. This was fine with Richardson, as the other kids had started to call him "mommy's boy." It was time for him to break free from his mother and vice versa. He welcomed the freedom to stay in his room and read. When his parents built the addition to the house, Richardson was given his own bedroom instead of sharing with Jameson, and this became his own private fort. From that time on, Richardson saw himself as on his own and alone.

Richardson was still friendly with Mickey as Katherine and Carol had stayed friendly. When Katherine and Carol would go out and take the two of them with them, Richardson and Mickey would be forced to play together. Mickey was an outside kid, Richardson was an inside kid. Richardson tried to go along with Mickey, as the other way wouldn't work. When Richardson was four, Mickey had got Richardson to ride his tricycle. William wouldn't allow Richardson to have one as he saw them as dangerous. Katherine was in Carol's house at the time. Richardson was trying to enjoy riding the tricycle, but it really wasn't happening. He was riding the tricycle along the sidewalk with Mickey running behind him when he started to daydream; he did this a lot. All of a sudden he and the bike fell off the curb. Richardson crashed into the street face first; he was bleeding all over. Mickey ran to the house and got his mother and Katherine. His mother was furious with him and sent him into the house. Katherine grabbed Richardson to her chest and rushed him into her car and to the hospital. He required six stitches over his eye and eight stitches on his knee. Katherine told William it was an accident at school; that he understood.

When Richardson was eight years old, the other kids started to ride small, two-wheel bikes. He wanted a bike of his own. This was the first thing in his life that he really wanted. With a bike he could get away by himself whenever he wanted. But, he couldn't ask his father. He tried to talk to his mother. She said she would talk to his father, but never did, as she knew what the answer would be. So he started riding on the handlebars of some of his friends' bikes and never told his parents. Sometimes Mickey would come over on his two-wheeler and offer him a ride to the store. Richardson always had money in his pocket; his father wouldn't let him go out without any. He would buy them sodas and sometimes cookies or cake. Katherine would see them ride off together, Mickey pedaling and Richardson sitting on the handlebars. She never said anything to Richardson or to William. She felt sorry for her son. She would get him a bike if she could.

Near the end of the third grade, Richardson was told that they would have to move to Connecticut for his father's work. He didn't love his life in

Columbus, but he resented his father always telling him what to do and expecting him to be obedient. By refusing to move and not talking to his father, he finally had a way of getting back. The truth, though, was that he was really looking forward to moving. He had no real friends at school, none that couldn't be replaced, and no real friends, other than Mickey, in the neighborhood. He could start over in Connecticut. He fantasized about how things would be so much better in their new home.

When they moved to the Connecticut in June 1972, Richardson had just turned nine years old. When he had gone to visit his father with his family to see the new house, it was all he could do to hide his excitement. The house was even bigger than those of his classmates at Edgemoor. He wouldn't have to feel poor anymore. He would have his own bedroom, larger than his parents' in Columbus, and share a den with Jameson. The next house seemed to be miles away from other houses, so there would be no pressure to have friends in the neighborhood. He would be able to be whoever he wanted to be.

The summer of 1972 was one of the best summers Richardson ever had. He was free to stay in his room and do whatever he wanted to do. His mother would sometimes take him, and Jameson and Elizabeth, to the country club with Mrs. Fogerty. He liked Mrs. Fogerty. She was funny and beautiful. He thought he would marry her when he got older.

Katherine had all the kids take swimming lessons. Richardson actually was a good natural swimmer, like his mother. He finally had something physical that he could do well and better than Jameson. Katherine would try to take him as often as she could to the club to swim. Richardson looked forward to it. Katherine was grateful that she had found something to get him out of his room. Sometimes, when Katherine couldn't take him, Mrs. Fogerty would. He liked being alone with Mrs. Fogerty. He fantasized about her. She would take him to lunch after his swimming lessons and he could order anything he wanted. This was his first "date." He hated it when his mother showed up to take him home.

This was the first summer that he didn't want to end. Since he started school, he couldn't wait for summer to end and for school to start. Summer had become an issue for him as to what to do. This summer was different. It could go on forever. William had researched private schools for the three kids, as Elizabeth would start first grade early. He wanted an all male school for Richardson and Jameson and an all female school for Elizabeth. He thought that would be best for their careers. He found an excellent boys school, Episcopal House, that almost guaranteed each student getting into the prep school of their choice. His boys would get the best education possible. He could already see them in Harvard or Yale or maybe even Roget. The school also had an athletic program so that Jameson could engage in non-contact sports and a swimming pool for Richardson to practice his swimming.

There was a sister school for the girls, Episcopal Gardens, which would be ideal for Elizabeth. They stressed the humanities, philosophy and literature, which would start to prepare Elizabeth for the right husband.

Richardson was apprehensive about starting a new school. However, from his first day at Episcopal House, he was happy. Most of the kids came from rich families, but they were less socially adept. The personal kidding stopped. He was actually looked up to by his peer group. The fact that he excelled at something physical such as swimming, a good preppy sport, also increased his stature. His only weak spot was that his father was only a plant manager, which was considered a laborer's job by his rich friends' fathers, while his classmates' fathers were presidents and vice presidents of large organizations. Sometimes he would get kidded about this, but nothing as cruel as the kids in Columbus.

Richardson was always at the top of his class; William would have it no other way. The school bus would pick the three kids up at their driveway and return them there after school. This made the kids independent in their schedules. If any of them wanted to stay after school for any reason, such as swimming, a club, using the library, meeting with a teacher or friend, and so on, the bus would bring them home later. This gave Katherine the day to herself. It didn't matter at this point how close their neighbors were. It was a good situation for all of them, including William. But, were they really happy?

The Episcopal House covered grades first through ninth. When Richardson was thirteen and in the eighth grade, his father was promoted to executive vice president of operations for Apex Industries. They were told about it at the country club by their parents. Richardson had never been so excited. There was now nothing that made him different from his classmates. His father now had a prestigious job. Many of his classmates' parents belonged to the same country club. He knew the news of his father's promotion would be spread around the school before he arrived the following morning. He was proud of his father; for once he finally did something right.

Richardson was a member of the school varsity swimming team. Usually, eighth graders could only be members of the junior varsity; however, Richardson was good enough to swim with the varsity. While he was still tall and thin, swimming had filled out his upper body and legs. He almost looked as good as his mother in his swimming team swimsuit. He was more on the people side like his mother and had many friends at school. His skills in academics and swimming were a perfect match for this school. In the ninth grade, he was elected captain of the swimming team. While this wasn't a high visibility sport for most schools, it was for schools like Episcopal House and the private prep high schools. In the ninth grade, the boys also started to go to dances with sister private schools. Richardson was able to get along fine now with his male classmates, but he had little experience with girls other than his mother and his sister and Mrs. Fogerty. Being one of the best scholars, captain of the swim team, and fairly popular helped some. The first dance of the year in September was at the Walford School for Girls. The school bus took the ninth grade boys to the dance and would return them to their school.

They were chaperoned by Mr. Harrison, who was there looking for female teachers, not much of a chaperone.

Richardson entered with his friends into the Walford school gym where the dance was being held. This was 1977 and the heart of the sexual revolution. Some of his friends bragged about their sexual conquests, but he didn't believe them. The guys who he might believe didn't brag. His group of six found a corner to stand in. While they all had had dance lessons at school (it was compulsory), none of them had really danced with a real girl.

Richardson looked at the Walford girls. They were a strange group. They tried dressing in mini skirts, high heels, and tight or low cut tops, as much as well-bred girls could get away with. He found them unappetizing, nothing like his mother or Mrs. Fogerty. He noticed one girl who attracted him. She was on the tall side with long blond hair. She was wearing the shortest of mini skirts and the highest of heels. Her face was made-up, like an adult's. She wore a low cut top, which showed off a pair of breasts that were larger than his mother's. As he stared at her, she started to walk towards him. She walked just like his mother used to walk back in Columbus. He looked away. The girl came up to him. He didn't know what to say as he had never been in this position before. She, however, knew exactly what to say; she had been in this position many times before.

"Hi. My name's Melissa Chance. You can call me Missy." She put her hand out for him to take. He shook it loosely. He said nothing. "Would you like to dance?" She led him out to the dance floor. He couldn't resist. They were playing a slow tune. "Great," thought Richardson, "I can't embarrass myself too much." Missy pulled him close to her. He tried to pull away and get in the proper dance position that he had been taught, but Missy kept him close. He saw his friends watching him, so he tried to be cool. She pushed her chest against him. He had never been this close to tits before. The guys talked about tits, but he didn't know anyone of his friends who had ever touched strange tits. Maybe he would get lucky.

When the dance ended, he tried to get away from her and return to his friends. He had enough to brag about for one night. Missy went with him. She introduced herself to his friends. They all blushed, particularly when she bent over to fix the bottom of her skirt and her breasts heaved out of her top. The next dance started, a fast rock number, and she pulled Richardson back on the dance floor. He tried his best, but he still felt foolish. It didn't matter, as all of the boys and most of the girls were watching Missy. When she danced her entire body talked.

When the dance was over, he started to return to his friends, but Missy took him by the hand and led him out of the gym and into a small room down the hall. As soon as they were in the room, she grabbed him and started kissing him. She had her tongue in his mouth and was moving it around. He was choking. He had never kissed a girl before. He found it anything but pleasant. While she kissed him, she took his hand and placed it on her breast inside her top. He grabbed at it, he didn't know what else to do. He found it anything but pleasant. She pulled back abruptly and her breast came out of her top. He looked at it with disgust. He touched it like he thought he was supposed to. She took his other hand and placed it on her other breast, it sprang out into his hand. He pulled away.

"What's the matter? Don't you like me?"

"No, it's not that."

"You have a girl friend?"

"No, it's not that."

"Then come closer." She pulled him back closer. She fumbled at his fly, but expertly unzipped it and grabbed his penis. Before he could stop it, she had his penis out and in her hands. She pulled her mini skirt up and took his hand and placed it under her underpants. He could feel the wet hairs; he was getting sick. She forced him to pull her panties down and moved her vagina against his penis. While she tried to insert his penis, he came all over her pubic hair, panties, and skirt. She wiped him off on her vagina. He gagged.

"I'm sorry," he said.

"It's okay, there will be other times."

He hoped not.

He went back to the dance, leaving Missy to clean herself up. He didn't see her the rest of the night. Other girls, less scary, seemed interested in dancing with him, but he had lost all interest. On the bus ride back to school, one of his best friends, Skip Walton, told him that he had found out that Missy was the class whore. She screwed every boy she could, including, it was rumored, some of the male teachers. She always had her pick; tonight it was Richardson. He hoped she didn't get pregnant. Luckily she didn't know who he was. She was also the daughter of Charles Chance, one of the vice presidents at Apex reporting to his father. She knew exactly who he was.

As the word spread on the bus about Richardson's exploits screwing Missy, his fame spread. Guys he knew, and didn't know, kept coming over to him and patting him on the back. They gave him names like Long Shot, Mr. Cool, the Seducer, Big Blade and so on. This was to be his shining hour. He didn't know if Missy picked him because of his appearance, his status as captain of the swimming team, or the fact that he was William S. Bradford III's son, who was her father's boss. It didn't really matter; he was basking in the limelight for the first time in his life and he liked it. What he had done with Missy was disgusting to him, but he didn't say anything to the guys, not even to Skip.

The next morning he thought he was going to school a hero, but when he entered the school and walked down the hall the cheers had turned to jeers. The other guys were laughing at him and calling him uncomplimentary names such as Quickshot, Preemie, Hotdick, and, sarcastically, Stud. He didn't know what had happened since the night before. Skip caught up to him and told him that Missy was spreading the story that Ricky Bradford couldn't get it in; he shot too fast. She had proudly shown her skirt to the other girls at school with Ricky's tracks on it. It was apparently her intent to embarrass him as William embarrassed her father. He was devastated. His only real contact with a female had been with his mother. Now, he was even ashamed to face his mother. The teasing by the other guys continued on; there was no honor among adolescents.

He withdrew from his friends and the other guys at school. At swimming practice, the other members of the team would wait for him to undress or dress and then poke fun at his penis calling it Quick Draw, Poor Shot, Leaky Hose and so on. Sometimes they would hide his clothes so that he had to run around naked looking for them. While he looked for his clothes, the other guys would point at his penis and laugh at him. Richardson wasn't very physical and abhorred violence and physical contact, so rather than fight he merely withdrew more.

He survived the swimming season by keeping to himself in school, at swim practices, and at swimming meets. He remained captain in name only. He would go to school, come home right after school, stay in his room reading, come down for dinner, and then go back to his room to read. He shunned all social activities, particularly those where girls were involved. He had always been a thin, gawky kid. Now, this became even more pronounced. He started to eat candy bars in his room so that he didn't have to face anyone. His complexion started to pale and the little bit of acne had intensified. As he withdrew, he was becoming less desirable to the others. His friend Skip tried to stay his friend, but Richardson pushed him away until he stopped trying. He had always been close with Jameson, assuming the role of big older brother, but now he ignored Jameson and left him on his own.

Katherine was getting very concerned about her son. They had always been close, and he would always be her favorite child. Now he shunned her and pulled away every time she got close. She expressed her concern to William. He told her that he was the same way when he was Richardson's age and look how he turned out. Richardson would turn out all right too.

Richardson was expected to continue with the Episcopal School into high school. However, when the time came, he refused to apply. He agreed to attend any other private high school but Episcopal. William and Katherine finally settled on Hawthorne Academy, a well respected academic boys' high school where all of their graduates were accepted to Ivy League colleges. This was fine with William and Katherine and with Richardson. He didn't know anyone who went there, and he didn't have a great need to know them. High school would only be a means for getting out of there.

In high school, Richardson found a group of similarly minded non-social boys as school friends. They might get together to go to the library or study together, but had little contact outside of school. This was fine with Richardson and it was safe. He gave up competitive swimming; the fun had left it. When he wasn't at school, he would stay in his room and read. Where he once looked healthy and virile in his swimming days, he now looked sallow and sickly. Hawthorne Academy prided themselves on developing well-rounded young men of the upper middle and affluent classes. They stressed socialization as well as academics. In their minds, they thought they were preparing young men for what they would face in the real world of privilege and upper class entitlement.

As part of the school's social program, they required each student to learn social dancing and graces with the opposite sex. To practice such social graces, the school had a series of weekend dances, some at the school, others at nearby girls' private schools. It was expected that each student attend these dances, either with a date or without. Richardson was uncomfortable with girls, particularly in 1977–78 when some of the girls were taking the lead in the sexual dance, after his experience with Missy Chance. He could go without a date and face his vulnerability to female persuasions or find a safe date for himself where the other girls would leave him alone and the other guys would leave his date alone.

There was a girl at the country club named Penelope Prentiss. The other kids preferred calling her Penny; she preferred Penelope. She had had her eyes on Richardson since they first joined the club five years ago. She had invited Richardson to a number of parties and social functions, but he had always refused.

She was extremely skinny, gawky, long faced and wore eyeglasses. Richardson found her unattractive and a pest. Now, however, he saw her as attractive as a date for the required school dances. He would be safe from other girls and needn't worry about the other boys trying to steal his date. Katherine liked Penelope and her family, but she was concerned about Richardson's choice. Penelope closely resembled what she looked like at that age.

He went through high school in this manner. He would go to school, come home and read, and date Penelope. There was nothing really happening anywhere. He had other boys call him to go over homework or talk about school projects, but he never socialized with any of them. William took pride that Richardson was turning out more like him than Katherine. He had always been Katherine's son and favorite. He would turn out all right, William was sure of that.

Richardson got mostly A's at Hawthorne Academy. William was expecting that he would follow in his footsteps and attend Roget Institute. Richardson, however, would arrive in a Mercedes, not on foot as he had. When the time came to apply for colleges, William applied to Roget for his son. As the son of a graduate, and with Richardson's academic record, he was readily accepted. William was pleased; Richardson was not. William wanted him to study business economics just like him. There would be a position at Apex ready for him. Richardson wanted to study literature and philosophy just like his mother. He had applied to colleges on his own and had been accepted at Princeton, Yale, and Columbia.

William tried to argue with him, but he got nowhere. Richardson wasn't worried about a job or making money. He had always been taken care of by his parents and had never really wanted for anything and assumed that would continue. He neither knew, nor cared, how one made money or how much was needed to live in the manner that they lived. Katherine had protected him from all that. She gave the impression that you just lived. He had no idea what his father had to do to make the money. He had very little contact with his father. He knew that he didn't want his father's life; he wanted his mother's. It was his mother who continually told him "be whatever you want." This is what he wanted. Nothing, not even his father's pressure, would change his mind.

William pressured him to at least visit Roget before he made up his mind. The entire family went to Boston one weekend. William hoped that by making it kind of a vacation, Richardson might be more impressed with Roget and the Boston area. He had set up for Richardson to spend all day Friday meeting with the President, the admissions people, a number of the faculty, and some of the students. He had tried to contact Ruth Selzer at both the office and at home, but she never returned his calls. Richardson was impressed with the people he met and the campus, but it made no difference as he had little interest in business and economics; he had seen what it had done to his father.

Katherine took the family on a tour of Boston, visiting some of her old haunts. Richardson appreciated his mother's attention. He agreed to reconsider Roget. William tried to talk to him about the world of business, what it was he did, and how Roget could help him in a business career. It only reinforced Richardson's decision about having no interest in business; it bored him. He had no interest in being like his father.

William had little commitment to take Richardson to visit Princeton, Yale, and Columbia, so Katherine offered to take him. William didn't object, but he made it plain that he would rather she didn't. This time Katherine stood firm. It was her eldest son's life and he should make the decision. On each visit, Richardson and Katherine talked about life, philosophy, and the world of literature. Richardson was excited. It was like old times with just him and his mother.

On their visit to Columbia in New York, Uncle Joey joined them. Joey took them out to dinner at a fancy New York restaurant and then to a Broadway show. They stayed overnight at Uncle Joey's apartment in the Village. Richardson wanted to be part of Joey's world. He told his mother on the way back home that he wanted to go to Columbia. He loved the school and he would be near Uncle Joey. Katherine nodded her head. She was proud of him for doing what he wanted to do. She was convinced it was the right thing for him to do. But, would William be?

With Katherine's support, he accepted admittance to Columbia. He told his mother. He expected her to tell his father; that was how these things worked in their family. He couldn't confront his father; he never had. Katherine talked to William about Richardson's decision. William at first said absolutely not, then said all right if that was the way it had to be, but he wouldn't pay for it. Katherine said she would. He then said of course he would pay for his son's college, but he would be no part of it. He then asked Katherine all about the program. He wasn't happy about Richardson's decision, but he was his son. He secretly wished that he had been able to do the same thing at Richardson's age, but he told nobody this.

Richardson started Columbia in the fall. Uncle Joey had gotten him an apartment near the campus. Joey knew the landlord and it cost less than student housing, and it was better. Richardson loved the school, the classes, the students, and New York. It was a new start for him. He quickly fell into a group of students and they became friends. They would go into Manhattan on the week ends, visit the main library, museums, walk through Central Park and so on. He would also visit Uncle Joey, alone or with friends, at his large apartment in the Village. He loved Uncle Joey, his partner Steven, and his lifestyle. He had finally found his life.

William rarely visited Richardson at school, even when his business took him to New York. He would meet him downtown sometimes at a restaurant for lunch or dinner. He would not talk about his business and Richardson would not talk about college. They had little else to say to one another. It was awkward for both of them. Their contacts became less and less frequent. Katherine would visit New York at least twice a week to see Richardson, Patricia, Joey and others. Richardson had more private time with his mother than when he was young. The more contact they had together, the closer they became. Patricia warned Katherine that Richardson was getting too attached to her. He would never find a woman for his own.

In fact, he had started to go to parties with his new friends, but was still resistant to getting close to a girl. When he had left for college, he had left Penelope as she had served her purpose. A number of girls were interested in him. He had filled out since he started college and had become more attractive in face and body. He had also started to swim again, not competitively but for conditioning. He was also running in the mornings with a group of fellow students. His enhanced appearance, together with his intelligence, made him quite attractive to the college girls.

He was attending a party at the off-campus apartment of one of his friends, Joel Bradshaw. Usually, he would sit with a group at these parties talking philosophy: what is truth, what is the meaning of life and so on. Others would drink, smoke pot, do drugs, or use one of the rooms for sex—sometimes they would have sex in the same room. He was sitting with a group in a large circle in Joel's living room. He was mostly listening as he usually did. He would speak every once in a while so that the group didn't totally ignore him. Sometimes he would be asked for his opinion, but mainly he stayed silent. While he listened, he would peruse the living room, watching other couples kiss, hold hands, make out, and go upstairs together. He would have liked to change places with the males, but he couldn't. While he was listening, he was looking to one side of the room at an attractive female and her not so attractive date thinking to himself, "If he can do it, why can't I? What's the matter with me?"

At that moment, he happened to turn his head and looked up to find an extremely attractive girl staring at him. She was tall and thin, with long black hair cascading down her back, just barely touching the top of her ass. She was absolutely exotic. She was dressed in a tight leather mini skirt, with a tight top, and long tapering high heel boots. She was the kind of girl who immediately intimidated him and rendered him speechless. Something about her, though, was familiar; he felt he already knew her. He looked back at her, and she smiled back at him. He turned to see if there was anyone behind him.

There wasn't, it must be him. She smiled even wider. She was beautiful when she smiled, and she was beautiful when she didn't smile. He could only stare back at her. She stood transfixed in his stare.

He couldn't speak, so he motioned with his head for her to join the group. As she walked, her body moved as if she were making love. He couldn't take his eyes off her. She stood above him with her left leg outstretched so that her mini skirt rode up to her thigh. He looked up into her panties and the outline of her vagina. His mouth fell open; he could only stare. She smiled down at him. She was enjoying herself, even if he was in agony. He motioned for her to sit down by patting the space next to him. She sat down in the circle next to him. There was hardly enough space for her, so she pushed in against him. He felt her breasts heaving against him; she was braless. Her breasts weren't large but they were solid. It didn't change his feelings. He didn't like large breasts; they made him gag. He would rather have a girl with no breasts. He leaned over to her ear and introduced himself. He whispered lowly, "Hi. I'm Ricky Bradford." He waited.

She couldn't stop staring at him. It was scary because she was so close. He coughed.

"Oh," she said, "I'm Sarah Kline." She looked down at her legs where her mini skirt had pulled up to reveal the tops of her thighs. She tugged on her skirt to pull it down, but she was sitting on it, the hell with it. Richard, the boy across from her, was staring at her exposed panties, the hell with him and the others.

The group continued the discussion. She nodded affirmatively at every-thing Richardson said. Her head bobbed up and down as he talked. She never took her eyes off of him. He was aware of this and talked more. Only Richardson and Sarah remained as the time got late and the group broke up. She got up to leave, but he didn't want her to. He got up with her. He called after her. "Sarah!"

She turned around. She smiled, but said nothing.

He could think of nothing to say. He stood looking at her.

She held out her hand. He took it. "Let's get some coffee," she said as she walked off with him. He followed. He said nothing.

When they were settled across from each other in a small booth for two, they just sat and looked at each other. He kept nodding his head as if to say, "I know you, don't I?"

Sarah finally spoke. "How come I haven't seen you in school before?"

"I don't know. I've been there. What's your major?" He continued to stare.

"Philosophy, and yours?"

"Philosophy," he said. They both laughed.

"Do you go to many of Joel's parties?" he asked.

"This is my first one. Usually our kind isn't invited to these parties."

"And what kind is that?" he asked.

"Jewish," she said. She added, "We have our own parties."

"I see." He really didn't. "So how come you were here tonight?"

"Joel wanted me to meet someone."

"So, did you?" Richardson thought it was he.

"Sure, but it didn't work out. He just wanted to go upstairs. He thought he was cool staring at my tits, like that would turn me on, and make me want to run upstairs with him. When I walked away, I could feel him staring at my ass. His loss. He was a creep."

"But you stayed anyway?"

"I was leaving when I saw you talking with the group. It looked interesting."

"So you stayed. Why?"

She hesitated. "I've never seen anyone like you. Something stopped me. I couldn't move. I don't know what I would have done if you had let me go." She squeezed his hand.

"I almost did. I'm not very good with girls."

"I know. Joel warned me."

"Oh, he did, did he? I need more friends like Joel."

The waiter came over to tell them they were closing. If they wanted anything they would have to order now. They looked at each other.

"Do you want anything?" she asked.

"I don't really drink coffee."

"Neither do I."

They left holding hands and walking closely. He walked her home.

"Would you like to come in? I don't have any coffee."

"I don't know. I'm not Jewish, you know."

"I know, but I don't care."

"Maybe next time. I have a mid term on Monday. I better get back."

He walked briskly away. He just wasn't ready. But he still couldn't believe it. Sarah looked exactly like his mother in her Columbus, Ohio, days, including the mini skirt, high heels, and long hair, although dark rather than blonde. He hadn't been this excited since his mother used to dress and walk like that, when he was eight years old. He didn't know what to do. He just wasn't ready. He took the bus to his Uncle Joey's. He would understand.

Jameson

Jameson was born in August 1965, two years and five months after Richardson. By the time he was born, Richardson was already Katherine's little man. There was not much room left in her heart for another son. Richardson had already bonded to her and her brother Joey. When Jameson was born, he wasn't given the attention that Richardson had been given at his birth. While Katherine couldn't wait to breastfeed Richardson, she was in no hurry with Jameson. His feeding time took her from Richardson. Where she went over six months breastfeeding Richardson, she got Jameson onto the bottle in less than three months. From the beginning she was very uncomfortable breastfeeding Jameson; he looked too much like William. Jameson was a chubby baby, eight pounds and twelve ounces at birth, with wisps of brown curly hair and a round face. Where Richardson had been long and thin, Jameson was broad and stocky.

In the two plus years of Richardson's life, his Uncle Joey had bonded with him. When Jameson came along there was no room for another favorite nephew. Richardson always reminded him of Katherine; Jameson reminded him too much of William. He would take care of Jameson when he had to, would bring him to Katherine for feeding, and would watch him in his crib, but he wasn't committed to it. Richardson resented Jameson taking his mother's time and would carry on until she paid attention to him. She would play with him while she breastfed Jameson. William paid no more attention to Jameson than he had to Richardson.

When Jameson was still an infant, Katherine had a mother's helper come in so that she could go out with Richardson, sometimes alone, sometimes with Patricia. The majority of her mothering time was spent with Richardson, as he demanded it. Jameson seemed to accept being alone. When Jameson got into his second year he wanted to come along, but Katherine wasn't ready to drag two kids along so, she continued to use the mother's helper. Jameson would cry and scream and run to his room. He would hide so that the mother's helper couldn't find him. Many times Katherine would just leave him like this.

As Jameson grew up he was always the tag-along to Richardson. Jameson always looked up to his older brother; he was bigger and seemed more important. As a toddler, Jameson wanted to do everything that Richardson did. Katherine couldn't do anything with Richardson without taking Jameson along. Somehow she resented Jameson for this and it pushed her away from him. At an early age he sensed this and became a loner. When Elizabeth was born almost two years later, Katherine's attention was split even further, and Jameson became even more alone.

When Elizabeth was a few months old, Katherine started going out with just Richardson again. She would leave the mother's helper to watch Jameson and Elizabeth. She would tell Jameson, "You are my big man. Stay home and help take care of your sister." Richardson was in pre-school then. Katherine would go out by herself during the day and then when Richardson came home from school the two of them would go out together. Jameson would stand at the window and watch them drive away from the house.

He would stand there crying until he couldn't see the car anymore. The mother's helper would try to soothe him by hugging him or getting him a cookie or some milk. He would pull away and run to his room. When he finally realized that it was easier to hate than to love, he wreaked his revenge. For instance, he would go to where Elizabeth was playing with the mother's helper and break one of her toys or take her cookie. Elizabeth would cry; he would hate her too. He then would go into the kitchen and throw his glass of milk in the air and watch it break all over the floor. He would smile at the mother's helper and go back to his room. The more he hated them, the more they hated him. He was happier.

Jameson was always a physically healthy child, naturally stocky and rosy. While Richardson preferred playing inside, Jameson was an outside child and very physically active. When Katherine took the two or three of them to the community playground, Richardson would play quietly in the sandbox while Jameson would play around the swings and gym equipment. Katherine would spend her time chasing after Jameson while Richardson played quietly.

Jameson would follow Richardson around wanting him to play with him. Richardson seldom did. When Richardson first went to pre-school and then elementary school, Jameson and then Elizabeth would be home alone with Katherine. When Richardson was home as well, they would always do things together. Now Katherine would get somebody to come in to watch Jameson and Elizabeth. Jameson would cause problems for the sitter and then for Katherine when she came home. This resulted in Katherine taking him even less. When Richardson came home from school, Katherine would take him out with her.

When Jameson was seven years old and in the third grade, his father was transferred to Stamford, Connecticut. Richardson didn't want to go, so he didn't want to go. He thought it was neat that Richardson wouldn't talk to his father. If the favorite son could get away with it, so could he. It was the first time that they had both been trouble to their parents at the same time. It made Jameson feel close to his older brother again. Jameson had many friends at school and in the neighborhood, but he always felt alone at home. It didn't matter to him where they moved. When they went to visit Stamford and he saw the house they were going to move to, he was ready to move. He could have a room away from everyone else; that was neat.

When they started the Episcopal School in Stamford, Richardson in sixth grade, Jameson in fourth, he would get on the bus with Richardson and want to sit with him and hang out with him at school. Richardson didn't want to have to babysit his younger brother, so he would move away. Jameson would try to tag along and Richardson would reject him. After a while, Jameson made friends, more than Richardson had, with kids in his grade and went his own way. He always considered himself the outsider in the family. As Jameson grew older, he became more robust. He would play sports, roughhouse with the other kids, and stay outside as long as he could. When he was in fifth grade, he was a tough kid. He got into a number of fights and always won them. When he was home, he stayed mostly in his room by himself.

Richardson was now in seventh grade and was easily picked on. One of the seventh grade bullies was harassing him in the schoolyard and enticing him to fight. Richardson would have nothing to do with fighting and violence. He started to walk away, and the bully hit him on the back of the neck. Jameson was in the schoolyard when this happened and jumped the bully. He expected Richardson to help him—after all they were brothers—but he continued to walk away.

Jameson was in up to his armpits and maybe for the first time in danger. The bully started pounding on him, and he started pounding back. The schoolyard had filled with kids, who started cheering for Jameson as the bully wasn't well liked. Jameson had never been encouraged to do anything before, and he stood his ground. He used all his might to punch the bully hard in the stomach and the bully doubled over. The kids cheered for Jameson to hit or kick him in certain places, but he backed off and waited. The bully got up and ran from the schoolyard. The kids cheered and thus began Jameson's reputation. He was never bothered again and neither was Richardson. Richardson never thanked Jameson for rescuing him. He was too ashamed of his fifth grade brother taking care of him.

In the seventh grade when Jameson was allowed to go out for sports, he made the junior varsity football and wrestling teams. In the eighth grade he made the varsity in both sports. Where Richardson was the scholar, Jameson was the athlete. In the ninth grade, he was the starting fullback (used mainly for blocking) and defensive end. By this time, Jameson had filled out into a real bull. He was big chested, muscular, and strong, much stronger than Richardson. In fact he scared Richardson, who stayed away from him, which was all right with Jameson. Jameson worked out every day at the Episcopal School and at night at home. He had a full set of weights and work out equipment in his room. For Katherine and William, it was always easier to give in to him than to fight with him; they, too, were scared of him. When Jameson asked for a two-wheel bike, he was given one. He would ride his bike back and forth to school and his parents didn't worry.

In the summers, Katherine would take the kids to the country club where they could use the swimming pool. By the seventh grade, Jameson was almost fully developed. He had a powerful upper body with a wide chest and muscular biceps. His legs were like steel. When he and Richardson would change in the locker room, Richardson would look away and turn his back on Jameson. Jameson had more pubic hair than Richardson and his penis was wider and longer. Richardson felt ashamed. Richardson would wear swimming trunks that covered his thin legs. Jameson would wear a small bikini which barely covered him. You could see the outline of his genitals; they were impressive for a kid his age. Katherine was embarrassed; Patricia was interested.

Richardson was the swimmer, so Jameson became a diver. He would stand at the edge of the diving board, posing, and flexing his body. When he did this, all of the young girls, and most of the old girls, would stop and lose their breath. As he dove, all female, and some male, eyes would be on him. While Richardson covered himself up in a towel and ran and lay down on a lounger next to his mother, Jameson would lie on the side of the pool still in his swim suit on his back with his genitals sticking up. The young girls would flock to him.

It was in the summer after seventh grade that Jameson first got laid. As he rode his bike in the neighborhood he would pass many large walled in houses such as theirs. At one of these houses, he noticed a well-built, attractive girl from the country club. He had noticed her watching him as he walked around the pool area. She tried not to be obvious, but she was. She wore dark Hollywood type sunglasses, but he could see her eyes looking down at his penis. Her name was Nancy Jones and she was in the tenth grade. When he first rode past her house, there was no sign of life, as it was walled and gated and you could hardly see inside. After a while, however, he noticed her sun bathing by the gate. She didn't look up, but he knew she was waiting and watching. This went on for three weeks.

One day as he rode past her house, she was on the other side of the gate sun bathing in a two piece bikini which left little to the imagination. He was looking for her inside the gate, and when he saw her it was too late and he skidded on the gravel in her driveway. She came swishing over to help him. He had skinned both knees. She offered him first aid in the house. He had never been in a house so huge before. Nancy lived in a wing all by herself. Her parents were traveling in Europe and she was alone with servants. She left him on her more-than-king-sized bed and went into the bathroom to get the first aid kit.

He heard the water running and then she came out with nothing on; she had taken a shower and was shining. Although he and his friends had talked about it enough, he had never seen a naked girl before. He had tried to catch his mother naked, but he never had. He was wearing tight bike shorts and a tee shirt. She looked down at his shorts, his penis had gone up to full size and it was immense for a kid his age, or a kid any age.

She came over and straddled his shorts, with his penis rubbing against her vagina. He didn't know what to do so he lay there and said nothing. She stripped off his shorts and played with his penis. He tried to stop himself from coming, but he couldn't, he came long and plentiful. She watched it spray on his stomach; it was an immense gusher. She was pleased. She rubbed it in and continued stroking his penis. It went up again, as long and as hard as before. She sat on it and it slipped right in.

She went up and down on his penis while he lay there. He tried to hold her by her tits, but she held his arms down. This time he didn't come so quickly. She was moaning, he said nothing. Finally, she lay back exhausted and fell off of him. He still hadn't come the second time. She finished him off with her hand. She got up and went into the bathroom. He could hear the shower running again. He waited but she didn't return. He got up and left— some first aid. He never said anything about this to anybody, and he never saw Nancy again. She had used him, but he didn't care. She had introduced him to the charms of girls. He liked his body being admired and touched.

When he returned to school it was 1978 and he was in eighth grade. His father had just been promoted to executive vice president at Apex. Jameson was proud and excited, as he figured it would help him get more girls. There would also be more money for his father. Although he went to an all boys' school, there were plenty of opportunities to meet girls.

Richardson had started high school at Hawthorne Academy, so Jameson was alone at the Episcopal School. He was also sometimes the fullback for the varsity football team. Over the summer he had grown even more. He was more than an eye full. William thought he looked like him with a similar build.

He started running around with the ninth graders from the football team. They were into partying and running with party girls. In 1978, there were more party girls than good girls. It seemed that the girls liked to screw more than the boys. Some of them would take on more than one guy in a night. He didn't care for that; he preferred a girl of his own. He would single out one girl at each party and go to one of the bedrooms. In the rich houses, there were very rarely any adults at home.

He quickly earned a reputation, and the girls waited to be picked by him. He would never pick an easy girl who pushed herself on him. One Nancy was enough. He tried to be discriminating. There was usually plenty of alcohol and drugs at these parties. He would drink some beer, but that was all. He was an athlete and had to protect his body. He was the first Bradford male to use alcohol. He was the first Bradford male to get laid and like it, but he wasn't sure why. In the ninth grade, when he was the starting fullback, the girls threw themselves at him. He was getting tired of girls. Many times on the weekend he chose to spend a night with the guys just bullshitting and carrying on. When he wanted to get laid, it was always available. He had become a legend like his father, but for different reasons.

Richardson had already withdrawn into his room and Jameson was always out. William and Katherine hoped that Richardson would go out once in a while, and they hoped that Jameson would stay home once in a while. Richardson was getting excellent grades, but not much else. Jameson was getting excellently laid, but not very good grades.

Jameson started hanging out with some of the high school kids, some who were old enough to drive. He was bigger and stronger than most of them. He never used his strength to take advantage of anyone; his size alone commanded respect. He had never had to get into another fight since fifth grade, as there was nobody who would challenge him. He was someone on the outside. He was no one at home. He was used to being alone at home and he didn't care. His parents gave him everything he wanted. What else did he need them for?

Jameson went on to high school at the Episcopal School. This was the final separation between him and Richardson and from here on in they went their separate ways. In high school, Jameson started to drift. He still played football and wrestled, but it didn't excite him any more. He would still party on the weekends, but he was tired of the same routine. He would drink and screw with girls, a different one each time, but he wasn't enjoying it. He had burned out at sixteen. There wasn't much for him to look forward to—how sad.

When he was sixteen, he was eligible to get his driver's license. Unlike Richardson, who had no reason to get his license and waited until he was graduating from high school, he passed his driver's test on the day of his sixteenth birthday. He knew neither of his parents would take him for the test, so he didn't ask them, and went with a friend. He had learned to take care of himself; he had learned to parent himself.

William, with a large Mercedes sedan, or Katherine, with a Mercedes convertible, didn't want him driving their cars. He knew to never ask them. He bought a used MG convertible like the one William remembered from his first trip to Roget. His parents never asked how he bought it. They didn't want to know.

He was out of the house even more now, every night of the week and most of the weekend. He came home to sleep and clean up. Katherine was surprised whenever he showed up for dinner. He was always polite to his parents but difficult to deal with. It was easier to let him have his own way. He was getting acceptable grades in school, B's and C's, and they just cared that he could get into college.

He would drive around in his MG and would show up at the country club with a different girl each time, most of them club members and from wealthy families. He loved to screw the rich girls; it gave him the most pleasure. It was like getting back at his parents, it felt good. They always looked pleased when he was with a girl from a good, rich family. Each time they hoped that he would settle with that girl. If only his parents knew what these girls were doing, they would be sick—it made him sick.

Jameson stopped playing football and wrestling in the eleventh grade; he had tired of them both. William had hoped that he might continue and earn an athletic scholarship to an Ivy League school, as he wouldn't get in otherwise, certainly not on his grades. He spent his senior year as a playboy, mainly taking out girls much older than he was. He had tired of the high school games. By the end of high school, he had laid many girls, but hadn't had a relationship with any of them. He really didn't like girls, but there was something that drew him to physically controlling them. He couldn't stop, but he didn't want to continue.

William thought about applying to Roget Institute on Jameson's behalf. With his clout as a distinguished alumnus and a member of a number of alumni committees, William knew that he could get him accepted at full tuition, but he knew that Jameson wouldn't want to go there. Even if he did, he wouldn't last the first year. It hurt William that there would be no sons to follow his path.

With Richardson he was really hurt, but with Jameson somehow he just didn't care, as he was too difficult. William had Jameson accepted to Roget anyway on the off chance that he might go. At the least, it might encourage him to take some action himself. As far as William, and Katherine, knew, Jameson hadn't even thought about what he would do after high school.

When William brought the Roget acceptance letter to Jameson, he was floored. It wasn't that he would even think about going to Roget; he hated the rich fat business types and their daughters from the club (screw them both) but he didn't think his father cared enough about him to be concerned. It was apparent that his going to Roget was important to his father. He would have preferred Richardson, but he'd take him.

He remembered the fights with Richardson about not going to Roget and now it was his turn. He didn't want to viciously hurt his parents, but he didn't know what else he could do. They had worked a system of living together in peaceful co-existence and his parents had allowed him to live a rich adolescent life style. But, he didn't want to get stuck going to a college he didn't want to, or to have a life he didn't want. He had seen his father do this and it wasn't pleasant.

Jameson took the acceptance letter from his father without a word. William could see that he was moved by his gesture. He sulked about his dilemma for over a week. To hurt his father or to hurt himself, that was the question.

Jameson had always been a fairly good artist since he was a small child; however, he kept it to himself. His parents, his teachers and nobody else encouraged him to pursue his art. When he started to grow and get bigger, he was ashamed of his art talent. He would sometimes sketch the more attractive girls he went out with, sometimes in not so favorable positions, and kept a sketchbook under his bed. He had accumulated quite a portfolio. He hadn't shown his sketches to anyone up to now.

Recently he took it into New York and showed it to his Uncle Joey. As Jameson had matured, he had become better friends with Joey. Sometimes he would take a girl with him to Joey's and sometimes he would stay over with him. Joey was quite excited with Jameson's sketches and found them really exceptional. Joey, as an architect, wished that he could draw like that when he was Jameson's age. It certainly would have made his college days much easier.

He asked Uncle Joey about architecture. It was possibly the first time in a long time that he had shown concern for anyone other than himself. As Uncle Joey explained architecture and showed him some of his projects and sketches, Jameson became fascinated. This was what he wanted to do. Uncle Joey promised to try to get him into his college of architecture. Joey was successful in getting him accepted on scholastic probation. Uncle Joey promised to work with him. They would get through it together.

He wanted to go to the college of architecture in New York. He could taste it. He tried to talk to his father, but the words wouldn't come out. He knew his father's heart had been broken when Richardson refused Roget. He didn't know if he could do it to him again. William had never been there as a father, but he had little else in his life since Raymond died. Jameson knew how important it was to his father to have one of his sons at Roget. He stalled and hedged each time his father asked him. But, the deadline for acceptance was getting close.

Jameson had never been close to his mother. He had always felt abandoned by her since he was very young. God, she had made him hate women something awful. She flirted, but she never did anything. He didn't like to flirt, but he did everything. He hoped that made her happy. But, Katherine had always been a gentle and understanding person. He knew she didn't like the way he had become, but she never showed him any disgust like his friends' parents, only love the best she could. He was her son and she wanted the best for him. She really hoped that one day they could be friends.

Jameson didn't know what else to do, so he came to Katherine. He tried to explain the situation, but it seemed that she already knew, she was just waiting for him to come to her. She never told him that Joey had told her about Jameson's visit to his apartment. Joey was thrilled about Jameson's talent and that was enough for Katherine. If Joey thought he was good, then he was good. She let him tell his story. He was near tears when he told her he couldn't go to Roget even though it would hurt his father. He showed more emotion and concern over this than Richardson ever had, which impressed her. He was much larger than she was, but nevertheless she held him close to her. He put his head against her breasts. She could feel the moisture of his tears against her shirt. She had never been moved like this by Jameson before in his life. She was glad that he had gotten some of William's sensitivity. She didn't realize that it was hers.

Jameson through his tears finally blurted out that he wanted to be an architect like Uncle Joey. Katherine couldn't have felt more proud and moved. He got his sketchbook, the nice pictures only, and he and Katherine sat on the sofa and went through it. She had kept a similar sketchbook when she was younger, but nothing of the caliber of what he had done. Joey was right. This was exceptional. Jameson and Katherine had never been closer. It was sad the time they had lost. Katherine agreed to talk to William on his behalf, as she knew how scary he could be to the children. He was grateful. He kissed Katherine on the cheek. She started to cry, but fought it back. He ran from the room with his sketchbook under his arm. He yelled back, "Thank you, Mom." He hadn't called her Mom since he was a toddler. He hadn't looked so happy and at peace as he ran from the room since that time either. There was hope. Katherine smiled.

When Katherine told William what Jameson wanted to do, he was extremely pleased. She didn't tell him of Joey's involvement. William wouldn't have thought that Jameson would be interested in architecture, but he was relieved that he wouldn't be going to Roget. That would have been a disaster for both parties.

William went into Jameson's room for the first time in a number of years. With all of his posters of sports stars, models, rock stars, and entertainers it was scary for him in there. He was amazed at how organized the room was otherwise. He had always seen Jameson as unkempt. There was hope. William smiled.

He told Jameson how pleased he was of his decision to go to the college of architecture. Jameson was relieved. William offered him his hand to shake and Jameson took it warmly. He felt part of a family for the first time. As William left the room he said to his son, "I'm always there for you. Don't forget that, son." He had never called him son before.

Jameson said lowly, "Thank you, Dad." He had never called him Dad before.

William and Katherine helped Jameson move into the dorms of the college of architecture in New York. Jameson wanted to live off campus like Richardson had, but his academic probation prohibited it. Somehow it was a happier occasion than when Richardson went off to Columbia. Jameson seemed to need help and welcomed it; Richardson didn't seem to need help and didn't want any. When they were leaving to go back to Stamford, Katherine cornered Jameson in the hall. She hugged him tightly and whispered in his ear "be whatever you want to be. We'll always be proud of you. I love you very much."

She was in tears as she heard him say "I love you too, Mom."

William offered him his hand at the door and said, "Good luck, son." Jameson took his hand sadly, knowing how hard it was for William to call him son.

Both Katherine and William visited Jameson as frequently as they could during his first year at college. He stayed mainly to himself and worked hard to do well. While many of his classmates wanted to party and talked of getting laid all the time, he preferred to be alone. He had gotten laid and partied himself out in high school; he was tired.

He found his classmates rather adolescent, like the kids he had left behind in high school. He spent as much time as he could with Uncle Joey, learning what he could from him. The three of them, Joey, Steven, and Jameson, would go out quite often to the opera, the symphony, the ballet, Broadway shows, and so on. There was so much that Joey wanted to make up to Jameson. He had misjudged him and he was sorry. At the end of the first semester, Jameson had earned two A's and three B's in his five classes. He was taken off academic probation. However, he still maintained his discipline. In the end, you find out that there is a little of each parent in each child, and you are responsible for yourself.

The next semester Jameson reversed himself; he earned three As and two Bs, not bad for a low C high school student.

His parents wanted him to come home for the summer. He couldn't have been more pleased, but Uncle Joey had offered him a summer job at his firm. He stayed in New York, but he didn't tell his dad who he was working for, only that it was an architecture firm. William couldn't be more proud of his son; Katherine couldn't be more satisfied if she were in love for the first time. He may have been a bad child and adolescent, but he was going to be a fine adult. William and Katherine felt that they must have done something right.

He worked hard that summer and the next school year. He moved into an apartment that Uncle Joey had arranged near the campus. He went to school and then worked at Joey's firm. Joey had become his mentor, and they were both enjoying the relationship. School and work, school and work, as much as William had done at Roget. One never knows how close, or how far, the acorn may drop. Each succeeding year, his grades improved until he was earning mostly A's. With his work experience at Uncle Joey's firm, he was far surpassing the other students in class projects, if not entirely in grades. He had no time for girls and he was relieved.

He graduated near the top of his class, not cum laude but respectable. Uncle Joey offered him a position with his firm, but he wanted to make it on his own. He knew he could always get a job with Uncle Joey. He needed to find out if he was really any good. He took a position with one of the middle tier architectural firms in the city. He avoided the arrogance of the large firms. His father offered to open the doors for him, but he refused. He also avoided the sloppiness of the smaller firms. He had a number of job offers, but he turned them down.

Jameson, with Uncle Joey's help, rented an apartment in the Village near him. This way they could be close and he could stop taking cabs to visit him. The savings on cab fares alone would pay half his rent. He worked hard and was soon assigned to important projects such as large office buildings, huge private estates, museums, churches, synagogues, and so on.

Whatever leisure time he had, he spent with Uncle Joey and Steven. They were becoming closer and closer. He had no time for other friends or girls. William and Katherine, in the beginning, would come down as often as possible to go out with him. After a while he asked them not to visit so often as he couldn't get his work done. William understood fully; Katherine was hurt. She had just gotten her son back and she didn't want to lose him so soon.

There was a girl, Rita Skinner, in Jameson's office, a fellow architect, who was quite interested in him. She would get herself assigned to the projects that he was working on. She could be quite seductive with the bosses. She was really quite attractive, pretty face and a most desirable body. All of the other men in the office were interested in her, but she was interested in Jameson. He was not particularly interested in her; she reminded him of his adolescent rich girls. Was his fate to never get over his adolescence and to always be alone? The project that they were both assigned to required that they work into the night. Jameson would come in earlier than anybody and stay later than anybody. Rita started to do the same. She would bring coffee and donuts for the both of them in the morning and would go out at dinnertime and pick something up for both of them. She expected him to eat with her, but he would take his food into his office and eat by himself, as he preferred it that way.

One night they were working particularly late, past eleven o'clock, to meet a client schedule. Rita waited until Jameson was finally ready to leave work. She somehow met him on the way out at the elevator. They got into the elevator car together. She tried to get his attention, but it was so obvious that he ignored her. He said nothing as he was tired and just wanted to go home and sleep. Rita had other ideas. As they were getting off the elevator and going their separate ways, Rita looked up at him.

"Would you like to get a drink, or something?" She smiled at him.

"I don't know, I'm really tired. Would you mind if we didn't. Maybe some other time."

Rita looked disappointed. "Why are you avoiding me? I've tried everything to be your friend."

Jameson laughed. "I don't know if I need a friend. But what did you mean by a drink?" He was trying not to hurt her feelings. A few minutes for a drink wouldn't hurt him. He was too tired to sleep anyway.

"Oh, I don't know. There's a little all night coffee shop two blocks away. Sometimes I stop there when I work late. It's not great, but it's open."

"Okay, two blocks it is."

They walked next to each other towards the coffee shop. As they walked Rita put her arm through his. Jameson minded, but he was too tired to care. The softness of a female felt good. He thought of his mother.

They talked about work while they drank coffee and ate a bagel with cream cheese and tomato. He was more tired and hungry than he thought. The only time he ate a good meal anymore was at Uncle Joey's, what a cook. Usually it was coffee and donuts or fast food. It felt good to just relax with someone. Rita turned out to be quite interesting. She was born in a small town in the Midwest, in Ohio not too far from Columbus where he was born. They laughed at the coincidence. She talked about how hard it was for a female to make it in the field of architecture. She wanted to do it on her merits, but the partners in the firm had all propositioned her. They would take care of her, if she would take care of them. She wasn't interested. She would make it on her own, or not at all. She tried to get on his projects because she thought he was the best in the firm including partners. He was flattered. She nodded at him. "So, why do you snub me?"

"I snub everybody when I have work to do," he said.

"You always have work to do. When don't you snub people?"

"Well, how about now. I'm not snubbing you, am I?" He smiled at her and she melted just a little bit.

"No, you're not. You're really much different when you're away from work, almost likable."

"I'll have to work on that. I don't want to be unlikable. Is that what the others say about me?"

"I've heard it said. Some call you the work Nazi. You can be quite scary, you know?"

"No, I didn't. I just try to do my job. Like I said, I'm not looking for more friends."

"You are quite physically imposing. Sometimes you scare me."

Jameson laughed. He had never been called imposing before. "Well maybe I was wrong. Maybe I do need a friend. Could that be you?"

Rita smiled and looked down. "It certainly could."

He reached across the table and took her hands in his. He looked into her eyes. "Thank you, Rita. I'd like to be your friend."

Rita held onto his hands. She would like to be more than just his friend, but she would settle for that for the time being.

He allowed her to hold his hands and did not pull away. Maybe for once he could have a female friend without screwing it up.

Jameson and Rita became good friends at work and outside of work.

When Joey and Steven were unavailable, they would go out together to a concert or a play with Joey's tickets. They would stop somewhere, sometimes back to their coffee shop, and talk into the night. Rita would invite Jameson up to her apartment, but he always refused. He wasn't ready for a heavy relationship just yet. Maybe he never would be, not until he proved himself as an architect. Rita tried to understand, but her hormones didn't allow it. They stayed friends, as Jameson wasn't ready to be lovers.

Rita invited Jameson over to her place for dinner. He couldn't refuse, as it was his birthday, August eighth. She had made a five course dinner for the occasion: shrimp cocktail, Caesar salad, filet mignon, baked potato with sour cream and chives, asparagus with hollandaise sauce, coffee, and an angel food birthday cake for the perfect angel. They both stuffed themselves. They ate and laughed about growing up in Ohio, architecture school, and the odd ducks at work. They were relaxing on the sofa after dinner with their second coffee. They were both full and mellow. Jameson was twenty-four years old. Actually, his birthday had been two days ago and he had celebrated it with his parents. Then, last night he celebrated it again with Joey and Steven. He didn't tell Rita this, though, as it would spoil her celebration.

They were talking and laughing. Suddenly they both stopped and looked at each other with hunger. Jameson took Rita gently into his arms and kissed her hard, harder than he ever had any girl; he may have waited too long. He had kissed her before, but more like a brother kissing his sister good night. This was serious and Jameson felt scared. He knew he could screw well, but he didn't know whether he could love well. He didn't want to lose Rita as a friend if he couldn't be her lover as well. He didn't know if he should screw his friend.

As they became more impassioned, neither one could or wanted to stop the inevitable. She led him into her bedroom. It was as neat as he had expected it to be. He felt like a rat invading her space. She had started to undress him and he did the same for her. She made slow love to him, tender and gentle. Her eyes went up when she first saw his penis. She had never seen one so long and hard. She was impressed — what an architectural tool.

She ran her hands and tongue over his body as he did the same for her. He avoided penetrating her vagina with his penis; something stopped him. Once they did that, could they still be friends? Rita couldn't stand it another minute. She pushed herself onto his penis. She smiled softly and said "nice." Jameson smiled and said "nicer."

He had always had great staying power. He pushed down hard like a jackhammer cutting through concrete, in and out, until he knew for sure that Rita had reached more than one orgasm. He wanted to please her so much. When she stopped screaming, he started up again until he came and then continued until she reached orgasm again. He went a third time until she finally pulled away from him and lay panting on her back. He came closer to hold her. His penis was still up, and it was imposing. It could be a tool of destruction.

"Please," Rita moaned, "no more. Happy birthday presents can go too far."

"Who was getting and who was giving the present?" He smiled at her.

She looked at him. "I thought I was giving you the present. Now I'm not so sure." She reached over and stroked his penis. It was still hard. "Where did you learn to screw like that?"

He smiled. "In junior high school."

She laughed, but he wasn't kidding. She stroked his penis softly and surely. He came again, this time gently in her hand. She rubbed it on both their bodies. It didn't matter; they were both soaked already. They fell asleep like that. He hadn't slept this soundly for years. It was a welcome relief.

Rita and Jameson continued to be friends. They would still go to shows and concerts, but something had changed. She wanted more than friendship. He did too, but he couldn't get closer. He enjoyed their time together, with or without sex, but he didn't know how to have a relationship. She would say many times, particularly during sex, that she loved him. He couldn't return it; the words choked in his throat. They had been seeing each other every day at work and most evenings after work. He started to avoid her at work and made excuses so that they didn't see each other so much outside of work. She sensed the change and pulled away herself. They started to argue; they had never argued before.

Rita asked Jameson to join her at the coffee shop after working late one night, the one where they had first become friends. When they were seated in their booth, she took his hands in hers. She looked at him lovingly.

"Jamey, we've become good lovers, but we've become lousy friends."

He looked at her lovingly. "I know. It's my fault."

"No, Jamey, it's both our faults. I love you too much." She hesitated and looked at him with tears forming in her eyes. "And you can't love enough."

He squeezed her hands harder. "I can't love at all. I'm sorry, Rita."

"I know, Jamey. I know how hard you've tried."

He couldn't keep the tears from his eyes. They squeezed out and ran slowly down his face. "I want to love you, I really do."

"I know you do." She was crying harder now, she couldn't stop herself. She knew she was losing her best friend and lover. She didn't know how to stop it.

"Rita, please, what can we do? We're going to lose it all."

"I'm afraid so. I wanted you to know, I'm leaving the firm. I've taken a position with a firm in Washington. I can't be near you right now. It's killing me to see what it's doing to you and to me. I can't live like this right now."

He had never loved anyone, including himself, before. He was scared to lose her, but somehow he felt relieved. He knew it wasn't the sex, it was her— it scared him. He nodded his head. He said nothing; he didn't know what to say. She held his hands and squeezed them again. She then got up and walked slowly out the door. She didn't look back, she couldn't. It was the first time that he didn't watch her walk away from behind, he just couldn't. He put his head down in his arms on the table and he cried into his arms. He couldn't stop her and he couldn't let her go.

He remembered their last time together. They had another argument after sex. He had hurt her vagina again. She said to him, "When we have sex, you don't make love, you hate." He thought that maybe she was right. There was something wrong with him; he knew it and she knew it.

"Will there be anything else, sir?" The waitress was talking to him.

He looked up at her. His face was tear-streaked, "No, I'm afraid there will be nothing else." He went home and sat in a chair in the dark in his living room. He cried uncontrollably. In the morning he was still sitting there. He must have slept, but he wasn't sure. He called in sick for work. He had never done that before.

Rita had said to him, "You can't love anything." He had answered, "I love my work." She responded, "No, you hate your work." Maybe she was right, but he didn't know what else to do. He took a shower and got into bed nude. He looked at his body; he was cursed. He hoped he could sleep. He didn't want to think of Rita cleaning out her office and leaving today. He wanted to call her and tell her how much he loved her, but he couldn't. He cried throughout the day. In the end, he let her go; he could do nothing else.

In the evening, he went to Joey and Steven's apartment. They were his only real role models of love; if only he could love like they did. As he entered their apartment, he started to cry again. They both held him and he cried into their shoulders. He cried until there were no more tears; he continued crying silently as his body heaved. Joey and Steven stayed with him throughout the night. He would stop for a moment and then start again. He tried to clear his mind of Rita, but he couldn't—he never would. He awoke in the morning after ten. His first reaction was that he was late for work. Steven came in with breakfast on a tray. He had stayed home from work to be with him. He had called Jameson's employer to tell them he wouldn't be in. Jameson couldn't eat and he wished he couldn't think.

He stayed out of work until the following Monday. He went in earlier and he stayed later. He did his work and he stayed away from people. He went back to his apartment or to Joey's. Sometimes when he couldn't sleep, he would stay over at Joey's. Joey or Steven would keep him company. He punished himself, "Why can they love and I can't?" He tried not to be alone but he was always alone with himself. As much as he tried to forget, Rita was always with him. He wanted to call her many times when his hatred for himself was overpowering, but he couldn't do it. He started to dial her number many times, but his fingers couldn't complete the dialing. His life became his work and his work became his curse. That was the only relationship he could afford; people were too difficult.

He would be alone in his office or at home, and suddenly he would find himself crying, not hard but with soft tears in his eyes. He would realize that he was thinking of something that Rita had said or done. He thought he was smiling or laughing to himself, but the tears were always there. After a few months of this, he realized that he hated her for making him feel this way. Hating was always easier for him than loving. He stopped crying—he missed it.

Sometimes he would see a girl passing by who reminded him of Rita from the rear and he would twitch. Sometimes he would hear her voice in his head and he would cringe. He would say to himself "bitch" and go back to work. He believed that he was all right again. He would go to work, work long hours, and then come back to his apartment late at night. He would sleep, or stare into space, a few hours and then go back to work. He spent less time with Joey and Steven as they reminded him too much of times with Rita. He discouraged his parents from visiting. He cut himself off from everyone. He dealt with the people in the firm but only around work. He had truly become a "work Nazi." He was very much alone, he hated his life, he was happy.

Elizabeth

Elizabeth was born in May 1967, less than two years after Jameson. Katherine had grown up with her mother always telling her how wonderful it was to have children. It was a woman's role and that was what her husband wanted from her. So Katherine had two children, both sons. Unfortunately, she didn't find it wonderful. She found it constraining. She felt her kids got in the way of her real life, which she was still waiting to begin. Her husband, William, didn't want children from her. In fact, it was difficult to know what he wanted from her. So she had, and was raising, two children. Then Katherine's mother told her that the greatest joy was in having a daughter. So, she was pregnant once again and this time she hoped it would be a daughter. Maybe then her mother would leave her alone and let her get on with her own life.

When the nurse told Katherine that she had a daughter, she was relieved. However, when the baby was first brought in to her, there wasn't joy. The baby was broad and stocky just like William with the same round face. She held the baby in her arms and suddenly realized she preferred sons. She named the baby Elizabeth Anne Bradford. Katherine picked Elizabeth because she recalled that this was a name of girls whom she had always liked; they all seemed to be happy. She hoped her baby would be happy as well.

She tried breastfeeding Elizabeth, but it made her too uncomfortable having a female version of William sucking at her tits. When the doctor asked her whether she was going to breastfeed, she quickly replied, "Not on my life." The doctor had her milk dried up; it made little difference to him. All three of Katherine's pregnancies had been relatively easy. Her father called her "the baby machine, just like your mother." For her mother it had taken four times to get her daughter. Katherine would stop at three. She had her tubes tied while she was in the hospital. She never told William. It would make no difference to him. While she was recuperating, she had little concern to see or be with her baby daughter.

Elizabeth stayed in the nursery and was fed a formula by the nurses. When her father came to visit he would wave to her through the nursery glass. When the nurse would bring the baby into the room and hand her to him, he would shy away or place her next to Katherine. She would lie next to Katherine, but she did little to comfort the baby. Her mother had called to say she wouldn't be able to visit for a couple of weeks—so much for having a daughter for your mother. Uncle Joey, who had been there for both boys, would come out later. He really wasn't very comfortable with baby girls, as they made him queasy. He would come out later on when the baby was bigger. Katherine's father and two older brothers, Robby and Alley, never visited until the kids were grown. So baby Elizabeth was all alone.

When Katherine brought Elizabeth home, her two brothers were excited to have a baby in the house. Richardson briefly held her and rocked her, and then he went on his way. Jameson looked at her, but wouldn't touch her, and ran to his room. Katherine had breastfed her two sons and stayed with them for at least the first year of their lives. With Elizabeth, she hired a mother's helper immediately, who would feed and change the baby.

As soon as Katherine felt fit from the delivery of the baby (the stitches bothered her less with each birth), and the tube tying operation, she was back to her life with Patricia and the club. She would leave Elizabeth and Jameson with Laura, the mother's helper, while she went out. She would always be back before Richardson got home from pre-school. Most times she would go back out with Richardson, leaving Jameson and Elizabeth once again at home with Laura. Jameson was becoming more and more of a problem each time she left, which only reinforced her decision not to take him. He was so close in age to Elizabeth she hoped that the two of them would bond as brother and sister, just like she and Joey had. She didn't know it, but the opposite was happening. Jameson resented and hated his sister, and she was to feel the same way.

By the time Elizabeth became a toddler, when William came home early, which was very rarely, she would run to him and grab him around the legs. William would pat her on the head and gently, and sometimes not so gently as she held on tenaciously, push her away. She would then run to her mother and hang onto her skirt. Katherine would pick her up and take her into the kitchen for a cookie, the answer to all mothers' prayers. When William was sitting at the dinner table or in his chair in the den, Elizabeth would climb up onto his lap and sit there. As soon as she was able to talk, she would look up at William, hold onto his tie and say, "I love you, Daddy." William would say nothing, but pick her up, put her on the floor, and call for Katherine to come get her daughter. His work always came first.

When Elizabeth was two, Richardson was six and already in elementary school. Jameson was four and going to pre-school. This was the first time that Elizabeth had the house to herself. She now also had Katherine to herself. Katherine really didn't know what to do with a girl. Katherine decided to join a playgroup in the Columbus development so that Elizabeth would have children her own age to play with. The playgroup consisted of about eight other children from the neighborhood—six boys and two girls. Katherine expected her to play with the two girls, but Elizabeth preferred playing with the boys.

The other two girls were too prissy for her. The boys were more fun. This was the first indication that she was to be a tomboy, a father's daughter with the wrong father.

Elizabeth would want to be on the swings and demanded that Katherine push her and be with her like the other mothers. Unlike the other mothers, however, she was into showing off her figure. She would wear tight mini skirts and tops, high heels, and her long blond hair flowing behind her down to the top of her ass. When she pushed Elizabeth on the swing, she would dig her left heel into the sand, spreading her left leg so that the bottom of her skirt rode up to the top of her thigh, exposing almost her entire leg up to her bikini panties. As she pushed the swing, her ass would float from side to side in a most sensual and provocative manner.

Elizabeth enjoyed making her mother chase her. When Elizabeth would run off from the playgroup, Katherine would have to chase her in her high heels. As she ran, her skirt would run up on her thighs exposing her entire leg. When Elizabeth would play in the sand box, Katherine would sit on the side forcing her skirt to ride up her legs. As she would cross and uncross her legs, she would expose her panties and the outline of her vagina. She didn't seem to notice.

The older men playing chess in the park or sitting on the benches and the grounds keepers would notice and would all stop what they were doing to watch the spectacle. Male attendance at the park greatly increased on those days when Katherine was there with Elizabeth. Elizabeth would sense the men moving to get behind her mother. She didn't understand what they were looking at, until years later, but the image remained in her mind. She had never wanted to be a woman like her mother, having to expose herself to men to get attention. She always wanted to be more like the other mothers, who came to the park just to be with their children She wanted to be approved of for her self.

As Elizabeth grew she looked just like William. She was broad across the shoulders, short and stocky, with William's round face and curly sandy hair. She would not be the kind of girl that Katherine had been growing up. In fact, she was just the opposite.

Katherine spent most of her time with Elizabeth chasing after her in her tight skirts and high heels. While she appreciated the male attention, this wasn't the place she was looking for it. She found it was really too much for her and realized the boys had been much easier. She was letting Elizabeth grow up as much on her own as she could. Katherine would leave Elizabeth alone with the playgroup during the day as much as she could, then with Laura the other times. This was her time with Patricia and the club, which was much more important than bonding with a daughter who was a stranger. When Elizabeth wanted anything, she went to her father. He gave her whatever she wanted, except himself.

It wasn't surprising that Elizabeth grew up by herself. She needed people and liked them, but she couldn't get that at home. She was drawn to children her age and made them her friends as if for life. Fortunately, she was extremely likable. When she started pre-school at four, she was invited to friends' houses and spent more time at other kids' houses than her own. She loved all kinds of animals. She would find stray dogs and cats and bring them home with her. Katherine would let her feed and play with them during the day. However, when William was due back home, she made her take them back where she found them. On those days, Elizabeth would get up on William's lap and ask him if she could have a puppy; that was all she ever wanted. He would always say "we'll see" and put her back on the floor. She would run off happily. She thought "we'll see" meant soon, but she never got her dog.

In pre-school Elizabeth befriended all of the social outcasts, those kids who didn't seem to get the teacher's attention or didn't seem popular with the other kids. She became the little queen of the misfits. She liked that as it made her feel important; she liked helping kids who were being ignored. Most of her friends, however, were boys. She would run with them, play on the swings and gym, and play ball. The other girls sat around and played with dolls, painted, sewed, cooked and so on. She found the girls boring. She didn't understand why she should play with girls who wanted to be like her mother. She wanted to be just like her father. Elizabeth would try to play with her brothers, but they pushed her away, so she found her own brothers.

When she was almost five and still in pre-school, her parents told her that they would be moving to a place called Connecticut. She was excited. Now she figured, she could have her puppy; "we'll see" was getting closer. She was looking forward to making a lot of new friends. She got up onto her father's lap and said, "Thank you, daddy. I love you." William nodded and put her back on the floor. Her brothers didn't want to move, but she couldn't wait. It was so exciting, and she just knew she would get her puppy.

The family moved during the summer. It was a big house surrounded by a wall. Elizabeth was to have her own, large bedroom, big enough to keep her puppy. Their new house wasn't as close to neighbors as their house in Columbus had been and there weren't any community play areas. So, Katherine would take all three kids to the country club to swim. The boys would go off on their own, leaving Katherine and Elizabeth alone. She really didn't know what to say to her daughter or how to entertain her. She looked for other girls her age for her to play with in the baby pool. Elizabeth played with them for a little while, but found them all boring. They just wanted to splash around or pour water out of their pails. In no time, she was back by her mother's side moping. Katherine would walk her around the pool area and the clubhouse in her bikini, not only to occupy Elizabeth but also to show off her body to the men at the club. Elizabeth found this disgusting. She wished she had another mother, one who was fatter and not desirable.

On one visit to the club, she met a little boy her age in the baby pool. His mother had placed him there; he wasn't happy. His name was Roger. He splashed the other girls and they screamed. He splashed Elizabeth and she splashed back; he cried. After that, though, he and Elizabeth became friends. They would meet in the baby pool and then explore the country club. They would find themselves in the kitchen and the help would give them food, in the bar and they would get drinks, in the card room and they would get money, mostly pennies and nickels. Elizabeth was now excited to go to the club, and Katherine could spend her day peacefully, reading and sunbathing, and being looked at by the men.

After Uncle Raymond's death, Patricia Fogerty moved to New York and would come to Stamford to visit or for the day. Aunt Patricia was fun for Elizabeth. She would explore with her and Roger, if he was there, and take them to lunch. Patricia was used to having daughters. Elizabeth was her chance to do it all over again, this time the right way.

After that summer, Elizabeth started elementary school. She wanted to go to the Episcopal School just like her brothers, but it was an all-boys school. She still didn't understand why she couldn't go, since she liked boys better than girls. William and Katherine enrolled her in the all girls sister school called Episcopal Gardens, a bridge to the best girls' prep schools and colleges. She hated it, both the girls and the girly things. She began hiding in her room when it was time to go to school. Katherine was getting exasperated. She punished Elizabeth by sending her to her room or denying her something such as cookies or ice cream. Elizabeth didn't care; she wasn't going back to that school. When she did go, she would do something to get herself in trouble: tie another girl's pigtails together, steal their milk, hide their coats, and so on. Katherine would get a call almost immediately upon Elizabeth entering school, to come get her. Katherine realized this had to stop.

They enrolled her in one of the best coed private schools in the area, The Learning Tree. Finally, she had boys to play with and she was happy. The teachers allowed her to do all of the activities for both boys and girls. They encouraged her to be who she wanted to be. Elizabeth was excited, she couldn't wait to get to school and never wanted to come home. She had much more fun at school than she could have at home. William and particularly Katherine were relieved.

Elizabeth made friends almost immediately at The Learning Tree. They were mostly boys and one other girl, Amanda Blake, who was just like Elizabeth. She, too, loved the boys' games and playing outside. Elizabeth and Amanda would play together with the boys while the other girls would stay inside. Most of the other girls weren't allowed to get dirty or their parents would punish them. If Elizabeth didn't come home dirty, Katherine would be concerned.

Katherine was happy for her daughter, as she had found herself and was being who she wanted to be. Katherine wished she had gone to a school like The Learning Tree. She was glad Elizabeth had the opportunity and was a child who knew what she wanted and fought for it.

Elizabeth started playing with Amanda after school. She would go over to Amanda's house to play or Amanda would come to Elizabeth's house.

Amanda had a swing set and an outdoor gym. They would play outside until it was time for Elizabeth to go home although she never wanted to. Sometimes, however, she would stay for dinner at the Blakes and she loved doing that, as she loved the Blakes. When Amanda came to play with Elizabeth, they would spend most of their time in the tree house. This became their secret hiding place and fort. They would stay there until they were called. Elizabeth would carry on when it was time for Amanda to leave. Many times her parents allowed Amanda to stay with Elizabeth for dinner and, sometimes, to stay overnight. When Amanda would stay overnight, they would talk until they fell asleep. They had so much to talk about; they always would. What Elizabeth couldn't find at home, she was finding elsewhere.

Elizabeth sometimes wanted to play with one of her boy friends after school. Katherine saw no harm in this if the other child's parents felt it was all right. Elizabeth would play with the boy just as she would play with Amanda. She didn't understand why she couldn't stay over at the boy's house, or the boy stay with her at her house, like she did with Amanda. One night William came home early and found Elizabeth playing rather roughly with a boy. He didn't like the looks of this. He told Katherine no more boys for Elizabeth. Elizabeth never understood. She wanted boys for her friends; she didn't like girls.

Throughout elementary school Elizabeth was extremely popular with the boys in the class. The prissy girls in her class would tease her about being a tomboy. They wouldn't play with the boys; good little girls didn't do that. They didn't want to get dirty. She was always dirty and she just loved it. Elizabeth's best friend, other than Amanda, was Kent Biddle. Kent was a very shy, sensitive boy whom the other boys ordinarily wouldn't play with. They would call him a sissy. However, Elizabeth and Amanda fought for his attention.

The years between first and fourth grades were the best years of her life. She played with the boys and some of the girls, and all her friends just liked each other. The prissy girls were the enemy and none of her friends cared to play with them. The prettiest girl in the school, Pamela Houston, would watch her and Amanda playing with the boys and would stick her tongue out at them. Sometimes Pamela would turn from them, lift her skirt, and show them the back of her underpants. Elizabeth and Amanda didn't care, but the boys would look at Pamela.

When Elizabeth was nine years old and in the fourth grade, she started dressing like her father. She would wear his old monogrammed shirts rolled and tied up with one of his old ties. She also insisted on having her hair cut short just like her father's. Her brothers found it spooky. They thought she was a little strange, but they had little to do with her anyway. Her male friends at school thought it was cool, but the girls at school moved further away from her.

In the fifth grade, the boys at school started to notice the prissy girls. Where once these girls were considered the enemy, now they were objects of desire. The boys would ask Elizabeth how they could win the favor of Pamela Houston. Elizabeth was disgusted. The Learning Tree started coed dances in the fifth grade so that the young masters and mistresses could begin their lessons in heterosexual social graces.

Initially, at the dances, all of her male friends would stay with her and Amanda on one side of the room, while the prissy girls would stay on the other side. The prissy girls would sneak looks over to the other side of the room to see which boys were looking at them. Elizabeth and Amanda would stare back at them and stick out their tongues. Some of the prissy girls, including Pamela Houston, would ask Elizabeth and Amanda if such and such a boy liked them or not. Elizabeth would tell them that the boys weren't interested in their type of girl.

This was 1977 when a number of the girls in Elizabeth's class had older sisters who were quite sexually promiscuous. The younger girls would learn from the older girls. Some of the girls started to wear lipstick and makeup, short tight skirts, tight tops, particularly those starting to develop, and short high heels. The boys were beginning to take an interest.

Pamela Houston was one of these girls. She had her eye on Tommy Thompson, considered the best looking, and most popular, boy in the class. He was one of Elizabeth's best friends. Tommy was shy and scared of the prissy type girls. Pamela was bold and determined. One day right after school, Pamela enticed Tommy back into their empty homeroom. She told him she needed help with her English homework, even though she was the brightest girl in the class and he was one of the dumbest. Tommy was flattered. Once inside the room, Pamela started to kiss Tommy as she had seen her older sister kissing her boy friend, with her tongue in the boy's mouth. Tommy was disgusted. She lifted up her sweater and teen bra and put Tommy's hands on her tits. Tommy ran from the room. Pamela told all the girls what Tommy had done to her. They were envious. Tommy said nothing. He neither denied nor confirmed Pamela's story. The other boys wanted to know what it was like. Tommy was a hero. He had broken the ice. At the next dance, almost all of the boys left Elizabeth's side of the room to dance with one of the girls. They wanted what Tommy had gotten.

Slowly, some faster, the boys stopped playing with Elizabeth and Amanda and became more attentive to the prissy girls. They were doing things with these girls that they had told Elizabeth they would never do. One of the boys, Andrew Tilden, stayed Elizabeth's friend. He was more comfortable playing like a boy than acting like a puppy to the prissy girls. The other boys would make fun of him, but he held his ground; Elizabeth was his friend. However, as most of the other boys started bragging about what they were getting sexually from the other girls, Andrew felt he had to do the same. He would tell them what he and Elizabeth did. Of course none of it was true.

Elizabeth had started to develop breasts in the fifth grade, and being heavily built, they were coming in quite large. While Elizabeth kept herself quite unattractive from a male perspective, her breasts were the envy of many of the other girls. They would look at them with envy in the shower at gym while hiding their flat chests. When word spread that Andrew was getting "bare tit" from Elizabeth, he became the envy of the other boys. He bragged that he could set it up for all of them to feel her up just like he was doing; he was getting tired of it anyway.

One day he persuaded Elizabeth to come over to his house after school in order to do homework together. As usual, they lay on the living room floor doing their homework. After about an hour, the doorbell rang and some of the other boys came in. They made a ring around Elizabeth and wouldn't let her out unless she took off her shirt and bra and let them touch her breasts, like she had let Andrew do. She looked around for Andrew, but he had disappeared upstairs. Elizabeth was scared for the first time in her life. She refused. She found these boys, her former friends, disgusting. She stood in the middle of the room and dared one of them to try anything. Not one of them moved forward. They stared at each other, until the ringleader, Tommy Thompson, said, "That prick Tilden lied to us. There's no bare tit here. Who would want hers any way? Damn dyke." They all left with Tommy. Elizabeth fell to the floor crying. She would never trust another male again. She spent the remainder of fifth and sixth grade with Amanda and Kent. They had become outcasts. Elizabeth's happy years had ended.

Elizabeth convinced her parents to send her to a junior high school where academics were stressed. She hoped that in that kind of environment she wouldn't be pressured to be the kind of girl that she didn't want to be—like her mother. She found girl and boy stuff and sex disgusting. She was more interested in who she was and who she could be. She had become very serious minded and goal directed, just like her father. William and Katherine found a very academically demanding coed prep school. Elizabeth wouldn't go to an all-girls school. Horizon Preparatory School started with the seventh grade and ran through twelfth grade. Elizabeth liked that she could stay there until college if she wanted.

Elizabeth loved the school. It was academically demanding so that she had no time for much of a social life. Her friend Amanda went to the school as well. Kent was sent to an all boys school to harden him up; his parents didn't like him having girls as friends.

At Horizon, both the boys and the girls worked together. There were no dances or social graces; if Elizabeth was with a boy it was to study or learn. They would go as a group into New York, sometimes chaperoned, sometimes not, to visit museums, do research or work on a project at the main library, attend a concert, and so on. There were no sports or athletics or parties to distract them. There was no pressure for the males and females to come together, date, or mate. They tended to do things in groups. This was the perfect way to grow up.

At home, the three children had pretty much evolved on their own. Richardson had isolated himself in his room, Jameson was out partying and chasing girls, and Elizabeth was maturing—possibly the only one in the house. Elizabeth and Katherine were now able to talk. Elizabeth realized that her mother was not just a dumb, attractive blonde looking to attract men, but was highly intelligent. She just didn't understand why her mother worked to hide it.

Katherine talked to her about what she had learned in high school and Jones College. Elizabeth became quite interested in philosophy and literature from talking to her mother. Katherine tried to encourage her in these areas. Elizabeth vowed not to waste her intelligence like her mother. She liked her mother more and more, but she still found her too female, too interested in flirting with men. As Elizabeth talked to her she realized that her mother was not being who she wanted to be, she was being who she thought her parents and husband wanted her to be. Elizabeth didn't want to be, nor could she be, that kind of female.

Elizabeth had always tried to spend time with her father. He seemed to be bright, successful, and everyone she knew looked up to him. They didn't always like him as he wasn't very social, but they respected him. That was how she wanted to be. She loved her father.

She started to talk to her father about his work and questioned him about what he did at Apex Industries. She had been quite proud of him when he was promoted to Executive Vice President, and now she wanted to know what he did. William found he was only too willing to tell his daughter. No one else in the family had ever asked him too much about what he did. He had always felt very alone with his work in the family. Now Elizabeth was taking an interest and he was pleased. Sometimes they would get together when William was home. He would explain how Apex worked and the systems that he had established. Elizabeth found it fascinating—she found her father fascinating.

During her high school years, 1982 to 1985, sex, alcohol, and drugs were prevalent. It was expected that if a female went out with a male, there would be sex, sooner not later. Elizabeth had no interest or time for any of this. She was quite serious about learning as much as she could from her high school courses and her life experiences. She had a special friend at Horizon, a boy named Tony Armento. He was of Italian heritage. His father was the CEO of a major wine distributor. Elizabeth, Amanda, and Tony would study and travel together into New York. They would visit museums, go to concerts, shows and so on. They were known at the school as the "three amigos."

When Elizabeth reached the tenth grade she began to lose her baby fat. Her body started to solidify, much as Jameson's had before her. As she trimmed up, her breasts became even more prominent. She had fantastic proportions for a girl her age, or any age, 36-21-36. Although the boys at her school were predominantly uninterested in females and sex, they couldn't help but marvel at Elizabeth's body. As her self-image as a human being increased at Horizon, her self-image as a female increased as well. She became less self-conscious of her body and secretly enjoyed the male looks she received, both at school and outside of school. She still found the physical aspects of a boy touching her body parts, or her touching a boy's penis, too uncomfortable and disgusting. Tony was her safe harbor.

She did catch Tony looking at her from time to time, particularly when she would wear a tight top. Sometimes she would stretch out her chest in class, or when they were walking together, to push her breasts out, and she would catch him staring at her breasts. She smiled to herself. However, she knew he would never try anything, but it was nice to know he was interested.

In the summers, between high school years, Elizabeth would go to the country club with her mother and sometimes Patricia. Most times Amanda and Tony would come with her as well. This protected her from having to interface with the shallow people her age who belonged to the club. Most of the females would wear the skimpiest of bathing suits and pose around the pool, in front of the young males, never going in except to wet their suits so they could be seen through. Most of them would do anything to have a boyfriend of their own. They had subverted their entire personalities and intelligence to attract a male. They were intent on being married so they could avoid having to finish college. Elizabeth and Amanda found them to be horrors. Neither one of them felt that they needed a male to determine who they were; they would be totally self-sufficient.

Elizabeth was not at all comfortable showing off her body. She regarded it as her curse, as it made her stand out. However, when she went to the club she would wear a skin-fitting bikini that showed off the grandeur of her breasts. With her muscular and trim upper body and her solid legs she was quite the spectacle. The boys at the club called her "Wonder Woman" and took bets as to who would be the first to screw her. If it weren't for her brother Jameson, and the fear he put in other males' hearts, all the males at the club would pester her. Her intent wasn't to attract the males or make the other girls envious, but to prove she could attract the males if she wanted to, just like her mother. Between her upper body and her mother's lower body there was an almost perfect female. Unfortunately, Elizabeth still had the face and hair of her father that was not particularly attractive on a female. Somehow the boys didn't notice this.

When Katherine and Elizabeth entered the pool area, all male eyes were on them. They smiled at each other. She was beginning to understand her mother better. The power that her body wielded was intoxicating. She liked it. Amanda liked being with her and the way she stood off from the frivolous club members their age, both male and female. Amanda had not been as physically endowed as she, so she enjoyed putting down the boys through Elizabeth. Academically, Amanda was far superior to any of the males in class, but got much less recognition. Tony would shield the two of them from any unwanted male attention.

There was a particular young male club member who would always sit across from Elizabeth and Katherine. He would stare directly at them over his sunglasses, surreptitiously but obviously. It made both of them uncomfortable. Katherine would try not to lie on her stomach so that her ass was apparent and would flaunt as little as possible in front of him. Elizabeth would try not to lean over in the front so that her breasts stood out. They would try changing their location around the pool, but he would follow them.

The steward at the club said that his name was Bartholomew Worthington IV. His family was one of the richest in the world and he was used to getting his way. If he wanted to stare at women around the pool, and he did no other harm, the club would not stop him. Katherine and Elizabeth felt that their freedom as club members was being impinged upon, but they were helpless to do anything about it. Elizabeth had always stood up for the underdog and fought injustice regardless of the consequences. She wouldn't let this one lay.

One day when they were at the club with Amanda, Tony, and Patricia, Bartholomew, "Bad Bart," was particularly leering at them. It was an extremely hot day and the women would have liked to go into the pool to cool off. However, none of them was willing to get wet so that Bad Bart could leer even more. They wouldn't get up either; they were prisoners on hot sweaty lounge chairs. Tony would get them drinks and towels to keep them cool. On one of Tony's trips back from the bar with a loaded tray, Bad Bart stopped him by standing right in front of him. Tony was not particularly big or strong, in fact he was slightly effeminate, but was never intimidated. Bart held him with his arm across Tony's body.

"You screwing the one with the super tits, dago trash?" Bart wasn't pleasant.

Tony held his ground. He looked Bart in the eye. Bart increased the pressure on Tony's stomach. "So, cat got your tongue, wop piss?"

Tony tried to move around Bart, but Bart held him in place. "I'll bet you got a spaghettini dick." Bart tried to pull Tony's bathing suit open in the front.

Instead, Tony pulled Bart's bathing suit open in the front and with a quick movement he dumped the tray of drinks into the front of Bart's bathing suit. The ice from the drinks froze Bart's genitals. He grabbed his crotch, let go of Tony, and ran to the men's locker room.

The entire membership of the club in attendance stood up and applauded Tony. Evidently Bart had been known as the club bully for as long as he had been a member. After that, any time Tony came to the club, there was a member offering to buy him a drink or something to eat. When Tony came back to join the women, Elizabeth gave him a big kiss on the mouth. Let the other girls wonder what their relationship was, she thought; for now let Tony be a hero.

Bart filed a complaint that the Bradfords were bringing in undesirable guests, in this case one of Italian descent. The club board vacillated between offending the Bradfords and the other Apex Industry members and the Worthington family. After much deliberation and hand wringing, the club board decided to ban young Mr. Armento—so much for social justice; exclusive country club style. Elizabeth stopped going to the club.

As Elizabeth's senior year approached, she was being pressured by the school, her parents, and herself to make a decision as to her college plans. She couldn't decide between a liberal arts education encompassing philosophy and literature, or one of math and science. She was equally adept in both areas. What she really wanted was a curriculum where she could learn to better help people, particularly underdogs who couldn't help themselves. She just couldn't hurt both parents; one wanted her to take a liberal arts program, the other a business program where she could use her math skills, preferably Roget Institute. Elizabeth wanted to make her own decision.

As the time grew near for applying to colleges, she submitted applications to most of the Ivy League coed schools and some of the private coed liberal arts colleges in New England. Neither parent had pressured her, but she knew she couldn't go to Jones College, her mother's alma mater. It was still pretty much a rich girls' finishing school, although they now admitted some males.

As acceptances came in, Elizabeth started to think that maybe she hadn't been fair to her father. She knew he had wanted his sons to go to Roget, but neither one did. He hadn't expected her to want to attend Roget. There were very few girls even at this time, and it was a rough curriculum. She knew, though, he would be extremely pleased if she did. She suggested that she and her dad go visit Roget as a possible college for her. William, of course, was elated. He suggested an entire weekend for Elizabeth, Katherine, and himself in Boston. Elizabeth told her father that she would rather it be just the two of them. They could talk about Roget on the way to and from. William set up a campus tour and a series of interviews similar to what he had done for Richardson. Elizabeth told herself that she loved Roget, that it was just an extension of Horizon school. When she told her father this, she could see how pleased he was. She would do this for her dad.

She went to Roget as a freshman. Since William had attended Roget, the industrial complex had changed. Many of the old-moneyed families had either sold their family-controlled companies to larger corporations or had gone out of business. The rich scions who were still out there didn't want to work that hard and had no interest in the economics of business, only in spending the money generated by the business. Roget was now more dependent on the sons, and some daughters, of the working class. It was indeed a sad state of affairs. Roget was glad to get the daughter of such a distinguished graduate.

Elizabeth found the basic student at Roget extremely tedious to be around. All they wanted to talk about was business, how they could make it work better and more efficiently so as to maximize returns. There was no discussion or consideration of the people involved. Elizabeth was appalled. All of the subjects were based on either economics or business; there was no room for philosophy or literature. What did it matter in the real world of business? She felt like a humanitarian trying to make sense of the diminishing of the human spirit. She knew almost immediately that she had made a big mistake. Now, how could she tell her father? It would break his heart.

She came home for winter vacation hoping not to return to Roget. She moped around the house for the first few days. On the fourth day, Amanda and Tony came over. Amanda was a political science major at Brown University. She loved it, but that wasn't for Elizabeth; it felt too indirect to make real changes. Tony, who loved people and animals almost as much as she, attended New York University's School of Social Work. He talked enthusiastically of what social workers did, how they helped people, and how good it made him feel. He was scheduled to work as an intern at a homeless shelter in Harlem during the next semester as part of his course work. He was really excited, and so was Elizabeth. This was what she had been working toward all her life; she just knew it was.

Katherine had talked to Patricia about how depressed Elizabeth seemed. It didn't seem right for someone so young just starting college. She remembered how excited she was when she first attended Jones College. Patricia suggested that they take her out to lunch in Manhattan. They could go to a Broadway show of her choice and then out to dinner at her favorite restaurant. It would be Patricia's treat for her favorite "niece." How could Katherine or Elizabeth refuse? Katherine was relieved, as Patricia was so much better with girls. Elizabeth didn't say much during lunch or the show. When either Katherine or Patricia asked about school, she would say very little, only that it was all right. On their way to dinner they happened to pass the administration building of NYU. She said she wanted to see where Tony was going to school and to pick him up something he had said he needed. Inside the administration building, she talked to the information person and put a number of things in her handbag. One was an application for admission and the other was the catalog for the School of Social Work. Patricia saw her do this, but said nothing. Katherine was in the ladies' room (she always seemed to be in the ladies room) and saw nothing. At dinner, Elizabeth was a little more talkative. Patricia noticed she kept her handbag close to her. After dinner, Patricia asked her what her plans were for after graduation, how she saw using her degree from Roget. She gave a very evasive answer, such as, "I'm not sure yet." Patricia finally asked her point blank, "Are you happy there?" Elizabeth said nothing. Patricia asked her what she really wanted to do. She hesitated. She slowly pulled out the catalog for the School of Social Work and handed it to Patricia and Katherine. They both nodded, they weren't surprised. Elizabeth talked about social work school and how she wanted to use her life. Katherine responded that she would talk to her father; Elizabeth should be what she wanted to be.

When Katherine talked to William about how depressed Elizabeth was at Roget and that she wanted to attend NYU's social work school, he was aghast. Why would anyone want to spend their lives trying to make life better for less fortunates? William had always been a proponent of self-responsibility, and the cause of social workers ran completely against his grain. There would also be humiliation for him at Roget, for his own daughter to reject it, and everything he thought he stood for. It was a slap at his life. But, if that was what Elizabeth really wanted to do, he wouldn't stop her.

She started the next semester at the NYU School of Social Work. She moved in with Tony. They were friends and they would always be friends. Neither of them was interested in a sexual relationship. Each one would keep the other safe from others, Elizabeth from males and Tony from females. It was a good arrangement.

Elizabeth told her mother what she was doing and where she was living. Her mother was happy for her; she was doing what she wanted. She didn't tell her father, though; she couldn't, he wouldn't understand. Her relationship with her father had cooled somewhat. He had lost interest in her. He would continue to pay the bills, but he became, once again, like the father he was when she was little.

Both Elizabeth and Tony graduated from NYU and took jobs with the parent agency that directed homeless shelters throughout the city. She was assigned to an agency in the Bronx, which was not far from where her father grew up. Life can be ironic. Tony stayed at the shelter in Harlem. Elizabeth worked the day shift and Tony worked the evening shift. It was almost a perfect roommate arrangement. They would spend time together on the weekends. Elizabeth was happy for now.

Elizabeth and Tony kept their small apartment in the Village. Neither family was happy with the careers they had chosen. However, neither of them would take any money from their families. They got by. Katherine would visit Elizabeth frequently. She tried to help her by bringing gifts and offering money, but Elizabeth refused. Katherine was living some of her own fantasies through Elizabeth. If only she had been able to do what she wanted.

Elizabeth became even closer with Patricia. Patricia was proud of what she was doing. She saw her as one of her daughters. She still called her Aunt Patricia. William would see his daughter once in a while for lunch or dinner when he was in the city, but she would never talk about what she was doing. William never talked about his business. It was a good business arrangement.

There were three different children, with three different stories, and they were all from the same parents. Yet they were all strangers to William and Katherine, and to each other, just as William and Katherine were strangers to each other.

8

HEADQUARTERS MAN

It was the fall of 1977 when William was promoted to Vice President of Operations for Apex Industries, a few months after his thirty-seventh birthday. Apex had always had a large market share of the domestic industrial fastener marketplace, close to sixty percent. The company had always been able to stay ahead of their domestic competition through efficient and economical operations. They were known for a top quality product that held up way beyond its life expectancy. William had been a prime mover for Apex remaining that way. From the time he had started with the company, some fifteen years ago, their sales had increased over 40% while market share increased over 20%, and net income had increased even greater by over 80%. Ingersoll, the CEO, attributed much of these gains to William, whom he considered as his protégé. From the standpoint of producing results for the company, William deserved the promotion. The other company executives resented William's promotion; he was capable enough but not well liked. And, he had replaced Daniel Flynn, who was one of them, one of the "good old boys." William was liable to shake the gravy train. Those at the top might have to really work again.

In the last few years, major competition in the manufacture of industrial fasteners came from the Asian countries. While a number of domestic companies had dropped out of the business, they were more than amply replaced by Japanese, Korean, and other Asian companies. These companies were able to produce the same products as Apex using less expensive labor and materials. Apex's market share was being compromised by their inability to match selling price. They were only maintaining market share as a result of fewer domestic companies in the market, the inability for foreign competitors to produce enough product at the right time, and their edge in quality.

Apex management was concerned about their primary marketplace. Their strategic plan was to reduce labor and material costs while at the same time increase quality. They believed that this was the only effective long-term way to combat foreign competition. They expected Daniel Flynn to be able to spearhead this plan. However, for the last two years he had only sputtered with necessary changes as Apex's market share continued to drop. In fact, its material and labor costs had actually increased while Japanese quality had increased. Apex had more production employees working for them now than they did five years ago. Mr. Ingersoll believed that William could turn things around. He knew that William wasn't afraid to say and do what had to be done. Look what he had done at the Hereford, Columbus, and Stamford plants.

On William's first day as Executive Vice President, Royce Mumford, who was Vice President of Personnel, gave him a tour of the headquarters offices. Normally, a Personnel Department assistant gives a new headquarters' employee the tour, but William warranted the Vice President. He got the VIP treatment. While William had visited there a number of times when he was at the Columbus and Stamford plants, he had always remained in one of the meeting rooms. The headquarters facility was extremely secure. It was a holding area for the company executives, a top echelon prison. As William walked around and saw one plush office or boardroom after another, he realized why employees in the company envied those who worked at headquarters.

Everything was nicer, finer, grander, and more expensive. While Apex was known to be stingy with the furnishings at their plant facilities, nothing was spared for the executives at headquarters. William's salary as Executive Vice President of Operations was more than double his salary as Stamford plant manager not including his potential bonus and stock options. William would be a rich man, but he cared more about his work. He thought he already had more than enough money for him and his family to live comfortably, and now they were giving him more. When he arrived that morning, they relieved him of his Mercedes sedan. It was only one year old, but it was too small and did not have sufficient status for an Executive Vice President. The company provided him with the largest Mercedes sedan, almost limousine size, with his own covered parking spot next to the side entrance and a driver whenever he wanted one.

At the end of the tour, Royce Mumford took William to his new office. On the way into his new office, Royce introduced him to his secretary, Gail Horwath. Gail had been Daniel Flynn's secretary and resented how the company had treated him. She liked Daniel and she knew she wouldn't like Mr. Bradford. She was 24 years old and fairly attractive. She had had an affair with Daniel Flynn that lasted only a few months. He had promised to make her his executive assistant. The affair ended when he left the company. He had called her a number of times after that, but she refused to talk to him. An out of work ex-Executive Vice President could do her no good; she had to get on with her life.

William looked down at her and offered her his hand. "Hello, I'm William Bradford."

She looked at his hand as it stood in mid air. He was ready to pull it back and move toward his new office when she took it limply. He shook her hand while she looked up at him; he already scared her. She remembered what the "girls" at the Stamford plant called him: WB, the Wicked Bastard.

"Hi," she said. "Gail Horwath. I guess I'm your secretary... if you want me."

The policy at headquarters was for each Vice President to choose their own staff including secretaries. William knew no one at headquarters and had no one from the Stamford plant to select. He had always worked through John Biddle to get things done. He saw no need for his own secretary, but evidently headquarters thought he did—so be it. He had brought John Biddle with him as a condition of taking the job as his Executive Assistant.

He stuttered. "Well sure...I'm sure it will work out." He went with Royce into his new office.

Gail went back to work. "He's kind of shy, but cute," she thought to herself.

He entered his new office with Royce. Royce stood in the middle of the room beaming. He was proud of the offices at headquarters, as his department was responsible for setting them up. The company used only top of the line carpeting, furniture, office accessories and so on. He wanted William to feel as proud as he was. It was William's company too, maybe even more so.

"So," said Royce, "what do you think?"

He looked around the office. It was larger than the entire office area at the Stamford plant. In the middle of the room with its back to a full length window wall overlooking the skyline of all of Stamford was an immense dark mahogany executive desk. There was nothing on the desk except a sterling silver water pitcher and goblet set and a matching pen and pencil desk set. He wondered how he would ever fill up the top of the desk. Behind the desk was an upscale African leather executive chair, over six feet tall. He would feel lost in such a chair. It wouldn't be him; it would be his boss. He forgot that now he was the boss.

At Stamford, his chair was an off-the-floor less than $200 "executive chair" that he had bought himself; it fit him perfectly. This new chair would take some getting used to. He wished he could have brought his old chair, but he knew it was against company policy and it would spoil the over-rich decor. On the side walls of the office were four floor to ceiling credenzas, two for filing documents and displaying books, one as an entertainment center with a stereo, radio, a large screen television, a VCR, and a CD player, and the fourth appeared to be a fully stocked bar with a variety of liquors, sodas, snack items, and drinking glasses. He wondered what he would do with all of this. On the other side of the room was a matching conference room table with ten enormous padded chairs. William thought to himself that he could run the world from this office. His immediate dilemma was exactly what he was supposed to do in this office. It wasn't made for work; it was made for living in. It was larger than his first apartment in Hereford.

Royce was watching him look around the room, eyeballing the overly thick carpeting, the silk brocade draperies, the furniture, and the accessory touches. Royce could see the overwhelming excitement and appreciation in his eyes. He didn't know it was an overwhelming feeling of dread. He let him take it all in. Royce felt so proud; William felt so dismayed. This wasn't him. This was corporate royalty.

"So," Royce said, "what do you think?"

What William thought was "what a showy disgrace of conspicuous consumption and a waste of the shareholders' money."

He looked askance at Royce. He didn't know what to say. Apex policy was one of austerity for their employees, adequate pay and benefits, but minimal working conditions. The cost of this office was more than the entire cost of furnishing office facilities at all of their plant locations. William believed in this policy of austerity and that fancy furnishings had little relationship to the work results that were accomplished. He would feel ashamed to bring visitors into this office; it wasn't the message that William Bradford conveyed. He wasn't sure that he could work in such an office; it was an embarrassment of riches that made him uncomfortable. How could he face the workers within the company? He would have to adjust, and it wouldn't take long.

"Impressive," William said. "Very impressive."

Royce beamed. His work was appreciated and by the new Executive Vice President of Operations. He knew that they would get along famously, William wasn't so sure. William didn't like supercilious people who really didn't add any value to the company. Royce was in that category; all polish but very little grit.

"Anything else I can do for you please let me know." Royce had his hand out and was ready to leave the room. "I guess I'll get back to my work."

William wondered what that was. He absentmindedly took Royce's hand. "I was wondering what one did with all of this."

Royce nodded his head. "Oh, you mean all the gadgetry. I'm glad you like it. Me and my staff designed it all." He beamed proudly and started showing William, like a bell person at a hotel, how everything worked. He showed him the lighting system with the control panel at his desk that turned on and off and dimmed all of the lighting in the room, then the control panel for the entertainment center, then the intercom system which rang his secretary and the other executives, and so on. William had been right. He could control the world from his desk.

William tried to stop him a number of times, but Royce couldn't be stopped; he was on automatic pilot. His routine had been programmed and it wouldn't stop until he had reached the end. His staff would be proud of him. Finally, after Royce explained how the curtain system had been designed for sun changes during the day and the seasons and how it could be set for automatic adjustment together with the heating and cooling systems, he stopped. He was out of breath and energy. He was ready for his morning break and then lunch with a prospective applicant. Royce hadn't paid for his own lunch, and not too many dinners, in the four years since he had been promoted to Vice President of Personnel. He had offered to take William to lunch, but he had refused. William would rather pay for his own lunch than prolong his time with Royce.

Royce plopped down in one of the six high back upholstered chairs sitting in front of William's desk as if he was used to sitting in such expensive chairs, which he was. The scene of the six high back chairs in a circle in front of the immense mahogany desk looked like the serfs come to pay homage to the king.

"Well," William started, looking down at Royce. "I really meant what do I do in this office?"

Royce looked puzzled. "What do you mean? You are the Executive Vice President of Operations, that's what you do."

"And you," said William, "are the Vice President of Personnel. You are responsible for all of the company's job descriptions, is that not so?"

Royce chuckled; there was a sign of human life. "Oh, I see. You want to know what you do, how to fill your time. Is that it?"

William smiled affirmatively. "Yes, that's it. What do I do?"

"You are the Vice President of Operations. You do whatever you want. If plant operations prosper, you prosper."

"So," said William. "There is no job description?"

"No, there is no job description."

"So," said William, "how does anyone know if I'm doing the right job or not?"

Royce looked baffled. "I really wouldn't know."

"But," said William, "you write everyone else's job description, including mine when I was plant manager. Is that not so?"

"Yes, we write the job descriptions. It is company policy, but we don't know if anyone really follows them. That's not part of our job."

William shook his head. "I see. So, how do I know what I should be doing?"

"Mr. Ingersoll didn't give you any indication?"

"Mr. Ingersoll assumed that I knew. I tried asking him, but he put me off."

Royce nodded his head. "I see. I guess usually there's a transition time when your predecessor explains the job to you, too bad about Dan Flynn. They just changed the locks on the office one Friday and delivered the contents of his office to his house when they picked up his car. No one knows what happened."

"Not even you—the Vice President of Personnel?"

"He outranked me, you outrank me. You do what you want to do."

He got up to leave the room. He put his hand out again. William shook it limply.

"You might," Royce began, "check with your secretary. She might have some idea of what you do. She was pretty close with Dan Flynn." He flashed a shit-eating grin. "Let me know if there is anything else I can help you with. We are a service department, you know."

"You've helped me quite enough already," William thought. If he was the CEO of this company, the first thing he would do to cut costs would be to get rid of this building and all of the people who supposedly "worked" here, starting with the Vice President of Personnel and his staff.

When Royce Mumford had finally left the office, William sat down in the chair behind his desk. The chair was too big or else he was too small. He felt like a Lilliputian sitting in a giant's chair. He put his head in his hands and tried to relax, but it wasn't happening. Finally, when he had calmed down, he looked at the intercom control. He pushed down on the button that he thought was for his secretary. The door opened and Miss Horwath put her head inside.

"You have to release the button or else it keeps ringing."

He looked down. His finger was still holding the intercom button. He could hear a loud ringing coming through the door. He picked his finger up and the ringing stopped. He would have to tell Royce about this, evidently a design flaw.

Miss Horwath smiled. "Did you want me, William?"

"Mr. Bradford, Miss Horwath."

"Yes, Mr. Bradford. Can I get you something?"

"Yes, I think you can. Mr. Mumford thought you might have some idea as to what the job of Vice President of Operations is all about. He didn't seem to have any idea."

She laughed. "He doesn't seem to have any idea about anything."

"I see," said William. "But you do."

"Oh yes, I worked very closely with Dan . . . that is Mr. Flynn."

He looked at her evaluating. "So I understand."

She said nothing. "I'll be right back."

She came back with a pile of folders in her arms. She came over to his side of the desk and placed them down in front of him. She began by opening the first folder; it was the weekly reports of each of the twelve domestic plant operations for which he was responsible. As she leaned over to show him each report and explain it to him, she leaned against him pushing her breasts into his side. He could feel her breasts digging into him at the same time that her leg dug into his. Miss Horwath was well endowed and evidently didn't mind sharing her good fortune. He pulled abruptly away. Replacing the friendly Miss Horwath would be the first thing that he would need Royce Mumford for. He hoped that Mumford could handle it.

When Miss Horwath finished going over the manner in which Daniel Flynn had done this job, William was even more perplexed. How could some-one run an entire manufacturing complex of twelve plants by sitting in this office and reviewing self-prepared reports? It was quite possible that William was the only honest plant manager of the entire bunch. With his knowledge of the other eleven plant sites, he knew immediately that these reports were complete fiction. They told headquarters what headquarters wanted to know, and the problems were kept to themselves. It appeared that Daniel Flynn very rarely visited a plant site, only when there was a legitimate headquarters problem such as William's promotion and Raymond Fogerty's status quo move or when he had been requested for an award ceremony or such. Much of Daniel's time was spent attending meetings at headquarters with other Vice Presidents or present and prospective major customers. William would change all that. He planned to be an integral part of each plant's operations.

The plant managers wouldn't like being held accountable after all these years, but William would do his job the right way and so would they.

William left his office immediately to find John Biddle. John, as Executive Assistant to William, had been assigned an office in the main section of the headquarters building. While William and the other Executives were on the top floor, the 22nd, John's office was on the sixth. This was the only open office at the time. Daniel Flynn had told top management that he didn't need such a person; it would save the company money. He was just fine with Gail Horwath, his administrative assistant; she worked quite well under him. The other Vice Presidents smiled knowingly; they knew exactly what he meant.

He finally found John in his office at the rear end of the sixth floor. His office was totally isolated from any others. It had previously been a storage room. It was no bigger than one of the credenzas in his office. There was only room for a small desk and one filing cabinet. Royce Mumford had done what he could on such short notice; he was proud of this. John was trying to settle in, but he had more things than the office accommodated. William grabbed what he could and told John to take the rest and follow him. He took John back to his office and settled him in there. There was enough work and storage space for both of them, probably the entire company. They would share the office temporarily.

He would request Royce Mumford to provide two small offices near this office so that he and John could get some work done; nobody could work in the office they gave him. Mumford would have to convert one of the many scarcely used conference rooms into two offices; he wouldn't like it but he would do it for the Executive Vice President of Operations, as he outranked him. Miss Horwath wouldn't like it, but she wouldn't be there for long. She couldn't work under him, not for a second. William felt he had accomplished quite a bit for his first morning. He had Miss Horwath order some lunch to be brought in for him and John. Then they got to work.

News traveled fast at headquarters. When the other Executive Vice Presidents heard about what William was planning to do, they merely shook their heads in unison. They said to each other, "He's still young; he'll soon learn the Apex headquarters way."

William and John

William and John worked together in William's office until the conference room near his office had been divided into two working spaces. He then used his office only when he needed the space to spread out their materials. Then he would use the large conference table. Royce Mumford got right on the conference room renovations. He originally told William that what he wanted would take at least two months. Somehow, for an Executive Vice President, the work was completed in just over three weeks. Position has power and Royce Mumford respected power and keeping his job. Royce knew that no other company, in its right mind, would pay him what Apex was paying him for what he did or didn't do. When the renovations were finished, William and John moved in. The new space became the nerve center for plant operations. William suggested to Mr. Ingersoll that the company use his large office for better purposes, such as an executive dining room or lounge or rent the space to another company. Mr. Ingersoll insisted that William keep this office as well; it went with the position.

As soon as William took over as Executive Vice President of Operations, he and John Biddle started to analyze the position of each plant location. From both of their knowledge of each plant facility they knew that the reports that they had been submitting to Daniel Flynn were fraudulent and overstated. The first thing to be done was to find out the true stories.

William realized that he didn't need a secretary as much as he needed an analyst. He and John were able to answer the phone and make their own appointments; they always had. He put in his request to Royce Mumford to transfer Miss Horwath immediately and to find him a production analyst as soon as possible. As there were no other openings for an executive secretary, Gail Horwath was assigned to the General Accountant; there was always work to be done in accounting. Gail wouldn't like it, she would have to work, and she wouldn't like William. He didn't care. Gail never forgot the "wicked bastard." William had stated his preference for a male production analyst, but Royce kept sending him female applicants. They ranged from the overattractive and overperfumed to the abject ugly. He found something wrong with each of them. He would rather not have female distraction and didn't feel that the plant managers would accept a woman. He didn't want to hire someone that would be doomed to failure.

Finally, he contacted Roget Institute on his own to determine if there were any recent graduates that they would recommend. They gave him three names. He had each of them come in for an interview. The first one, Hunter Richmand, was too upper class. The second one, Desmond Diamond, was too aggressive, as he wanted John Biddle's job and then William's. The third one, Brad Myers, was just right.

Brad came from a working class background in Queens, had gone to Roget on a Blanchard scholarship, and had worked his way through college. He had come to work and to learn and would be William's protégé. He was twenty-two years old, the same age as William was when he started at Apex. William would train him in his way of doing things before he acquired any Apex bad habits.

As William and John, with Brad's assistance, put the pieces together for each plant site, it became obvious to them that the real story was exactly the opposite of what was being reported. Where each of the plant locations, other than the Stamford plant, told a story of increased production and productivity and decreased costs, after William and John redid the numbers as they should be it was a story of decreased productivity and increased costs. Its always astounding what you can do with numbers and statistics once you are aware of what your audience wants to hear.

William developed a visitation schedule for each of the plant locations other than Stamford. He and John and Brad would visit each plant location and identify what needed to be done to bring each plant up to expectations. Each of the plant managers was aware of the positive results that William had achieved at both the Columbus and Stamford plant locations. They despised his success as it made them work harder and do the right thing and fictionalize their reporting of their operating statistics. Now the "wicked bastard" himself was the Executive Vice President. They had always had little trouble deceiving Daniel Flynn; he didn't care as long as the reports were favorable. But William would be another story. He was actually coming out to visit them to review their operations and tell them what they should do, and they were scared of being found out.

Katherine was hoping that William wouldn't have to do as much traveling in his new job. She didn't like it when he told her that he would have to visit each of the plant locations requiring at least a one-night stayover. He had planned to stay at each plant location for two days and then leave John and Brad there for as long as it took to clean things up. He would help them analyze operations and provide direction for those areas that needed to be looked into. John and Brad would then deal directly with plant operations and the people involved. It was William's formula all over again; he would deal with the technical aspects and John would deal with the people.

Each of the children, Richardson, Jameson, and Elizabeth, were having problems. Katherine had hoped that William would be around more often to help her with the children. They all respected William, but none of them could communicate with him. She had expected that the new job would allow him more time for the family. However, once William saw the enormity of the situation at the plant locations, he had to spend even more time at work, initially a considerable amount of time out of town and then a considerable amount of time at headquarters. Work was his life; family and children were Katherine's work. He told Katherine that once things were settled down at the plants, he would be able to spend more time at home. Things never settled down at the plants and never settled down at home. William would continue to choose work, and Katherine would continue to have no choice.

Ethel Biddle was used to John coming home at reasonable hours and spending the weekends together. It was only the two of them as she had not been able to have children. John was her child, and they had always had a close relationship. Until John accepted the job as Assistant Plant Manager to William at Stamford, he had worked as a plant industrial engineer working a regular eight-hour shift with weekends off. Working with William, he worked at least a sixty-hour week including all day Saturday and most of Sunday. While he was at the Stamford plant, he at least came home every night. Now it looked like he would be out of town quite often. Ethel was scared being in the house alone at night. She was used to having John sleep beside her; she got cold without him. They had recently purchased a larger house and new cars with John's increased salary and they were locked in. William had made sure that John was more than adequately compensated for his time. John was now 49 years old. If he worked until retirement he would be a very rich man, richer than he had ever imagined. Ethel didn't want the money. She wanted John. She blamed William and would never forgive him for this.

Executive Vice President

William scheduled their first plant visit for Bueno Verde in central California, the farthest plant site from headquarters. He would get the farthest away done first and then gradually move east, with the Stamford plant the last one to review. By the time they visited the Stamford site, he expected bad habits would have arisen since he had left. He was sure that there would be things to improve. He figured it would take the three of them the best part of a year to visit all twelve plant sites and implement their recommendations.

The Bueno Verde plant was similar to the Hereford, Alabama, plant in that the employees were mostly ranchers and farmers and Apex was the largest employer in town. It was ironic that William had started his career at Apex in Hereford and now Brad would be starting his career in Bueno Verde. The plant manager at Bueno Verde was named Dale Higbee. Dale was a local boy who had risen through the ranks at Apex, having started as an eighteen-year old apprentice machinist over fifteen years ago. Dale also owned a small cattle ranch, which was his priority. The job at Apex helped him to afford the ranch. The Bueno Verde plant was important to Apex, as it was their only plant in California, which was close to many of their large aerospace customers. These same customers were major targets for their Asian competitors.

William led John and Brad through a review of the plant's operations. For William and John it was Hereford deja vu. The employees came to work and left for the day as demanded by their ranch or farm operations. It was apparent that productivity wasn't even close to what it could be. The numbers that Dale Higbee had been reporting were a complete fiction. He had been reporting quarterly totals as monthly totals. When William's team worked through the numbers, they found that the plant was really operating at a loss of over $300,000 per month. At the same time, they were sitting on major customer orders in backlog, weren't able to ship anything on time, and had built up excessive inventories as a result of canceled orders and inaccurate production schedules.

Their market share for the California market had eroded from over 70% to less than 30%. Dale attributed the slide to foreign competition. William attributed it to inefficient management and operations. Daniel Flynn hadn't been at this site for over five years, and then it was to present a gift of appreciation to Dale for ten years of service. Daniel didn't like long flights or California.

After the first three days of reviewing plant operations, it was apparent that this plant couldn't be saved. There was no more that William needed to do. He left John and Brad to finish up gathering numbers and statistics to justify their recommendation to close the plant. William went looking for a replacement plant closer to their major customers and a more reliable labor force. It was also an opportunity to pay a courtesy visit to Apex's major California customers.

Of Apex's six major customers in the aerospace industry in California, four of them were located in Orange County within sixty miles of Los Angeles and the other two were located in the San Francisco Bay Area. Daniel Flynn had chosen Bueno Verde, as it was half way between each of these areas, but close to nowhere. William's first visit was to their largest customer, Innovac Inc., located in Lake Pontoon outside of Newport Beach. He met with their Vice President of Operations, Harold Borden, who was most cordial and pleased to see William. No one from Apex had been to see them in over three years, not even a sales person. Their purchases from Apex had dwindled each year, and Apex sales management had decided they would be flogging a dead horse.

Harold told him that they would love to be buying more from Apex, but they couldn't live with Apex's unreliability of on-time deliveries and receding quality. Harold agreed that the Asian companies were able to sell at lower prices, but after adding back shipping and port charges their prices were not significantly lower than Apex. He got a commitment from Harold that if Apex could guarantee full quality and on-time delivery at the same prices as foreign competitors, Innovac would commit themselves to long term contracts for all of their major components. Harold would much rather buy locally if he could, but Apex had made this impossible. It wasn't foreign competition; it was domestic incompetence.

When William contacted the Apex Vice President of Sales, Roland Boxley, to share his experience with Innovac, Roland was furious. How dare William call on one of his customers? The sales department had done fine without his help all these years. When William started to read Roland the unpleasant statistics as to the erosion of sales at Innovac and all of California, Roland abruptly interrupted him. Roland was aware of the entire situation; there was nothing Apex could do with unfair Asian competition. They had conceded the market.

If William could clean up the Bueno Verde plant operations, then maybe they could recover some market share. Leave the sales end to the sales people. Roland hung up on him. William called back and spoke directly to Mr. Ingersoll, who stood behind Roland Boxley. He told William to stick to operations and leave sales to Roland. This was the first doubt that William had that possibly Apex management wasn't as together as he thought they were.

Harold Borden put William onto an available plant site that one of their domestic competitors, Flexible Fasteners, had recently closed as a result of foreign competition. The site was strategically located within forty miles of their four major customers in this area. Harold suggested that he go over immediately as he was aware that one of the Japanese conglomerates was negotiating with them. He knew the management at Flexible and assured William that they would much prefer to sell or lease the site to Apex. William contacted them immediately and set up a meeting for that afternoon. They told William that they were very close to an agreement with the Nagasaki people, but if William could obtain a binding commitment from Apex within the next two days they had a deal.

He again called Mr. Ingersoll for a quick decision. Mr. Ingersoll said that he couldn't make such a decision on his own, but for William to talk to Don Crawford, the Vice President for Capital Acquisitions. He called Don and was told Don wasn't available. Don called back and he missed his call. He called back and Don wasn't there. This went on all that day. They finally made contact late the next day. Don told William that the capital budget for the year was pretty much expended or committed. Apex didn't operate in this manner. It would take at least six weeks for a decision like this. He would set it in the works if William wanted him to. William told him to forget it. He called Mr. Ingersoll to explain the situation. Mr. Ingersoll supported Don Crawford. William would have to learn how the company worked. He couldn't just be making decisions on his own. He would have to figure how to improve Buena Verde plant operations, that was his job, and leave sales and capital acquisitions alone. Mr. Ingersoll was starting to think that maybe he had made a big mistake; William didn't seem like he was a team player. William started to think that maybe he had made a big mistake, that maybe Apex wasn't a winning player.

William returned to Bueno Verde and assisted John and Brad in determining what could be done to make the plant more efficient and economically operated. They developed an entire plan consisting of equipment replacement, revamping of hiring and training procedures, plant layout changes, quality control procedural enhancements and so on. William left at the end of the week, with instructions to John, Brad, and Dale Higbee as to what needed to be done and by what date. It took them three months to implement their operational recommendations. Dale was cooperative, but not committed to the changes. He had told William that these changes would result in massive employee leavings. William felt if that happened, it would be for the best. Sure enough, over 40%, about 308 employees, of the plant employees left Apex within the next two months. William had estimated that they would only have to replace one third of these employees. With John Biddle on site to review all new hires, William was confident that they could quickly replace these employees with ones who sincerely wanted to work. After three weeks, John had interviewed over eighty prospective employees and had found only two that he would even consider, and he wasn't too sure about those two. In the meantime, operations had worsened. William decided to close the plant. He didn't call Mr. Ingersoll or anyone else. He was the Executive Vice President of Operations—let the Japanese have the business. The result of the plant closing was that company wide net income increased by over eight percent and over 800 employees had lost their jobs. William was the company hero once again. Mr. Ingersoll knew now that he had made the right decision.

Company Acquisition

By the time that William, John, and Brad had reviewed the other eleven plant sites, four other plant sites were also closed resulting in over three thousand employees losing their jobs. There was nothing else that William could do without the cooperation of other departments within Apex such as Sales, Capital Acquisitions, Accounting and so on. With the seven remaining plants, overall sales decreased by 28%, with overall net income increasing by over 40%. William had succeeded in making more money for Apex with a lot less cost. Apex had become a much smaller, but more profitable, player in the industrial fasteners market. They stuck to specialty products where they could deliver on time with top quality at competitive prices. William was a hero to the stockholders, including Mr. Ingersoll, who owned thirty percent of the stock. He was the devil incarnate to the other operating departments of the company as well as his own. The company had reduced overall employee levels from a high of 30,000 plus when William took over as Executive Vice President to less than 12,000 four years later.

After four years on the job, he had operations where he wanted them. Each of the seven remaining plants was operating efficiently. Apex had carved out a number of niche markets with quality products with minimal price competition. Their net profit margin had risen from less than eight percent to over seventeen percent. They were exceedingly profitable. John or Brad would visit each plant site at least quarterly to provide assistance and ensure that quality was maintained. William would receive weekly reports from each plant site to ensure that results continued to improve. He rarely visited a plant site himself except for special occasions or award celebrations. He had John and Brad, but he was getting bored. He had moved back into the large office and attended a number of weekly meetings.

Somehow, he still went into work early and returned home late. Katherine was happy that he had stopped traveling, but she wished he were home more often. His salary and benefits, including increased stock options, had increased greatly over the four years. Where he had thought he was well paid then, he was now being exorbitantly paid at the expense of those employees who no longer worked for Apex. He never saw the connection. He still enjoyed problem solving and making the numbers work. There was just less of that to do as operations had been made so efficient. John and Brad could take care of maintaining operations, but there was little room for William to employ his innovative problem solving skills. He had become a part of the executive team whose goal was to protect their assets (e.g., share value), only William wasn't aware of it.

He had evolved into a new routine. He would awake at five and shower and shave and then dress in the suit, shirt, tie and shoes that Katherine had set out for him the night before. He would kiss Katherine on the top of the head as he left the bedroom and pull down her nightgown (she had begun to wear unattractive but warm granny gowns) and pull up the covers. He would leave the house immediately and be at the office by six. There would be an executive meeting in one of the executive offices until eight. There was more horsing around, joking, and kibitzing than work discussed, but he didn't notice, as he had become part of the team. The executive whose office was being used for that morning's meeting provided the breakfast food, each one attempting to outdo the one before.

After the meeting, he would meet with one of the other vice presidents to discuss strategy, whatever that was. Sometimes he would meet with John Biddle or Brad Myers if they were in the office, but they rarely were. The rest of the morning usually consisted of telephone calls to and from the plant locations, many of these merely courtesy calls, some trouble shooting. He liked these but they were far too few, and fewer all the time.

He had gone without a secretary for over three years. Just the past year when he moved back into his large office, he was forced to hire one so that there was somebody outside of his office to shield him from unwanted interruptions, they were all unwanted. After interviewing a large number of applicants, Royce Mumford and the personnel department gave him an ultimatum to select one within the next month or they wouldn't work with him anymore. He remembered a diminutive, unattractive young lady with impressive academic and work credentials whom he had interviewed a number of months ago. At the time, he thought he would find someone better; that is with the same quality credentials but with smaller breasts. He had personnel bring her back in and she was still interested in the job. He hired her immediately—personnel wouldn't threaten him. This is how Harriet Gregson was hired. She was 25 years old in 1981 when she was hired, just a little younger than Brad Myers.

Interestingly, as the number of personnel in operations had greatly decreased, the number of employees working at headquarters had greatly increased, from about three hundred to over a thousand. Everyone had secretaries and some of the secretaries had secretaries, administrative assistants, staff analysts, specialists, trouble-shooters, and so on. William had John, Brad, and now Harriet Gregson.

As he became more and more involved with the executive team and its large number of required meetings, he started to delegate more and more of the daily work to Miss Gregson. She was eager to learn and was glad to take on as much as she could. It was better than sitting idly at her desk waiting for the phone to ring or for William to ask her to get him something. The other secretaries told her she was insane, all that work for the same pay. William, however, made sure that Miss Gregson was more than fairly compensated. The other secretaries told her that this wasn't fair. They didn't like Harriet and she didn't like them. She liked working for William and being responsible. Harriet began to come in early with William and leave late with him. He would confide in her, as she knew as much as to what was going on in operations as he did. She had become indispensable; in a large sense she was doing his job. He had become a true executive, but he didn't like it.

Apex operations continued to run smoothly with each month's results surpassing the month before. Mr. Ingersoll and the other executives of course, gave William credit for these results. John, Brad, and Harriet were, of course, doing the bulk of the work. William was being removed farther and farther away from actual operations. It was now 1983 and takeover fever was rampant in the country. Apex was continually being rumored as a takeover candidate. The Apex board of directors passed resolutions to protect themselves, and their shares, and the executives should such a thing happen.

It was only the other employees who would be vulnerable. A number of companies had considered acquiring Apex, but the board had successfully deterred them as they thought they could get more. In 1984, Diamond Industries, a conglomerate who manufactured industrial adhesives, PVC piping, and pretzels, made an offer that the Apex board couldn't refuse. The members of the board and the executives would be extremely wealthy individuals. Mr. Ingersoll and the board convinced the other stockholders that accepting this offer would be in their best interest, and well it was. It just wasn't in the best interest of the Apex employees. Many of the executives took their stock earnings and left the company, including Mr. Ingersoll.

Diamond Industries wanted William to stay as part of the deal. He was one of the reasons that Apex was attractive. They made him an attractive offer that included increased compensation and stock options. He insisted that his team, John, Brad, and Harriet, be similarly compensated. As part of their purchase, Diamond had planned to reduce costs at Apex and sell off pieces of the business. As William was the main remaining Apex executive, they put him in charge of carrying out their consolidation plan. William started with headquarters and with John and Brad's assistance they were able to reduce personnel from over 1,200 to less than 400, with a freeze on hiring. Many departments were eliminated or greatly reduced. William had earned his nickname of "the wicked bastard" even though John and Brad carried out his orders. After the selling off of less profitable pieces of the operations, anything providing less than ten percent net income, and with William's consolidations and increased efficiencies, operations personnel were reduced from 12,000 to less than 4,000. William enjoyed problem solving once again. He was promoted to Executive Vice President of Diamond Industries. What he had been able to do for Apex in the industrial fasteners business, he could do for Diamond Industries and industrial adhesives, PVC piping, and pretzels.

William kept John, Brad, and Miss Gregson with him and he stayed in his same office. After a period of review with John and Brad, they were able to implement numerous economies and efficiencies in these other businesses to the tune of over 6,000 out of 15,000 employees no longer needed. William's reputation as a ruthless businessperson, the wicked bastard, was increasing. He still saw himself as a problem solver with people just one factor of the equation. After three years, in 1987, things once again had settled down. Diamond Industries was now considered "lean and mean" with net income and earnings per share on a continual rise. William was now back maintaining systems and getting bored again. He would attend more and more meetings, now most of them out of the building. He was being used to work with vendors to get them more economical and efficient and with customers to get them to buy more products after he showed them how to use their products for increased uses. He was getting farther away again from the actual operations, which were left to John, Brad, and Harriet. Diamond Industries had effectively constricted their operations, fewer facilities, fewer employees, but more profits. By 1992, they had become a takeover target themselves. They had become too good at what they did. William was becoming expert at building up companies so that they could be bought out attractively. William was made part of a team to prevent this from happening. Their job was to make Diamond less attractive to a potential purchaser. William couldn't think this way, as it was against his principles of efficiency and economy.

James Corcoran

With the acquisition of Apex by Diamond Industries in 1984, William became one of twelve Executive Vice Presidents and was able to promote John Biddle to Vice President of Operations (at that time there were 34 Vice Presidents), Brad Myers to Assistant Vice President (there were 87 of these), and Harriet Gregson to Executive Assistant (there were only four of these). Each of these promotions came with substantial increases in pay and made the three of them eligible for the company stock option plan William rewarded loyalty and hard work, compensation commensurate with results. When William and his team were through eliminating, reducing, and consolidating there remained only three Executive Vice Presidents; William for Operations, Leroy Holmes for Human Resources, and Harold Satinsky the chief financial officer, six Vice Presidents, eight assistant vice presidents, and three executive assistants—one for each executive vice president.

While job titles, status, and compensation changed for John, Brad, and Harriet, their functions remained the same. William was still very much the boss; the others carried out his orders. At this point, the three of them had no complaints. William had indeed taken care of them. The other executives, however, who were downsized didn't feel the same way. Although William made sure that those downsized in the company were well compensated, particularly for those years where they were well paid but provided minimal results, they bore resentment towards him. He was the survivor, and they were the losers. William, on the other hand, had no survivor's guilt. Those let go were given more than they should have as a reward for raping the company for years.

One of the ex-Executive Vice Presidents, James Corcoran, of Sales and Marketing, had given his entire working career to Diamond Industries, right out of college at 21 years old. He had worked side by side with William as part of the streamlining team to eliminate unnecessary people and costs. He never imagined that he himself might be one of the victims. How could the company function without him or someone in his position? He felt safe in recommending others for displacement. However, when William's team developed numbers and statistics that showed that the company was not selling the right products to the right customers at the right prices, the CEO John Armstrong and the board decided that the Sales Department needed revamping. James fought back and defended his position; however, he became the first to go. James blamed William, but William blamed James himself. James was sixty-two years old with nothing to do and nowhere to go.

When Harriet was promoted to the management position of Executive Assistant, William also made sure that she got her own office. As he needed her near, he converted some of his space into an office so that Harriet was right outside his door. She was only the third woman in the history of Diamond Industries to be promoted to a management position; the other two were accounting managers. The other women in the organization resented her for this. Harriet didn't care, as this was her life. As a result, she became closer to the men (William, John, and Brad) and avoided the women in the organization. The other women said she looked like one of the men anyway. She was in the right place.

Shortly after James Corcoran had been helped out of the organization, he began drinking heavily. James had been a devout Christian and teetotaler when he first joined Diamond. However, it was soon apparent that it was expected for Diamond sales people to take major customer personnel out to lunches and dinners with heavy drinking before and after the meal. James soon realized that if he was going to be successful as a sales person he would have to drink along with the customer personnel. In his first year, his sales manager admonished him for not drinking with the customers. He was told, "a drinking customer is a happy customer." So James started drinking. At first he couldn't stand the taste or the smell. However, it wasn't long before he enjoyed the effect of the drinking. He could laugh along with the customers and tell them what they wanted to hear; promise them anything, but get the sale. James quickly became a heavy drinker and an extremely successful sales person. The more he drank and his tolerance for liquor increased, so did his sales. Ultimately he became sales manager, then Vice President of Sales, and finally Executive Vice President. As James rose in the organization, so did his girth. He was a big man, six foot three and over 200 pounds, and he kept getting bigger. He would always have a ready joke, usually off color, and would laugh along with his audience, usually customers, so that his entire body shook the room.

At the time of his dismissal, James was living alone. His wife of thirty-six years had died of breast cancer three years before and his three children lived in other parts of the country. James had never been a womanizer; he had always been one of the boys. However, with the loss of his job, he lost his friends from Diamond and was too ashamed to maintain his other friends. He was too ashamed to leave his apartment, so he stayed alone and drank. James had never drunk alone before. He stayed unkempt and ate very little.

One of his children became concerned about him and called the company. He talked to Leroy Holmes in Human Resources. Leroy would typically patronize such phone callers as once an employee had left the company they were no longer his responsibility. Besides, there had been too many employees let go to deal with all of them. However, James had been an Executive Vice President and a professional colleague. He had personally counseled James through his grief when his wife, Helen, had died. He assured James's son, Jimmy, that he would personally look in on his father and get back to him. However, Leroy put off calling or visiting James until his son called him back the following week; James was getting worse. Leroy promised Jimmy he would visit his dad immediately.

When Leroy arrived at the apartment, he found days of newspapers stacked in front of the door. It appeared that either no one was home or James hadn't left his apartment in days. He rang the buzzer; there was no answer. He held the buzzer down just to make sure. If anyone were home they would hear it and answer the door just to shut it up. Leroy continued ringing for a good five minutes. He was getting quite concerned. Jimmy had told him he had talked to his father the evening before and he was quite incoherent, cursing at the company and someone he called the wicked bastard. Leroy went to find the custodian for the building.

When they opened the apartment, it smelled horrible, both toilets stuffed and dirty clothes and garbage lying all around. They found James lying on the living room rug, passed out in his own vomit. Leroy called for an ambulance and James was taken to the hospital. James spent three weeks in the hospital to allow him to dry out and regain his strength. When William heard the story, he just shuddered. He would have never thought that James couldn't be self-responsible.

Three days after being released from the hospital, he showed up at William's office. He had to enter William's office through Harriet's office. He had always gotten along with her and she had always liked him. He always had a joke for her, not one of his off color ones, and he always made her laugh. Fortunately William was out of the office when James asked to see him. There was no joke today.

Harriet told James that William probably wouldn't be back for another three or four hours, maybe not even that day. He asked where William was, but she wisely didn't tell him. He said that he would wait. He sat on the sofa and stared straight at Harriet. It was unnerving. After a while she excused herself and made the sign to James to indicate the women's room. James nodded his head and continued staring. When Harriet left the office, James tried to go through her desk drawers, but Harriet had wisely locked them. James then tried to get into William's office but the door was locked. He kicked at it and rammed his shoulder against the door but it wouldn't budge. James only succeeded in hurting himself.

Harriet went immediately to Leroy Holmes's office. She had kept her cool with James, but was now quite concerned. What if James had a gun or a knife, what if William returned while James was there, what if James decided to use her as a hostage, what if he started shooting up the place and so on? Leroy was initially concerned as to how James had gotten into the building, as it was a secure facility. Leroy called security and was going into the whole routine of lapsed security and he would find out who was responsible and take appropriate measures and so forth. Security reported to Leroy.

Harriet was frantic. She didn't care about breaches in security; her immediate concern was what to do about James. She finally got Leroy to focus on the situation, not the blame for the situation. He agreed to go with Harriet back to her office with two security guards. When they arrived at her office, James was still sitting on the sofa staring straight ahead. It scared Leroy. He decided to take a cordial approach. He extended his hand. "James, what a pleasant surprise." The guards moved closer, but Leroy waved them off. Harriet stayed in the back.

James looked up at him. "Like Hell it is."

"James, why don't we go down to my office and talk about this."

"I'm waiting for the wicked bastard. I have no business with you."

"Please, James. You can wait for William in my office. Harriet will let us know when he gets back."

Leroy tried to move closer to James. He could smell the alcohol on his breath.

"Like Hell she will. She's in it with the wicked bastard."

Harriet cringed and moved further back.

Leroy moved closer to put his hand on James's shoulder to help him up. "Come on, Jim, we'll talk about the old days."

"Fuck the old days. They don't exist anymore. Nothing exists anymore. Fuck Diamond Industries, fuck William S. Bradford III, and fuck you!" He pulled his shoulder away.

Leroy persisted. "Come on, Jim. Don't be like this."

James stood up. He was at least a head taller than Leroy and fifty pounds heavier. He looked down at Leroy and breathed in his face. Leroy moved away. The guards moved closer in. Leroy motioned them back. He knew James; he wasn't violent. "I'll be anyway I want. You still got your fucking job. It's easy for you to talk."

Leroy took James by the elbow and tried to get him to move. As the guards watched, James quickly grabbed Leroy around the neck. James nodded at the guards. "Tell them to leave us alone."

He motioned for the guards to leave. As they hesitated, Harriet stepped forward. "Please, James, take me. Leroy had nothing to do with your losing your job."

James looked over and became befuddled. He released the pressure on Leroy's neck while he thought about it. At this moment the guards ran at James and were able to knock him down. They subdued him on the floor, while Leroy telephoned for the police. He could hardly talk.

They found two long knives in James's pockets. Whether he would have used them, nobody knows. The company decided that it was best not to press charges. They did however change all the locks. They never did discover how he entered the building. Leroy increased security; it was all he could think of to do. James agreed to seek help and went to live with his son Jimmy in Idaho. He would never be the same. William was eternally grateful to Harriet. She may have saved his life with her quick thinking. This brought them even closer. The incident confirmed William's and the company's decision that James had become a liability.

Harriet Gregson

It was around this time that one of the Diamond employees took a personal interest in Harriet. At the time of the merger between Apex and Diamond, William's team and the Diamond industrial engineers were required to work quite closely together. One of the industrial engineers, Herman Whiteside, was assigned to the same project as Harriet. Herman was a rather non-descript man, short, heavy set, slovenly, poorly dressed, with a face like a bull-dog. His shirt was always coming out of his trousers and he always had a full pencil protector hanging from his shirt pocket. He never kept his suit jacket on; it was usually food stained. His tie was pulled away from his collar; it choked him, as his neck was too fat. He was not the image that headquarters liked to portray. However, Herman was one of the best industrial engineers at Diamond's largest plant facility and had been transferred to headquarters to work on the transition team.

Herman had never worked this closely with a woman before. At first, even Harriet found Herman somewhat repulsive. However, as they worked together, she began to find him extremely sweet. He started by bringing her coffee and donuts in the morning. He would come into work early with Harriet and work late so that they could leave together. As they worked closer together, each one began to appreciate the mind of the other. After a while, their lack of physical beauty became less important to each of them. They would have coffee in the morning, lunch, and sometimes dinner together in the office. William noticed them getting closer even before Harriet did. He was concerned that he might lose Harriet. Sometimes when he walked through her office, he would find Herman and Harriet sitting close together while they worked, with Herman's hand slightly touching Harriet's leg.

Herman and Harriet were becoming an item for gossip in the office. Some wise guy in sales, as a joke, had started up an office pool as to the day when they would finally do it. Many of the employees saw their relationship as a joke; others saw it as wonderful and heart warming. Herman and Harriet were moving towards love; even ugly people have the right to love. They were spending all of their time together, even outside of work. Harriet was glowing. She dressed and acted differently, she had her hair done, she used more make-up. She was alive. She was now 32 years old and this could be her last chance. Herman was 38 years old and had never expected to find a woman for himself. Harriet was his picture of the perfect woman. He would never meet another like her; there wasn't another like her.

When the consolidation was completed near the end of 1988, the consolidation team developed a list by department of those employees who were to be displaced—some transferred, some early retired, and some let go. William, as Executive Vice President and consolidation team leader, was responsible for finalizing the list and making any adjustments. He noticed a few departments that were getting rid of the wrong people and called them to task. For some, he reversed positions, and recommended keeping the employees and getting rid of department management. As he perused the list, he came to the industrial engineering department and noticed that Herman was listed for transfer back to the Nebraska plant.

William thought hard about what this would do to Harriet. He knew she wouldn't leave her job to move to Nebraska, even for Herman. He wanted strongly to be able to recommend Herman for a headquarters position, but in the end his principles wouldn't allow it, Herman just wasn't headquarters image. He let the transfer stand.

When Herman received the news, he was personally devastated. Admittedly, he had done an excellent job on the consolidation team. The results he had achieved warranted a better reward. Other less competent industrial engineers had been retained at headquarters, why not him? When he got his official notice, he went immediately to Harriet. He was close to tears. He didn't want to leave her. Harriet said she would talk to William.

She went immediately into William's office. She had never before entered his office without first asking. William looked up from his work. He was taken aback, but not surprised.

"Mr. Bradford," she stammered. "Can I talk to you?"

He put his work aside. "Of course, you know that. What's it all about?"

Harriet sat down in one of the visitor chairs. She crossed her leg and he looked away. She gulped down the saliva in her throat. "It's about Herman."

He nodded his head. "I thought it might be."

Harriet was approaching tears. "They're transferring him back to Nebraska. Is there anything you can do to keep him here?" Her eyes misted over; the scene was surreal to her.

He looked at her sternly. "You know I approve of all consolidation moves. I'll see what I can do."

She brightened up. "Oh, thank you, Mr. Bradford." She ran out to tell Herman. William could see them hugging through the opening in the door.

The CEO and board of directors gave William one last review to make any changes before they approved of the final consolidation list. He looked at it, went through it one more time, and then signed his name. He let it stand as is. In the end his work principles won out. Herman went back to Nebraska, Harriet kept her job at headquarters, and William kept Harriet. Herman and Harriet vowed to stay in touch, but after a few months he stopped calling. Harriet went back inside herself. Her life became her job again. She never forgave the wicked bastard. She did her job well because she knew no other way to do it, but she became the enemy within.

Brad Myers

Brad Myers had been an honor student and academic overachiever all his life. Coming from a lower middle class background, his father was a department store clerk; his mother worked in a greeting card store. They impressed upon him the value of an education. Neither one of them had gone to college. He would be the first college graduate in the family. This would be his ticket out of the neighborhood. His parents both worked hard so that he could have a better life. When he was a teenager, they wouldn't allow him to work; his studies came first. He was able to get into the high school for math and sciences, where he excelled academically. He was given a Blanchard scholarship to Roget Institute. Ironically, William was a member of the scholarship committee. The scholarship required him to work during college in the field of economics. When it came time for employment in 1978, his counselor at Roget recommended Apex Industries and William Bradford.

When Brad came to the interview with William, he was dressed exactly as William would have dressed for a similar interview. He was highly recommended by Roget and his field placement. He was extremely polite and eager. He made sure that he called William "Mr. Bradford," which impressed William. Since Brad would be the first assistant to the vice president in the company, his formal title would be production analyst. There were no guidelines for compensation—it would be up to William. William remembered when he first started work and how grateful, coming from a poor background, he was to receive a fair starting salary. William checked with personnel to see what they were paying recent college graduates and offered Brad $10,000 more. Brad was ecstatic. It was more than his parents combined were earning. He knew immediately he was going to like William.

Brad was an apt pupil. He quickly learned, from William and John, the principles of economic and efficient management and operations. As with William, it was the real life application of what he had studied at Roget. William was pleased, as Brad had no time to pick up bad habits elsewhere. Brad would be his unspoiled protégé. For a number of years, this was exactly the way it was. William and John would set up the parameters and Brad would carry them out. Brad never questioned their authority or what they asked him to do. He was obedient and was rewarded for it. He was alone with William and John for three years until Harriet Gregson was hired in 1981. She was only slightly younger than he was, and he now had someone close to his age to talk to. He and Harriet became work friends. They would try to support each other.

Brad had always kept his personal life to himself. When he was out of town with William or John, he would start work early and end work late. As far as was known, he went right to his room to sleep. When he was in town, he again started work early and ended late six days a week. On Sunday he came in a little later and left a little earlier. He really had no time for a personal life. His life was his job and making as much money as he could. He would never live like his parents. As far as anyone at the company knew, he had no friends outside of the company. He worked and went back to his small efficiency apartment in downtown Stamford, which he used mainly for sleeping. He was out of town over 70% of the time.

Brad spent very little money. When he was out of town, the company paid his expenses. When he was in town, he was always working. This allowed him to accumulate quite a sum of money, but there would never be enough. He had been with the company for six years when in 1984 William promoted him to Assistant Vice President. With this promotion and the increased salary, he was able to finally start saving substantial amounts of money each month. This allowed him to give himself permission to live somewhere nicer. He purchased a new relatively high-end two-bedroom, two-bath, living room and den condo apartment that was half again as large as his parents' house where the three of them had lived. He had squirreled his money away for six years; now it was time for him to live a little. He was now 28 years old.

In 1988, when Herman was transferred back to Nebraska, it was Brad whom Harriet turned to for comfort and he was there for her. This was the first time that he had ever questioned William. He thought it was a bastardly thing to do to anyone, especially Harriet. It was over this incident that he started to move away from William as a mentor. He began to question whether he wanted to be like William.

After the incident with Herman, Brad started to have a social life. He could see himself becoming a male version of Harriet and he didn't like the picture. He was now 32 years old and it was time to have a life. He still wanted the money, but maybe he could have both. He would go into New York on the weekends to dinner, shows, concerts, opera and so on. He contacted some of his old friends from Roget and made new friends in the city. One of his new friends, Mike Morgan, was a plant manager at a defense contractor on Long Island. He confided to Brad that his job was killing him. He was tired having to lie to the government inspectors and falsifying cost records. He wanted to get back into the private sector. Mike was kind of a gruff individual who made himself familiar with a new acquaintance almost immediately, particularly males.

There was an opening at their New Brunswick, New Jersey, plant for a plant manager. William told Brad that it would be more desirable to find someone from the outside, as the present employees were too close to the bad practices of the previous plant manager. Brad thought immediately of Mike Morgan. He set up an interview with William.

Mike arrived punctually the following Wednesday. William was busy in his office and Harriet asked Mike to wait a few minutes. Mike was dressed in a new suit, shirt, tie and shoes, as advised by Brad. He felt very uncomfortable, as he normally wore slacks and a sport shirt to work. He sat on the sofa in Harriet's office. He smiled at her, and she smiled back. He picked up *Forbes* magazine. He could look like a Republican if that would get him the job. Harriet smiled at him.

"So," Mike began, "you're Miss Gregson."

"That's right." It said Miss Gregson on her nameplate. She continued to work.

"Oh, no. I mean Brad's told me about you."

"Oh," said Harriet. "What did he tell you?"

"Oh, you know, about you and Herman. I'm sorry."

Harriet grew crimson. How could Brad tell a stranger about her? She was so embarrassed. She got up and left the room immediately. The nerve of that jerk. She hoped he didn't get the job.

William called on the intercom for Harriet to send Mike in, but there was no response. He went to her office and found Mike sitting alone on the sofa.

"Where's Miss Gregson?" asked William.

"She had an emergency. You know woman's stuff." William didn't know.

He extended his hand. "Hello, I'm William Bradford."

Mike grabbed his hand firmly, too firmly. "Hi, William, I'm Mike Morgan." William cringed at the mention of his first name.

Normally, he would have ended the interview right there with some kind of excuse. But, as Brad Myers referred him, he gave Mike the benefit of the doubt. "Mr. Morgan, would you like to come into my office?"

"Sure," said Mike as he pushed past William.

Mike was sitting down in front of William's desk by the time he sat behind the desk. It wasn't the chair William would have had him sit in, but he let it go.

He looked down at Mike's resume. "I see you've had experience in both the private and public sectors. Impressive." He was going to continue, but Mike interrupted him.

"Yeah, I've been around. Started out in the schmata business in New York. We made rags, you know. for little princesses."

William nodded. Mike continued. "Then I moved into the metal fabricating racket, you know, converting dreck into product. It was a mitzvah to be out of the schmata trade and into dreck." Mike laughed. William remained stern and silent.

"Next I was plant manager for a precision parts maker. It was a quality outfit, but a meshugina family operation. If you know what I mean." William didn't.

"For the last five years," Mike continued, "I've been plant manager at Kopsky and Company, out on the Island, making radar parts for the government. I'm tired of being a goniff, so I'd like to get out. Brad said you had an opening in Brunswick. It's a good town, has a good deli."

William stared at Mike. He wasn't sure that Brad wasn't having fun with him.

"I see you graduated from CCNY. What was your major?"

"No major, just a bunch of courses. Did take some Jewish engineering, though; you know, accounting courses. Been helpful to me."

William got up from his desk. Mike sat there. William extended his hand. Mike took it limply.

"So," said Mike, "that's it?"

"That's it, Mr. Morgan. We'll let you know. We're still looking at other applicants."

"Yeah, sure," said Mike. "I can start whenever you need me. No big magilla."

"Thank you for coming in, Mr. Morgan." William tried to raise him up out of his seat. Mike finally understood.

"Yeah, thanks, William. Look forward to working with ya."

When they reached Harriet's office, she had returned, grateful that Mike Morgan was no longer there.

"Miss Gregson, would you take Mr. Morgan back to the reception area."

Harriet made an ugly face at him. William quite understood.

On the way out Mike turned around and said to Harriet, "I hope you find someone else. Shitty thing for that putz to leave you like that." Harriet turned and ran back to her office.

Later on, Brad asked William how the interview with Mike Morgan had gone. William told him that it was strange. Mike kept using yiddish words and not listening. It was almost as if Mike was conducting the interview, kind of pushy. This wouldn't go at Diamond Industries. Mike wouldn't fit in. It wouldn't be fair to hire him. What had Brad told him about Diamond Industries and William?

When Brad asked him about how the interview with William went, Mike said he thought it went well, but that William . . . uh Mr. Bradford . . . was a little stiff. That seemed strange for a Jewish guy; usually they were all so out front. And, he looks just like Henry Kissinger, awesome. Brad looked at Mike. "William isn't Jewish!" Mike look confused. "Does this mean that I didn't get the job?" Brad understood why William wouldn't want to hire him, but he thought Mike was also being discriminated against. William might be discriminating against Jews, but Mike wasn't Jewish; he was a homosexual just like Brad. Brad wouldn't forget this.

9

WILLIAM REDUX

I n 1992, William had all plant operations within Diamond Industries running quite efficiently and economically. He had established fairly foolproof weekly reporting systems, which allowed him to monitor results so that he could catch any potential slippage while it was happening. He had also helped design an online computer system directly tied into each plant so that he could see, on a real time basis, exactly what was occurring at each plant site. The system would instantaneously flash a message on William and Harriet Gregson's computer screens if any operational result at any plant site exceeded (plus or minus) the expected criteria. This allowed him to closely control all plant operations from his desk at headquarters. If he desired, he could automatically call that plant site to make sure the proper remedial action was being taken and to ensure that it wouldn't happen again. William was quite proud of what he had accomplished. However, since the real work had been accomplished, he now just watched.

He still had John and Brad continually visiting each of the plant sites on a revolving basis. Between these ongoing plant reviews and the computer monitoring systems, he felt quite confident about each plant site. As added insurance, he would visit each plant site on an annual basis just to see for himself. As a result of his visits, he would always develop a list of improvements for the plant manager to implement, with follow up reviews by John and Brad on their next visit. He would rotate John and Brad's plant visit assignments on a semi-annual basis so that neither of them got too close to any one plant location. Twice a year, he would have all plant managers, together with John, Brad and Harriet, attend a two or three day meeting at headquarters so that he could go over his plans and expected results for the next six months. These plans also established the criteria upon which each plant would be evaluated.

He had trained Harriet Gregson to interpret the computer reports and prepare a summary of any areas that he should look at himself and any action that he needed to take. He expected Miss Gregson to take care of anything of less importance. He had also trained her on the detail operations of the computer monitoring system, so that if he wasn't available, she could take care of the problem. In many respects, she was performing his job.

As Executive Vice President of Operations, he had basically designed himself out of a job. It was only his presence and reputation as the "wicked bastard" that kept everything in line. John and Brad were covering the on-site reviews, Harriet was covering headquarters' concerns and monitoring, and he was just in place. For the past four years, his job had been primarily delegated to these others. He had worked himself out of a job. Ironically, he was earning more money now for much less work than when he first started with the company. He wasn't problem solving anymore; he remembered the days at Hereford and Columbus, and was just maintaining and waiting for something to happen. If nothing happened, it meant everything was all right and there was nothing for him to do.

He still came in to work early and left late at night. But now, instead of actual problem solving work, he was involved more with headquarters' concerns. The first thing in the morning, at six o'clock, was the executive group meeting. The group consisted of the six other executive vice presidents and Mr. Wagner the CEO. The stated purpose of the meeting was so that they could review the prior day's happenings and their combined plans for today. It had begun as a consultant's idea as to how to get the various functions to communicate and work together. The actual purpose for the meeting, though, had become a free executive breakfast and a forum for the Sales EVP, Tommy Tolliver, to share his latest jokes. It seemed that was the main product and purpose for the sales department; in reality sales were generated automatically through the computer system. William found these meetings a waste of his time. He would report yesterday's results and today's expectations from plant operations, but he felt that nobody really listened, as they were too busy having side conversations. In truth, he didn't hear much of what the others had to say either, he was thinking of his own concerns at the plants. The meeting usually lasted until seven thirty, providing these busy executives a half hour to get ready for the day, before the employees were due in to work.

After this meeting, William would go to his office. Miss Gregson was already at her desk. Her work hours, like all other employees at headquarters, were eight to five, with a strict fifteen-minute morning and afternoon break and an hour off for lunch, a full eight-hour day. Harriet would come in by seven o'clock in the morning to review the previous day's plant reports and prepare her summary for William. At seven thirty, she would meet with William to review the reports and outline any actions that he needed to take. In reality Harriet could take the same action. Her meeting with William usually ended by eight o'clock; then she would go to her desk to monitor the computer system. She would save any messages that she couldn't handle herself for William, which were very few. If there weren't any that day, she would route some of her own to William. She would also handle any correspondence in or out, any inquiries, and prepare any special reports. Harriet always had more than enough work to do. She would stay until at least eight o'clock at night to monitor the West Coast plants and finish her work for the day. She didn't mind. After Herman had been transferred to Nebraska, she had nowhere else to go. This was better than going home to an empty apartment and eating dinner by herself. This way she would have dinner at work, either from the company cafeteria or ordered out, and the company paid. This had become her life, work and William. She hated them both.

The rest of William's day consisted of various meetings with other vice presidents, customers (present and prospective), vendors, other headquarters' personnel and so on. Because of his position, William was in great demand for lunches and dinners. Typically, he would leave for lunch at eleven thirty and not return until two; sometimes he left earlier and returned later. If he had a dinner engagement, he would always get back before Miss Gregson left so that they could review the day's happenings and any items that he had to attend to personally and go over the following day's schedule. Many times this meant that Miss Gregson didn't leave until after nine, sometimes ten. He would stay another couple of hours to clean things up. This was really when he did whatever real work had to be done. The days had begun to merge together, looking similar.

William had his own executive bath room with a double sink, toilet and tiled shower with a massaging head, a large, fully stocked medicine cabinet, a towel closet, an electric shoe shiner, a hair dryer, a telephone and so on. He had maintenance add a large closet so that he could store additional suits, shirts, ties, underwear, socks, and shoes. This allowed him to shower and change his clothes prior to lunch, dinner, or important meetings. The joke in the office was that the bathroom was really his office and the large office was really Harriet's. The rare times when he would meet Katherine for dinner or after work, this would allow him to clean up first. Usually, when he met Katherine it was for a related business purpose where it was important for the spouse to be present. This was an important obligation for the corporate wife, and Katherine never disappointed.

In the fall of 1992, a leveraged buyout group, Consolidated Unlimited, as a potential purchase candidate, approached Diamond Industries. Consolidated was known in the trade as a buy and slash outfit. That is, they would buy the company, get rid of all unnecessary or duplicate employees (including vice presidents) and sell off pieces of the company where they could make a quick profit. If they were clever enough, they could sell off enough pieces so that the purchase of the remaining parts cost them almost nothing, sometimes less than nothing. Their goal, in effect, was to have the purchased company pay for its own purchase either by immediate turn around sell offs or by on-going profits. Diamond Industries was a perfect candidate for their type of deal.

When Consolidated Unlimited first approached the Diamond Industries CEO, Albert Wagner, he tried to stall them by ignoring them. He would refuse to accept their phone calls and ignore any correspondence. Diamond corporate attorneys advised him that if he continued this way he would only bring on a hostile takeover from Consolidated. If they really wanted Diamond

Industries, they would get it one way or another. Albert Wagner told the attorneys he didn't care what they did; they wouldn't get Diamond Industries.

Consolidated Unlimited had gone through this same scenario many times before. Their CEO, Harold, affectionately known as "Hardball," Simmons was a professional at getting what he wanted, and he always did. Al Wagner used all the defensive tools at his disposal, such as golden parachutes for the executives, increased stock options (more for the executives, less for the employees), employment contracts with large termination bonuses, misleading financial reporting and so on to prevent a takeover. None of this fazed Hardball Simmons as he had seen it all before. Consolidated initially offered $60 per share for Diamond stock when it was trading for $48 per share. The Diamond board of directors turned the offer down; their company was worth more than that and a higher offer would enrich all of them.

When the market price of Diamond went to $60 based on the offer, Consolidated upped their offer to $72. When the market price of the stock rose to this level, they upped their offer again to $80. At this point, the market took notice, and Al Wagner was able to coax Best Brands to enter the bidding. Al put the story out that he favored Best Brands as they were more ethical and there would be a minimal loss of jobs. The truth was that he was using Best Brands to force Consolidated to raise their offer. At this point he didn't care who bought the company, as he had done his best to enrich himself.

Best Brands, who thought they were seriously in the running, offered the Diamond shareholders $95 in cash—no junk bonds or stock swap. Al Wagner came out as supporting the offer. Consolidated countered with an offer of $120 per share, $80 in cash and $40 in stock. Best Brands couldn't better it. Al Wagner admitted defeat and recommended acceptance of the offer to the board and to the shareholders. Consolidated Unlimited wholly owned Diamond Industries by the end of 1992.

Consolidated Unlimited was in the food and consumable goods business. They owned a number of small to large food processors in the condiments, frozen foods, snacks, fruit juice, and carbonated beverage businesses. This was their first foray into the industrial products business. Typically, when they bought a business, they would immediately sell off those less profitable pieces where they could get a good price to help pay for their purchase. In this case, due mostly to William's diligence, all of Diamond Industries product lines were doing well.

Instead of selling off pieces, they decided to close plant locations by consolidating the sixteen locations into three and terminating over 8,000 employees. Manufacturing was outsourced to Asian companies, which guaranteed on time, quality products at less cost than William's plants. The remaining three plants were used for emergency and specialty orders, one time versus repetitive production. There was no longer a need for William's monitoring procedures or for that matter for William and his team. William could see his work life coming to an end, but he needed the job for his identity. The job, together with its power and status, had become William.

Once the plant locations had been dealt with, against William's wishes, Consolidated management concentrated on Diamond headquarters. At the time of purchase, there were over 800 employees working at Diamond Industries' headquarters. The first employee to go was Al Wagner himself. He didn't care as he was a very rich man and if he wanted another CEO job he would have numerous offers; once a CEO, always a CEO. Consolidated brought in Richard Sprague to be CEO of the food and consumable division and the industrial division. Consolidated decided to use the Stamford building as their headquarters building instead of Consolidated's building in north New Jersey, which was much shabbier. Besides, the Stamford building was fully owned while they paid high rent in New Jersey. Let the New Jersey employees relocate if they wanted to keep their jobs.

The next level that Consolidated attacked was the Vice Presidents. There were seven executive vice presidents and twenty-two vice presidents. Almost immediately, the executive vice presidents were asked to submit their resignations. The company accepted all of them except William's and the CFO, Kenneth Crockett. With the termination of the executive vice presidents came the termination of the twenty-two vice presidents. Consolidated had only six vice presidents; operations, sales, engineering, human resources, information technology, and finance. They would consolidate their management structure with that of Diamond's. Consolidated then took each level in turn and merged their employees with Diamond's, eliminating all duplications and redundancies, always favoring their employees. By the time they were finished, they had reduced headquarters' staff to under 300, and going down.

As part of the consolidation effort, Consolidated management recognized there was little need for William in the industrial division, as they had effectively eliminated in-house manufacturing. They believed that William could effectively apply his production principles to the foods and consumable products division. Manufacturing is manufacturing, isn't it? Food processing was less susceptible to outsource manufacturing. William was asked to become Executive Vice President, Foods and Consumable Division. They wanted, and expected, him to do for that division what he had done for Diamond Industries industrial plants.

William knew relatively nothing about a food processing plant. Consolidated's philosophy was that a business was a business and that all the same principles applied. Many of the old Diamond employees blamed William for making their company so attractive for a takeover. If it weren't for him they would still have their jobs. William felt that if they had done their jobs, they would still have them. William was his job, so he accepted. He still expected to one day be the CEO, but now of a much larger company.

He was told that he could bring one assistant with him, either John or Brad, but not both. The company would take care of the one not selected so he shouldn't worry. He fought to keep Harriet Gregson as well and the company gave in. He then only had to choose between John, whom he considered his best friend, and Brad, whom he considered his protégé and successor. It was not a nice decision. John was 59 and loyal, Brad was 36 and ambitious. He had a week to decide and he agonized. He wasn't good at people decisions, especially when he knew the people.

By the end of the week he had decided. He had Human Resources prepare two contracts, one for the job of Assistant to the Vice President, Foods and Consumable Division, and the other a termination contract with the most liberal severance pay and benefits. He would fill in the names later. He knew both John and Brad would be happy with his decision; it was the best for each of them. He called them to his office at four o'clock that Friday. They could both leave work immediately after signing their contracts to celebrate.

When John and Brad entered William's office that Friday afternoon, he was busy at his desk finalizing the two contracts. He was waiting to fill in the names. He still wanted to make sure. He looked at both of them over his eyeglasses. In his early forties, he had started wearing glasses strictly for reading. Now he kept them on all the time as he thought they made him look more like an Executive Vice President. He motioned for them to sit in the visitor chairs set up on the other side of his desk. He took his glasses off and looked at them.

"I guess you both know why I called for you." He lifted his shoulders and tried to release the tension that had built up in the cords in his neck and across his shoulder blades. He didn't like dealing directly with people. He had John and Brad for that. But who was there to deal with John and Brad?

John and Brad nodded their heads. They were both nervous. They knew the power that William possessed in the organization and their fates were in his hands. John kept crossing his legs from the right to the left side and then back again. Brad exhibited a facial twitch on the right side of his mouth when he was nervous. He was in continual twitch.

"You've probably heard the rumors. Consolidated management wants each of us to cut staff as a sign of good will to the areas that have had severe cuts. They've told me that I can keep one assistant." He nodded at John and Brad. "That is, one of you. And, let the other go." John and Brad started to squirm; it was getting uncomfortable. "I want to be fair to each of you. You've both done excellent jobs, and if it was up to me I would keep both of you." He looked at them. "Does each of you want to stay?"

Neither one answered. They shook their heads slightly signaling the affirmative.

"I see." He looked at both contracts and then at each of them. He picked up his pen and hesitated. Then he quickly wrote the corresponding names on each contract and put each one in a separate envelope with one of their names on it.

He balanced the envelopes in each hand. He tried to hold onto them, but he knew it had to be done. He slid the respective envelopes across the desk toward each recipient. He got up from the desk and left the room. Somewhere along the line, he had become Daniel Flynn.

John and Brad sat there immobilized, delaying the inevitable. Brad finally picked his up and opened it. He read it slowly.

"I can't believe this. This is a crock of shit! There must be some mistake. This must be for you." Brad kept repeating himself. He got up and paced the room.

A wave of relief settled over John. William hadn't disappointed him. He still had his job and his life. John opened his envelope with relief. He read the contents slowly and then read it again. He looked over at Brad. He signed the contract, left it on William's desk, and slowly left the room. That was the last time he would be in William's office, or his presence; the wicked bastard had terminated him. John couldn't believe it; his life was over. William had killed it.

As John left the room, Brad walked over to shake his hand. John walked right past him.

"Look," Brad began. "I wanted the termination, the money and the benefits. I have to get out of here. It's killing me! I'm too young to become William. I don't want to be William. Please, John, I'll tell him he's made a mistake. Take the job! I'll take the money!" Brad knew he couldn't give up this job on his own. He was too important. Fucking Assistant to the Executive Vice President at 36 years old. He was one termination away from being the fucking Executive Vice President.

John had already left the room. Brad continued shouting. It wasn't the loss of the job for John; it was the betrayal by William. William may have thought he lost a friend; John felt he had never had a friend. He would miss that and the position. Now, what would he do?

John walked fast. He couldn't get out of there fast enough. As he walked past Harriet's desk, she looked up at him. He continued walking. As far as John knew, Harriet was in on the plot. Harriet said to him as he walked past, "Have a nice weekend, John." She smiled at him.

He brushed right past her. "The bitch was in on it," he thought. "Screw them all."

John went to the company garage and got his Mercedes. He was always friendly with the garage attendants; this time he was brusque. He thought to himself, "If they got rid of all of these unnecessary frills, I'd still have my job." Funny, John had never thought of that before. When his car came, he pushed the attendant out of the way, jumped in the car, and raced off spinning his back tires. He was always such a cautious driver. He sped off Consolidated property.

John had no idea of where he was going. It was only four twenty and he wasn't ready to go home and face Ethel. She expected to go out to celebrate his promotion, not his termination. He was driving fast in the wrong direction. On an impulse, he pulled abruptly into the large shopping mall parking lot, turning from the far right hand lane into the far left lane, cutting off cars in his wake amidst the chorus of honking horns. He thought he better get off the road while he still could. He didn't know where else to go as he didn't drink much, particularly alone, and he knew he wouldn't be able to eat anything the way his stomach felt. He would walk around the mall to get his head together.

He walked aimlessly, oblivious to the stores or people around him. Slowly his anger subsided and he started to notice his surroundings. Other people seemed to be walking as aimlessly as he was. They all seemed to be bored and depressed, going through the motions of shopping, but not really enjoying themselves. The only ones who were having fun were the young kids and the teenagers. They still looked forward to the future. He wondered how many of them dreamed about being the Vice President of Operations; probably none of them. He had done the impossible; maybe life wasn't as bad as he thought. He had achieved his dream; now he could have his life. He left the mall. He still had Ethel. He would go home.

When he got home, Ethel was dressed to go out and celebrate. He was feeling better, but he dreaded disappointing her. He thought she gloried in his position. She would be ashamed of him for losing his job. He looked at her and didn't know what to say. She looked at him. He looked like the little boy who lost the grocery money. He didn't have to say anything.

"They didn't give you the promotion, did they?" She spoke gently as a mother.

He put his head down. "No," he whispered.

"Those bastards!" Ethel cursed very rarely, but she was mad.

He sat down and put his head in his hands. He was dejected.

"It's all right, Father." She patted him on the head.

"No, it's not. I gave them my life; they gave me the back of William's hand."

"William did this to you?"

"Who else? It was Brad Myers or me. He picked Brad. And, Brad didn't even want the job."

"And you, John, you wanted the job?" She stroked the back of his neck.

"Sure, didn't you want me to get the job? Isn't that why you're dressed up?"

"Oh, John. I only want what you want for yourself. That job was killing you—and us. I want you back. Fuck the job!" She looked down at him tenderly. God, she really loved this man.

"I thought you were proud of me . . . you know, being Vice President and all."

"Of course I'm proud of you. But no more than when you ran the tractor on your parents' farm. I'm proud of whatever you do. But, I want you back."

He stood up and held onto her. He put his face on her shoulder to stop from crying. He held her tight. He felt his strength returning. "You really mean that? You'd still love me without being Vice President?"

"Why are men such fools? I'd love you if you were homeless and penniless."

He pulled away and looked at her. She was crying softly. He started crying as well. They stood like that looking at each other crying. Suddenly she started laughing hysterically. He looked at her and started laughing with her.

He finally spoke. "You mean I put up with that shit all these years thinking it was what you wanted? That it was important to you?"

"Oh John, and I put up with it because I thought it was important to you."

They couldn't stop laughing. It was so sad it was funny.

"So, Mother, shall we still go out? We could stay here you know."

"Oh no, I'm dressed to go out. If we stay here, you'll rip my clothes off."

"I'll do it later anyway. So what shall we celebrate?"

"How about your freedom?"

"Freedom from what?" he asked.

"How about celebrating your sentence being commuted from Consolidated Unlimited, time off for bad behavior. We should thank the wicked bastard."

"Please, don't call William that."

"Still protecting him. That's all right."

"He's been a good friend."

"Uh huh," she said.

They went out to celebrate at their favorite restaurant. They ordered a bottle of champagne before dinner and a bottle of wine with dinner. They hadn't felt this liberated since college. They really had something to celebrate; they had their lives back. Hallelujah!

They returned to their house. As the door closed behind them, he did indeed rip her clothes off and she did the same for him. They wouldn't need those clothes again. They belonged to two other people. They made love like two teenagers who had an empty house for a night. When they were done, he looked at her and began to cry again.

"What is it, Father?"

"I've been such a fool. My life was here all the time."

"Maybe so," she said, "but you had to take the journey first."

"Yeah, but I don't anymore. No more traveling to places I don't want to be and no more terminating good people that I don't even know. I saw some of their faces this afternoon in the mall. I didn't like what I saw. I can't crush dreams anymore." He started crying again.

"Oh, Father. It must have been terrible for you!"

"I never knew. William did me a favor, didn't he?"

"Yes, he did. Let's go to bed. I have more celebrating to do." She smiled at him.

They didn't talk to William after this. Ethel saw and talked to Katherine once in a while, but they couldn't be close friends anymore. This hurt Ethel, but she had John back and the trade was more than fair. Within the month, they moved into New York City to begin their lives anew. It was this incident with John that was the final push for Katherine to move into her own bedroom. She couldn't stay in the same bedroom with the "wicked bastard." William thought it was because he promoted Brad. He knew Katherine never liked him. She thought he was too ambitious, aggressive and pushy.

William got right to work on his new assignment. Consolidated management had assumed that since the pretzel company, Twist Delites, under Diamond Industries had shown steady growth and better than competitive profit margins and net income, that William must have had something to do with it. In truth, William and his team had ignored Twist Delites. None of them knew anything about food processing and saw Twist Delites as the idiot son of the company; it didn't belong. Twist Delites was started as a hobby by one of the original Diamond Industries buyouts. He had a successful industrial adhesives manufacturing business, but always wanted to produce a better beer pretzel, crispier and non-fat. He had no idea that his idea would be such a huge success; he got lucky. When Diamond Industries purchased his industrial adhesive company, the pretzel company became part of the purchase. Diamond allowed him to continue operating the pretzel company as long as it showed steady growth, and it always had. Diamond looked at Twist Delites as an on-going profit center requiring no attention. They didn't know what else to do with it.

Consolidated Unlimited had 24 food processing plants spread across the country. There were six condiment, four frozen food, eight snack, four fruit juice, and two carbonated beverage plants. With the pretzel company added, there were now 25 plants. Each food processing business was different, so William didn't know where to start. The condiment business was the largest in terms of number of plants, sales, and contribution to overall company profits so he decided to start there.

William and Brad tried to apply the same manufacturing principles to the food processing business as they had successfully implemented in the industrial fasteners business. However, they didn't take into account some of the major differences in the two types of businesses. For instance, the industrial fastener business leant itself to producing directly for customer orders while working toward eliminating inventories, while the food processing business was geared to maximizing production yields, the most product for the least cost, and shipping from inventory. William couldn't figure out how to adjust his formulas and equations for these differences. The production demands that he had developed just didn't work in the food processing industry. There were numerous complaints, all anonymous, about his methods to Richard Sprague, the Division CEO. The plant managers and employees quickly learned to hate William.

William's life had been regenerated. He was out in the field with Brad problem solving. Harriet Gregson was taking care of office operations. Her new position was chief administrative assistant, a lesser title, no longer management, but a little more money. Brad had hired Emily Bryson, whom he knew, as an administrative assistant to work with Harriet in the office and coordinate with them in the field. William continued working long hours developing his formulas and then testing them. When he left each plant site, he left established production standards, cost expectations, and manufacturing profit margins. He expected each plant manager to meet his standards. He set up daily and weekly reporting criteria and linked each plant location into his computerized real time reporting system. Based on his calculations, he directed each plant manager to reduce their production and administrative staffs. As usual, he never got to know any of the employees except the plant managers. Brad Myers had the assignment to ensure that all of their recommendations were put in place.

By the fall of 1994, William had been in his new position for over a year. He and Brad had installed their systems in each of the twenty-five food processing plants. Although costs had been reduced in each of the plant locations, sales and net income, too, had decreased. He trusted his formulas as they had always worked in the past, so he figured there must be something else wrong. He instructed each of the plant managers to reduce costs even further. The reduction in costs should increase net income. But, the opposite started to happen, sales and net income decreased even further. William had neglected one of the most important factors in any production formula, the people. And, the people from the plant managers on down were angry. Whatever he would come up with, good or bad, they would sabotage.

He had a standing meeting with Richard Sprague on Thursday afternoons. They would have lunch in one of the private rooms in the executive dining room and then continue their meeting in Richard's office. This particular Thursday Richard seemed less than his usual sociable self. He would always ask after Katherine, he was one of her dancing partners, but this time he didn't. And, he would have a cute story or joke, never off color or offensive, to tell. Today he was very somber as they had lunch. They always had the same waiter, Jonathan, and Richard was always gracious with Jonathan. This time he yelled at Jonathan for the food not being there timely. "How long do you think we would be in business if we delivered that late!?" Jonathan, of course, was only the messenger. William realized that Richard was annoyed about something and he hoped it wasn't him.

After lunch, William and Richard went back to Richard's office. Richard always had coffee service and dessert cakes waiting for them, but this time there was nothing. Richard took his seat behind his huge desk in his huge chair Richard was a small, slight man, about five foot six and 140 pounds, and always looked ludicrous behind his desk. He tended to elevate his chair so that he looked bigger behind the desk; his feet didn't reach the floor and they rested on a stool. He had the power, but he didn't have the size. He motioned for William to sit across from him in one of the massive visitor chairs. Richard liked everything large. They usually sat in Richard's conversation corner for special guests. Their meeting was typically informal; however, today it was to be formal.

Richard took out an official looking folder from his right side desk drawer, the confidential drawer with the double lock. He looked it over while looking over his glasses at William. He put his hand to his mouth and coughed. It was obvious that Richard was anxious and uncomfortable.

"William, some things have come to my attention that I need to share with you."

William nodded.

"First of all." Richard looked down into the folder. "Do you remember an employee named Gail Horwath?"

He felt relieved. "Sure, she was my first assistant when I became Executive Vice President, when the company was still Apex Industries. She was transferred to accounting. She married Riley Hawkins the CFO. I sent them a nice present."

"Aha. Did you know that she filed a sexual abuse claim against you? That you had her transferred because she wouldn't comply to your advances."

William was shocked. What was this all about? "And you believe this?" Richard shook his head. "It doesn't matter. Let's go on."

"Did you also know a Herman Whiteside?" Richard waited for an answer.

"Sure," said William. "He was an engineer assigned to headquarters for a while. He was sent back to the Nebraska plant."

Richard looked over at him. "That's right. Was there anything else about him?"

"Um. I remember him being friendly with Miss Gregson, my assistant."

"That's right," said Richard. "He claims you sent him back to Nebraska to get him away from Miss Gregson. That you wanted her to yourself." Richard looked at another letter in the folder, hesitated, and then decided to pass it by.

William was starting to get the gist of what was going on, and he didn't like it.

"Why that's ridiculous. Look, what's this all about?"

Richard put his hand up. "How about a Mike Morgan? Do you remember him, a friend of Brad Myers, came in for a job interview?"

William wasn't sure who he meant. He looked puzzled. "I don't know. I interview a number of applicants. After Brad has passed on them."

"This particular one worked in the defense industry on Long Island."

William got an insight, his eyebrows lifted. "Oh yeah, the Jewish guy. I didn't think he would fit into our organization. He talked in bad Yiddish."

"He claims you discriminated against him. He wasn't Jewish, he was homosexual. He says you made a pass at him and he wasn't interested."

William was starting to shake. Where would this all end. "Look, Richard, where did you get that folder? What's this all about?"

Richard looked at the cover of the folder. "This is your unofficial record from Human Resources; it was started by Royce Mumford. You remember him?"

William nodded.

"Evidently, he never liked you, or anyone else. He started folders like this for all of the executives. His successors continued to add to it."

Richard leaned closer to him. He put the folder down. "Let me tell you a little story. It begins with a small poor boy from Brooklyn. He was the son of a single mother and an alcoholic father. He had less than nothing as a child. He worked his way through city college, no fancy Roget Institute for him, as a bus boy at a storefront Chinese restaurant in a bad neighborhood. Many times he got mugged on payday. When he graduated college, without honors, the best job he could get was with a pickle producer in Brooklyn Heights. He helped build that pickle company into a national concern, Shurpack Pickles. When Shurpack was bought out by Consolidated, he was the President of the company. He is now your CEO. I'm still protecting that little pickle company. I don't want to be a poor Jew again."

William was taken aback. Richard had never said anything about his personal background, and it had never mattered to William. He was his boss; that was all that mattered. William said nothing.

"Look, William, I never liked you, you and your kind, rich WASP socialite types. But I was willing to give you a chance. If you produced for us, I couldn't care if you screwed your computer or masturbated at board meetings. You've been the executive vice president of the food and consumables division for over a year and the results are horrible." He picked up a stack of letters and held them up in his right hand. "These are all complaint letters, some signed, most of them anonymous, about you. I can ignore these and the other complaints, and there are more, but the fact is you are screwing up the division. I can't allow someone to take a fist full of money and not produce results." Richard hesitated and looked down at his desk. He said quietly, "I'm going to have to let you go."

William didn't quite hear him. "I'm sorry, what did you say?"

Richard banged his fist on the desk. "Are you fucking deaf? I'm firing you!"

William was shocked. He had never heard Richard lose his temper before. There was no point in William trying to defend himself, as the die had been cast. He sat there stupefied. His life was over, what did it matter?

Richard got up from his desk. He threw some papers at William and left the office.

William sat there for a considerable time. He finally picked up the papers. They were his termination contract. He looked it over and the terms were more than fair. It didn't matter to him, though; he was already a wealthy man. He was more concerned with who he would be without the job and position. He would never be CEO, but who would he be? He signed the contract and walked slowly back to his office with his head down. William walked right past Miss Gregson and into his office. This was possibly the last time he would be in this office.

PART FOUR
THE FOOTPATH BACK HOME

10

THE LIGHTS GO ON

William became aware of an incessant banging in his ears. He thought it must be someone banging on his office door. He had just sat down at his desk and was looking at all of the important papers lying there. Somehow they no longer were of significance to him. The banging continued. He felt himself calling out "come in, come in, and take everything away." He heard himself hysterically laughing; he never laughed out loud. Was it him or someone else? The banging continued. "God damn it," he said, "come in, come in, it's all yours. Just stop the banging."

He heard a loud voice. "Are you all right, sir? Please open your window."

He couldn't understand the message. His office had no windows that opened. He looked up. "My God," he said to himself. "What am I doing in my car?" He didn't remember how he got here. He looked out the driver's side window. There was a very large, menacing police officer staring down at him. The sight of the police officer shocked him back to reality. He remembered losing his job. He remembered putting his head down on the steering wheel. He remembered watching his life unfold. He remembered people saying that at the moment of death your life would pass before your eyes. Was he dead? Had he killed himself? Was the large police officer the angel of death, there to take him away to pay for his sins?

The police officer was speaking again. "Please open your window. This is the Stamford police."

He knew there was no way that Stamford would be in heaven, maybe the other place, but not heaven. "Son of a bitch," he thought, "I must still be alive." He didn't know if that was good or bad. Either way, his pain wasn't over.

"If you don't open the window immediately, we're going to have to bust it." The police officer looked over at a police car where another officer was ready to get out with a crowbar in her hands. They were evidently serious.

He hit all of the automatic window buttons at once. First, the windows in the back went down and then the passenger's side window. The police officer rushed from window to window, but as he did William would correct himself and close each one. He finally got the driver's side window to go down. The officer ran to the window; he looked angry. The police officer stared down at him. William could read the name on his badge—Lt. Robert C. Calhoun.

"Do you know who you are?" Calhoun asked him.

"I'm trying to find out."

"Uh huh," said Officer Calhoun. "And, do you know where you're at?"

He really didn't know. He remembered pulling into this strip shopping mall, on the bad side of town, the one he passed quickly every day going to and from work. But he never noticed the name of the shopping center.

"On the road to oblivion?" ventured William.

Officer Calhoun was getting angry and frustrated. If William weren't extremely well dressed and sitting in a top of the line Mercedes, he would have had him out of the car and spread across the car frame looking forward to a strip search. This was a common procedure in this part of town. He would give William a break, but not for too much longer. The poor son of a bitch seemed disoriented, probably coming down from a cocaine high. He could be someone important.

Officer Calhoun took the police officer's officious pose. "Can I see your driver's license and auto registration?" He waited patiently, staring down at William from beneath his cap.

William was befuddled. He knew his response to this request should be automatic, but he really didn't know where to look.

"All right, get out of the car!" Officer Calhoun's patience had snapped. Important or not, he didn't have all day to diddle with this rich fancy pants. He ought to just run him in. It would serve him right. Asking for it, parking here. It's a wonder he hadn't been mugged and his car stripped. God watches out for the rich and the lucky. Calhoun reached in and opened the car door.

William tried to get out, but he was stuck. Calhoun reached over and released the seat belt. William slid from the car onto the pavement. Calhoun caught him and straightened him up against the car. He looked down at his trousers and realized he had urinated on himself. William put his hand on it and it felt sticky. The other officer, a female, had come over from the police car. William tried to cover his crotch with his hands.

William read her badge, "Officer Carol Oliveri." She said something to Calhoun. She tried to whisper, but he could hear her. She thought he was out of it.

"I checked the registration. It's registered to Consolidated Unlimited."

Calhoun nodded his head. He should have known. Their executives were like big kids. This wouldn't be the first one that he had to take home discreetly.

"His name is William Bradford. He was an Executive Vice President. He was terminated yesterday. No wonder he's in a stupor." Oliveri felt sorry for him. She remembered when her dad had been terminated from the Apex plant some years before. He had been devastated. She didn't know that this was the wicked bastard that he had cursed at the time, the one responsible for his losing his job at age 48, after 26 years of service. He had never been the same since.

Calhoun patted William down. He found his billfold in his right hand suit pocket. He flipped through it and found William's driver's license. He looked at the picture and at William. They matched. He read the name. "You won't believe this. This is William S. Bradford III. Another one of those rich pricks. Probably hasn't worked a day in his life. And now he has no job. Poor slob."

"You got an address? Should we take him home?" Carol was concerned that William might yet kill himself.

"Oh, yeah," said Calhoun. "You're going to like this one. 161 Crescent Lane."

"The big house on the hill?" asked Carol.

"That's the one. It's where what's his name lived, the punk in the MG. The one who screwed all the girls. You remember him?" Calhoun was smiling.

"Oh yeah. I remember the night he was drunk. Found him and the rich guy's daughter, Tiffany something, nude in the MG. He was talented. That was one position I couldn't believe any human being could get into." Oliveri was shaking her head. "He asked me for my phone number, with my flashlight on his dick."

"That was quite a dick as I remember, for a kid that age." He rolled his eyes.

Carol smiled. "For a guy any age."

"And," said Calhoun, "how would you know?"

Carol smiled. "I had four older brothers, remember?"

"Uh huh," said Calhoun. "So what do we do with the big dick's father?"

Carol looked at William. "Do you know where you live?"

He pointed vaguely in the direction of his house; it was a lucky guess.

"He seems okay, just a little shell shocked. I remember my dad when he lost his job. Took him a couple of months before he could function. Let's just make sure we get him out of here. Not a safe place with that car and the way he's dressed."

"It's okay with me," said Calhoun. "I've got better things to do than babysit some rich shit who can't find his way."

"Oh," said Carol. "And what would those better things be?"

"Never you mind," said Calhoun.

They helped him back into his car. "You be all right now, Willy?" said Calhoun.

"That's William."

"Of course it is," said Calhoun. "You be careful now. Get away from here quick. The store's just opened. Once we leave, the teenage punks will be all over you in a matter of seconds."

William looked over Calhoun's shoulder and saw a crowd of rough look-ing teenagers eyeing him and the car. He looked at the clock radio. It read 8:12 AM. He couldn't remember when he parked there. If he had left his house at his normal time, then he must have been sitting here for over two hours. He started the engine. The keys were still in the ignition. He realized he could have been in real trouble. He sat motionless.

"Go ahead, Willy. We'll follow you out of the parking lot. You'll be okay."

William thought, "that's William," but decided not to say anything. What was the use? He didn't know who he was anyway.

William moved slowly, past the crowd of teenagers, and out of the park-ing lot. He had an idea that his house was to the left, so he turned right.

Calhoun and Oliveri were right behind him. Calhoun, who was driv-ing, said to Oliveri, "The stupid shit is going the wrong way. Should I pull him over?"

Carol chuckled to herself. "Nah, let him go. It's his life now."

At the next corner, William went straight and the police car turned right.

As soon as he saw that the police car wasn't trailing him anymore, he pulled over to the side of the road. He sat there motionless for some time. He was immobilized; he didn't know what to do or where to go. He no longer had an office to go to, and he wasn't sure he still had a home he wanted to go to.

As he was no longer an Executive Vice President, he saw no reason why Katherine would stay with him a second longer. They were hardly much of a couple as it was. She could have whatever she wanted; he didn't care. She had her friends, he had nobody; he was alone, he was used to that. He had started with nothing and he would end with nothing. In a strange way he felt free for the first time in his life. He had nowhere to go and no one to please.

He looked at the car phone. If the company hadn't cut off his service already, he could call anyone in the world. He sat there thinking. He laughed to himself. There wasn't a soul he could think of calling. He picked up the phone and called his home number. He hoped that Katherine wasn't home. He would leave her a message on the answering machine. Although it really didn't matter if she was home or not, as she had taken to letting the answer-ing machine pick up all messages. She said she had been getting obscene calls and didn't want to answer the phone as it scared her. He knew, though, the real reason she screened her calls was she didn't have to talk to him; that's what scared her. If she needed something, she would leave a note on his desk. She was so sure he would work when he came home, no matter what time. He always did, but not any more; he had no work to do. He waited for the three rings and for the answering machine to pick up. He listened to the message in Katherine's voice. He wondered where things had gone wrong or if they had ever been right. "This is the Bradford residence. If you wish to leave a message for either William or Katherine, do so after the beep. We will call you back as soon as we can. Love."

He hoped that the love at the end of the message included him, but he wasn't too sure. He left his message. "Katherine, this is William. I have to go out of town for a couple of days. I should be back by Sunday night." He didn't know why he said, "this is William." Was it a habit or was he not so sure who he was anymore?

He started the car and continued in the direction he was going. Any direction that took him away from his home and the company and Stamford seemed fine. He drove aimlessly for a number of miles. He found he was enjoying riding in the company car. He never did when he felt it was part of his job. Now that he was finally free of that job, the car felt good. It felt good to be getting one on the company. Fuck them. Fuck them all! He laughed to himself. He didn't laugh very often, now he couldn't stop. He noticed things along the road that he had never noticed before. He had always been in a hurry to get to work. He had missed so much and given up so much for those bastards, but no more. The question was what to do now. Was there any life left or had he killed anything that really mattered? He looked at himself in the rear view mirror. He didn't recognize who he was looking at. Where was the young man who had left home to go off to college and a new life?

It appeared that he was being pulled in the direction he was traveling. After driving a number of miles, he realized that it was the direction towards New York City. He kept driving in that direction, not sure of where his destination might be, anywhere but Stamford. When he reached the city limits of New York, he just kept driving. He followed once familiar signs and landmarks, but things had changed. He remembered the streets being clean, kids playing in the streets, people looking happy, the hustle of pleasant activities and talking and so on. Now there seemed to be dreariness, a pallid gloom, which had descended over the area. Houses were boarded up, people appeared to walk cautiously, kids were hanging out and harassing passersby, trash covered the streets, sidewalks, and small lawns. Where he had remembered a bright sun, there were now dark clouds in the sky. Had he really been away that long? It seemed like such a short time, those years between eighteen and fifty-four. What had he done with those years?

He pulled onto a street, the one that he had seen almost every day since he had left. Every other house seemed to be abandoned with broken windows, signs of vandalism, trash strewn about, and young adults and teenagers loitering about. Even with his car windows closed and fairly sound proof, he could hear the loud sounds and vibrations of heavy rock and rap music. Whatever happened to school and work? Is this what he had missed by working all of those years? There must be something other than the extreme of work and the extreme of nothing to do.

He slowed down. He didn't want to miss the house. There it was, between an abandoned house and one with a group of youngsters lying about. He pulled the car in front of the house. It looked no different than when he had left, the same house in his dreams all these years. Slow tears came to his eyes. He wiped them away with his sleeve. There looking out of the front window was his mother. She didn't look much different than when he left years ago. It was like he had just gone out for a newspaper, still looking out that front window. He still didn't know why.

He sat and looked at the house and his mother in the window. He had been moving towards this day from the day that he had left. It was inevitable. The void in his life was what he had done in between. He hesitated. Should he go in or just drive away? He had been driving away for years, maybe it was time to stop and go in. He was tired of running away. It was time to stop and find out who he was.

He slowly got out of the car. The youngsters who had been lying about the house next door came down to check him and his car. Cars, and people like William, didn't come into this neighborhood. In William's world, they were the freaks; in their world, William was the freak.

"Look at this dude, man," one of the bigger kids was saying.

"Yeah man, cool."

They had surrounded William and his car. Not long ago, he would have been scared for his life. But then, he wouldn't have been here. Now he didn't care. The least valuable thing he had left was his life. They could take the car. It wasn't his; let the company worry.

The largest of the group—the largest always seems to be the leader—was looking him over. He noticed William looking up at the house.

"You here to see the German lady?" he asked William. Some things, it appeared, had stayed the same.

William was daydreaming as he looked up at the house. The leader said again, "The German lady. You here to see the German lady?" The leader had pressed himself closer to William.

William looked at him, not knowing who he was and why he was here.

"Oh yeah, I guess I am. Here to see the German lady."

"Listen, man. Don't you know no better than coming here like that? Why you're lucky you got this far in that car. You go in there, there won't be no car."

William looked at him. He hesitated. Maybe he had made a mistake. His mother's expression hadn't changed. She just sat in the window looking out. What was going on in the street in front of her house seemed to have little interest to her. She would be all right whether William went in or not. But, would he be all right? He moved closer to the house. He started to walk toward the front door.

"Listen, man. You want us to watch your car or not? Cost you two bucks."

William turned. "Oh, sure." He reached for his wallet. As he did so, he sensed that he was probably making a big mistake showing them where his wallet was. "The hell with it," he thought. "They want to rob me, they can have my money. It hasn't done me too much good." He looked in his wallet. He pulled out a bill. He extended it towards the leader. "Here's ten dollars. Watch the car and this house."

The leader snatched the bill. "You okay, fancy pants. We watch the car. We already watch the house. She okay, the German lady."

"Uh huh," said William.

He walked to the front door. His legs were shaking, his stomach was talking, and his bowels were loose. "Jesus Christ," he thought, "she's only your mother." But that thought had never stopped him shaking before. He rang the bell, but he heard nothing. He would have to fix the bell again. He knocked on the door, no response from inside. He knew she was there. Did she know her son Wilhelm was there? He knocked louder, still no response. He thought he better leave. His mother didn't want to see him. He didn't blame her; he had left her. As he was about to leave, he tried the door. It pushed open easily. He would have to fix that as well.

He entered his boyhood home for the first time in over thirty-five years. Little had changed, older but still the same. He walked into the small living room. His mother was sitting in the same chair as when he had left, staring straight ahead out of the front window. He walked slowly over to where she was sitting. This was the most difficult thing he had done in all that time. CEO's, boards of directors, other vice presidents didn't scare him, but his mother did. She always had.

"Momma," he said. "It's Wilhelm."

His mother didn't move. "I know who it is."

He stood, his mother sat. Was this it? Was this all there was going to be?

He looked at his mother. Had he done this to her? Had she been sitting like this all these years? Had he killed her soul as well? He turned to go.

"Wilhelm, you just got here. Where is it you got to go now?"

"Nowhere, Momma. I came to see you …to see how you were."

"So, you see. So, that's it, ya?"

"No, Momma. I came to tell you how sorry I am for leaving you."

His mother said nothing. She was still staring out of the window.

"Momma, I want to make it up to you." He stood looking down at his mother. It was he who had made her like this.

"Make what up? Children leave, they have their lives. I knew you would leave. Your life was good, ya?"

"No, Momma. I don't think it was."

"I'm sorry, Wilhelm. I always wish you a good life."

He walked over to his mother. He put his hand on her shoulder. He stroked her gently. She turned her head towards him. She was crying, slow, happy tears. He had never seen his mother cry before. He tried, but he couldn't stop his own tears. He kissed his mother softly on the cheek. She took his hand.

"So, you stay for tea, ya?"

"Ya, Momma, I stay for tea."

"Good," said his mother. She got up and went to the kitchen.

He sat in the same chair at the small dining room table that he had sat in as a small boy. His mother brought his tea to him, always in a glass, just like when he was younger. His mother sat in her seat. She passed the cream, sugar, and lemon to him. He fixed his tea, cream, no sugar, with a wedge of lemon, and then he passed the cream, sugar, and lemon back to his mother.

Only when she had prepared her tea, cream, sugar, and lemon, did he start to sip his tea. His mother brought some sugar cookies, the ones that he had liked as a child. He took some and passed the plate back to his mother. They both sat silently sipping their tea. It was as if thirty-six years had not passed since their last meeting.

"So. Wilhelm, what about your life?"

"My life is over, Momma. I never should have left here and you." He looked down at his tea. As old as he got, he would always be afraid of his mother.

"Nonsense, Wilhelm! You are still a young man. Your momma, she is old."

"I know, Momma. I'm sorry. I made you old."

"No, Wilhelm. I get old. I do it myself."

"But, momma, I walked out on you. I left you sitting by the window."

"Oh no, Wilhelm, I let you go. It was time. You had your life to start."

"But, momma, I wrote you from college. All of the letters came back. I stopped writing you."

"Ya Wilhelm. I get these letters. I have no one to read them to me. So, I think maybe you would like them back. Enough that I know you're there."

"And you never cared where I was all these years."

"Oh ya, Wilhelm, I care. You're my boy, always you be my boy. You need your momma you come home, like now. You never forget your momma, ya?"

"Ya, Momma, I never forget. I think about you every day. Sitting in this house, by the window."

"Ya, Wilhelm. And where else, but this house? I wait for you. I know you come back."

"Momma! It's been over thirty-five years. You've been sitting in the window all this time, waiting for me?"

"Oh no, Wilhelm. I keep house so you know where I am."

"So, Momma, why do you sit by the window?"

"Today?"

"Yes, Momma, today."

"Today I sit waiting for Beckman, the baker."

"Mr. Beckman, the Jewish man, from down the street?"

"Ya, that Beckman, from down the street."

"Momma, why were you waiting for Mr. Beckman?"

"We go out. Friday we go out."

"So you didn't see me when I drove up?"

"Oh I see you. Talking to Raymond and the others. I was pleased. You come to see your momma."

"Yes, Momma, but it's been over thirty five years."

"That's all we have, years."

"Yes, Momma."

They were silent for a while. Each one sipped tea and nibbled on sugar cookies. His mother was no different than he remembered her, older but no different.

"Momma, why do you sit at the window and stare out?" He had to ask the question. It had bothered him all of these years.

"Today, like I say. Waiting for Beckman, like always on Friday."

"No, Momma. When I was a boy, until I left?"

"Oh then. I look at America, hoping no Nazis here. And I look for Karl, make sure he no return." She was pleased with her answer. She sucked on a lemon rind.

He smiled at his mother. She always made life so simple. "So, Karl, my father, never returned?"

"No, Wilhelm, not your father."

"My father never returned?" He was confused.

"No, Wilhelm, Karl never return and he not your father."

He couldn't believe what he was hearing. All these years dreaming about Karl and his abuse and now he was not his father. Karen told him slowly about her childhood and her parents. As she told the story of her childhood (it was a happy one) her face beamed. He had never seen his mother so happy. She hadn't ever told anyone the details. Now she felt her son had a right to know. He held her hands and looked at her fondly with large tears in his eyes. She was so beautiful and he felt so ugly.

Karen's Story

I was born in 1923, in Munich, Germany, between the two great wars. My parents were Gustav and Sarah Guffmann. My father was German and Lutheran. My mother was Austrian and Jewish. When they married, both sets of parents disowned them. My mother's parents sent her a notice of her death and they sat shiva, the Jewish tradition of mourning for a dead family member. My father received a Hummel piece for a wedding gift. He smashed it into little pieces and sent it back to them. He never talked to them again. My momma was sixteen and my poppa was nineteen.

Seven months later I was born, without grandparents. My momma went on to get a doctorate in literature and my poppa a doctorate in philosophy. They loved each other deeply and hated the world of intolerance. They lived in the world of ideas. They hoped they could save some souls from the Nazis of the world through their teaching. They won a few battles over the years but in the end they lost the war. They raised and protected me from the unloving outside world. I grew up among books, concerts, lectures, music and art lessons, nannies and tutors. I was a child of the intelligentsia of Munich and knew little about the world outside.

I was sixteen years old in 1939. Munich remained the cultural capital of Germany, while the rest of Germany was in turmoil. Momma and Poppa were afraid for me; to the Nazis my worth could only be measured in terms of a Jewish mother and a non-Nazi professor of philosophy. So, they made arrangements through friends, Sally and Sigfried, to get me safely out of Germany to America. I was to live, temporarily, with an aunt of Sally's in

New York. That was Sophie. Momma and Poppa felt they couldn't leave their students in the middle of a semester, but planned to join me as soon as they could.

I was scheduled to leave on a Russian ship in October of 1939. However, within a week of the scheduled departure, the sailing date was canceled by the Nazi party; no reason was given. Sigfried, who it turned out had some connections with the Nazis, was able to get me on a Portuguese ship leaving that very night. Momma and Poppa had to decide quickly. Since they didn't know when such an opportunity would present itself again, they said yes. Sigfried arranged for me to travel with a female cousin of his who was also desperate to leave Germany. The cousin, Lili, was over 20 years old and would provide protection for me. There wouldn't be any other passengers on board, but Sigfried guaranteed my parents it would be safe. Also, Momma and Poppa paid the Captain a lot of money to further assure my safety.

A very bad thing happened on that ship, Wilhelm. It is hard, even now, for me to talk about it. Let me just say that Lili and I were the only females on board. We were given a cabin way below deck and far away from the crew. We were safe for the first three days, as we kept to ourselves. The only other human we saw was the deck hand, Laslo, who brought and picked up our meals. By the fourth day, we both needed some air, so we went up on deck. This was the first glimpse and knowledge the crew had that any women were on board. One of the crew passed by and tipped his cap to us. We smiled at him. The name on his shirt said Tony.

The Captain had instructed us to double lock the cabin door and not to open it for anyone. We slept uneasily but undisturbed. About three in the morning one night there was a knock on the door. We sat up in bed and pulled the sheets over us.

"Come on, I know you're in there. Laslo told me. It cost me plenty. Come on, it's Tony. I'm your friend from the deck."

We cowered together on Lili's bed. I was scared. This was nothing like Munich.

"Go away, you ugly man, or we'll tell the Captain." Lili spoke shakily.

"Go ahead, tell the Captain. I only wanted to say hello."

"Sure," said Lili, "just go away."

"All right, but I'll be back."

We heard his footsteps leaving. We couldn't sleep the rest of the night. Lili held me close in her bed, but Tony never returned. The next day we told the Captain and he said he would talk to Tony and not to worry, we were safe on his ship. Never been any trouble before in his eighteen years as a Captain. Of course, there had never been any women on board.

The next night we couldn't sleep, so we talked about our new lives in America. I told Lili about my parents and how much I missed them. Lili told her story of parental abuse. How her parents were alcoholics and forced her into a life on the streets. When she got into trouble, how her parents threw her out of the house. She told me of the horrors of living off the streets, never knowing whether she would ever eat again. When her cousin Sigfried approached her about going with me to America, she seized the opportunity.

As we talked and hugged into the night, there was a scratching at the door. Our bodies tensed and we held each other more tightly. I was petrified, but Lili put on her street face. We watched from the far reaches of Lili's small cot as the bottom lock turned and opened. We thanked God for the double bolt on the top of the door. This would keep him out and he would eventually go away. The fear, however, did not go away.

There was a crashing at the door. We cowered into the corner of the room. I held onto Lili for my life. We heard Tony speaking through the door. Our worst fears were realized.

Tony was shouting. "Get back, let the big Polack do it. Come on, Stosh."

There was a loud crash and the door burst and an enormous sailor fell into our small room. Tony, and four other men, came into the room. They glowered and salivated. We moved closer to the corner of the room. You can get out of Germany, but you can't get away from the Nazis of the world. My parents were so right, but it was too late.

The room was really too small for all of them. Stosh had moved to the doorway to make room for the others, but there was still no room to move, nor for us to escape. I couldn't stop screaming and crying. Lili tried to be brave for both of us, but she knew it was hopeless.

"Leave us alone, you filthy pigs." Lili shouted at them and spat at Tony.

Tony grabbed at Lili, but she was able to push him off.

"Heinie, give me a hand here. I have a little German Nazi tiger by the tail."

Tony with Heinie's help pulled us apart. We hit, kicked, spat, screamed, and fought as hard as we could, but we were no match for two hardened sailors. Heinie and one of the other sailors held Lili down, while the two other sailors held me down. Stosh stayed by the door, while Tony looked over his choices. He looked at Lili and then at me.

"Take the Jewess, leave me alone," Lili screamed. Once again the gentile betrayed the Jew, and once again there was nothing the Jew could do.

"A Jewish virgin Christ killer. I think I go for revenge this time. Age and experience can wait. I do the whore next." He looked at Lili. She knew he knew.

Tony moved toward me. I struggled as best as I could, but the two sailors had me pinned down. My parents had sent me off to safety, but where was that for a Jew at that time? Tony moved closer, his sailors arms tightened about me, and my eyes left my head.

Tony straddled my body. I squirmed as much as I could, but there was no way I could get away from him. He had a knife in his hand with a long, sharp blade. One of the sailors had his enormous hand over my mouth so I couldn't scream out loud, but I heard my screams in my head, I still do, until I lost my entire sense of reality. I watched terrified as if it was someone else as Tony cut my clothes off and stood back and savored my body.

"Very nice, very nice indeed—pure virgin meat. The best for Tony."

He ran the knife blade up and down my body, caressing but not cutting. As the blade ran across my breasts, he let the knife tip pierce the nipples so that a trickle of blood flowed. As I squirmed and screamed internally, Tony bent down and licked the blood from my nipples. My eyes were frozen, my mind gone. As he sucked the blood from my breasts, he let the knife blade caress the opening of my vagina. I was frozen with fright.

Tony jumped back suddenly and tore his clothes off. He stood naked casting a large ominous shadow over my small body. I was terrified and completely out of my mind.

Tony had an enormous penis; he stuck it straight in my face. He ran his penis over my body exactly as he had caressed me with his knife. One was as terrifying as the other.

At Tony's signal, the other two sailors pulled my legs far apart so that I was in extreme pain. As I screamed from the pain, he suddenly thrust his penis into me. I screamed out of my mind and my soul died that very moment. I lay there, but in reality I wasn't there. They could do this thing to my body, but they couldn't get my soul. Only I owned that and I let it die.

I had never felt pain like this, but Tony took his time. With each thrust, I lost a piece of myself. When he was finally finished with a long gasp and fell from me, there was little left of the girl who had got on this ship of hope. It may have killed my soul but it was over and I was still alive.

Tony nodded to the sailor holding my right arm and leg. Tony took his place holding me down, and the other sailor raped me. By this time I had lost all fight and they didn't need to hold me down or gag me. They repeatedly raped me until all the sailors, with the exception of Stosh, had their turn. As I moaned out of my mind, they left me and started working on Lili.

Lili saw no way out, so she lay passively as each one had their turn. Getting raped was unavoidable, but at least she could give them the least possible pleasure.

When they were all done, they left us curled up on our beds. Only Stosh remained at the door. As Tony left he yelled over his shoulder

"They're all yours, Stosh," and laughed cynically.

When they had left, Stosh slowly moved into the room. He was at least twice as large as any of the other sailors. We cowered at was in store for us. If Stosh had his way, it would kill us. He came over to my bed and looked down at me. There was pity and a trace of a tear in his eyes. He reached down to touch me and I instinctively pulled away in horror. I expected the worst and protected myself with my knees. I didn't know what I could do, but I would do something. I heard Lili screaming.

"Get away from her, you big dumb ugly Polack fuck. Haven't you shits done enough?" She screamed over and over again. I started to scream with her.

Stosh moved closer to me and had his hands out to touch me. The nightmare continued and I was helpless and so was Lili. Stosh had my clothes in his hands; he handed them to me.

"They shouldn't have done this to you. You're so beautiful. I shouldn't have helped them. They said you were both sick and couldn't get out so I helped them. I'm sorry." Stosh, the gentle giant, was crying.

He sat on the floor while we slept. He made sure none of the others would return. He did this each night for the rest of the journey. He fixed the door and the locks. I spent my days locked in the room reading books. Lili and I never spoke to each other again. Stosh would come each night and sit by my bed until the morning. We never told the Captain. Tony would kill us as he had promised and the Captain too.

Upon arrival in New York, Stosh walked us down the gangplank, each of us holding onto one of his enormous arms. He made sure we both got down safely and wouldn't leave our sides until he knew we were with those we were meeting.

Sally's aunt Sophie was waiting right in front of the boat, with a bright red scarf tossed around her neck, as promised. We recognized each other from photographs exchanged through the mail, but there was no mistaking Aunt Sophie. She was an imposing woman, almost six feet tall, while I was much shorter at five foot one and a half inches. Sophie hugged me so hard that tears came to my eyes. When Stosh had me safely in Sophie's hands, he finally let go of me. I reached up and gently kissed him on the cheek. He blushed and backed away. As he went back up the gangplank, he waved feebly to me and then disappeared. I have never seen him again in person, but he has been forever in my memories and dreams.

Lili was met by an elderly, weathered-looking man. They recognized each other by looking at photographs and searching the features of each other. The elderly gentlemen seemed pleased and they walked off hand in hand. I never saw Lili again. I later learned, from Sophie, that this was a mail order bride situation and that Lili killed herself two years after her arrival in America.

I went to live with Sophie in her little house in the Bronx section of New York City. This was the only neighborhood that I would ever know in the great land of America. I would sit for hours in my little bedroom just staring at the walls or reading one of the books my parents had given me for my journey. This was my one and only connection to the world. Sophie would go to work each day and I would take care of the house, an acceptable arrangement for both of us. In the evenings, after dinner I prepared, we would sit in the parlor and talk about our days in Munich. I talked to no one else.

I wrote my parents at least twice a week, telling them how wonderful America was and all the things I had seen and done. The details were taken out of newspapers and magazines; they were all some other person's life. My parents wrote back telling me of their plans to join me. However, each time they set a date to depart, something seemed to come up that prevented their departure.

I had been moping around the house more than usual for a number of days and Sophie became worried. She called in a doctor. He examined me in my room and came out with a sad expression on his face. Sophie was quite alarmed. She had come to like and love me. She understood my resistance to leave the house in a new country with a new language, but she was sure this would eventually pass. I was only sixteen and had only been in this country for about a month. Sophie knew that everything would be all right. I was too lovely a girl.

"So, Doctor?" Sophie asked hopefully.

"She'll be all right, she's still young. She'll get over it. She's not the first one."

"Not the first one what?" Sophie was always direct.

"Not the first young girl to be pregnant. I thought you knew. That's why you called me, no?"

"I didn't know. She's only sixteen and she's been in the house since she got here."

"She's almost two months pregnant. This didn't happen in your house."

"That big, dumb Polack, I'll bet it was him."

I had to tell Sophie the entire story of the rape, minus some details. Of course, she was shocked. When I was done and had stopped crying, Sophie made some calming tea and sat on the edge of my bed stroking me until I calmed down and stopped shaking.

"So," said Sophie, "what are we going to do about this?" She paced the room shaking her head and muttering to herself. I remained, drained, on the bed.

"I know," she finally said, "we must get you married before the baby. We don't have much time left."

"No, I can't have another man, never, never. Please."

"But, Karen, what else can we do? You can't have this baby alone."

"You'll be here, won't you?"

"No, no babies, no. I'll write your parents, they'll know what to do."

"No," I pleaded, "you can't ever tell my parents! Promise?"

"All right, all right, we come up with something else."

Sophie found a man, not much older than I was, maybe twenty years old. He said he was the son of a friend of Sigfried's, from a little village not far from Munich. His name was Karl Broadfort and he had been in America only a short time and knew few people. It turned out that he was eager to get married because he was convinced that that would help him stay in this country. Sophie contacted Sigfried and he confirmed that he had known Karl and his family since his childhood. However, he warned that Karl's father was a member of the Nazi party and Karl was probably one as well. Also, Sigfried wasn't certain, but he heard a rumor that Karl had stolen money from the Nazis and his father had helped him to escape to America. If the Nazis caught him, they would kill him slowly and painfully. Apparently Karl felt he had no choice but to remain in America, and a wife would enhance his chances to be able to stay.

Sophie impressed upon me that I must get married right away and this nice young man from Munich was interested. I agreed to meet him. He seemed surly and very quiet, but it was nice to talk to someone else about Munich; he knew so many of the same people and places.

Sophie set the wedding for the following week; things had to move quickly. She coached me on how to get Karl to seduce me on our wedding night; we had to have intercourse to legitimatize the baby. I was worried that he would be concerned about my not being a virgin. But, Sophie instructed me on how to get Karl drunk and how to get blood on the sheets.

Although scared throughout my mind and body, I performed well on my wedding night. Karl, who was extremely drunk, placed little sexual demands on me. Thankfully, he was in and out before the nightmares started. I was grateful, as I didn't know if I could ever do this again.

Karl and I moved onto the same street as Sophie. I would move no further away. I now had Karl and Sophie. This was my world. After our wedding night, I would have nothing sexually to do with Karl. I avoided him for the next few weeks and then announced that I was having a baby. Karl now knew that he would be allowed to stay in America. He was so delighted; he let up on his sexual demands. I said it wouldn't be good for the baby and he accepted this.

You were born less than seven months later in July of 1940, weighing over eight pounds. Karl was so proud of his son, a big boy just like him, that he didn't question the early delivery. We named you Wilhelm Sigfried Broadfort. I never told my parents about my marriage or the birth, their grandson. I just kept writing them as usual, using Sophie's address. I continued telling them about the wonders of America. Some wonders, huh?

After you were born, Karl was happy just to be with the baby. I took to wearing large, unattractive housedresses and lounging around the house. I did little to entice Karl; however, eventually he turned his attention to me. He was my husband and it was his right. I did all I could to refuse him, always making excuses. He started staying out late and coming home drunk. He tried to push his drunken body on me, but I successfully fought him off. I then moved into the other bedroom and kept the door locked.

One night Karl came home even more drunk than usual and demanded his rights. He banged on the door and screamed while I cowered under the covers. I was back on the ship and nightmares came back. I would survive this night, but how many more? His drunken behavior continued with, at least, weekly banging at my door. I didn't know what to do. I talked with Sophie, but she had no remedies. She said that I was lucky and would be worse off elsewhere, maybe so.

You were now almost a year old. I had started to keep you in my bedroom, and you started to cry every time Karl banged on the door. I thought by having you with me it would stop Karl. It did for a while, but one night he didn't even bang on the door, he came at the door with the claw of a hammer and quickly broke through. I clung to you in the corner of the bed, but it was Tony and the ship's nightmare all over again. He came in, pulled you from my arms, tore my nightgown off, and raped me for the first and last time. When he was done, he rolled to the side of the bed and looked apologetically at me.

"Karen, I'm sorry, this is not right. But, neither is denying your husband. What is wrong with you?"

"You damn Nazi!" I spat at him.

"So, you knew. So, that's it. Sophie tell you?"

I said nothing to him. I stared at the walls and tried not to think. I didn't talk to Karl after that. I went about my business during the day when he was working and stayed locked in my room at night. He stayed out late getting drunk, and he never came for me again. I now had the safety I was looking for, and Karl was officially allowed to stay in America. We both became United States citizens shortly thereafter so you wouldn't be ashamed of us.

I continued writing my parents, although life with them seemed like a faint memory. I lived my fantasies of the American life through my letters. Nothing was true, but what did it matter? They continued to write about their plans to join me, but now I didn't want them. My life was over. My parents couldn't protect me now.

It was now 1942 and the war in Europe was accelerating. There were rumors that the Nazis were rounding up all of their internal enemies and putting them into concentration camps. There were stories of mass murders and atrocities. I should have been more concerned about my parents, but I found it difficult to care about anything anymore. A little after this, a letter arrived from Sally. I hadn't heard from her since my arrival in America and was afraid to open the letter. What could she want? It was a short note, probably written and posted in a hurry. The note simply said:

"Your parents were taken by the Nazis. Jews and intellectuals are no longer welcome in our homeland. We are escaping to France tonight. God bless."

The letter was simply signed Sally. No last name, no address.

I never heard from my parents again. After this, I never read another book. I ripped each book given to me by my parents, page by page, and fed each page into the fireplace. I thought, so much for the world of ideas and ideals. I was alone now, a Jew in a Nazi world.

Karl met a woman at one of the bars. He hadn't been with a woman in such a long time that it was easy for him to be persuaded. She was a whore and dirty, but he didn't care. He started going from one woman to another, after the first one, and would come home later and later. He paid little attention to you and even less to me. However, I didn't care; let him have his women and leave me alone. He wasn't a bad person, just a man and that was enough.

I lived in my housedresses. I felt sorry for you, but I couldn't love you and neither could Karl. You were becoming as alone as I was, but I didn't care. This life continued for another five years. I was just waiting for something to happen, thinking death would be pleasant. Then came Sophie's funeral and I went out for the first time in years. Although I hadn't spoken to her much in the last few years, Sophie had remained the only friend I had in America. They said she had died of melancholia for the loved ones who had died in her once beloved native Germany.

I stayed after the funeral to sit shiva with Sophie's friends and family. When I came home, Karl had moved out. You were sitting up alone in your bed with all the lights on.

I asked you, "Where's your father? Isn't he watching you?"

"He left, with a woman. The one at the ball game."

I ran to his bedroom. It had been stripped. He had removed all of his clothes and things. The suitcases were gone as well. I ran back to you.

"He's gone all right. Did you try to stop him?"

"What for, Momma?"

What for, indeed. I was better off alone.

The next day I went to see Sophie's brother, Bernard. He owned a men's pants factory nearby called Rufkin and Son. Years ago he had said to me that if I ever needed anything I should ask him, so I asked him for a job. Although I had no skills, he was kind enough to give me a job in the office as a helper. I was now 25 years old and had the rest of my life to go back and forth from our little house in the Bronx to Bernard's factory three blocks away.

The more he heard, the more he loved this little old German lady. When she was finished telling her story, they were both crying, wiping their eyes on their napkins. He sensed, maybe for the first time, that he wasn't who he thought he was. It was as if his entire life had been someone else's.

"Momma, why didn't you ever tell me this?"

"You never asked. I not know what you know, and what you don't know. You had your life. I give you your life, ya?"

"Yes, Momma, you gave me my life. Thank you." He reached over and held her small hands in his. She didn't pull away.

Through tear-filled eyes, he told her his story from the day he left this house. He told her about his days at Roget and working with the Selzers. She smiled knowing that Wilhelm was in good Jewish hands. It made her remember her mother. He told her about Rebecca Goodman and how much he cared for her and how he couldn't marry her. He still didn't know why, but Karen nodded knowingly. He told his mother about his marriage to Katherine. She asked him what she looked like and about her background. She grimaced sadly when he told her of Katherine's Italian family; she remembered Mussolini. He tried to relate in detail the birth of each of his three children. Karen wanted to know all about each of them. He tried to describe them and tell her what each of them was doing, but he realized that he didn't know any of them very well. Karen glowed as she heard about Katherine and each of the children. It was good for her Wilhelm.

"So, Wilhelm, you a good husband and father, ya?" asked Karen.

"No, Momma, I could have done better."

"Ya, we all could have done better." She looked tenderly at her son.

"So, Wilhelm. I meet them, ya?"

"Ya, Momma, you'll meet them, all of them. Come with me now."

"No, Wilhelm. I wait for Beckman; it's Friday. We go out."

"Soon, Momma?"

"Ya, Wilhelm, soon."

She started to get up to clear the cups and plates. He motioned for her to sit back down. He told her about his work, how he only wanted to do the right job, to work hard and please his bosses and how he had gotten caught in being responsible for people losing their jobs. His mother looked at him sympathetically. She knew what he must have wrestled with in his mind and in his soul; she remembered her own poppa. How in the end, he had lost his own job and then his life.

"So, Wilhelm, you lost your job. Me too. You still have your life, ya?"

"But, Momma, I was a corporate Nazi."

"No, Wilhelm, you were a good boy, always a good boy."

Somehow, telling his mother made him feel better. He had unburdened himself and his mother didn't leave him. She still loved him—and he still loved her. Life was simpler than he had imagined. He said good-bye at the door. He kissed her on the cheek and tasted her tears. He held her, not wanting to lose her again.

"I'll come back, Momma. Take you away from here. It's dangerous here."

"No, Wilhelm. I stay here. Raymond and the others, they watch out for me. This is where I live in America, this is where I die."

"Sure, Momma. We'll see." He wanted to do everything he could for this little, old lady, to make it up to her—maybe then he would stop dreaming of her.

He stood outside the door, him on the stoop, her holding the door. He thought for a moment. "Momma, do you remember a classmate of mine, Howie Eskin?"

"Ya, he come visit me. Right before I stop work at Ruskins."

"And when was that?" He assumed that his mother had stopped work a long time ago. She was over seventy years old.

"Maybe two, three years ago, I work as long as I can. Mr. Ruskin die and I work with young Ruskin. He keep me on, but I no do computers. We agree to nice retirement, two, three years ago. That's when Eskin visit me. Looking for you."

"So you know where he is?"

"Maybe. You wait." She went back into the house. He waited on the stoop for what seemed like a long time. His mother came back, walking very slowly with her old bandy legs and heavy oxford high top shoes. She handed him a ragged card.

"Here. Eskin's card." He took it and shook his head. Howie was the CFO of a small pants manufacturer. The card listed his work number. On the back, Howie had written his home address and phone number. He lived in Brooklyn Heights.

He stepped back and kissed his mother on the cheek again. "Thank you, Momma. I'll come back tomorrow. You wait for me, in the window."

"Ya, Wilhelm. Tomorrow, Saturday. I wait for you. I be in the window."

Karen watched her son go down the steps to his car. She watched as he engaged Raymond and the others. Her little boy had become a man. She watched him get into his big German car. She hadn't said a thing about it before and she wouldn't say anything now. She felt sorry for her Wilhelm. She had tried to keep him safe from the world and the Nazis. He had become a corporate Nazi anyhow. So be it. She felt sorry for him. The world had not been kind to him.

He drove away from his mother's feeling much better. All these years he had felt guilty for leaving his mother out of hate. His mother felt that she had let him go out of love. What a remarkable woman, he thought. And he had been ashamed of her all of his life, the German lady. It was he that he was ashamed of now.

11

TAKING CARE OF BUSINESS

It was two o'clock in the afternoon, and William had more calls to make, but most of the people he planned to see were probably still at work. He decided to drive toward Howie Eskin's house in Brooklyn. On the way, he stopped at a shopping plaza. He would walk around, maybe get some lunch, maybe do some shopping, until after six, and then he would call on Howie.

After a lunch at a salad bar in a mall food court, he walked around. He passed one of the chain stores that his two sons used to shop at; they specialized in jeans and casual clothing. He would never go into a store like this on his own. All of his clothes, suits, shirts, and ties, were custom made. He looked in the store window. He could see his reflection in the glass; he didn't know who it was. It was an old man in a suit.

He entered the store. Immediately, a sales woman approached. She was tall, slender, well made up, and very attractive. She reminded him of a young Katherine with dark hair. He felt more comfortable. She looked at William with a slight smile at the corner of her mouth. "Can I help you with anything, sir?"

"I don't know. I was thinking of changing."

"Changing to what, sir?"

"Oh, changing my wardrobe, to something more casual."

The sales lady looked him up and down. It was apparent that she didn't like what she saw. The clothes were expensive looking, but drab and boring.

"I see. My name is Lilly. I'd be glad to help you." She extended her hand.

He extended his hand. He took her hand in his. "I'm William."

"So," she said, "Lilly and Willy." She smiled at her little joke. He didn't smile, but he didn't correct her either. "Where shall we start?"

He hesitated. "How about head to toe, or toe to head."

She nodded her head. "Good choice."

They walked around the store. They picked out shoes, loafers and sneakers, white sweat socks and ankle length prints, slacks, jeans and khakis, shirts, tees, band collars, sport shirts, jackets, denim, casual, and sport jackets, three full sweat suits and caps. Lilly helped him take it all to one of the dressing rooms. He liked everything and bought it all. He dressed in a pair of jeans, a long sleeve tee shirt, loafers, one of the caps which said "New York I love you," and a casual outdoor jacket.

"What shall we do with the clothes you were wearing?" she asked him. "Shall I put them in a suit carrier for you?"

He looked at her while she rang up the sale and took his, not the company's, credit card. She wasn't surprised when his credit card limit was sufficient to handle the purchase total. He looked extremely attractive in his new clothes. Where she was somewhat afraid of him when he first walked in, she was now somewhat interested in him. He looked at his old clothes lying on the counter. Lilly was packing them.

He put his hand out. "Oh no, let's just give them away. I'm through with them. No more."

She looked at him and smiled, this time seductively. "Whatever you say." She placed the old clothes aside. "Can I help you out to your car?"

He didn't know how he was going to get all of the packages out, and he appreciated her offer. He noticed that she offered to help him herself; she didn't enlist one of the male sales people. She was keeping this one to herself. He had just spent over a thousand dollars on casual clothes on a whim. What would he spend when he was serious? She wanted to keep him as her customer, and maybe more.

He went out to pull his car in front of the store. Lilly was waiting for him with a cart loaded with his purchases. She smiled knowingly at the size of his Mercedes. She batted her eyes at him. He opened the trunk of the car, and he and Lilly loaded the purchases into the back. She made sure that she got as close to him as possible as she placed items in the trunk. He drank in her perfume as she moved close to him. She was nicely shaped with small breasts like Katherine. He liked that.

"Thank you, Willy." She said as he got in the car. "Please come see us again."

He thought he might just do that. He was starting to enjoy his new life.

It was getting close to six o'clock. He drove toward Howie Eskin's house. He whistled to himself. William never whistled. He was feeling better. He drove slowly onto the street in Brooklyn Heights where Howie Eskin lived. The houses were large brownstones. They were the types of houses that he envied while he was growing up in the Bronx. Now, compared to where he had been living in Stamford, they looked shabby. Life is a matter of perspective, he thought. He saw the number of the Eskin house. The house was a large corner home with a front and a side yard. In a neighborhood such as this, this type of house was always considered at a premium. Howie wasn't doing as bad as he thought.

William parked his car in front of the house. As he did, the outside lights leading to the front door went on. He got slowly out of the car and looked up at the house. He could see Howie in a house like this with a wife and family. He smoothed out his slacks and jacket. He wasn't used to dressing casual. He felt like he had become someone else once again. Was he never to find out who he really was?

He rang the doorbell and waited. He fidgeted with the chain on his jacket. He was more nervous than he had thought he would be. He had thought about doing this many times before, especially since they had moved to Stamford, but he always found a reason why he couldn't. The door opened and a rather dowdy woman appeared. She looked at William as if she knew him from somewhere.

"Yes?" she said. "Can I help you?" Her first response was that it was somebody selling something.

"Does Howie Eskin live here? I'm an old friend of his."

The woman looked at him quizzically. She hadn't heard her husband, Howard, called Howie for many years, not since high school.

"Who should I say is calling? I was just preparing dinner." The clear message being that this was a bad time to come calling.

"Oh, I'm sorry;" said William. "I can come back another time. That is, if this is inconvenient."

"Oh no, I didn't mean that. Come in. And, who did you say you were?"

"I didn't. Tell him it's William...that it's Wilhelm Broadfort, a friend from high school." He said this proudly. He hadn't used that name for over thirty years.

"Oh my God, Wilhelm! You don't remember me? Eleanor Bernstein. I was two grades beneath you and Howard in high school."

He didn't remember her for his life. He didn't remember much from high school, particularly the people. "Of course, Eleanor Bernstein. You've changed a little; you're much more attractive."

She blushed. "Thank you, Wilhelm. Howard's in the living room reading the newspaper. Every night he comes home, changes his clothes, and reads the newspaper while I prepare dinner. That's our life. Nothing exciting, nothing bad."

William thought, "Isn't that everyone's life?"

"Why don't you go in and say hello. Surprise him. He talks about you all the time. His successful friend." Some success, thought William.

Eleanor went back to the kitchen talking to herself. "Wilhelm Broadfort, in our house. Wait till I tell the kids."

William peeked into the living room. Howie was sitting in a black vinyl reclining chair with the newspaper in front of him. He tiptoed directly in front of him.

"Hello, Howie," said William.

Howie was startled. He put the newspaper down suddenly. He looked up at Wilhelm. A small smile started at the corners of his mouth.

"Holy shit! It's you, it's really you!" Howie jumped off his chair. He went to hug William, but remembered his aversion to being touched.

William moved closer to him. "It's all right, Howie." He hugged Howie.

"Wilhelm ...or is it William now? What are you doing here?"

Howie was quite impressed at the success of his old high school friend. Most of the kids that they had gone to school with still lived in one of the boroughs, working stiffs like him. He was more successful than most of them. William was the exception.

"So," said Howie. "What brings you here? I never thought I would see you again. Not in your circles anyway. I thought you would want to forget your old life."

"I did," said William. "But, I've never been able to forget what I did to you. It's preyed on my mind all these years."

Howie had no idea what he was talking about. "Wilhelm, you were a good friend. You got into Roget, I didn't. It's nothing to blame yourself for."

He looked Howie over. He looked pretty much the same, except he was paunchier, balding, what hair remained was gray, and he wore eyeglasses. It appeared that life had been good to him.

Howie looked William over. He looked pretty much the same, except he was wearing casual clothes. Howie remembered Wilhelm always in dress clothes. A little gray maybe but the same.

"No, Howie it's not that. Well, it's that too." He hesitated.

"So," asked Howie. "What is this terrible thing you did to me?"

William looked down at his feet. "I didn't give you the five hundred dollars for college. I should have. I was selfish."

Howie looked perplexed.

"You asked me for the money at the celebration, at the market where I worked." William tried to explain, but Howie still didn't understand.

"I asked you for money?"

"That's right. And, I should have given it to you."

"Wilhelm, if you say so. I asked everybody for the money. You were probably my last resort. I hated myself. I should have worked in high school like you did, but I thought I was smarter than you and didn't have to work, that I would get a scholarship. But you got the scholarship. I couldn't have taken your money even if you had offered it. It was my fault, not yours."

"So," said William, "you didn't hate me for not giving you the money?"

"Of course not. I may have, for a little while, at the time. But, I knew that I would have hated myself more for taking the money."

"Really. You mean that?"

"Absolutely. So what happened to you? You seemed to have disappeared."

"I just went away and never came back. You know about my name change, but I changed everything. I became a socialite snob. Just like the guys we used to hate."

"You never contacted anyone from your old life? Your mother said she hadn't heard from you in a long time. But she knew you were all right."

"When was the last time you saw my mother?"

"Let me think. It was right before we moved from the old neighborhood, about eight or nine years ago. It was getting too dangerous, too much crime and drugs. It was bad for the kids. They kept getting beat up. I told your mother that she better get out of there. I hope she did."

"No, she's still there. I saw her this afternoon."

Howie nodded his head. "Is she okay?"

"She's fine. The neighborhood toughs protect her. She still sits at her window."

"A remarkable lady," said Howie.

"Yes, she is." And he meant it. "So, you married Eleanor Bernstein from our old high school. She looks great. You two must be living good."

"You remember her?" asked Howie. "She'll be so pleased. You know she had a terrific crush on you. Whenever we have an argument, she always brings you up. How things would have been different if she had married you."

He said nothing. It would serve no purpose to say he really didn't remember her. "And kids, you have kids?"

"Oh yeah, a son and a daughter. Both engineers. Did what I couldn't do. I'm proud of both of them. Roy's in South America building bridges and Gretchen's in Texas building oil refineries."

William told Howie about his wife Katherine and their three children. Every time he talked about his family, he felt he knew them a little better. Maybe it was time to pay attention to them; he soft-pedaled talk about his money, possessions and life style. William was never a braggart and saw no reason to lord his material success over Howie. In many ways, Howie was much more successful. William was glad he was wearing his new casual clothes.

Eleanor entered the room and looked at the two of them, old friends. Life was good. "Howard, dear," she said, "dinner is ready."

"I better be going," William said. He started to move toward the door.

"Oh, no, Wilhelm, you can stay for dinner, can't you?" She looked at him like a young girl. She still had a crush on him.

"No, I better get going. I was just in the area."

They both walked him to the door, with their arms around each other's waists. William thought that they looked very happy, and they were. He didn't tell Howie about his losing his job. It wasn't necessary.

Eleanor made William promise that he would stay in touch. Thirty years was too long a time. He promised that he would and that he would bring Katherine. He hoped she was still talking to him. Losing his job might be the last straw for her. But he promised anyway.

Howie and Eleanor watched him get into his Mercedes. Eleanor turned to Howie and looked appreciatively at him. "What do you think he wanted?"

"Just to make amends...to an old friend."

"He doesn't look good, does he?" asked Eleanor.

"With all his money and his big car...no, he doesn't look good," said Howie.

"He's dying, isn't he?" asked Eleanor.

"I don't know, but he isn't a happy man."

"No, he isn't," said Eleanor. She kissed Howie on the lips. He held her tightly. You can lose the thing you love so quickly, he thought. They walked back into the house, hand in hand, each clutching the other. They were the lucky ones, weren't they?

William had always wanted to be a wealthy socialite as he didn't like being poor, and now he was one and hated himself. He walked away. He envied Howie and Eleanor. He sat in his car in front of the Eskins house. He really had more friends than he had ever thought he had. People seemed to like him, rather than dislike him. Where had he been all of his life? And he liked Howie and Eleanor; they seemed like good people. He was sick of the other kind and their world. He turned on the car and listened as it purred quietly. German precision, he thought, I gave my life to German precision. I gave no quarter, no error — human error. And I, Wilhelm Broadfort, may have made the biggest error. I was so smart, and yet so dumb. He pounded the steering wheel and then drove off towards Manhattan.

He pulled up to the address he had been given. It was a prestigious apartment building facing Gramercy Park, quite impressive but understated. There was no parking allowed so he drove around the corner and parked in an indoor parking lot. William always felt a bit scared walking around Manhattan, especially in closed parking garages with no attendants. He walked quickly back to the apartment building. He found the name on the register inside the building. This was a secure building; you had to be rung in. He had come this far. He rang the button next to the name. The door buzzed without anyone asking who was there. He rushed for the door and grabbed it just as the buzzer stopped. The apartment number was 618. He took the elevator. There were a number of people already on the elevator elegantly dressed. This was Friday night, and wealthy New Yorkers went out on Friday night. They looked at William in his casual clothes like he was a delivery boy who had forgotten the pizza. Usually it was William who looked at people this way. This made him feel good. Let them look. He got off on the sixth floor and looked for 618. The numbers were going in the wrong direction, so he reversed himself. When he came close to 618, he noticed a person waiting at the door. He walked over; he had never been so nervous. He flashed a sign of recognition. He was ignored. He wasn't what was expected.

"Hello," he said, "remember me?"

The person looked at him without recognition.

"It's William. William Bradford." He waited.

There was a slight smile and then a deeper smile. "William! It's really you."

"I'm afraid so. You still look good, after all these years."

"And so do you. Oh my God, it's really you."

He moved closer and hugged Rebecca Goodman. He was coming home. She held onto him and began to cry. He tried not to, but tears formed. He brushed them aside slyly with the back of his hand. He hoped that she didn't notice, but of course she did. He hadn't realized how much he missed her.

They were standing in front of her door hugging, neither one willing to let go. Neighbors passed them and looked at them suspiciously. One didn't show their affections in the hall in a building like this. If this persisted, they might ask Rebecca to leave. Rebecca and William didn't care.

She was holding tightly onto him, pressing hard against him. Her breasts were pushing into his chest. Only yesterday this would have made him feel extremely uncomfortable. Today he couldn't let go of her, breasts and all.

"Come in, come in," she said. "We don't do things like this in the hallway. We're sophisticated here. We do it behind triple locked doors."

She took his hand and led him inside. She held both his hands and looked at him. "My God, William ... or should I call you Wilhelm ..."

"Either one. I'm between identities."

"I see," she said. "I can't believe it. You look better than I remember. Age has been kind to you." She hugged him again. He was learning to like this hugging.

"Maybe, but not everything else. Age hasn't harmed you much either." He hugged her harder, breasts and all.

She blushed. She still wasn't comfortable with male compliments. There was always something expected of her when a male complimented; usually to feel her tits. She hated those things, she always had.

"With a little help from Revlon. So, William . . . William is okay?" He nodded.

"Come, sit in the living room."

"Weren't you waiting for someone? Maybe I should go."

"Not so fast William S. Bradford III. Whoever I was waiting for will wait. You won't."

She took him into her living room. The apartment was decorated and furnished with top of the line materials; a far cry from her old dorm room. She was a slob in those days. He sat on the plush sofa, she in an easy chair facing him. She smiled at him and kept shaking her head.

"So, tell me what's happened since I saw you last. Must be what, thirty years?"

"Thirty-two . . . almost thirty-three."

"My God, that long?"

He looked down at the rug. He knew it was his fault. "Afraid so. I haven't been a very good friend. I wasn't a very good friend."

She looked at him and smiled. "Just like the William I knew. Always blaming yourself. Never trusting that someone could just like you."

He flustered. "I'm sorry, Rebecca, I was never good with people. It was always easier to just move away." He thought of his mother; tears came to his eyes.

She moved next to him on the sofa. He sensed their bodies touching but he didn't mind. He didn't even think about it. It was good to be with her again.

"You never moved away from me," Rebecca said.

"Rebecca, I married another woman!"

"I know. She was a friend of mine too! Remember?"

"I can't forget. I've thought about it all these years." He didn't tell her about his dreams and her role in them. He didn't have to.

"And you think I've forgotten you. I've missed you dearly. I've tried, God knows, but I've never been able to replace you as a friend." She squeezed his hand.

"I know I should have married you, but I just couldn't." He couldn't stop blinking. It was either that or cry uncontrollably. He still didn't lose control.

"No, you did the right thing. Katherine loved you, she still does. I never loved you in that way. You'll always be my dearest friend, and I'll always love you as a friend, but we could never be lovers. I would rather have you as a friend." She kissed him softly on the cheek. He wiped it off.

"You didn't want to marry me?"

"William, of course not. Katherine was perfect for you. She was the kind of wife you needed. I would have killed the William you wanted to be."

"But, you moved away. You didn't come to the wedding. You didn't give us a gift. I thought I had hurt you badly. I couldn't face you…all these years. You never got married. It was all my fault. I ruined your life, didn't I?"

She looked fondly at him. "No William, I ruined my own life. I didn't run away from you. I ran away from me."

"How so? We were so close. And, I turn around and marry your girl friend…without even telling you." He looked down at his lap. Her body heaved up and down and her breasts heaved, but he didn't look. She looked over at him. She noticed what he wasn't looking at.

She cupped her breasts in her hands. "It's these things. I thought these were all the boys wanted. You were the only boy who wasn't interested in my tits. They disgusted you. They disgusted me. We could be friends without these things (she pushed them toward him, he backed away) getting in the way. When you married Katherine, I lost two friends."

"But you didn't return my calls, you didn't come to the wedding, you didn't send a present, you didn't…"

"Hold on, William. I did return your calls, and I talked to Katherine. I was in New York interviewing for a job with publishers. I got the job; I still work for them."

"I know, that's how I found you."

She nodded. "When Katherine told me you were getting married, I was happy for both of you. You were both my friends. I didn't come to the wedding because I was never invited. I found out later you were already married . . . it was too late. And, I did get you a present. I sent it to your room at Roget, but it was returned. You had already left. Stay here." She went into the other room and returned with a large package, an aging wedding gift. She handed it to him. He looked at it.

"What's this?" he asked.

"Your wedding gift. I've kept it for you. I expected it to be sooner rather than later. Go ahead, open it."

He opened the card. The card had a wedding couple on the front. The groom looked like William, the bride looked like Katherine. She had written their names over the figures. He opened the card and read the message to himself.

"To my two best friends, the best in life. William and Katherine, husband and wife. Both of you, please stay as you are. And please don't go too far. Love always, Rebecca."

He held the card and just looked at it.

"Go ahead, open the present. I've schlepped it around with me. This is my sixth move. I always hoped you would come for it. I wanted to give it to you."

He opened the gift. It was a bagel and lox server exactly like the one that Herman Selzer had given them. Herman's was still sitting in their attic unused. He laughed when he saw it.

"I wanted to give you something that would always remind you of me and us."

"Rebecca, it's lovely." He couldn't stop the tears. "It's been a lot of years without this, and you. I'm sorry. We'll use it this Sunday. Why don't you come out and join us?"

"I think maybe you should talk to Katherine first."

"You're probably right." He placed the gift, the card, and the wrapping on the floor. They were all keepers. He would use the gift gladly. William had saddened.

"What is it?" She could always tell when William was bothered.

He hesitated. "Oh, Rebecca." He blurted it out. "I've always held myself responsible for your never marrying. If I had married you, everything would have been all right. It's all my fault. Oh, I'm so sorry. I've hated myself."

"What for? I could have gotten married many times. I was your friend because you were no threat. You weren't interested in me physically, these things disgusted you (she cupped her breasts), and I wasn't interested in you physically. My God, you were always so pale like a ghost. You kept me safe from other boys and I loved you for that. It wasn't you that kept me from marrying, it was me. I always thought I hated males and you hated females, a perfect match. I thought we could just go on being friends the rest of our lives. It didn't work out that way."

"I know, it's all my fault."

"Stop saying that. It's nobody's fault. It was the way it had to be. We each had to find ourselves, without the safety net."

"But, I disappointed you."

"No, William. You did what I expected you to do. If it wasn't Katherine, it would have been someone like her. She's always loved you."

"I know. I just haven't been able to love her."

"I'm sorry."

"Now you're sorry." They both laughed, as well as they could through tears.

She got up and went into her bedroom. She returned shortly with a picture frame in her hand. She handed the picture frame to him. The picture was one of Rebecca dressed in an evening gown on the arm of a distinguished looking man in a tuxedo. They both looked like they wanted to be together. She looked happy and it made him happy. He looked over at her.

"That was my husband. Oliver Guest."

"The famous author?"

"The very same."

"You said "was." You're not married anymore?"

"Oliver died three years ago. He was over twenty years older than me. He died of author's disease."

"What's that?" He was still looking at the picture. He was glad for Rebecca.

"Too much smoking, drinking and coffee. He died of lung and stomach cancer."

"I'm sorry, Rebecca."

"Don't be. We had eight wonderful years together. This was Oliver's apartment. As long as I stay here, I'll be with him. He was a wonderful man. Other than you, he was the only man who wanted the inside me and not the outside me."

He reached over and held her hand. "I'm glad for you."

"That's much better than being sorry." Rebecca smiled at him. He turned away.

"Any children?"

"No, I never wanted any. I was over forty when we got married and Oliver was over sixty. He already had a family, two sons and two daughters. They became my children too. Oliver's wife had died of lupus in her early forties. He raised the children himself until we got together. They're all the family I need." She looked at William. "Except you. So, tell me about you."

He started at the beginning from his wedding day to the ending, his termination from Consolidated Unlimited and his activities of that day up to his visit to her apartment. She felt so sad for him. He got the life he wanted, but it didn't give him what he wanted.

"So, William S. Bradford III, what do you do now?"

"I wish I knew what to do and who I am?"

She looked him over. "Your new wardrobe is certainly a start. I like it. I don't think I've ever seen you not in a suit."

"I don't think I've ever seen me not in a suit. I thought I was born in one."

She laughed. "I like you with a sense of humor. You were always so serious."

"I guess so, until this afternoon."

The buzzer rang. "That must be Stacy." She got up to push the ring in button.

"Stacy?"

"Stacy Guest, Oliver's son, that's who I was expecting. We're going out to dinner. Why don't you join us? I'm sure you'll like him, you're so much alike."

"Oh yeah. Serious, stodgy stuffed shirt with no sense of humor with no interest in your body, only your mind."

She laughed. "You're really quite funny, I mean the new William."

"The new William. I like that. I better go. Maybe the next time."

"I'd like that. I mean a next time." She came close to him and hugged him and kissed him softly on the lips. It was the first time their lips had touched. He liked it. She opened the door to let him out. At the door she hugged him again.

"I've missed you William S. Bradford III." She hesitated. "I love you."

"I love you too, Rebecca Goodman." He said it and he meant it. Now if he could only say that to Katherine. Maybe it wasn't over yet.

As they were holding each other, Stacy came to the door. He did indeed look something like William, as did his father. Stacy looked at them. His face took on a smile of pleasure. William could tell he liked (and loved) Rebecca as he finally realized that he did.

Stacy looked at Rebecca as if to say "what do we have here?"

"Hello, Rebecca," he said.

She had been daydreaming on William's shoulder. She remembered doing that a lot when they were younger. Once again she was proving that dreams could come true, even if it took over thirty years to happen.

"Oh, Stacy. There you are."

"Yes, Rebecca, here I am." He did have the new William's sense of humor.

"This is a very dear old friend of mine, William S. Bradford III. You may have heard me speak of him."

"Not often. Maybe less than three thousand times."

She looked at William. "See, I told you that I hadn't forgotten you."

He extended his hand, still holding on to her. "You can call me just William."

"Well, hello just William. Will you join us for dinner? It would be flattering to have the real William S. Bradford III with us rather than the memory one."

"I would really love to, but I need to be somewhere else. But, we'll get together real soon."

"I hope so. Please bring Katherine with you." Stacy was sincere. William didn't know how Stacy knew his wife's name. Rebecca must have told him.

She hugged William once more, pressing him against her breasts. Somehow it didn't bother him. He was home again and their souls once again were intertwined.

She whispered in his ear, "I've missed you dearly."

He whispered back, "I've missed you too."

He slipped one of his cards in her pocket with his home address and phone number on it. She looked at it quickly and nodded. She was eighteen again. She, too, was home again. She was already thinking of trips to the museums, concerts, late night coffees, long talks, and William.

William slowly released her. He could have stayed there forever; it was always a safe place for him. It was like the years had slipped away. What a mess he had made of things.

He walked slowly away. He looked back at Rebecca as he walked towards the elevator. He was happy that she was happy. The elevator was full, all dressed to go out on a Friday night, as he would have been dressed himself. They all moved back as he entered the elevator. They didn't want to touch or be touched by one of the working class. He laughed to himself. There, but for the grace of Richard Sprague and Consolidated Unlimited, go I, he thought.

In the lobby, he waited for the others to get off. He walked behind them as it should be and as they would want it to be. He had never felt better in his life.

He found his car in the parking garage and sat there thinking about Rebecca, Katherine, and his life. He drove out of the garage. He had no place to go. He just wasn't ready to go out with Rebecca yet. He had more work to do.

He pulled into the parking garage of a high-rise cooperative apartment building. He was getting used to life on his own in Manhattan. He had always had a driver on his company trips to New York. It made things easier for getting around the city. The driver would take care of letting him off and picking him up and the God-awful problem of parking. Now he would have to do all this for himself. He was enjoying himself. There was something good about doing things for yourself. He had forgotten how good it felt.

He took the elevator up to the lobby from the parking garage. He was greeted in the lobby by a security guard. Why do they always look so officious? William thought, like they have ownership in the building. When he wore his suit and fancy overcoat, nobody gave him a second glance and stopped him for anything. He was realizing the difference dressed in his casual clothing. He was looked at differently, more suspiciously, and his very presence was questioned. He had gone from being invisible to being suspect. In a strange way it felt good to be recognized; he felt alive.

"Can I help you?" the guard asked him as he looked William up and down, mentally frisking him. William looked at the badge pinned to the guard's jacket. It read "Bud Doyle, Security."

William pointed to a name on the owners listing. "I'd like to see them."

"Are you expected?"

"Probably, but maybe not this soon."

"I'll have to call up, before I can let you in. Whom shall I say is calling?"

He handed him one of his business cards. He might as well give them away; he didn't need them any more. They wouldn't do him any good.

The guard looked at the card and back at William. He was impressed. Amazing the power of a business card—and the position that went with it. William hadn't changed, but his stature had. Somehow his dress mattered less. The guard made the call. William sensed some hesitation on the other end. The guard hung up.

"It's okay. Go on up, the elevator on the right. Number 1862."

"Thank you, Bud," he said. He was enjoying his new identity.

He rang the buzzer at apartment 1862. He waited. He could sense some hesitation on the other side of the door. Eventually the door opened a crack.

"What do you want?" It was Ethel Biddle. She had a bathrobe on. Evidently he had come in the middle of something. He could only guess what.

"Hello, Ethel. I wanted to talk to John if I could." He had no more reason to talk to Ethel than she did to him.

"Wait here. I'll see if he wants to talk to you."

He waited in the hall. He felt like a gatecrasher at a whorehouse. He heard muffled talking going on inside. Finally the door reopened. It was Ethel again.

"You can come in, William. I don't know why, but John agreed to talk to you. You can stay for a short time. We were right in the middle of something."

John sat in the living room waiting for him. It was apparent that he had dressed hurriedly. His shirt was half sticking out of his trousers and he had no belt on.

"Hello, John," said William.

John said nothing. He had been well instructed by Ethel.

William stood looking at him. "Is it okay if I sit down?" John nodded. He was wary of William. He was sneaky enough in his business suit. John had never seen William in casual clothes. He wasn't sure what to expect. William sat in a chair across from John. He noticed that the apartment had been professionally decorated.

"Look, if this is a bad time, I can come back." He was trying to be nice.

John hesitated and looked over at Ethel. She nodded. "No, it's all right."

"Okay. I just stopped by to say how sorry I am, the way I treated you. I thought I was doing the best for you. I handled it badly. I'm sorry, John."

John said nothing. William got up to go. He started for the door. Ethel opened it for him. She was still scowling. He was going through the door when John spoke.

"Wait a minute, William."

He turned to look at John. "Please," said John. "Come back and sit down."

He sat back in the same chair. He stared at John waiting for him to speak. He had done what he had come for. He never expected that he and John could be friends again, if they ever were, but they didn't need to be enemies.

"William, what you did to me is unforgivable. To decide for me that I was ready to retire and to give the job to that pip-squeak...I gave you and the damn company a lot of good years. I deserved better."

He looked at John for the first time as a real human being and an equal. "Yes, you did, John. I'm sorry. I never could deal with people. That's why I had you."

Ethel sneered sarcastically. "Jesus Christ, William. He's worse with people than you are. You, you son of a bitch, had him traipsing all over the country dealing with people and getting rid of people. Do you have any idea what that did to him?" Ethel came over to sit next to John. As she did so, her robe opened at the top and William could see that she had nothing on. He turned his head. These were breasts he absolutely didn't want to see.

William put his head down. "No, I never knew. John never said anything. I just thought he liked being out of town."

Ethel started "Liked . . ."

John interrupted her. "Please, Ethel, it's okay." Ethel had pleaded with John so many times to talk to William about all of his out of town travel. John had told her he had and it would just be for a short time longer. It wasn't, and John had never talked to William about it. He was afraid he would lose his job.

"I'm sorry. I should have talked to you. Ethel's right, it was killing me and she said to talk to you. I just couldn't. I didn't want to lose my job. I did anyway."

"So did I," said William.

They both said "what" at the same time.

He told them the story of his termination. They listened without saying a word.

"Those bastards," said Ethel. "After all you gave them."

"I'm sorry, William," said John. "It appears that we now belong to the same club, the unemployed executives club. How about a drink to celebrate?" John knew William didn't drink, but what the hell. This was a special occasion.

William hesitated. "Celebrate? We're both out of work dinosaurs."

"William you did me the best favor of my life getting me out of that place. I lost my job, but I got myself back and my wife." He squeezed Ethel on the side so that her robe opened at the top again. William saw more than he wanted to and then looked quickly away.

"What do you do? I got through today but I don't know what else to do."

"It'll come. Take some time and then decide. You don't have to work, you know."

"So what is it that you do, John?"

"Well, we have this apartment right in the middle of Manhattan and we have museums, the library. Ethel volunteers at the main library—concerts, shows, restaurants—you name it. I'm working with a group of retired executives. We offer free consultation to start up minority businesses. I'm really enjoying it. And, oh yeah, we bought a farm in upstate New York. My brother Ronald's son, Rollie, operates it for us. We go up as often as we can. Our problem is we can't find the time. We love the city, but we miss the farm. We got the best of both worlds."

"And what do you do for money?" William asked.

"Money, we don't need money, we never did. But, thanks to you and the company we have more money than we'll ever need. Plus, I'm making more money on our investments than I made on salary."

William thought about that. He had always tried to live on what he earned. All of the bonuses, stock options, investment income and so on had always just sat there. He had always made enough salary so that he, Katherine and the kids always had everything they wanted. Accumulating money had never been his thing. He just wanted to be able to buy whatever he wanted, never to be poor again. He had liked being William S. Bradford III; he didn't know if he would like being just William. Since the children had graduated from college, not one of them had asked him for money. He would have given it to them gladly had they only asked. He wondered what he was worth.

"John, I'm glad that things worked out for you."

"Losing my job was the best thing that ever happened to me. It should have only happened sooner."

William laughed. "Now you tell me."

Ethel smiled; the ice was thawing.

"William, please come again. Now that we're both old retirees."

"Who's old?" William asked. He got up to leave. He nodded at Ethel's robe. "I better go, you have things to do."

"Don't feel you have to leave," Ethel said. William was surprised. "Don't get me wrong, I've hated you for a long time. It's going to take some time to like you. But, Father here, he's missed you."

William looked at them both. "I've missed you too, both of you."

"Thank you, William," said Ethel. "You didn't need to say that."

"Now you tell me," William said. They all laughed.

William got in his car; it was ten at night. He was tired of seeing people. He would see the others in the morning. He had never been alone in Manhattan before with nothing to do. It had always been for a meeting, a conference, or some other company business. It felt good to have nothing to do. He drove around the city for a while watching the people going places and basking in the lights. He pulled the car over to the curb on Broadway and watched the activity. He really loved the energy level of New York.

He drove slowly over to Park Avenue and parked the car in the garage of the hotel where Consolidated Unlimited kept rooms for visiting employees and guests. He was known there and felt certain that they would find a room for him even this late at night on a Friday. William took the elevator to the first floor lobby and was greeted by Jimmy the Bellman.

"Hello, Mr. Bradford. Can I take you up to your usual room?"

He meant the company suite. "No, Jimmy, I think I'll take a room of my own."

"It's no trouble, Mr. Bradford. The company suite is open. You can have it for the entire weekend."

He thought about it. The temptation was great. The company had screwed him. Why not screw them? "I know, Jimmy, but I'll feel better this way." And he would.

"Okay, Mr. B. Let me get you registered." Jimmy led him over to the registration desk. William had never been there before; he hadn't needed to. It was a new feeling for him paying your own way. It was feeling good. He liked it.

"Can I get your luggage, Mr. B?" Jimmy had his hand out for William's car keys, and a tip.

He handed him the keys and a five-dollar bill, the same tip that the company usually gave Jimmy. He could be as generous as those bastards. Jimmy ran off to the garage. William called after him. "The car's in space number 38. Bring up all the packages." Jimmy gave the okay sign. He thought it strange that William didn't park in one of the company spaces, but who was he to question executives? They were all a little screwy. And how many used their company suites on the weekends to bring their girl friends or boy friends. Jimmy knew how to keep quiet; if Mr. B wanted to play for the weekend, that was his business.

William checked in. The desk clerk—it said Maria on her badge—was extremely efficient and quite attractive. He hadn't noticed before. Exactly what you would expect in an exclusive small hotel catering to company and executive suites.

"You won't be staying in the company suite, Mr. Bradford?" She was being discreet.

"No, I'd prefer not to. Is that all right?"

"Certainly, we have execs like yourself staying here on their own all the time."

He wondered what treatment he would get when they knew that he was no longer an exec.

"Can I get an imprint of your credit card?"

"Of course." He automatically reached for the company credit card. Anything that could be was charged to the company, but no longer. He would have to get used to paying his own way. He handed his personal credit card to the desk clerk. She looked at it suspiciously. The only time company executives paid for a room themselves was when they didn't want the company to know they were here. Usually they would have a woman with them, who never looked like a wife. This was the first time for Mr. Bradford. She wondered who would be joining him. She wouldn't mind herself. He was kind of cute, especially in casual clothes. She had never seen him in anything other than a business suit. He seemed different somehow, almost likable.

"Would you sign the registration form to verify your agreement as to the rate?"

He looked at the form. It said $280 plus tax per night. She noticed him staring.

"Is everything all right, Mr. Bradford? I gave you our executive weekend rate, 20% off and no charge for parking."

He pondered. "Oh yes, of course. I just never knew what your charges were. Kind of shocked me." He could well afford the charges; he just wasn't comfortable paying excessive costs as if he was rich and it didn't matter. He didn't like being taken advantage of; he never had.

Maria thought to herself, "Another rich executive bastard. Will buy you anything you want on the company expense account, but nothing on their own account. Wouldn't want the wife to find out. At least he's never propositioned me."

Jimmy was back with William's packages and had them sitting on a cart. Maria gave William's key to Jimmy. In these kinds of hotels, you weren't allowed to bring your own bags to your room. Jimmy probably made more money than the head of the hotel, most of it non-tax reportable.

He followed Jimmy to his room. The room was a suite, really like a small apartment. It had an entrance hall, a living room, a dining room, a small fully stocked kitchen, two full bathrooms, and two large bedrooms. The larger bedroom had a whirlpool tub. Even though he had stayed at the hotel many times, Jimmy always went through his routine as to what was in the suite and how to use everything. Jimmy tried to earn his tips.

"Will that be all, Mr. B?" asked Jimmy.

William was used to eating late at night and tomorrow morning he had no reason to get up early. It was almost eleven o'clock and he was hungry.

"Can I still get something to eat?" he asked Jimmy.

"For you Mr. B anything, anytime. What would you like?"

"Is Donagan's still open?"

"I think so. Till two a.m. on the weekends."

"How about a nice porterhouse steak, a baked potato with the works, some green vegetable, Caesar salad, coffee, and some New York cheese cake." William considered cutting back on his eating now that he was out of work. However, tomorrow would be soon enough; tonight he was celebrating.

"You got it Mr. B. Leave it at the door as always?"

"Sure, Jimmy." Once he got into his room he didn't like to be disturbed. He would be working. He and Jimmy had a code, two long knocks and one short one, to let him know the food was there. He gave Jimmy a twenty dollar bill for his service. The food would be charged to his bill when he checked out. He couldn't cheat Jimmy of his normal tip just because he had lost his job.

"Thank you, Mr. B. If anyone asks for you, I'll send her right up." He winked.

"Thanks, Jimmy." William winked back at him. Boy, this was really fun.

When Jimmy left, he ran the water for the whirlpool tub. While the tub was filling, he went through his purchases. He held the clothes up to him as he looked at himself in the mirror. He took the clothes off that he was wearing. He stripped down to nothing. He looked at himself in the full-length mirror. He had really gotten chunky on that job, eating and sitting too much. He would have to do something about his shape; he didn't like what he saw. He thought of Katherine watching herself in the mirror. God, he missed her.

He took a bottled-water from the small refrigerator and got into the tub. He felt the last two days evaporating into the tub. He let the whirlpool jets hammer at his body. He knew everything would be all right, he just wasn't sure how. He reached out of the tub for the telephone. He dialed his home number. The tape came on. Either Katherine was home and not answering or she was out for the night. She was out quite often lately. He left his message. "Hi, it's William. Just to let you know I'm okay. See you Sunday night." He reached over to hang up the phone. As he did he added, "I miss you." He really did.

He put on his new pajamas, 100% cotton, no silk anymore. He ate his dinner while he watched television. He flipped the channels, but found nothing he wanted to watch. It confirmed why he never watched television. He finished his dinner, every last bit, and got into bed. He put his hands behind his head and looked up at the ceiling. He felt his life beginning. He slept soundly. He only had good thoughts for the future on his mind.

He slept until he was ready to get up. This was the first time he had stayed here that he hadn't placed a wake up call for six a.m. He looked at the clock; it was 8:14. Ordinarily, he would be panicked. This would mean that he had lost over two hours of work time. This morning, he couldn't care less. He had nothing to do today but deal with people. After yesterday, he was actually looking forward to it.

He stretched out in bed; boy, did it feel good. William hadn't slept like this since he was a young boy, maybe never. He reached for the phone and dialed the bell station. Jimmy was off on Saturday, so he got Johnny, who didn't know him. He ordered breakfast: two fried eggs, bacon, hashed browns, rye toast, a large pot of coffee, and a New York Times. He would change his eating habits on Monday; this weekend he was on vacation. While he waited for the breakfast, he took a long shower and shaved. He was still in his underwear when Johnny arrived with breakfast and the newspaper. Johnny treated him like any other guest, unlike Jimmy. William felt initially discounted, as he liked being treated as someone important. He would miss that. But it was nice to hide behind a cloak of anonymity. He could see where he might like that as well. There were some advantages in being the common man. He gave Johnny a two-dollar tip. One of the advantages was that it cost less to be a common man. He liked that.

He had his breakfast on the balcony in his underwear. It was a little chilly, but he didn't care. He had always wanted to do this and to hell with appearances. He took his time eating. He hadn't enjoyed food this much in years. He savored the coffee as he read every page and every column of the Times. When he was done, he did some stretching on the balcony as he looked over the skyline of Manhattan. He could understand why people wanted to live here. Even the skyline was charged with energy. New York had always scared him with all of its people. It was the people and their diversity that excited him now. He finally felt like one of them. As he was stretching, an elegant lady, a dowager from his past, appeared on the balcony in the building across from him. She looked down her nose at him in disapproval. He continued his stretching and waved at her. She ran back inside. He smiled to himself. He was going to enjoy this common man stuff.

He rummaged through his bags of purchases looking for what to wear. This was the first time in years that his clothes hadn't been put out the night before by Katherine. As he thought of this, he missed her. He wished she could be there to share his metamorphosis. It was always more fun to share things with someone else, especially someone you love. He hadn't thought of loving Katherine for a long time, but he always knew he did. If he could only tell her and show her. He was having fun deciding what to wear. On the road to oblivion, he had missed simple steppingstones of pleasure. He had a lot to make up.

He decided on a pair of khaki slacks, a multi-colored sport shirt with no collar (he would never wear a solid color button down shirt again), white socks (no more solid color stretch socks), and sneakers (he had never worn sneakers before in his life), with a V-neck cashmere sweater. He looked at himself in the mirror and he looked good. It was almost ten o'clock. This was a more appropriate time to start a Saturday.

He sat on the bed and made some phone calls. The first one was home to Katherine. The tape message picked up again. He found himself whistling as he listened to the message. He never thought how good it would be to hear her voice. Normally he gnashed his teeth while the message played. He left his message. "Hi, it's William. Just wanted to hear your voice. I miss you." He almost said the "L" word, but something stopped him, possibly fear of non-reciprocity. He didn't know whether she was there, had been there last night or had been out all night into the morning. He didn't care. As long as she was still living with him, he felt he had a good chance.

He walked for a while, enjoying the day and watching the people. He was always a quick walker as time was money. Today he walked slowly. He didn't need the money. It was a glorious sunny summer day for the middle of August. He looked each person in the face. He nodded or said hello as he passed them. Some looked at him as if he were a loony tune, but most of them smiled at him and returned his hello. He walked to the parking garage and drove slowly out.

He proceeded to his first visit—his son Richardson's apartment. It wasn't far from the hotel, but parking was a problem. He found a garage within a few blocks and left the car. Richardson lived in a four-story brownstone just north of Greenwich Village. The building had been converted to eight apartments, two on each floor. Richardson lived on the third floor. He had only been here a couple of times, never having gone upstairs. Richardson would come down and meet him. Normally, he met Richardson at a restaurant for lunch or dinner, on the company. He rang the buzzer and waited. The name on the buzzer said "Ricky Bradford." He smiled; his son had changed his name.

Richardson's voice came over the intercom. "Who is it?"

William talked into the holes next to the buzzer. He always felt awkward doing that, not knowing if anyone heard him or not. He would speak too loudly to make sure. Sometimes people walking by would stop and stare at him. Today he didn't care. He yelled into the holes, "It's your Father . . . er, your dad." He thought he heard an "oh, shit" on the other side, but he was willing to ignore it. After a moment's hesitation, he heard, "I'll be right down." He quickly responded, "That's okay, I'll come up." There was silence on the line as if he had suggested he wanted to come up and share his venereal disease. After a long pause, he heard his son say, "All right, come on up." He didn't feel particularly welcomed, but the old William probably deserved it.

The three floors required a lot of steps to get there. He was surprised that he could do it at all. He would definitely start his diet and exercise program on Monday. When he got to the apartment, his son was waiting at the door. He was dressed in a scraggy sweat suit outfit with no socks or shoes. His hair was in total disarray. William wondered if he had awoken him; it really didn't matter.

"Hi, Dad. Good to see you," said Richardson. William doubted it.

Richardson was amazed to see his Dad on a Saturday without a suit on.

"Hello, son," William said.

Richardson hadn't moved from in front of the door. He seemed to be guarding the entrance and view into his apartment from William. William stood awkwardly in the hallway.

"So, Dad. What brings you here on a Saturday?" He leaned against the doorframe and scratched his crotch. It was evident he wasn't glad to see his father.

William tried to look past him to see inside the apartment. He couldn't see in. "Can we go in? I've never seen your apartment."

"That's not my fault. I've been here for five years. You've always been welcome."

"Like now?"

"I'm sorry, Dad. I don't usually expect unannounced visitors on Saturday. This is usually my time to read papers and grade exams. But, come on in."

He followed his son into the apartment. It was a large apartment, somewhat run down, but spacious. There was a mug of coffee on the living room floor with papers scattered all around. There was a pair of pajamas thrown on the floor. Richardson must have dressed quickly as he came up. He had interrupted his son's Saturday morning. To William, Saturday was just another workday. He had to get used to its being a day off for other people that now included himself.

"I'm sorry, son. I see you're busy."

"No, Dad, really it's all right."

"You're sure?"

"Absolutely. You just surprised me." Richardson spoke in understatement.

They stood looking at each other. Richardson had had very little to do with his father since he hadn't gone to Roget Institute. William looked at him awkwardly. He finally remembered. "I brought you something."

Richardson waited. Nothing materialized.

"Oh, it's downstairs. You want me to bring it up? I left it there in case things didn't work out."

"No," said Richardson. "I'll go down with you."

Richardson slipped on bedroom slippers and followed his father downstairs. Sitting right outside the front door was a top-of-the-line racing bike. Richardson looked at the bike and then at his father.

"This is for me?" Richardson asked. His father had never gotten him a present before in his life. William always paid for it, but his mother always got it for him.

"That's right, son, it's for you."

"Dad, it's beautiful. But you shouldn't have left it sitting outside like this. You're lucky it wasn't stolen."

He hadn't even thought about its being stolen. He had a lot to learn about New York. They brought the bike inside, and Richardson locked it to the hall radiator.

Richardson didn't know what else to say. "Would you like to come up for some coffee? I was just finishing a mug. There's more in the pot."

The last thing he needed was more coffee. "Sure, son, I'd like that."

When they were both settled in the living room, Richardson sitting on the floor, William in an easy chair by a small table, Richardson looked up at his dad. "So, Dad," he said. "Why the gift?"

"I just felt badly that I didn't allow you to get a bike when you were little. I was afraid you would get hurt. You were so fragile, like your mom. I wanted to make it up to you."

Richardson swirled some coffee around in his mouth. He was contemplating what to say. He chuckled. William wondered what was so funny.

"I remember the day when I came home and asked you, really asked mom to ask you, for a bike. When Mom told me no, I hated you for days. I was the only kid without a bike. I would come home from school and cry in my room while the other kids rode their bikes."

"I never knew, son. I should have. I'm sorry. I know how it is to be the odd kid, first hand."

"It's okay Dad. It lasted less than a week. Mom took me to the store and I picked out the bike I wanted. I kept it at the Cohns'. It was the envy of all the other kids. I stopped hating you for a while."

"Until the next lousy thing I did" William said.

"Yeah, I guess so."

"I'm sorry, son. I tried to be a good father. Discipline was all I knew. I wanted you to be able to do better in the world than I have." Small tears formed at the corners of his eyes.

"You okay, Dad?" He had never seen his father vulnerable.

He wiped his face and picked up his cup of coffee, not to drink it but to have something in his hands. "I think so. I'm just trying to undo the mess I created."

This was the first time that Richardson realized that his father was just another human being. William had always been superhuman, above human frailties.

He told Richardson about losing his job and trying to find himself, to reconnect with those who should be close to him, but were not.

"Those bastards," said Richardson.

"It's okay, son. They probably did me a favor. I wouldn't be here today."

"That's true. Does Mom know you're here?"

He picked up the cup of coffee and hesitated. "No, I'm here on my own."

Richardson looked pleased. His father had given him little attention from the day he was born. He had tried all his life to get close to his father; it wasn't to be.

"Does Mom know where you are . . . in New York?"

"I don't know. I left her a message on the tape machine, but I don't know if she got it or not." He turned the cup in his hands. "We're not getting along too well right now." He looked down. He had never confided in any of his children before.

"I know, Dad. Mom's very unhappy. She loves you so, she always has, but she's not liking you." He looked away from his father.

"I know she does, son. And I love her too. I just can't seem to tell her."

Richadson chuckled. "I suffer from the same disease. I never think I'm good enough."

"I'm sorry son. I didn't give you the best of genes."

"I think those genes might be Mom's."

William shook his head. He might be right.

"But," Richardson continued, "you gave me a lot of good things. I've never been ashamed to be your son. I just wish we could have been closer."

"That was my fault. I let my insecurities with people affect my family."

"I got that one too, Dad."

"From now on we're going to be a family—dysfunctional, but a family."

Richardson swirled some more coffee. "So, what are you going to do now without a job? That was your entire life, that job."

"You hated that job, didn't you?"

"I hated that it kept you from us. It was always the job, never us."

"I know, son, but no more. I'm free."

He looked at his dad and his clothes. "I like you in those clothes. I always hated those suits and those monogrammed shirts."

"So did I," William said. They both laughed.

"Would you like some more coffee?" Richardson got up to refill his cup.

He hadn't taken a sip. "No, I had better be going. You look like you're busy."

Richardson looked at the pile of papers strewn about the floor. "Student papers and exams and administrative crap. It all piles up for the Chair."

"Chair?" asked William as his eyebrows went up.

"Mom didn't tell you? I'm the Chair of the Philosophy Department at NYU."

He looked bewildered. "I thought you were teaching economics at Columbia."

"That was two years ago when I was at Columbia and I taught literature and philosophy. You wanted me to teach economics. I can't even balance my checkbook. I don't even bother."

William laughed at himself. How little he knew about what was going on in his family. "So, Chair of the Philosophy Department. I'm proud of you, son."

"Thanks, Dad. You're still not mad that I didn't go to Roget?"

"No, that was for me, not for you. You're where you should be. Where I wanted to be."

He looked at his dad. He had learned more about him in these few minutes than he had in all the years before. "Come on, Dad, I'll walk you out." They walked down the stairs together, as close as they had ever been. In the bottom hallway, Richardson stopped to unlock the bike. He looked up at his Dad. He hesitated. He rolled the bike toward the back of the hallway. "Dad, you got another minute?"

"Sure." He followed Richardson down to the basement.

Richardson wheeled the bike over to his storage locker. He opened the door and turned on the light. There were three racing bikes sitting in the front of the locker. He looked at the bikes and then at his son.

"Thanks for not saying anything." He thought he had screwed up once again.

"It's all right, Dad. With this bike, I'll be the envy of all the other guys." They both laughed.

"What do you do with all those bikes?" He thought one bike was enough.

"I race them; in rallies and speed races, mostly in Central Park. I came in fourth last weekend. Not bad for an old college professor."

"Not bad for a Bradford."

"You gave me that too, Dad."

"Not everything was bad?" He looked at his son.

"No, Dad." Richardson looked at his father, maybe for the first time as an adult.

They went back upstairs and Richardson walked William to his front door. They stood looking at each other awkwardly. William moved to leave and then turned back towards Richardson. He started to say something but the words choked in his throat. He hugged his son instead. Richardson was startled. His arms were caught under William's. He kissed him softly on the cheek and whispered, "I love you son." Richardson said nothing. William pulled away and went out the door. As he watched his father walk away down the street, tears came to his eyes and he said softly to himself, "I love you, Dad." He went back upstairs, but he couldn't work. He went back to the basement and took out his new bike. He drove it as fast as he could. He was breaking it in for his dad. Someday, they would go riding together. Richardson hoped that it would be soon.

Jameson lived within a mile of Richardson, so William decided to walk there. He needed the space and the fresh air in his lungs. Jameson lived in a fancy newly renovated building in the heart of the Village. William was enjoying walking through the small parks and watching the people enjoy the beautiful Saturday. He had missed too many beautiful Saturdays; he didn't want to miss any more. He passed the administration building of NYU and decided on a whim to pick up a catalog; he wanted to see his son's name listed as Chair of the Philosophy Department. There it was on page 64, Dr. Richardson Bradford, Chair, Philosophy Department. He felt proud. He kept the catalog.

Jameson was home when he rang the buzzer. He buzzed his father in immediately and came down to the lobby to meet him. Jameson was dressed in a suit and tie. He looked like a young William. He had just come from work to pick some things up and was on his way back. They could talk on the way. His office was only a few blocks away. Time is money.

William tried to walk slowly so that they could talk. Jameson was in a hurry to get back to work. He had an important job he was working on.

"So, Dad. What brings you over this way on a Saturday? No work today?" He looked over at his dad. "I like the new duds." Jameson had never seen his father out of a suit and tie. He was rarely out of a suit and tie, and he wouldn't be caught dead in William's new clothes.

"No work any day. They let me go."

Jameson stopped abruptly. "You're kidding. That was your life. When did this happen?"

"Two days ago. I'm trying to decide what to do next."

"I'm glad you came." And Jameson was; he just wanted his father to approve of him. "You looking for a job? I'll see what I can do. We have a lot of big clients."

William laughed. "No, no, never again."

"Okay, Dad. So what can I do for you?"

"Nothing, son. I brought you something."

They had stopped against a building. William took an envelope out of his pocket and handed it to Jameson, who took it and opened it up. There were two tickets inside. Jameson looked at them strangely.

"They're season tickets to the Giants games. Just in time for their first home game."

Jameson looked at the tickets. "Why, Dad?"

"I guess it's my way of saying I'm sorry. For not letting you go to the games when you were younger."

"Dad, I was fourteen years old. I'm twenty-nine now. I go to concerts, opera, stage shows. I haven't even watched a football game in years."

"I didn't know what else to get you."

"It's okay, Dad. I'll give them to some clients. Your coming here is all I need." And it really was.

"Thanks, son. Is there anything else I can get you? I don't want to continue to be a lousy dad."

"You were never a lousy Dad. But I was certainly a lousy kid."

"So," said William, "what can I get you?"

"Dad, there's nothing I need. I have everything I need. Believe me."

William didn't believe him for a moment, and neither did Jameson. William thought of Jameson, so much like him, yet he would never see it. Neither one ever needed anything. William had nothing more to say; there was nothing more to say. They stood there awkwardly.

"Look, Dad," Jameson finally said, "I better get back to work. Are you going to be around for a few days? We can get together for lunch."

"Sure, son. That would be nice."

"Okay, Dad. Thanks for the tickets. Let me know if you decide to go back to work." Jameson walked on toward his office.

William turned back the way he had come. He had a luncheon date in twenty minutes. He would just make it if he hurried.

He kept saying to himself as he walked "so much like me, so much like me." He wondered what he could do for Jameson before he wound up completely like him. It hurt him to see his son so alone in the world. There were so many people out there, why couldn't he make some connections? The

Bradford curse, thought William. There had to be more in life than work, and he was determined to find out.

As he approached the small intimate restaurant that he had chosen for lunch, he saw his luncheon date walking in. He slowed his pace so that he wouldn't arrive at the same time. It might be awkward for both of them.

This particular restaurant, La Scala, was one that William had been to many times with business associates and clients. He was well known here. The owners and employees were known to be discreet. Many deals were consummated here, business and otherwise. Top business executives were known to rendezvous with their secretaries, girl friends, and other assorted lovers. It was an unwritten law that no one spoke of whom they saw someone with here. It was very expensive. If people talked, it wouldn't survive; it would lose its reputation.

When he entered the restaurant, the owner, Luigi, immediately came over to greet him. Luigi loved to swarm over his guests and William hated it. The food and service was excellent, so he endured Luigi.

"Mr. Bradford, how nice to see you." Luigi held him by the arms as a gesture of affection; some of the guests he kissed on the cheek, but not William. He noticed how William was dressed, but would never comment. If his rich clientele wanted to come in naked, it was none of Luigi's concern. If they paid their bills, he was glad to see each of them.

"Thank you, Luigi. Is my table ready?"

"Of course, of course, Mr. Bradford, the little booth in the back as you requested. Your guest is already seated." Luigi winked and led him to the back.

Patricia Fogerty was already seated and sipping on a martini. He came around to her side and kissed her softly on the cheek. She was still a good-looking woman. He had started to notice such things.

"Thanks for joining me, on such short notice."

"Of course, William. You were Raymond's best friend, maybe his only friend. And, you've made me a rich woman. You sounded like you needed a friend on the phone."

The waiter was hovering. "Would you like a drink, Mr. Bradford?"

Patricia was impressed, the waiter knew him by name.

He thought, "Why not?" He looked over at Patricia. "What are you drinking?" He didn't know one drink from another. Whatever she drank must be relatively mild.

"A vodka-tini. Martini."

He thought for a moment. "Let me have the same thing, and a glass of ice water with a lemon. And some bread."

"Certainly, Mr. Bradford. Right away."

She looked at him. She mimicked the waiter. "Certainly, Mr. Bradford. Right away. I'm impressed. Is that why you guys like your jobs so much? It's not what you do, it's the power?"

He looked at her. He had always liked her even though he felt that she had never liked him. He was Raymond's friend and Katherine's husband, nothing more.

"I don't know. I don't have a job anymore."

She was shocked. William's job was William. "My God, what happened?"

"They let me go. I was costing them too much money for what I was producing. I understand the system. I used it on others for too many years."

"I see. I hope you handle it better than Raymond." She wiped her eyes with the napkin. It still wasn't easy for her to talk about Raymond. He touched her hand. She held his hand in hers.

The waiter came back and placed William's drink, water, bread and olive oil in a fancy gold rimmed dish on the table. When the waiter left, he took a sip of the drink. My God, he thought, this is awful. He gulped some water and ate some bread dipped in the olive oil. He caught his breath. He would have to work on this drinking thing. Maybe a tini wasn't the drink to start with.

"I don't know Patricia. I sat in my garage for a long time yesterday. Thinking that maybe Raymond had the right answer."

She dabbed at her eyes again. "Oh, William, don't even think like that. I'm glad you called me. Maybe I can help."

"I'm sure you can. You've been a good friend of Katherine's and mine."

She smiled. "Maybe not as good as I could."

"I know that you're Katherine's friend first and mine second. I know she confides in you. I would never ask you what she tells you. But that's not why I called you."

She was concerned. She squeezed his hand; she expected the worst. "What is it, William?"

"I just wanted to apologize to you."

"What in the world for?"

"For not being a better friend when Raymond was having his problems. I always thought I was too selfish. If I had been more aware of what was happening with Raymond rather than relishing my grandiose position as Stamford plant manager, maybe I could have done something."

She squeezed his hand again and looked into his eyes. "William, believe me, there was nothing you or anyone else could have done for Raymond." She dabbed at her eyes and swallowed a gulp of her martini. "He did it to himself. Nothing mattered, he had to do it. He had ruined his life and he knew it. He just took the coward's way out. Please, don't you do it." The tears were falling down her face. He handed her his napkin. She blew into it and wiped her eyes, but it didn't help.

"I'm sorry," he said. "I didn't mean to make you cry. I was looking forward to a nice lunch."

"Me too," she said between tears and sobs.

He took her hand. "Don't worry. I think I'm over it. I feel like I'm on the way to recovery."

"I'm glad, William." She got up to go to the lady's room. He watched her get out of the booth leaning her breasts on the table as she did so, then her ass in a tight skirt as she stood up, and then her body as she walked to the rest room. Yes, indeed, she was still an attractive woman, physically and otherwise. Raymond had been a lucky man to have her love him. If only the poor son of a bitch had realized it. He hoped he didn't make the same mistake with Katherine; he hoped it wasn't too late.

While she was in the lady's room, their lunches arrived. William had pre-ordered the veal Marsalla, the specialty of the house and always excellent. He waited until she returned . He watched her walk back and get into the booth. He was starting to feel, and it felt good to be alive.

She looked at the food. She was thinking of just a small salad. Where did this food come from? She sat down and looked across at him.

"I'm sorry. I didn't want to spoil our lunch. We've spent so little time alone together all these years. But I still think of Raymond. I just can't help it. I bawl every time."

"Don't worry about it. I understand. I'm learning to cry again myself."

She took his hand again. "Thanks, William." He noticed her looking at the food.

"I hope you don't mind. I took the liberty of ordering for us. The veal Marsalla is Luigi's specialty. I hope you like it."

She stared at his drink. He followed her stare. "Are you going to drink that?"

He looked at his drink. He had taken just the one small sip. "No, I guess not."

She reached over and grabbed the martini. She swallowed it in one gulp. He was amazed. He would need more practice at this. He ate his entire meal, while she nibbled at hers. He could eat and she could drink. It was the world of specialization.

They talked of many things, but mostly what he was going to do with the rest of his life, either with Katherine or alone. Patricia explained to him that Katherine wasn't angry that John Biddle was let go, since Ethel was hoping for that anyway, but the callous way that he had handled it. She knew that William was insecure and insensitive with other people, but John deserved to be treated better. She thought that John had been a loyal friend of William's for many years. He should have been consulted; William shouldn't have decided for him. He had been doing that to Katherine for years, and it was time to stop. They were having coffee and feeling mellow. William never realized how nice it was to have someone to talk to, especially someone unconnected to his work.

"Thank you, Patricia."

"What for?"

"For listening to the ramblings of an unemployed executive vice president."

"That's what friends are for." She reached over and squeezed his hand.

"I'm beginning to realize that. Thanks."

Luigi brought them the check. It was an expensive lunch. He had never realized that when the company was paying. "Should I bill the company as usual, Mr. Bradford?" He winked at William as he said this.

"No, Luigi, this one's on me. Just leave the check."

"As you wish, Mr. Bradford." He winked at him again as he left.

"So, this is what you guys do. Is this a client lunch? That's what Raymond used to say."

He didn't know if she knew of Raymond's out of town, and sometimes in town, sexual habits. He said nothing about this. "Not this one," he said. "This is lunch with a friend, a very beautiful, old friend." He winked at her. They both laughed; it felt good to laugh.

"Thank you, William, for saying that."

Outside the door of the restaurant, she leaned over and kissed him softly on the cheek. "You know Katherine loves you."

"That's what everyone is telling me. I hope it's true."

"Oh, it's true all right. The man is always the last to know. Good luck, William. I love you too."

She walked slowly away. He stood and watched until she was out of sight. He had tears in his eyes. "I love you too," he said to himself. And it was true. Now he just had to say it aloud, and to Katherine.

He walked slowly back to his car feeling free. He watched the people walking by chattering and hurrying to mundane activities. He wished he could be like them. He was still worrying about the undone items that he had left behind in his in-basket. He better call Miss Gregson on Monday to let her know. Otherwise those items might not be taken care of correctly. He hated himself for feeling this way, but he couldn't stop himself. It was as if his mind had control over him. He would have to fight these mental demons. The first step would be not to call Miss Gregson on Monday. To hell with the company; they would have to survive without him. He felt better already, or did he?

He had one child left to visit, his daughter Elizabeth, the child who loved him the most, and the one who gave him the most trouble. He knew the other two loved him in their own way, but they made little demands on him. If he didn't display his love for them, they might not like it, but they lived with it. Elizabeth, on the other hand, demanded his love; she always had. When he withdrew from her when she left Roget Institute to enter social work school, she withdrew from him. They hadn't had much contact in over five years. He vaguely knew what she was doing. He had taken her address and phone number from Katherine's address book. He had it in his pocket scheduler for over four years. He'd intended to phone her or see her on numerous trips to New York, but somehow he was always too busy. Other than his mother, she was the one person in the world who scared him the most. Somewhere (could it be his heart?) he knew she was right.

Elizabeth lived in a three story older structure deep in the heart of the Soho district. It wasn't far from where William had parked his car, but it took him a relatively long time to get there. The other cars just wouldn't move. It gave him time to think—some good and some bad. He found the building with little trouble. It was in the middle of a block with some newly renovated buildings, some boarded up buildings, possibly housing the neighborhood rats and drug dealers, and some vacant lots where buildings had been demolished.

He shuddered at the thought of his child living in this neighborhood. He had stopped for a package for her, a kind of a peace offering. He lifted the package gently from the back seat and walked up the steps to the front door. The steps were crumbling. He almost toppled but righted himself before the package flew from his arms. There was a deteriorating name plaque by the front door. He could just make out the names through the spray painted graffiti. He identified what he thought was a Bradford in apartment 3B. There was no security system or buzzer in this building. The front door was hanging on one hinge and the inside hallway was dark and gloomy. There was one light bulb hanging from a wire, but the bulb was out. He could smell urine on the fading carpet.

He gritted his teeth and aescended the rickety stairs. He didn't dare hold onto the railing, as he feared it would come off in his hand. He reached the third floor after three steep flights of twisting and turning. There was a little dark landing with two front doors facing each other. He peered at both doors. It took him a minute to discern which was A and which was B. He knocked on the door he thought must be B. He heard solid footsteps. A young man opened the door. He was scraggly with long hair in a ponytail tied back with a rubber band, an unkempt beard, a bushy mustache, and blossoming sideburns. When William saw him, his first thought was that he must have the wrong apartment. The young man was looking at him. William was carrying the package in both hands and felt vulnerable. What if the young man pulled a knife?

"I'm sorry to bother you. I was looking for Elizabeth Bradford. Do you know where she lives? I think she used to live in this apartment."

The young man was still staring at him. He hadn't said anything.

"I said, do you know where she lives?"

The young man was still staring. He spoke quietly, almost in a whisper. "She lives right here."

He wasn't sure what he had heard. "I'm sorry, what did you say?"

The young man spoke quietly again, as if he was afraid to speak. "She lives right here."

"Elizabeth Bradford lives here, in this apartment?" William had to clarify.

"That's right, right here!" The young man continued to stare.

"And, who are you?" He asked, afraid of the answer.

"I'm her roommate." He said no more.

"Do you know where she is?" William asked, again afraid of the answer.

"At work." He said nothing more.

"And where is that?" he asked.

"In the Bronx." The young man offered no more than what was asked.

"Do you have the address?"

"1615 Boyer Street," the young man quickly mumbled.

"Was that 1516 Breyer Street?" William wasn't sure what he heard.

The young man stared down at him, he thought with disdain. He said nothing. Finally he said very clearly "1615 Boyer Street." He had decided that might be the quickest way to get rid of this man.

"Thank you," said William. He knew exactly where that was; it was within a mile of his mother's house in the Bronx. He turned to go. He would deliver his package to Elizabeth in person.

The young man closed the door abruptly. He never asked William who he was; he already knew of the wicked bastard.

He drove into the Bronx for the second time in two days, and the second time in over thirty-five years. Yet it seemed as if thirty-five years ago was just like yesterday. Except now he was a grown man in a luxury automobile. He drove past streets, houses, stores, parks, and buildings. It was all strangely familiar. They had aged as he had, but they were still the same. Older, dirtier, more corrupted, tainted, jaded, and so on, but the core was still the same.

He turned into the 1600 block of Boyer Street; 1615 would be on his left side near the far corner. He watched the numbers decrease, 1663, 1661, 1659 etc. Stores that he had remembered were no longer there. They had been replaced by other stores, video stores, convenience stores, newsstands, coffee shops, or had been torn down, boarded up, or renovated into apartments or double properties. Number 1615 turned out to be two previously existing buildings that had been turned into one large building with a doublewide entrance. The sign over the entrance said "Last Hope Shelter, The Footpath Back Home, 1615 Boyer Street, A United Way Agency, Serving All Those In Need." When he had lived in this neighborhood there was no need for such an agency; individuals were taught to be self-sufficient, or the family or the community helped those in temporary need.

He pulled his car into the small parking lot. There were six parking spaces, three of them filled with older, smaller cars. The spaces weren't designed for a car as large as his. If he parked in the lot, no other cars would be able to park and those parked wouldn't be able to get out. He backed out of the lot and found a parking spot on the next street. It would be better if Elizabeth, her coworkers, and clients didn't see her father in a large Mercedes sedan. He thought that would be best. The cost of his car could probably fund this agency for over a year.

He left the package for Elizabeth in the car and walked back to the shelter. He noticed large amounts of dirt and litter, graffiti, urine and feces stains, beer, wine, and liquor bottles strewn along the pavements and cluttered in the curbs. He remembered when he lived in the neighborhood that each of the neighbors would take responsibility for keeping the area in front of their houses clean. The neighborhood was poor, but it was never dirty. The changes he saw were comparable to the changes he had seen, and been part of, in the corporate world. Was there a connection between the decline of corporate America and the rest of America? He was beginning to see the connection.

He entered the large glass door of the shelter. The door had been shattered and taped over. If someone wanted to break into the building, though he couldn't think of a reason why, they could easily pull off the tape. The metal door handle was caked with grime and dirt. He resisted touching it with his bare hands; he grabbed it with the flap of his jacket, and then wiped the jacket clean. As he entered the building, he could readily see it was in a perpetual state of disrepair. It made him sad to think that his daughter had to work here. It was a far cry from the Consolidated Unlimited corporate offices, or even the worst of their rest rooms. There was a large black woman sitting at a small metal desk in the center of the entry room. Around the circumference of the room were old sofas and chairs, many of them with the stuffing and springs sticking out. A number of what he assumed to be clients were sitting in these sofas and chairs. They were poorly dressed, dirty, and shabby looking. He thought that the cost of the suit that he had left at the store yesterday could have adequately clothed all of them. And the cost of one of his client lunches could feed them all for a week. He felt shabby.

He walked over to the receptionist, the large black lady. On her desk was taped down a piece of paper that said "Ms. Regina Brown, Intake Worker." Nobody had thought to get Ms. Brown a fancy plaque that said "World's Greatest Intake Worker."

"Excuse me," he said. "I was looking for Elizabeth Bradford."

The large black lady looked up at him. She started to say, "Do you have an appointment?" when she noticed his dress and cleanliness. They rarely got other visitors to the shelter except some local politicians at election time looking for publicity photos. It was obvious he wasn't a client, far from it. The large black lady looked at him; he was the enemy. She thought who Elizabeth might be. They didn't have any Elizabeths working there.

"Who was that?" she asked him. "Is she a client or a worker?"

He laughed. The way she lived with that boy she might be a client. "She's a social worker."

"Let me see." Regina took a tattered list of names from her drawer. The drawer stuck and she had to pull it hard to get it out. The drawer and its contents fell to the floor. "Oh, fuck," she said. William turned away. She put the tattered list on the top of her desk. She went down the list slowly placing her finger under each name. He could hear her faintly pronouncing each name as she went down the list. She made sure that she hid the list.

"No 'Lizabeth Bradford here. Sorry." She looked up at William.

"I was told she worked here."

"I'm sorry. You can wait over dere if you like. Some of da social workers are meetin' now. They should be out soon. One of dem might know this 'Lizabeth."

He walked over to where he was told to wait. He would wait until the meeting broke, but he wouldn't sit down. While he waited, he watched the people interact. Most of them were barely functioning, much like the employees at corporate headquarters, he thought to himself. In a few minutes, which seemed like hours, a group of more together people came out of one of the doors off the reception area. These must be the social workers. They looked to William like they needed as much assistance as the clients. He hoped he would be able to recognize Elizabeth. One of the last to come out of the room was a young girl who had to be his daughter. She was thinner than he had remembered her and was dressed rather shabbily. There was no mistaking, however, that she was his and Katherine's daughter. She looked just like a sandy haired Katherine. William thought, thank God she had gotten Katherine's looks, but with breasts. She had his broadness and solidity of body. He walked over to approach her before she got away. She was talking to two others when he came over. She continued to talk, ignoring him. She knew immediately who he was. She had tried, but she couldn't forget her father. He stood on the fringe of their conversation. When they were through talking, she started to move away. He went after her.

"Elizabeth!" he called.

She turned around. She wanted to ignore him, but the sound of her name automatically stopped her. She was, above all, still an obedient child. She looked at him. He looked much the same except his face and demeanor seemed somewhat more inviting. He was dressed casually, instead of in those awful suits and shirts he wore. That would have totally embarrassed her. She said nothing.

"Elizabeth," he said, "it's your father!"

"I know who you are," she said. "What are you doing here?"

"I came to see you, you're my daughter."

"Now I'm your daughter. When I wanted to quit Roget and go to social work school, I was Mom's daughter. Why the sudden change?"

He looked down at his feet. She looked down too and saw his sneakers. She smiled; she couldn't help herself. Somehow she still loved this silly man.

"I was wrong," he said softly.

She couldn't hear him or wasn't sure that she heard right. "What did you say?"

He thought he was being questioned. "I was wrong!" he yelled.

"Please, Dad, this is where I work. You wouldn't want me yelling in your fancy office, would you?"

"No, of course not. I'm sorry. Look, can we go out somewhere? Get some coffee or something?"

She thought that her father was minimizing what she did, as he always did. "Look, Dad, I don't drink coffee. I don't have time for coffee breaks like you do. This is where I work. You see all of these people waiting? They're waiting for a social worker or a counselor. I'm a social worker and a damn good one. Most of these people are homeless, many of them victims of abuse. If it weren't for our agency, they wouldn't eat today or have a warm place to spend the night. We are their last hope. I know you don't care, it's not a corporate problem, but I care."

He didn't know that problems like this existed. He remembered Karl physically abusing his mother and his mother having no place like this to go. She would sleep in William's room and cry all night. The next morning she would go downstairs and make Karl his breakfast as if nothing had happened. Maybe he cared for these people more than Elizabeth gave him credit for and more than he knew.

He said nothing; he knew she was right. He bowed his head. He looked sad. He was ready to just leave.

She had never wanted to hurt her dad, but he had hurt her, so she hurt him back. She rejected his values of wealth and superiority. She had decided on a career of working with the less fortunate, the very ones that her father's corporate world exploited. It was her way of apologizing to the world for what her father did.

"Okay, Dad, I guess I have a few minutes. I owe you that much. Let's take a walk outside."

He knew she wanted to get him out of there, and that was all right; he wanted to get out of there too. On the way out, she noticed a man about her dad's age sitting alone talking to himself and playing with his fly. He would zip it up and down.

"Dad, come on over here. I want you to meet someone."

He walked over to the man with her.

The man looked at Elizabeth and then at William. He was dribbling.

"Dad, this is Rodney Wilson. We call him Buddy. He used to be a Vice President with Reynolds Electric. He lost his job three years ago. He went downhill immediately. He was found living in a cardboard box under an overpass. He was drinking hair lotion and cheap colognes and anything he could find in the trash that had alcohol in it. He was brought here for rehab. He sleeps and eats all his meals here. We hide him from the community. Someday, with our help and vocational rehab, he might be able to get a menial job in the neighborhood."

William knew very well why she brought him over. If it weren't for people like him, there wouldn't be any Rodney Wilsons. He nodded his head. His daughter was indeed a good social worker. She made people care; that was important.

They stood outside the door of the building. Neither one of them said anything.

"Can you take a little walk?" he asked.

"There's nowhere to walk around here. Most of the stores have closed up. Those that are open are used for drug dealing."

He cringed. He didn't like the idea of his daughter working in an area like this, but he felt it was mostly his fault.

"Can you walk me back to my car? I have something for you."

She looked at him, exasperated. "Okay, Dad." She was tired of him buying her things rather than giving of himself. But, what the hell, she owed him a walk to the car. When they got to the car, there was a gang of teenagers sitting all over the top of it. He was lucky that they hadn't stripped it down. He wanted to call the police, but he didn't say anything. While he was contemplating what to do, Elizabeth walked over to the gang.

The kid sitting on top of the car, who was evidently the gang leader, spoke up.

"Hi ya, Lizzie, are these your wheels?"

"No, Ramon, they're my Dad's."

Ramon looked over at William. "Hey Dad, cool wheels."

William said nothing. He knew enough not to encourage conversation.

"Hey, Lizzie, what's a nice white girl with a Dad with wheels like this working with us poor folks?" Ramon was grinning, the rest of the gang was grinning.

"That's none of your business. Now, come on, let's get off the car."

"Okay, Lizzie, but only because it's you."

Ramon slid down from the car scraping his heels and the taps on his shoes across the paint finish. William heard the sound of scraping and saw the gash being formed, but he didn't care, as it wasn't his car anymore; it had never been. The rest of the gang slid off with him. There were scratches all over the car. It actually made William feel good. As Ramon passed Elizabeth, he patted her, not so gently, on the ass. It made William feel dirty. Elizabeth seemed to take it in stride; it was just part of her job.

"See ya, sweet cakes," said Ramon, as he and his gang moved on.

"See you, Dad," Ramon and the gang said in unison as they passed by William.

They all smiled slyly. If they were trying to get William angry, they had succeeded. This was probably the reason why the so-called good folks had given up on neighborhoods like this.

"Dad, you shouldn't have parked your car here. They could have easily vandalized or stolen it." She was relieved, however, that he hadn't parked this symbol of decadence in the agency parking lot.

"It doesn't matter. It's not mine anymore."

She looked at him strangely. Things like this had always meant so much to him. Material things were his world. "What do you mean, not yours?"

"It's the company's car. I don't work there anymore."

"Since when?" She never knew her father without his job. She had hated that job all her life. A victorious smile appeared at the corner of her mouth.

"Two days ago."

"I'm sorry, Dad. I didn't know."

They looked at each other. She moved closer. She wanted to hug her Daddy, to make him feel better, but she remembered all of the times that she had tried to get close to her father and he had rebuked her. All she had ever wanted from him was a loving relationship, but he made that impossible, so she had hated him instead.

"Is that why you came to see me? To tell me that?" she asked.

"No, yes. I wanted to tell you how sorry I am. You were right, I was wrong."

She had never heard her father say he was sorry before or admit he was wrong. This softened her. Maybe there was a heart in the wicked bastard.

He continued. "I wanted you to go to Roget for me, not you. You wanted to be a social worker, not a corporate executive. It should have been all right. I made it wrong. I just want you to have the best life possible. And, I should

have been of more help. I'm sorry, Elizabeth. I wasn't a good father for you."
He felt tears in his eyes once again.

He was such a sad case. He never could express himself, but he was trying. She loved him so, in spite of what he stood for. She went over and held
him in her arms. He didn't resist or pull back. He put his arms around his
daughter for the first time. He kissed her softly on the cheek. She could feel
his soft tears on her cheeks.

"Thank you, Dad," she said. "I love you." She was crying, too.

He whispered, "I love you too."

She wasn't quite sure what she had heard, but she would accept it as an "I
love you." If she was right, it was the first time she had heard her father say this
to her or anyone else. She was happy. She could go home again, to her Daddy.

He looked at her, but he said nothing. He opened his car and took out the
package. She could hear noises coming from the package. He handed the
package to her. She looked at it.

"Go ahead" he said, "Open it."

She pulled the paper off. Inside was a pet carrier with a little puppy
inside. It looked exactly like the puppy that she had wanted as a little girl, the
one that her father wouldn't let her keep. "Oh, Daddy, he's so cute."

"She, it's a she. I didn't think you would want a male."

"She. What's her name?"

"Whatever you want to name her. It's your puppy now."

"Mine? You mean that?" She was jumping up and down with the pet
carrier.

"Of course. I hope it makes up for the puppy I didn't let you keep."

"Dad, I was five years old. I kept the puppy anyway. Mom arranged to
have the Remingtons keep the puppy. I brought it home every day and played
with it. I hated you, but Mom helped me get over it. That was a long time
ago."

"I never felt good about what I did. I just wanted you to know." He hesitated. "Now I know why I smelled dog and thought I found dog hair in my
den!"

They both laughed. She hugged her dad again. "You were the best Dad."

"No, I wasn't. But I'm going to try from now on. If you'll let me."

"I missed you, Daddy."

She didn't tell her dad that she already had two dogs, two large
wolfhounds that she kept in the basement during the day. That was why she
lived where she did, as the landlord allowed her to have her dogs. She would
keep the puppy at the agency until she was big enough to stay at the apartment alone.

"I'm going to call her Little Lizzie. Is that all right?"

"It's your dog now. You call her whatever you like. I noticed that they call
you Lizzie. Is that something new?"

She thought as to how she could be tactful. She knew that her father
preferred formal names, not nicknames. "I thought Elizabeth Bradford

might be too formal for this population. I call myself Lizzie Angel. I hope that's all right."

Ordinarily, this would have greatly irked him. Today, somehow, he didn't care. She was his daughter; she could call herself whatever she desired. "I think that's a fine name. Your mother would be proud."

"She is," said Elizabeth. "I hope you are too."

"Very," he said. He could say no more; he had a lump in his throat.

She leaned over and kissed her father softly on the cheek. He didn't move away. "Good bye, Daddy. Thank you."

"Good bye, Elizabeth ...oh, I mean Lizzie." They both smiled. "Oh, by the way I met your roommate. Seems like a nice boy."

"No, he doesn't. I'm afraid I convinced him to hate you too."

He pondered. "I see, even if he never met me?"

"Oh, he's met you. You didn't recognize him. That's Tony."

"Tony?" He looked confused.

"Tony from the club!"

"Your old friend Tony? That was him? I thought he was robbing your apartment."

She laughed. "That's his statement against his parents. He doesn't talk to them. He's ashamed of their wealth and they're ashamed of his poverty."

"And you?" he asked.

"And me what?"

"Are you ashamed of your parents, of your father?"

"No, Daddy, I was never ashamed of you . . . or Mommy. I just didn't like you."

He nodded his head; he understood quite clearly.

"I'm hoping I can change that."

"I hope so too." She held up the pet carrier. "This is a good start."

She walked back to the agency. He watched her go. She reminded him so much of Katherine when she was that age. He wondered what Katherine could have been, if she had been allowed to do what she wanted to do, if he hadn't stifled her. He hoped that Elizabeth was doing what she really wanted to do, not just getting back at him. He got in his car. There were tears in his eyes. This must be love. He couldn't think of anything else it could be.

12

FAMILY MATTERS

William looked at his car clock. It was three seventeen. He had an appointment downtown at four. He had time to stop at his mother's for a quick hello. As he drove up to his mother's, Raymond and his gang came to the curb to meet him. He could see his mother sitting in the window watching. Raymond gave him the okay sign that he would watch his car, the same deal as last time.

He went to the house. This time he didn't knock. He just walked right in. It seemed that his mother never locked her door. After what she had lived through, she wasn't afraid of much for herself, only for her Wilhelm. And, what would they steal from her? She had very little of material worth; she liked it that way. Karen stayed in her chair looking out the window. He came over and kissed her on the cheek. She smiled. She said nothing.

He asked her whether he could get her anything. She said no. She wanted to get him something, a little tea, cookies, some cake, a piece fruit and so on. She would do anything for her Wilhelm and asked for very little for herself.

He had just enough time to get back into Manhattan for his four o'clock appointment, but he got his mother to agree to go out with him that night. He would be back for her at seven thirty. She said she would be watching for him, in the window. She would wear her "new" evening dress. It was only twenty-two years old. She had last worn it at young Ruskin's bar mitzvah. He told her that whatever she wore would be fine. She would always be beautiful to him. She was his mother, no matter what she wore.

He kissed his mother on the cheek and went to leave. She held onto his arm.

"Wilhelm," she said, "you are a good boy. Good to your mother."

"Yes, Momma" he said. He didn't want to correct her. But he hadn't been a good boy or a good son. He would try to make amends.

He arrived at his destination, back in Manhattan, just in time for his four o'clock appointment. He parked his car in the covered garage under the building. He checked the apartment number on the slip of paper he had written it on earlier in the day, number 3550. He pushed number 35 on the elevator pad; it was the top floor. When he reached the thirty-fifth floor, the elevator door opened onto an imported marble hallway decorated with large oriental vases with large tropical flowers, oriental rugs, credenzas, and so on. He was quite impressed, as it was rich without being gauche. He wished he had such a tasteful decorating touch. Katherine would love this. There were only two apartments on this floor, one on each side, number 3500 and 3550. The doors were double heavy, dark wood with large brass knockers in the shape of the angel Gabriel blowing his horn. He pushed on the knocker and he could hear a Mozart piece playing on the other side of the door. He was trying to figure out its name when the door opened.

"Hello, William. Just on time." The chimes from the clock were just ending the fourth chime.

He extended his hand. "Hello, Joseph...er, Joey. Thanks for seeing me."

Joey was dressed casually, but elegantly, in a silk tee shirt, stretch designer jeans, and Gucci loafers, no socks. William wished he could dress like this; he had so much to learn. It wasn't easy being casual.

Joey looked at William. He had never seen him dressed in anything but his boring suits and monogrammed shirts. He nodded his approval. For William, his change in dress was an enormous leap. He had miles to go, but he was finally on the right path.

Joey shook his hand firmly and sincerely. "Thanks for calling me."

They stood there looking at each other. They had never been friends. William hadn't allowed it for him and his family.

Joey shuffled his feet. He had always been uncomfortable around William. He was much too stiff for Joey. And, Joey suspected that William was homophobic. Ever since his wedding, William had not said more than two words to him. Whenever Joey visited them, William was busy or out of town. He had never visited him in New York. He loved his sister Katherine and her kids, but William was tough to love; William was tough to like.

Joey shook his head. What the hell he thought, I'll give it a chance.

"William, it's really good to see you." A little lie never hurt an incompatible relationship. "How long has it been, four, five years?"

William knew exactly when the last time was; it was Elizabeth's graduation. He felt like a stranger, but Elizabeth revered Joey. All of the kids liked Joey; it was he that they didn't like. He thought it was because he discouraged them from seeing Joey. He was only trying to protect them, especially the boys. It had been over five years.

"Five years," William said. "At Elizabeth's graduation."

Joey remembered. William wouldn't talk to him. They both nodded at each other, but neither one spoke. Joey thought it was because Elizabeth, and Richardson and Jameson, liked him. But, maybe it was because William didn't like him. He remembered that William didn't come to the graduation party that he gave for Elizabeth. Katherine had made excuses, but Joey had always wondered what the real reason was. Elizabeth had told him that her father wasn't happy about her becoming a social worker, maybe that was all it was. Regardless it seemed very strange, not coming to your own daughter's graduation party.

"I remember now," said Joey. "So, how are you?"

Joey motioned for William to follow him into the apartment. The decor was startling. The theme from the hallway was carried throughout the apartment. On one side of the living room there was a large glass double door leading out to an immense balcony. William noticed Joey's partner, Steven, sitting on a chaise lounge reading the Times and sipping on a drink. Joey motioned for Steven to come in. Steven was dressed similarly to Joey. Steven came over to Joey and placed his arm around Joey. William cringed from old instincts.

"Steven," Joey said, "you remember William, Katherine's husband?"

"Sure," Steven said. "How are you, William?" They hadn't seen each other since William's wedding. He wouldn't have known Steven if he had come to him for a job.

Joey motioned for them to sit down. Joey and Steven sat together on a small love seat, which forced them to sit close together. William wondered why he and Katherine couldn't be that close.

"So, William," Joey said, "how can we help you?"

He explained what he wanted. Joey and Steven nodded their heads. They would do what they could. He couldn't believe how easily they accepted him. They couldn't have liked him, the way he treated them. As if they were sick creatures to be kept away from him and his family. William would have never forgiven them if the tables were turned.

He got up to leave. He had a lot to do before he picked up his mother in the Bronx at seven thirty. Joey and Steven got up together. This was as close to real love as William had ever gotten. He was impressed and he knew he had been wrong. Joey and Steven walked him to the door. They held each other closely. Love emanated from their very beings.

Joey touched William on the arm. He didn't pull away; somehow he was extremely flattered. He had a long way to go, but he was resolved to get there.

He arrived back at his mother's house right at seven thirty. As promised, she was waiting patiently at the window. He entered the house and walked over to his mother. She was still sitting in the chair staring out. He bent down and kissed her softly on the cheek. She didn't move.

"Well, Momma, are you ready?"

"Ya, Wilhelm, I'm always ready."

She held onto his arm and raised herself from the chair. She was wearing a black evening dress that showed off her body. He had never known how well his mother was built. She was an extremely attractive woman for seventy years old, or any age; she was a young seventy.

"Momma, you are very beautiful."

Karen blushed. He had never seen his mother blush before. He had never thought of her as a woman, always as Momma.

He helped his mother on with her coat. It was in good condition, but out of style and shabby. He thought about how much he could do for his mother. He had a lot of making up to do.

As they left the house, he instinctively went to lock the door.

"No, Wilhelm. No lock."

"But why, Momma? You could get robbed."

"No, Wilhelm. I lose key. No lock door."

"Momma, you're not worried."

"What can they steal? I'll be with what's valuable. This (she waved her hands) they can have."

He knew his mother was right and he was wrong, once again.

As he held the car door of his Mercedes open for his mother, she hesitated. She had avoided anything German for too many years. It wasn't easy breaking old habits, especially those based on prejudice. She grunted and pushed past her prejudices. For her son, she would do this, but she still feared anything German. She would hold her breath until they got to where they were going. She had been in America over fifty years now. She had been watching at her window all that time; the Nazis hadn't come. Maybe it was time to stop watching, she would see.

They arrived at Angelo's restaurant a little before eight. William had reserved a private room in the back. Angelo's was another place where Consolidated had a company account. He had used it numerous times for business meetings. He knew Angelo personally. Angelo greeted him. He was glad to see William. He had given him a lot of business in the past, all on the company. Angelo's had excellent food and was very expensive. Tonight William would be paying, but he didn't care. Last week he would have cared greatly.

Karen was impressed that her son knew such important people. He must be important too, she thought. Her Wilhelm had done well; she was proud.

Angelo took them to a private room in the back. In the room was a long table with ten places set. She wondered why such a long table, but said nothing. She had never been to a place such as this. She was too engrossed in looking around at the pictures on the wall, the frescos on the ceiling, and the crystal chandelier over the table. She was a princess in a movie. It felt good.

"Something to drink tonight, William, for you and this lovely woman?"

Angelo knew William didn't drink, but he was ever hopeful. The bar was his big profit operation.

Karen blushed for the second time that night. "Ya, a little schnapps, Wilhelm?"

"Sure, Momma. What would you suggest, Angelo?"

"Ah, William, this lovely woman is your mother? I should have known. So, this is where your good looks come from?" Angelo, always the flatterer. Flattery always equaled more tips and subsequent visits. Angelo knew his business.

"How about some nice peach schnapps? To help cleanse the palate before dinner."

He looked at his mother. She nodded.

"And for you, William?" asked Angelo, the ever hopeful.

He looked at his mother for approval. She didn't care. She was having her schnapps.

"I think I'll have a vodka martini."

Angelo was ecstatic; he had another drinking customer. "Good for you, William. Up, dry, or on the rocks?"

He hadn't realized there was so much involved in this tini drinking. He really had a lot to learn. "What do you think, Angelo?"

"For you, William? On the rocks, half and half, with a twist of lemon."

"Good," said William.

"Ya, good. Me too," said Karen.

They were sipping their martinis and munching on bread sticks when the first arrival appeared. It was Richardson. He didn't know why he had come, but his father had insisted. In the dark room, all Richardson could see was that his father was sitting at the end of the table with a woman other than his mother. He started to walk out, when William got up and caught him.

"Thank you, son, for coming. Come over, I want you to meet someone."

Richardson wanted to disappear, but William was holding him by the arm and steering him over to the woman. As he got closer, he could see that it was an old lady, hardly someone that his father would be romancing.

"Richardson, this is my mother." He turned to his mother. "Momma, · this is your oldest grandson, Richardson." Richardson didn't know what to say. He thought his father's mother was dead. All of a sudden he had another grandmother.

"Dad, where did she come from?"

He looked at his son straight faced. "From the Bronx."

"You mean you've had a mother living in the Bronx all these years?"

"I used to live in the Bronx too, with my mother." He squeezed her hand.

Richardson had never seen his father so affectionate, not even with his mother.

"Ya, we live in the Bronx." She patted the seat next to her. "Please, sit next."

Richardson sat down next to a grandmother he never knew he had. She took his hand. "Ya," she said. "You good boy like my Wilhelm."

"Wilhelm?" thought Richardson. His new father was becoming more than he could handle. Next he would find out that he wasn't a Bradford, from the New Haven Bradfords.

She held onto Richardson's hand. It felt good, not like holding his other grandmother's hand, which she would never do. She tried to pronounce Richardson and it just wouldn't come out. "Ya, I call you?"

He understood. "Call me Ricky, Grandma."

"Ya, call me Bubbe, Rickeee. I always want to be called Bubbe."

He was going to like this grandmother. He looked at his father and his grandmother. Ya, he thought, this was his father's mother. He would get the details later from his father. He noticed drinks set before his father, who never drank, and his newly found grandmother. She noticed him looking.

"Ya, Wilhelm," Karen said, "a tini for Rickeee?"

William looked at Richardson. "Sure, Dad, why not. A tini for Rickee."

By the time the next arrivals entered, the three of them were on their second tinis and Bubbe and Richardson had bonded. They would stay that way. Richardson had found what he was looking for, a surrogate mother, and Karen had found a surrogate son.

Elizabeth and Tony entered the room with Angelo. He always escorted the ladies or couples. Angelo prided himself on being an Italian charmer, everything short of pinching the ladies' asses. Katherine had always enjoyed coming to Angelo's, not so much for the food, which was always good, but for the attention given to the ladies, especially by Angelo himself. He would always personally pull out the chair for Katherine, make sure she was well seated, then push it back in, and then spread her linen napkin on her lap, always lightly rubbing her lap slightly with the back of his fingers. Angelo made such simple gestures absolutely sensuous. He always watched as Katherine's ass settled into her seat and moved across the seat as he pushed her in, a simple gesture that to Angelo was sensuous. They each had their own thing going.

Angelo brought Elizabeth and Tony over to William.

"William," Angelo said, "this beautiful young lady claims to be your daughter. If it wasn't for your lovely wife Katherine I would doubt her claim."

Elizabeth blushed automatically, but felt uncomfortable. She didn't like being compared to her mother or being evaluated solely based on her physical appearance. She was a full human being, with a mind and a soul.

Elizabeth bent down to kiss her father and Richardson on the cheek. She stared at her grandmother, as she didn't know who she was. Tony was much more cordial than he had been that morning. Evidently, William had redeemed himself to some extent. He was dressed like he was in the morning, except that his jeans, sneakers, and shirt were somewhat cleaner, though frayed. Elizabeth was also dressed in jeans (but tighter than Tony's), sneakers and a loose sweater top to de-emphasize her breasts. One would never guess that either one of them came from wealthy parents; this was the way they liked it.

William noticed Elizabeth staring at his mother, who was holding hands with Richardson. Elizabeth had never enjoyed games; there was always a bluntness about her. "Elizabeth, this is my mother . . . your grandmother."

Karen smiled up at her. "Y,a" she said, "come sit next to Bubbe."

Elizabeth looked at her perplexed. She hoped that Richardson would provide some explanation. But, he merely held up his hands in a gesture that said, "I don't know anymore than you do."

William moved over so that Elizabeth could sit next to her grandmother and Tony could sit next to Elizabeth. As Elizabeth went to sit down, Angelo rushed over to help her with the chair. She looked back at him with such a look of disgust, that he quickly took his hands off her chair. He would have to content himself to watching her ass sit down and wiggle on the seat. He handed Elizabeth her napkin and walked away. She said nothing; she didn't have to, her face said it all. Karen took her by the hand.

"Ya, such a good girl," said Karen. Elizabeth smiled. She liked this lady, whoever she was.

A few minutes later Jameson entered the back room by himself. Angelo didn't accompany males. They could find their own way and seat themselves. Jameson blinked until his eyes adjusted to the dark. He had expected that he was meeting his father alone for dinner. He quickly noticed his brother and sister and that Tony character sitting there with some strange old lady sitting between them. He walked over to his father, sitting on the far edge of the others. He was dressed in well tailored and pressed trousers, with a dark blue blazer, and black, tight, silk, turtle-neck shirt, with freshly shined expensive, black loafers. Jameson looked very impressive in clothes. He waved weakly at Richardson and Elizabeth. He had never gotten along too well with either one. He saw very little of them. He was his father's son.

"Ya," said Karen. "So who is this one?"

William put his arm around Jameson's shoulder. Jameson pulled away. "This is my other son, Jameson."

Jameson, looking cool, said "ya, so who is this one?" nodding at Karen.

"This one," William said, "is my mother, your grandmother."

"Really," said Jameson. "I thought she was dead."

"No," Karen said. "I here."

"So I can see," said Jameson.

Karen tried his name, but she couldn't quite pronounce it.

"Please," Jameson said, "call me Jamey."

"Ya, Jamey and you call me Bubbe."

"Ya, Bubbe," Jameson said as he waved to her. He didn't get up.

Jameson asked his father what he was drinking. He had never seen him with a drink in front of him before. He told him a vodka tini. Jameson was impressed; he nodded his head affirmatively. He ordered a double scotch and soda, and water with lemon on the side.

Karen held Richardson's and Elizabeth's hands, while she told them all about herself and their father. Tony, Jameson, and William sat quietly. They were waiting for something to happen. William looked up and was the first to see them. "It looks like our last guests have arrived."

Standing in the entrance to the back room were Uncle Joey and a dark haired, sensuous-looking young lady. Richardson and Elizabeth were shocked to see Uncle Joey with a woman, especially one so attractive and sexy. William, of course, knew who it was and so did Jameson. He hid his face in the glass of his drink. Angelo was lurking behind the young lady. He took them to William's side of the table. William and Joey shook hands warmly and actually winked at each other. The young lady sat down next to Jameson. He looked the other way; Angelo did not.

"Hello, Jameson," she said.

Jameson looked away. He couldn't face her. "Hello, Rita."

He swallowed the rest of his drink in one swallow. He tapped on the top of his glass. "Angelo," he said, "another please."

"Certainly,"said Angelo and he was off.

Jameson turned to Rita. "So, what are you doing here?"

Rita looked over at Joey and then at William. They both nodded okay.

"Your father called me. He said you needed me. So I came. I can see he was wrong."

"Oh he did, did he?" Jameson scowled at his father.

William realized once again why he was so uncomfortable with people; they never made it easy to do good things for them. He looked down at his drink.

"I'm sorry, Jameson...Jamey," William stammered. "I thought this would be a happy surprise."

Jameson turned to William. "Dad, she left me. I was too hateful."

Rita turned to William. "Tell him," she pointed to Jameson, "that I didn't say he was hateful."

"Well," said Jameson again talking to William, "ask her what she did say."

Before William could say anything, Rita spit out, "I said that you hate the ones you love. It was too much for me."

"And," said Jameson, "how about me? Maybe it was too much for me too."

"Was it?" asked Rita.

"No," said Jameson, "but you hurt me."

She started to cry. "You hurt me too. I loved you so much and you hurt me."

Tears were slowly rolling down Jameson's cheeks. William had never seen his son cry before. He was always the tough guy. "I loved you too," he said through his tears.

Rita took his hand in hers. "I know you did. I was hoping you had changed."

He tried to control himself, but his body was heaving. "I have, I really have."

"Uh huh," Rita said. She squeezed his hand more firmly.

"There's been no one else since you, there couldn't be" Jameson said.

"No, Jamey, there couldn't be. I've been waiting for you to call."

"I couldn't."

"Goddamn male pride," said Rita, smiling. "Son of a bitch, you would have let me go, wouldn't you?"

Jameson was silent. He sipped on the ice left in his drink hoping to wring out some more scotch.

"I guess so," he said slowly.

"Well, thanks to your Dad, you can't now."

Jameson lifted her hand in his and kissed the back of it. "No, I can't."

Rita turned his way and he grabbed her and kissed her with his mouth open; she kissed him back with his mouth open. The rest of them applauded.

Jameson had his hands all over her as he kissed her again and again. They both cried on each other neither one cared.

Rita looked up at Jameson. "So, is anyone going to buy a lady a drink, a lady who traveled many miles to see the man she loves?" She ran her hand over Jameson's thighs and lap. She felt a familiar friend, Mr. Long and Hard. She was home and so was Jameson. He raised his hand for the waiter. The waiter came over and waited for Rita to order. Rita looked at Jameson. "What are you drinking, Buster?"

"Double scotch and soda."

"Bring me a triple of the same," she said. "She looked down at Jameson's lap. "I think I'm going to need it."

Jameson nodded. "Same here."

Steven walked in. He sat down next to Joey and automatically their hands intertwined. William looked around. Richardson was holding hands with his Bubbe, Elizabeth was holding hands with Tony, Jameson was holding hands (and more) with Rita, and Joey was holding hands with Steven. He was the odd man out once again. He was alone, but he was happy. He smiled at his family; he felt good.

William nodded at Joey. This was the signal for him to remove some papers from his pocket and pass them over. William took one set of papers and passed them to Elizabeth. She looked at them, but was confused. "Dad, what is this?"

He looked over at his daughter and smiled. It was time to let her go, for her to be fully on her own. "It's a lease to your new apartment."

"But, Dad, this is in the fancy part of the Village. We can't afford that and they won't take our dogs. Not three dogs. The wolfhounds just love the puppy. Thank you, Dad, but it won't work."

"Did you read the lease?"

"I can't understand legalese." She passed the lease to Tony. The first thing he noticed was that it was in both their names. His first thought had been that the wicked bastard had figured out a way to separate them, but maybe he had changed. Tony perused the lease. He shook his head affirmatively as he read.

Elizabeth was getting itchy. "So, what's it say?"

"It's a condo unit, two bedrooms, two baths, fully furnished."

"And?" said Elizabeth.

"Dogs allowed . . . and the same rent that we pay now."

"This can't be. Let me see that." Elizabeth knew her father's tricks. He would lock them in so that they couldn't get out. She would be dependent on him again.

"What is this, Dad?" asked Elizabeth.

William smiled. "It's all there. Joey arranged it with a friend of his. He's been reassigned for a period of time and just wants someone to stay in the apartment. He only wants to recover expenses. You can move in anytime you want to."

Elizabeth looked over at her Uncle Joey. "Is this right?" She could trust Joey.

Joey nodded. "It's all as your father said."

Elizabeth looked at Tony. "What do you think?"

"Let's go for it!" Tony had never liked living poor; he just never wanted anything from his family and Elizabeth wanted nothing from her family. This was perfect.

Neither William nor Joey told them that William was the new owner of the condo unit and the friend of Joey's had been reassigned permanently. The lease said that William had paid the required deposits. It didn't say that he owned the unit and was subsidizing the difference between the rent and the cost of maintaining the unit. There was no need to. Elizabeth would never accept it on those terms.

Elizabeth came over and kissed both her father and Uncle Joey. William beamed; he was becoming a different kind of problem solver and he liked it even more.

William passed some papers over to Jameson. He and Rita had been too absorbed in each other to pay attention to what was happening, something about Elizabeth getting a better apartment. Jameson had just assumed she had an okay apartment. He thought he was the only child who didn't take from his parents. He never even considered that Richardson and Elizabeth could live well in New York on their salaries. He was right, they didn't live well, but they didn't take either.

Jameson looked up at his Dad and then over to Uncle Joey.

"This is a partnership agreement for Uncle Joey's firm. Is this serious?"

"Absolutely," said Joey. "Your dad convinced me this afternoon. It's the logical way for the firm to stay in our family's hands. Your dad is quite persuasive."

Jameson looked askance at his dad. "Always has been." Jameson looked at the terms of the agreement. He looked over at Uncle Joey. "Are you sure that you want to do this? You're being quite generous."

"I think you're worth it. If you don't produce, I'll throw you back on the street. Just read clause number 18. I'm well protected."

Jameson looked at the contract; there was no clause number 18. Jameson smiled at his Uncle.

"We won't need clause number 18." Uncle Joey winked at him.

Jameson shook his head. "I don't know what to say."

"Just sign it," William and Joey said simultaneously.

He put his hand on his son's shoulders. He handed him a pen from his pocket.

Jameson signed both copies of the contract and handed one back to Joey.

Neither William nor Joey mentioned to Jameson that William had become a silent, but substantial, partner in Uncle Joey's firm; there was no need to.

William handed some documents over to Rita. It was an employment contract with Uncle Joey's, and now Jameson and William's, architectural interior design firm. The compensation and terms of employment were quite generous, a great deal more than she was getting with the firm in Washington.

She knew she was underpaid, but at the time she needed the job to get herself away from New York and Jameson. She put the contract in her handbag. She looked over at Joey.

"I'd like to wait until the morning, see how the night goes."

William passed the one remaining document in his hand over to Richardson. Richardson looked it over and nodded to his dad.

"I'm sorry son. We" (he nodded at Joey) "did our best to find Sarah."

"That's all right, Dad. It wouldn't have worked anyway. But I know this will."

The document was William's admission application into the graduate philosophy program at NYU. Richardson folded the application and put it in his pocket.

"I wish I could have done more for you, son."

Richardson smiled at his father, not something he had done often in the past.

"You've done enough for me. You've given me my father back," and he looked at his grandmother, "and a new grandmother. That's enough for the first day of your return. Oh, and the bike I never had." He smiled at his father and kissed his grandmother on the cheek.

William had no more documents to distribute, the remainders were his and he put them in his pocket. "Shall we order?" he asked. The waiter had been hovering right outside the room for the longest time. Now he automatically appeared. They ate and drank joyously. William had a real family for the first time. He smiled internally through the entire dinner.

Jameson and Rita were the first to get up to leave; they were eager to renew acquaintances. When Jameson got up, William put out his hand to shake it. Jameson looked down. Inside his hand William had placed two sets of keys. Jameson looked at his Dad. "What is this now?"

William looked at his son and Rita. He had never seen his son so happy. In fact, he had never seen his son happy. He picked up the first set of keys. "These are for the Mercedes." He picked up the second set of keys. "These are the keys to my suite."

"So," Jameson asked, "what do I do with them?"

Rita understood, but she said nothing, just held onto Jameson's arm and looked up into his eyes. William could feel the love between them; he was jealous.

William hugged his son. "You take the car and get to the suite as quickly as possible, before the Jacuzzi gets cold."

"And where are you going to sleep?"

"At Uncle Joey's, where else?" said William.

Jameson raised his eyebrows. His world was going upside down.

"You're serious, aren't you?"

"Of course I am. Now get out of here before Angelo steals your girl."

"Fat chance," Jameson said. He held tightly onto Rita and his dad.

"I love you two." Jameson left before he cried again.

William said to himself, "I love you, too." It was getting closer to coming out.

They all made arrangements to meet the next morning in Central Park. William wanted to take them all out for a brunch before he returned home. He wanted to see them all once more before going home to face Katherine. He knew he was delaying and he was scared. He had come a long way on the pathway home, but the last mile was always the toughest. He had the most to make up to Katherine. He didn't know if he could ever do it.

The next morning they all met around ten thirty at the carousel in Central Park. William, Joey, Steven, and Karen were the first to arrive. Joey and Karen had become good friends from the night before. They held hands and talked like they had known each other all their lives. William and Steven found that they had much in common. Steven was a corporate lawyer and William was a recovering corporate executive. They both hated corporations.

Richardson arrived next, riding one bike and holding another. The other bike was for his dad. William had never ridden a bicycle in his life. His mother had made him scared of things like that. Richardson told him that he would teach him before the others arrived. William looked at his mother.

"Ya, son," she said, "this is good. Rickee teach you."

He was apprehensive, but then figured "what the hell, this should be nothing for an executive vice president."

Richardson ran along as his father pedaled just like he would with a little kid.

After less than ten minutes, he let go and William continued to pedal on his own. When he looked back to find Richardson, he wasn't there. William toppled into the bushes. Richardson laughed and so did William.

He yelled from inside the bushes. "Did you see, I was riding on my own?"

"Yeah, Dad, and you fell on your own, too."

He got back on his bike and they rode slowly around the park. Richardson was a speed racer, but he didn't mind riding slowly, not next to his dad.

Elizabeth and Tony were next to arrive, on roller blades. They buzzed past the family before anyone realized who they were. They made a wheely and turned back, taking off their helmets. They both wanted to teach William to roller blade, but he thought learning to ride a bike was sufficient learning for one day. He promised them that next time he would try roller blading.

The last to arrive were Jameson and Rita. They walked slowly arm in arm, unaware of their surroundings. If Jameson could learn to love then maybe William could too; he certainly hoped so. When Jameson saw his brother riding his bike and his sister on roller blades, he felt sad that something was missing in his life. He had always been the athletic one of the siblings, and now things were just the opposite. Rita had kidded him about getting chunky and he knew that he was. He called to his dad as he went past them on the bike, "How about jogging with me sometime?" William called back, "I'd love that, just you and me?" He looked at Rita and she nodded her head. "And Rita too." William circled back and rode around them. He could feel their love and it brought tears to his eyes. He told himself it must be the wind in his face. "I would love that even more." As he rode off, they both called out "Thanks, Dad, for just being you."

They made a funny group as they went around the park. Richardson and William riding slowly on their bikes, Elizabeth and Tony circling them on their roller blades, Joey and Steven walking hand in hand, and Jameson and Rita walking in the clouds. Jameson had his other arm around his grandmother. Love can be contagious.

As they rode around the park, Richardson talked to William about the graduate philosophy program. He had never seen his son this excited about anything. He had always been a loner just like William. He wished that someday he could feel the same way. He felt like he was finally doing what he wanted to do for himself, what he was destined to do. He was all questions and Richardson was all answers. They kept forgetting that they were on bikes in Central Park and continuously stopped short of running into other bikers, roller bladers, and people just walking. William had given Richardson the best gift of all, a father that he could love.

William's body wasn't ready for too much bike riding on his first day. After about forty-five minutes, his crotch started to hurt. He hadn't been using that area of his anatomy in a long time, for any purpose. He looked at his three children. They had an awful lot to teach him and he had an awful lot to learn.

He walked with Jameson and Rita, and his mother, for a while. It was evident that they were all in love and there was little room for William. Jameson and Rita kept thanking him over and over again. They didn't want to talk; they just wanted to be close to each other and their new grandmother. Karen kept repeating "ya, Wilhelm, you are a good boy." William kept nodding his head. He caught up with Joey and Steven. He tried to talk about business with them, but this was Sunday, their day off, and they were in love too. There was no real place for him. He would have to find his own love. He hoped to and he knew who it was.

Elizabeth and Tony came running up to William. Tony had the two wolfhounds on leashes, and she had the new puppy on a leash. The puppy was pulling her along, trying to keep up with Tony and the wolfhounds. She gave the leash to her dad. "Here, Dad," she said, "you take Sweet William for a while." They had renamed the dog after William, even though it was female, using Katherine's pet name for him. He really missed Katherine and wished she could be here. She had been forced to miss her children all these years all on account of him. He didn't think it possible that she could forgive him for all he had wronged her. But, she was an Angel; there was some hope. He dreaded seeing her, though. The kids and his mother and Joey were easy compared to making it up to her. He had been a dog just like Sweet William.

Elizabeth put her arm in his and leaned her face against him. This time he didn't pull away. She looked up at him. "You've always been my Sweet William too." He didn't know what to say; he didn't need to. He put his other arm around his daughter. He felt there was hope that he could learn to love.

If Richardson could teach him philosophy, the others could teach him love. It seemed like a fair trade.

They all stopped about twelve thirty for lunch. He had made reservations for them at a different restaurant. This time it wasn't one of Consolidated's expense account places. It was one that Uncle Joey had recommended. It was time that he got used to being just another human being and not an executive vice president. He would have to hack it on his own. With a family like this, he would rather be Dad anyway. It was a much more important title.

Uncle Joey had reserved the back room of one of his and Steven's favorite restaurants. William had expected a certain clientele, but it wasn't a gay place, it was a people place. He would have to work harder on exorcising a lifetime of prejudices. When they sat down, the waiter poured them each a glass of champagne. They offered one toast after the other. As their glasses emptied, the waiters kept filling them. By the time that Elizabeth and Tony had returned from putting the dogs back in their apartment, they were all pretty sloshed.

They had been toasting each other for close to a half hour. First, to Bubbe and her family, then to William and his family, then to Jameson and Rita and their family to come, then to Joey and Steven and their family, and then to Richardson and his dad, the family philosophers. Karen kept interrupting the toasts with one of her own: "To Wilhelm, such a good boy." Every time she made this toast the others would say it along with her. It became a family joke. They would lift their glasses and say together (even William) "To Wilhelm," (with a V), "Such a good boy."

When they saw Elizabeth and Tony arrive, Joey put two filled glasses in their hands. They all lifted their glasses and toasted. "To Wilhelm, such a good boy."

After brunch, it was almost three o'clock and William couldn't delay the inevitable any longer. They all walked him back to the hotel, to pack his bags and check out. They walked him to his car, each child carrying a piece of his luggage. At the car, each one in turn hugged him and kissed him. The last to do so was his mother.

She held onto him. There were moist tears in her eyes, as there were in the others'.

"Ya," she said, "such a good boy."

"Ya," the others said, "such a good boy."

They all waved as he drove off. He turned the corner and had to stop the car. The tears in his eyes made it impossible for him to drive. He sat there crying. He didn't care. He wished there was someone who could help him with Katherine. He gritted his teeth. "The hell with it," he said to himself. "She's my wife and I'm William the Conqueror." He turned the car around and headed for Stamford.

He found himself whistling to the music as he drove along. The trip had never seemed so short. The car didn't slow down until he arrived at his house. All of the lights on the outside were on, from their automatic timer, but he didn't notice any lights on inside. Maybe Katherine wasn't home, maybe he was granted a reprieve. He pushed the remote and the garage door opened. He could see Katherine's car in the garage and his dread returned. He pulled his car in and hesitated, then got out and walked into the house. He was home; it would be all right.

13

COMING HOME

William entered the house cautiously, and as he entered each room, he would turn the lights on. He had spent his adult life yelling at the kids and Katherine to turn the lights off if they weren't in a room. He forgave the kids, kids are thoughtless, but he knew Katherine did it to spite him. It was against his natural instinct to be wasteful. Now he didn't give a damn; let the electric company get a little richer. It was only money and he had accumulated quite a large sum of it. As he went from room to room through the downstairs of the house he called out, "Katherine, are you here?" There was no answer; the house was silent except for the tick of the clocks and the normal house creaks. It was eerie.

His den and home office was at the back of the downstairs, almost a separate wing. It was the last room downstairs. He called once again "Katherine, are you here?" before entering. Again, there was no answer. He flipped the light switch for the overhead lights. There was Katherine sitting on the love seat with her feet propped on his working table with an over half empty pitcher, of what looked like martinis, sitting on the table. Ordinarily, he would have rushed to put a coaster of some sort under the pitcher to protect his valuable tabletop. He didn't care anymore; it was just a piece of furniture.

She had a large glass in her hand filled half way. When she saw William she gulped down the remainder and refilled her glass. She looked up at him cockeyed. She had been having her own party. "Hello," she slurred, "how's my sweet William?" She looked at him. "Turn off the damn light!"

He did as he was told. He looked down at her. Normally, he would have been screaming mad. She knew not to put her feet, or anything else, on the furniture. This time he looked down with kindness.

"So, William the Conqueror has returned. What news has thou brought?"

He walked slowly to the other side of the room. He picked up a drinking glass from the set on his sideboard. He walked back slowly towards her. She giggled as she slurped her martini.

"What's so funny?" he asked.

"You are." she slurred as she continued giggling.

"Do you mind if I join you?" he asked as he sat down beside her. He raised the pitcher and nodded his head for approval to take some.

She couldn't stop giggling. "William doesn't drink martunis."

He poured himself a full glass and swallowed about one third in one gulp.

"William's going to get drunk." She continued to giggle.

"William should have got drunk years ago. William is making up for lost time."

He took her hand in his and kissed the back of it.

She turned to William and looked at him quite confused.

"Who are you?" she asked.

"I'm your husband, William," he said.

"No, you're not," she slurred as she dribbled martini down the front of her blouse.

She tried to lick up as much as she could. "My husband dresses funny, he doesn't drink and he certainly doesn't make love. I don't know who you are, but you better leave. My husband's coming home. I've been getting ready for him."

"And I've been getting ready for you." He reached over and kissed her softly on the lips. She returned his kiss with an open mouth, as did he. Without thinking, his hands went around her and he started to caress her body. She leaned into him and kissed his neck and ears. He didn't pull away this time; he let it be. He held her tight as he had always wanted to. He now knew that everything was going to be all right; he was finally home.

She started to rip his shirt down, button by button. His first inclination was to stop her as this was a new shirt, but he stopped himself. He could buy thousands of these shirts if he wanted to. She slowly massaged his upper body and ran her tongue along his chest. She caressed each nipple with her tongue and held each nipple in her mouth. He wanted to scream knowing he should hold it back, but he screamed anyway. This only encouraged her. She threw his shirt to the floor and began to open his trousers; his penis was bursting. She abruptly pulled his penis out and looked funny at it. "Umm, nice," she said as she put her tongue on it. He screamed again. As he did, she gulped his penis into her mouth. He burst quickly, slow and full. She kept it in her mouth while he screamed and dug his fingers into her back. She looked up with his penis sticking out of her mouth and smiled.

"I've wanted to do that to you for years," she said slyly.

He looked down at her face, with white dripping from her lips, in his lap.

He smiled. "I've wanted you to do that to me for years. I just couldn't let you."

She giggled. "I couldn't do that to an executive vice president, now could I?"

He stroked her hair. "No, you couldn't."

She was stroking his penis using his come as a lubricant. He was up again. She nodded at it. He nodded back. She pulled up her skirt. She was wearing no panties and she was wet all over her vagina and down the front of her thighs. He looked. It wasn't disgusting, it was beautiful; it was for him. She slowly inserted his penis; it went in easy like it belonged there. She moved up and down on him slowly and methodically, moving from side to side so he could feel it all.

She had tossed her blouse off; she wore no bra. He pulled her close to him and fondled her upper body with his hands while his tongue caressed her small breasts. He was surprised how easily her nipples went into his mouth. As he did this, she began moaning. This had always sickened him, but this time it excited him. She moved his hands down so that they cupped her ass on both sides. She pushed his hands against her cheeks to let him know that was how she wanted to be held, the harder the better, as she moved her vagina up and down on his penis. In moments in that position she began to scream. He found himself screaming with her. He came again, this time quickly and forcefully. He felt her coming with him, her liquids against his penis. She clutched his upper body and pushed down on his penis as hard as she could. It was hurting him, but the pleasure far outweighed the pain. She finally stopped. She was making up for years of self-denial. She wrapped her bare wet thighs around him and looked up at him. There was love in her eyes. He could see it clearly. There had always been love in her heart, but he had never seen it. The sticky body fluids didn't seem to bother him.

"So," she said again, "just who are you?"

"I'm the guy who used to be your husband and Executive Vice President of Consolidated Unlimited. Now I'm the unemployed guy who makes love to you."

She smiled and licked the stickiness from his penis. "I like that guy much better. Is he going to stick around?"

"You bet. I left the other guy in the garage." She knew exactly what he meant. "So you know about losing my job?"

"Your office called Thursday morning. Miss Gregson wanted to know what to do with your stuff."

"Uh huh, so what did the dutiful wife tell Miss Gregson?"

She giggled. "To stuff the stuff, you know where."

"Good for you, dutiful wife. So, why didn't you answer my calls?"

"I just couldn't. I didn't know what to say to you."

He nodded his head.

"That's when I started drinking," she said.

"Because I lost my job?"

"No, because I thought I was going to lose my husband. I heard you in the garage that morning. I was scared."

"Of losing me?"

"Yeah ...well no, of losing what we never had. I'm glad you came back."

"Me too. It was the hardest thing I've ever done. I was afraid to come home and face you and afraid of not coming home and facing me."

She stroked his chest. "I know, me too."

"Are you hungry?"

He stroked her nipples softly and gently with the palms of his hands. "Only for you. It feels like this was the first real meal I've had in my life."

She purred in his lap and moved her nipples against his hands. She increased the pressure of her thighs against his body and rubbed her vagina against him. "Yes, and I'm hungry again."

They looked at each other. It was the first time that he had really been able to look his wife honestly in the eyes. His body trembled, starting in his toes and running up his spine. He shivered and held her as tight as he could. He was free to love; he would try to do so. She stroked his body to stop the shivering. It only made him shiver more.

"So, my sweet William," she said as she leaned against him, "what are we to do? We can't stay like this forever?"

"I don't see why not. I have a lot of time to make up with you." He kissed both of her nipples. She shuddered and pulled closer to him.

She stroked his chest running her long fingernails down his body, causing him to continue to shiver uncontrollably. "I didn't mean this. I meant what are we going to do? I've never known you without working."

"Oh that. Not to worry" he said slyly.

"William! We can't just do this the rest of our lives. I might get tired of it, in a couple of years."

"True, me too." He pulled the papers from his pocket and handed them to her. She looked at the first one. It was his application to the graduate program at NYU.

"William, what is this? You're going back to school? In Richardson's program?"

He smiled at her as he stroked her thighs and clitoris; she shuddered again. He was afraid that she was concerned that Richardson wouldn't like it. "It's okay. Richardson has a copy."

"Oh, I know," she smirked.

"And"—William continued stroking her—"How do you know?"

"I know because Richardson called me, and it seems the rest of the world called me, all wanting to know what had happened to my husband."

"Really? Who else called you, and what did you tell them about your husband?"

She placed her left index finger to her lips. "Now let's see, there was Richardson, and Jameson, and Elizabeth and the Biddles, Patricia, and Joey."

"That all?" asked William.

"Oh yeah, Becky Goodman. She was the first to call."

"So, it bothered you that she was the first one I went to see after all these years? That she might still want me."

"No, William, it bothered me that you might still want her."

"And how did you know that she wouldn't want me?"

She smiled. "Oh, I've stayed friends with Becky. She was my best friend at college, maybe my only friend. I knew why she was your friend in college. And why she didn't want to marry you."

"And why was that?"

She rolled her tongue around in her mouth and seductively licked her lips and kissed the top of his penis. "Because, she used you for protection from the other boys and you used her for protection from the other girls. You were afraid of girls, even me. But I was safe."

"Not any more," he said as he rubbed his thumb around her clitoris.

"No, William, not any more." She looked pleased.

"Rebecca told you all this after I saw her the other day?"

"No, silly, I see Becky . . . and Patricia and Ethel and Joey and the kids at least once a week when I go into New York."

"Rebecca said you never invited her to our wedding; that is why she wasn't there. Is that true?"

"It's true. At the time I still thought you had made a mistake. That it was really Becky that you wanted to marry. I was too scared and insecure of losing you to have her at the wedding. You could have changed your mind."

He stroked her body. He was enjoying making her shudder. It was a new kind of power for him. He was going to like it. "Never. You were always the one I wanted. I just didn't know how to be a husband and a father."

"And now you know?"

"No, but I'm trying to learn."

"So I hear." She kissed him on the face, on the eyes, the nose, the cheeks, the neck, and finally hard on the lips.

"The more I know about you, the more I like you. You've been a good wife. I didn't deserve it, but you did it anyway."

"Oh, and Herm Selzer called you a number of times. He said he called the office and Harriet Gregson told him that you were working at home. He thought it sounded strange. He seems quite worried."

"He was probably calling me back. I needed to consult with him on some business matters, but those don't matter any more. I'll call him later, when we're through here."

"Oh," she grinned, "we're not through, there's more to come?"

He handed her some more papers. She looked at them and then picked up her martini and drained the glass. She continued sucking on the ice cubes as she read over the papers. He sipped at his drink; it felt good, and so did Katherine.

"William, what does this mean? You bought a condo in Manhattan?"

"Well, not quite. Not until you approve of it. It's for both of us, I hope."

"Oh, of course I approve. I can't wait to get out of this prejudiced little town."

"I thought you always liked it here, the big house, the country club, the money."

"No, William. I've hated it from the beginning, and the roles I've had to play. Your wife, the kids' mother, the matron of the manor; it was never me."

"Katherine, I'm so sorry. I thought you had everything that you wanted."

"I had everything, but not what I wanted."

"And what was that?"

She squeezed him harder between her legs. "What I have right here. The man I saw when I married you. When can I see the condo?"

"Let me see." He put on a pondering look. "I don't think I have any meetings scheduled for tomorrow. Would that be okay?"

She grabbed him around the neck. "Oh, William, I'm so happy. I won't even get mad that you picked out the condo without me."

"The building was highly recommended by two expert New Yorkers, Patricia Fogerty and Joey Angel. And your unit faces Central Park with a large balcony to do more of this on."

She smiled and licked his chest while she looked up at him. "I certainly hope so. I'm not through with you."

They held and stroked each other. If they had never known love before they were learning to know it now. He thought how everything in his life was not as he had thought it was. He was learning.

"So William the Conqueror goes back to school. What does the dutiful wife do?"

He looked at her. "Whatever she wants. Be whatever you want to be." He smiled at her. "This is what you told the children all their lives; now it's your turn."

"You really mean that? I'm free to be whatever I want to be?"

"That's right, anything you want to be."

"William, are you sure we can afford all this, without your job? The apartment itself is very expensive. It's not like you to spend money like this."

"You don't know that yet. This is only our first night together."

"I see. And how much money do we have? I've never asked before."

"And I've never told before. I was always afraid you would leave me and take the money with you. I would have to marry a young trophy wife and she would get the rest. So, I just let it accumulate."

"And how much has accumulated?"

He hesitated. He took an envelope from his pocket with some numbers written on it. "As close as I can come, somewhere between twelve and fifteen million dollars, not counting this house and the stock options I still have to cash in."

"Are you kidding?" She screamed. "We're rich!"

"More money than we'll need for the rest of our lives and the children's lives."

She looked at him incredulously. "You accumulated all that?"

"I guess so. I never stopped to look. While I was investing for Patricia, I was also investing for us. It never meant that much to me. It was just numbers, once we had enough to be financially independent."

"Why didn't you quit that job years ago? It was killing you, and me and the kids."

"I know. I thought that was who I was, corporate executive vice president."

"And who are you?"

"Just Wilhelm, a poor boy from the Bronx."

"Wilhelm? What does that mean?"

Just then the doorbell rang. "Oh my God! What time is it?"

He looked at his watch. "A little after nine. Why? Are we expecting someone?"

"Yeah, Brad Myers. He's been over twice a day since you left and calls about every two hours. I told him you would be home tonight. He said he would stop over around nine. Just look at us."

"Don't worry. He probably just wants to gloat and take over the Mercedes. I'll talk to him through the door and get rid of him."

"No, you let him in. I'll sneak upstairs and clean up and then join you. He seemed sincerely sorry about what happened to you. Said he wanted to talk to you personally."

"Okay, but I hope there's more to come. You promised."

"Oh yeah, later." She smiled and gathered up her clothes in her hand. She didn't bother putting them on. What was the use? She walked away from him with her most seductive walk. This time he noticed. This time he knew it was meant for him.

As she went from room to room, she noticed that all the lights were left on. This was the man that she had married. She smiled and left the lights on.

He dressed himself the best he could and went to the door. He looked through the peephole and saw Brad Myers grinning back at him. "The complacent bastard," he thought and he opened the door just as Katherine was at the top of the stairs. Brad looked up and saw Katherine's bare ass moving across the landing and into the upstairs. He was quite impressed, even for a gay guy, at what he saw and what William had.

William followed Brad's glance to the top of the stairs. His glance was just in time to catch Katherine's last cheek descending into the innards of the upstairs. As he retold the story, he would swear that her cheek winked at him mischievously. This was the woman he had married and he was glad, now, that he had.

When he turned back around to face Brad, he was grinning appreciatively. A few days ago, he would have been ashamed, embarrassed, and angry, not for Katherine but for himself. Now he was proud that she was his wife and that she really loved him in spite of what he had been all of these years.

He grinned back at Brad and ushered him into the den and offered him a seat. Brad started to sit down on the love seat but William quickly brushed him aside. He didn't want Brad sitting in the wet spots. He sat down with Brad around his desk, both of them on the same side as they were now equals, or was Brad now his superior? William tried to look angry, but he didn't really care about losing the job. It was becoming more and more of a blessing. He did realize, however, that he was still angry at Brad for sabotaging him with Sprague and maneuvering himself into his old job. He put on his stern and angry mask, hopefully for the last time.

"So, I guess you came for the car now that it's yours... and the credit cards?"

"No, William," Brad was actually smiling (the son-of-a-bitch) "I really don't give a shit about the car, the credit cards, or the fucking company."

William was confused. "So, what are you doing here?"

"I came to apologize, if you blamed me for what happened."

"Of course I blame you. That bastard Sprague had information about me that only you could have told him. What should I think? And then he tells me you're the new Executive Vice President. "

Brad shook his head. "I thought so. I'm really sorry. He asked me about that interview with Mike. I thought he was trying to make a case about you being prejudiced about Jews, him being a Jew, so I told him the full story and made sure that he knew that Mike wasn't a Jew but a homosexual. I tried to defend you. The bastard used it against you. I'm really sorry."

"I didn't care what Mike was, he wasn't employable. I don't care what anyone is as long as they do their job. Jesus Christ, I didn't even know that Sprague was Jewish until he told me. Made me feel like shit."

Brad smiled at him. "I know William. You've been my mentor, my protector, my coach, and I always hoped my friend. I would never do anything to hurt you. You're the most brilliant man that I've never known. You solved the problems, set the strategy, and I did the work. I know that I wouldn't be anything without you. I feel horrible about what happened." He had tears rolling down his cheeks.

"But you took the job?"

"The hell I did!" He pounded his fist on the desk. "I'm no fucking Executive Vice President, you're the Executive Vice President. I can't kid myself. I walked out less than an hour after you did. They wanted me to go after you and get the car back. They had all your shit packed up in my car. It's all outside if you want it."

"You really turned them down? Good for you. How about the money?"

"Money. I never wanted their fucking money. I wanted to work with you. I still do. The money only protected me from ever being poor again. I've accumulated more money than I ever thought I'd have, thanks to you. Fuck them. I got my life back, I'm going to live."

William nodded. "So what are you going to do?"

"I'm not sure. I'll look around. Maybe help other poor kids, I'd like that." He wiped his face with the back of his hand. He was wearing his compassion.

"You gonna stay here in Stamford? Keep the apartment?"

"No way. I just bought a coop unit in New York, me and my partner."

William knew very little about Brad's personal life. He wondered where his heart had been all of those years. He let his head make all of his decisions.

"Really. Where in New York?"

William had never asked him a personal question before. He had only asked him about the job. As long as Brad had done the right job at the right time, William was happy and Brad got rewarded. It was a fairly easy working contract, but it had never been a relationship.

"Across from the park, Central Park East."

"Really? You won't believe this, but we just bought a condo on Central Park West. We'll be neighbors. That will be nice."

"I'm moving tomorrow. That was why I wanted to see you tonight. I hope I didn't interrupt anything with you and Katherine."

William smiled. "Nothing we can't do later."

Brad nodded. "Uh huh."

"Good luck to you and your partner, with the move. Is she with you? I'd really like to meet her. She's getting a beautiful person." He looked him in the eyes.

"He," Brad said. "It's a he. I'm a homosexual."

"I didn't know. I'm sorry."

"I know you didn't and it's nothing to be sorry about."

"I'm just sorry I didn't know. You worked with me for a lot of years. I should have known more about you. I should have been the friend you thought I was."

"William, you were my best friend. Believe me."

He looked at Brad. "I'm going to be better."

Brad beat back the tears with his eyelids. "I know you are."

"I've been thinking of a venture. Something we can all feel good about, give something back. I've already talked to John Biddle about it and he's interested. We're meeting tomorrow in Manhattan at John's place."

"I'd like that. It'll be good working together again, the three of us."

"Yes, it will." William said.

They exchanged addresses in New York. Brad got up to go.

"I'd better go. Mark is coming in from New York; he's going to help me pack. Look, do you want any of that stuff in my car, from your office?"

William thought about it. "You can throw any work stuff in the sewer or burn it. Did you bring my suits and stuff, you know my extra clothing?"

"Yeah, it's all in the car. You want me to get it for you?"

"No," William said. "You said you're going into New York tomorrow. Do you have enough room to take my clothes with you?"

Brad thought about it. "Sure, why not, we'll make room."

He wrote the name and address of The Last Hope Shelter on a piece of paper. He handed the paper to Brad. "Could you deliver the clothes to this address?"

Brad looked at the paper. "Sure. It's a little out of the way, but why not. You want a receipt for tax purposes?"

"No, just deliver them anonymously, that's receipt enough."

He got up to walk Brad to the door. Brad stopped short. He put the bag he had come in with on the top of the desk. "I almost forgot. Harriet wanted you to have this." He took out the plaque that said "The World's Greatest Executive Vice President." "She wanted you to know she agreed with the plaque and how much she appreciated working for you. I think she really loved you, in her own way."

He looked down. "Even after the way I treated her by sending Herman back to Nebraska?"

Brad put his hand on William's arm. "She knew that would never work out. Oh, she was mad at you for a long time, but I think in the end she knew you were right. She just wouldn't let you know that. She was as rigid as you are."

"I suppose you're right. That's probably why we got along so well."

Brad smiled and grasped William's arm. "No doubt."

"Without you and me, what happens to Harriet?" He was going to miss her.

Brad laughed. "When I quit they disbanded the office of the Executive Vice President. I think they would have done that anyway. Probably in a few months I would have been out on my ass just like you. They offered Harriet a job in Personnel, as an assistant. She turned them down, just walked out on them. She probably has more money than the both of us combined."

"Probably does. Never spent anything on herself. I hope she learns how to live." William was hoping the same for himself.

"I'm gonna miss her. She was like a mother to me." Brad fought back his tears. "And you were like a father to me, the one I never had. Thank you William."

At the door, Brad leaned over to William. William thought he was going to kiss him; he didn't know what to do. Whatever Brad wanted to do was all right. Instead Brad whispered softly in his ear, "Your fly is open. And I love you." Brad was out the door before he could respond.

He watched him go and fought back tears. He would do what he could to keep Brad in his life, and Harriet Gregson. Jesus Christ, he thought, nothing seems to be what it seemed. He looked down at his fly; it was indeed open. He never remembered his fly being open before. He saw it as a good sign and left it open.

He could hear Katherine moving around upstairs. He went back to the office and called Herman Selzer. He tapped anxiously on the desk while he waited for the phone to ring. Over the years, he had always called Herman at work so that there was no chance of Ruth answering. Herman had been his mentor from the first day he started work at Apex. It was Herman who had developed the formulas and recommendations for the Hereford, Alabama, plant study. It was Herman who had provided guidance to William throughout his career. It was Herman that he owed his success to. He usually thanked him, now he wasn't so sure. He would consult with Herman a number of times a week on the telephone and would meet with him periodically when he was in Massachusetts at his office at Harvard or when Herman was in New York. In the beginning, Herman helped William as a friend and surrogate father and to appease his guilt as to how Ruth had harshly treated William. In the latter years, William contracted with Herman as a consultant to the firm through his discretionary monies. Nobody needed to know about the arrangement, especially Ruth. Herman would have continued to help him regardless, but William wanted to reward him for his efforts and he rewarded him extremely well.

William heard the phone being picked up on the other line. He didn't know what he would do if Ruth was on the line. He was ready to hang up, or was he ready to talk to her? He wasn't sure what to do.

"Hello," he heard, "this is Herm Selzer."

He breathed easier. He wasn't built for tension. "Herman, it's William."

"Of course it is," Herm said. "What's going on? I got a message Consolidated was canceling my consulting contract. I called for you and they told me you were no longer there. Strange people."

Strange people—that was an understatement. "They let me go, then disbanded the whole office. Brad and Harriet quit right after I left. I'm afraid dinosaurs like us are no longer needed by the corporate geniuses."

"Bullshit," Herm said. "Corporate dunces is more like it. They're going to kill themselves."

William cringed. That was almost him. "I'm sorry about the contract."

"William, don't worry about it. I never needed their money and I never needed them. I only worked with them to help you."

"I know, Herman. It was just the only way I had to thank you."

"Don't be a putz," Herm said. "Being my friend was all I ever asked you for."

"I know Herman. I never thought that was enough."

"William, believe me, that was more than enough. So, boychik, what are you going to do now?"

He told him about the condo unit in New York, the changes in him, Katherine and the children, and the new enterprise he was thinking about. He told Herman about his thoughts on his new enterprise and his meeting with John and Brad for the next day.

There was a pause on the other end. "Would you like another partner?"

"Sure," William said. "Who are you thinking of?"

"Schmuck," Herm said. "I was thinking of me."

"You, really? Sure. Can you meet us tomorrow?"

"Why not? The bastards canceled my contract. I have nothing else to do. I'll charge them for the day and expenses. A fitting footnote to my final bill."

"Okay," William said, "I'll see you tomorrow."

"Ciao, boychik." Herm hung up.

William sat staring into space when the phone rang. He picked it up on the first ring so that it wouldn't bother Katherine. "Hello, William Bradford."

"William, is that really you?" He would never forget that voice. It was Ruth Selzer. Ruth, who had cast him out of her house for taking the job at Apex, over thirty years ago. Ruth, who had ignored and snubbed him on the numerous occasions when he went back to Roget to work on various committees and alumni functions; Ruth, whom he and Herman had hidden their relationship from.

William said nothing. He didn't know what to say to the woman who had mothered him through college and had been his first friend and mentor. There was an uncomfortable pause.

"William," Ruth said. "You still there?"

He heard himself say, "I'm here." He waited for Ruth to say more.

"Please, William, don't say anything; just let me talk."

He couldn't argue with that.

"I just talked to Herm. He told me what happened to you. I want you to know how sorry I am. I never wanted that to happen. I was mad at you for taking that job with those Nazis. But, I had no right to be. It was your life, your decision. I was trying to run your life. I was mad that I couldn't control you. I was being a Jewish mother and I shouldn't have. I had no right. You were right, I was wrong."

He finally spoke. "No, Ruth, I was wrong, you were right. They were corporate Nazis. I became one in the end. I would have stayed if they hadn't got rid of me. They were killing me. You told me they would."

"I told you that to make you change your mind. I didn't want to be right. I wanted what was right for you. I always saw your Jewishness, your humanity; I didn't want you to lose that."

"I'm afraid I did. I'm sorry, Ruth. I should have listened to you."

"No, William. You should have listened to your heart, not mine."

"I only recently realized that I have one. I guess you knew before I did."

"William, I'm an old lady with no children. My crime is I loved you too much, as a mother when I should have been more of a friend."

He fought back his tears once again. "You were the best at both. I've never forgotten what you did for me. I never will."

"William, I was such a stubborn old fool chasing you out of my life. Can you ever forgive me?"

"Only if you can forgive me for being a stubborn young fool."

"You got a deal," Ruth said.

He looked up to see Katherine coming into the room. She was dressed in one of her old mini skirts, a tight sweater, no bra, and black, spike heels. She had her hair up and was made up to look her best. He gasped. She was beautiful and his penis was rising once again. She came over close to him and he could smell her perfume; she was intoxicating. She got close to him and lipped the words "who's on the phone?" He lipped back "Ruth Selzer" and put his finger to his lips to signal her to be quiet. She said "Oh" with a surprised look on her face. She took his finger from his lips and placed his hand on her thigh under her skirt. She moved up and down to give him the idea to fondle her thigh. He got the idea. She pulled her skirt up to show him she had no panties on.

He said "Oh" and looked surprised. She moved his hand onto her vagina. She was wet again. She moved his hand around until he did it himself. She smiled while she moved on his hand. She had never been so happy and neither had he. He was distracted. He couldn't do this and talk to someone, especially Ruth Selzer after all these years, and do this to Katherine. His penis was pushing its way out from his underpants. She helped it out the rest of the way. She fondled it with her hands.

"Ruth," William asked, "can I call you back?"

"I just wanted to know if I could come with Herm tomorrow to New York. I'd like to be part of your project, if you'd want me."

"Ruth, of course."

"Thank you, William. I've missed you."

"I've missed you too."

Ruth gently put down the receiver. William felt the tears over the line, and he felt his own.

He stood there holding the receiver in his hand while Katherine stroked his penis. He put the receiver down gently. He looked into space. She gently pulled him by the penis. She led him out of the room, through the house, up the stairs, and into their bedroom. As they passed each room, they both looked at the lights on and ignored them.

She pulled her skirt all of the way up and placed his penis between her legs so that it caressed her clitoris. She moved on it gently. She put his arms around her and placed each hand on each side of her ass. She pushed down on his hands so that he would know to grip her hard and pull her against him. She pulled off her sweater to expose her bare breasts. She pushed his head against her so that his mouth was close to her nipples. He licked her nipples as she moved against him. She moaned deeply and placed his penis deep inside her. They stood like that not wanting to disturb the feeling. She came; she couldn't stop it. Her body throbbed with love for the moment and their future. She didn't think of the wasted years. She didn't have to; William thought of those lost years for both of them.

She fell onto the bed with William on top of her. He liked just lying there with his penis inside her. She grappled to take his shirt off and threw it to the floor. She had placed some warm massage oil on her night table. She poured some onto her hands and began massaging his back and shoulders. He melted into her. He took some of the oil and massaged her chest and breasts and manipulated her nipples between his fingers. She shuddered with pleasure and closed her eyes. He pulled out of her just long enough to pull her skirt off. She kicked her shoes off, and he pulled his pants off. He threw them on the floor. He put his penis back inside. She moaned deeply as he did and kissed whatever she could of his. They lay silently like that. She felt herself drifting off to pleasurable sleep. Before she did, she looked at him with all the love in her heart and kissed him deeply.

"I love you," she said as she fell asleep.

"I love you too," he said. He wasn't sure that she had heard him. She wasn't either, but she fell asleep with a satisfying smile on her face.

For William it wasn't so much a blending of their bodies, but a blending of their souls. His closeness with Katherine had allowed him to stop waiting for his real life to begin. His life with Katherine became his real life. He could stop sitting in his chair and looking out the window of life waiting for something to happen; it was already happening. As he slept, he pulled her to him as close as he could. As long as she was there, he was there. He would never be alone again.

EPILOGUE: LIFE BEGINS

The next morning William moved the company Mercedes out of the garage and placed it on the side of the road. He called the company and told them where it would be if they wanted to come get it. He left the keys in the ignition. He didn't care if they came or not. He was through with that life. He had his own life, finally, to worry about.

Katherine drove them in the Mercedes convertible to New York. William was too exhausted to drive; his eyes weren't working right. She was too excited not to drive. She put the convertible top down and drove with one hand and stroked William with the other hand as he closed his eyes. As they drove towards New York life was exhilarating as it should be. They were just a man and a woman in love, nothing special.

As they approached Manhattan, William directed her to the condo building. Katherine missed the turn for the underground parking garage and said out loud, "Oh shit! I was doing so good." He looked over at her and said, "Yes you were. You always will." They smiled at each other. She came around the block and pulled into one of their assigned spaces. There already was a sign up with their name on it, "The Bradfords." She liked that. She felt at home.

They walked arm in arm to the parking garage elevator. William inserted a small key into the elevator and it started up noiselessly. Katherine pressed herself close to William and motioned with her head "Should we?" He shook his head negatively. There would be other times, many other times. He didn't want to be black balled from the building before the sale was final. Before they realized it, the door opened at their floor.

Katherine looked around for the hallway, but there was only a door facing them across from a small landing. He opened the door to an immense entrance hall. She looked at him. "This is ours?" she said. He smiled. "This is the entry; the apartment's behind it." "You're kidding," she said. He said nothing. He opened the double doors beyond the entrance hall and the immensity of the apartment was displayed in front of them.

"Oh my God!" she yelled. "This is all ours?" She ran from one length of the apartment to the other, looking in every room. She came back screaming. "William, what have you done? This is larger than our house in Stamford!"

He held her and smiled at her. "Not quite, but almost."

"My God, William! What are we going to do with all of this space? I thought we were condensing our life space."

"I know. I just couldn't turn it down. Joey set it up for me. It belonged to one of his former clients. His firm did the decorating. The owner fell on bad times. Lost his job, but had never learned how to accumulate. It's been on the market for over a year. Joey was able to get it for us direct from the bank at less than we're selling our house for in Stamford. I thought it was a good trade."

"Four bedrooms?" she asked. "What are we going to do with them?" She smiled slyly and let her tongue circle her lips.

"Oh, we have friends and children and their friends and maybe their children."

"William! You know something I don't?"

"No, just forecasting."

"You're always forecasting." She motioned with her head to follow her into one of the bedrooms. She licked her lips again. She was pulling him with her; he offered minimal resistance. Just then the buzzer rang. It startled them both.

She looked at him. "Are you expecting anyone?"

He grinned, with his mouth shut, and tongue in his cheek. "Maybe."

"You are just full of surprises. Where have you been all these years?"

"Waiting for my life to begin."

"And?"

"It began last night."

"Yes, it did, and it continues."

"Yes, it does," he said as he pulled away to buzz in the visitors. He went into a little room where there was a remote television, an intercom system, and a security panel for the front door and the elevator. No one could get to their apartment unless they wanted them to. This was the only way that he would feel safe with Katherine in Manhattan.

He waited with Katherine by the front door. The elevator door opened and Richardson and his mother stepped out. Richardson went directly to them and hugged them both. Katherine looked at the elderly lady with Richardson and wondered who she could be. William stood with his arm around his mother. He looked at his mother and then at Katherine. "Katherine," he said "I'd like you to meet my mother. Momma, this is my wife, Katherine."

"Ya, Wilhelm," Karen said. "You a good boy and she a beautiful girl."

Katherine looked at William bewildered. She thought he was an orphan, which usually meant that your mother and father were dead. Her husband had become a man of surprises. "William," she said, "your mother is dead."

"No, this is my mother. Her name is Karen Broadfort and she lives in the Bronx."

Katherine shook her head incredulously and looked to Richardson for help. "Is this true, son?"

Richardson was enjoying surprising his mother; he always had. He loved the look on her face when she was confused. "That's right, Mom. This is Bubbe."

"Oh, and how long have you known Bubbe?"

Richardson winked at his Dad. It was fun to be co-conspirators with his father. "Oh, for a long time . . . at least since Saturday." He kissed Bubbe on her cheek.

Katherine finally got it. "William!" she said. "This really is your mother!"

"The only one I've ever had."

"So where's she been all these years?"

"In her window in the Bronx."

Katherine gave up trying to make sense of any of this. She went over to Karen to shake her hand. Karen looked up at her; there were glad tears in her eyes for her son and his wife. She hugged Karen instead. Karen held onto her.

"Ya, Wilhelm. You make good choice. I like this one," Karen said.

"And," Katherine said, "I like this one, and this one, and this one." She included all three of them.

Katherine looked at William. "Does this mean there are no Bradfords of New Haven?"

"Oh," said William, "there might be, but I'm not related to them. My ancestors are the Broadforts of the Bronx. Right, Momma?"

"Ya, Wilhelm."

William went to the front of the living room. It was covered with an extravagant floor-to-ceiling drapery. He turned a control on the wall and the drapery slowly opened to reveal a double door opening onto a large outdoor patio. With the drape opened, sunlight flooded the apartment.

"So, what do you think?" William asked them.

"It will have to go. It's too ornate, too many different colors, too . . . too Italian. It reminds me of my father and my two older brothers. It goes." Katherine was referring to the drapes.

"No, Katherine, not the drapes, the view."

"Oh, the view."

He opened the double doors and stepped out on the penthouse patio and the others followed. Their building was the tallest in the area. They could look down at other buildings, but others could only look up at them. Katherine liked that. She thought of the possibilities.

He led them to the front of the patio. It overlooked Central Park and the New York skyline. The view was breathtaking even in the middle of the afternoon. On a small table they found a tray of hors d'oeuvres and an ice bucket with a bottle of champagne. There were four glasses ready to be filled. Each one took a glass. William offered a toast.

"To life and love!" he said.

William and Katherine went to the meeting at the Biddles. He loved his life, he loved this woman, he loved these people, he wanted them all to know.

They walked to the Biddles'. They were only three large blocks away. Patricia Fogerty was less than five. Katherine was going to love being here. They walked arm in arm like the young lovers they were. When they reached the Biddles' apartment, everyone else was already there. William had always been early; it wasn't like him to be late. They all looked at the two of them and understood.

Ruth Selzer was waiting when they came to the door. She hadn't realized how much she missed William. She went to hug William, but she remembered he wasn't fond of hugging so she held back tentatively. He opened his arms and she melted into them. William kept his arm around Ruth and Katherine as they went into the living room with the others.

Herm Selzer was the first to extend his hand. "William the Conqueror," he said. Ruth sat down next to Herm and she pulled William down next to her; she held his hand warmly. John and Brad were sitting together on the other side talking old Consolidated war stories. Brad had brought Mark along. He was sitting at Brad's feet. Brad had his legs around him. Mark was stroking his legs. William was glad that Brad had found love too.

Katherine was busy in the other room telling Ethel all about their new apartment. She could be like a small child sometimes; he loved her even more for that.

They all waited for William to start. He called out for Katherine and Ethel to join them. There might be something for them in this as well. William told them about his visit to The Last Hope Shelter and his talk about it with his daughter Elizabeth and her friend Tony. They had told William about the services that they offered to the homeless and the destitute. They provided shelter, room and board, but they couldn't do much to sustain their clients. They were forced to send them back to the streets so that they could provide service to others. They were always living from hand to mouth, so to speak, as funding was always insufficient. Many of their clients returned again and again hoping for help. When William had met Buddy, the downsized executive, he had the idea of starting a program to get these people back into the mainstream of life. They could then take care of themselves and not be dependent on handouts and charity. He had signed a tentative agreement on a building less than two blocks from the shelter in the Bronx. He wanted all of them to work on the project with him. They would teach them life skills, work skills, grooming skills, people skills, and so on.

"So," he said when he was done explaining his idea, "who wants in?"

"Who would want out?" Ruth asked. She looked over at Herm. "I told you there was a mensch hiding in there somewhere. So, William, when do we start?"

William explained his plan and how he thought each of them could contribute. He told them that he had spoken to Harriet Gregson and that she would be pleased to be included. William thought that Harriet could be the overall administrator running day to day operations. She would be the only real paid employee. The others agreed. He didn't expect that the project would make a lot of money, but it would make a lot of lives. The money didn't matter to any of them; the lives did. The group came up with a name for the project, The Life Light.

William looked at each of them. They were all nodding their heads enthusiastically. They were each talking about what they could contribute to the project. William let them talk; he wanted this to be their project. He was tired of being the boss and telling people what to do. He got up from his seat. "If you'll excuse us, we have a date with a sunset." Katherine looked over at him. "Who is this man?" she thought, but she didn't argue.

Ruth walked them to the door. At the door she reached up and kissed William and Katherine.

"Thank you, William, for forgiving a foolish old Jewish lady. And thank you, Katherine, for taking care of our William, in spite of him." She took Katherine's hand. "It's nice," she said, "to love the same man with you." Katherine squeezed William's hand. She couldn't agree more.

William was busy with his classes three days a week. Two mornings a week he would ride bikes with Richardson in Central Park. William enjoyed these times talking to his son, about his classes, philosophy, and his son's life. Another two days a week, he would jog in the park with Jameson and Rita. On Sunday morning, he would roller blade with Elizabeth and Tony. During his breaks at school, he would walk Elizabeth's and Tony's dogs in the park. In between these activities, William would run over to The Life Light to do whatever he could.

For the next three years, this was his routine. He and Katherine would visit the Biddles, Patricia, Rebecca, Joey or one of the children some evenings. Other evenings they might go out to dinner, go to a show or concert, or some other event. Most of the time they would stay home. William would read or complete his school assignments and then they would just be with each other. They never got tired of each other; they didn't need other people.

Katherine was spending as much time as possible at The Life Light. She was helping Harriet and Karen in the office and teaching classes on grooming, literature, and female self-image. She had also taken a part time job at the Museum of Modern Art, the thing that she wanted to do. She contributed her salary to The Life Light.

In June 1997, William graduated from the master's philosophy program at NYU. He had enjoyed the contents of the program and the stimulation with the professors and the other students. He was going to miss all this. He still had Richardson to discuss philosophy with, but it wouldn't be the same. Richardson suggested that he submit a syllabus for a course that he could teach in the undergraduate program. Richardson assured him that it would be reviewed objectively, no special treatment because he was the Chair's father. Richardson suggested a course on economics and philosophy, two subjects that William now knew well. The proposal was accepted. William was now a college professor. Who would have thought it? Karen was proud of him; her mother and father had also been college professors.

In September 1997, at the age of 57, William was poised to start his new career as a college professor. On the morning of his first class, he met Richardson in his office. Richardson assured him that he would be fine. William had never been so nervous. Richardson agreed to sit at the back of the class for the first day.

William entered the room wearing dress slacks, a dress shirt, a plain tie, and a sport jacket. It felt strange to be entering this room as the teacher when only a short while ago he was a student. A number of students were already sitting in the room. Some had been in classes with him as a student; now he was their teacher. He went to the front of the room to get ready. On the teacher's desk was the class list, there were to be over thirty students in the class. He busied himself in the front of the room looking over his notes.

When they were all in and it was time to start, he picked up the roll sheet. As he read each name, he looked to see where each student was. He nodded at those that he knew. As he was getting to the bottom of the list, he noticed Richardson entering the back of the room with someone William assumed was another student. At the end of the roll sheet, there was a handwritten name added to the list. He looked at it and looked to the back of the room. He read the name "Karen Broadfort." From the back of the room came a response, "Ya." Richardson had his arm around her. She never looked so proud.

William turned his back to the class and wrote his name on the blackboard. He stepped back and said, "My name is Wilhelm Broadfort." He looked back at his mother and winked at her. He threw his sport jacket on the desk, pulled his tie off, and opened his shirt and tossed it aside. He was wearing a tight tee shirt underneath. Some of the young girls whistled. Some of the boys whistled as well and shouted out, "Take it off, take it all off." On the front of the tee shirt was a picture of the old William in his business suit with the caption "Free Willy." "Free" was meant as a verb and a command. William turned around and displayed the back of the tee shirt as he shook his bottom. More whistles and shouts. The back of the tee shirt was a picture of William in his workout clothes with the caption "Free Willy." This time "Free" was as adjective. The class applauded.

He looked at the class and grinned. "You can call me Willy."

The class had quieted. From the back of the room came a distinctive voice with a distinctive accent. "Ya, Willy."

The rest of the class repeated, "Ya, Willy."

They all laughed, even Willy. "So, let's turn to some Plato. Life begins there."

"Ya, Willy, life begins."

The class in unison: "Ya, Willy, life begins."

William established a college scholarship fund for GED graduates of The Life Light program. Raymond, the gang leader watching Karen's house, was the first scholarship recipient. Working with William and the Selzers, Raymond was accepted on a probationary basis to NYU. Richardson was one of the primary volunteers in the GED program, and he and Raymond had become good friends. Richardson had Raymond accepted to his program at NYU based on his sponsorship. At NYU, he had Richardson and William as mentors. While Raymond attended NYU, he worked as a crew leader on the center's rehab projects. By the time he graduated, he had established, with the Selzer's help, a construction business of his own. He continued to work with the center, but he also accepted other rehab jobs on his own.

Four years after she started, Karen received her bachelor's degree at the NYU graduation ceremony; she was the oldest graduate. Richardson and William presented her with her diploma. The audience gave her a standing ovation. Richardson brought her over to the microphone to speak. Standing on her tip toes she still couldn't reach the microphone. Richardson picked her up. She looked at the crowd with tears in her eyes. The crowd applauded. She was now a college graduate just like her momma and poppa, her son, and her grandchildren.

William reserved Angelo's back room for his mother's graduation party. The room was hardly large enough, but that was where Karen wanted her party. All of the family and friends came bearing gifts even though Karen had requested that they make contributions to the center. All of the center staff and clients were invited, they all came. Karen was much loved. Raymond, who had graduated in the same class, was the co-guest of honor. He was extremely grateful for the honor and to be considered one of the family, but he was greatly concerned. He said to William, "If I'm the co-guest of honor, who's gonna watch the cars?" Raymond's building rehab business was now grossing over five million dollars a year, and Raymond had his own Mercedes that needed watching.

Richardson announced that Karen and Raymond had been accepted to the NYU graduate program. Raymond also received a minority business person of the year award from the city. He was now twenty four years old. Richardson had one more award to make. He called for his father to come up on the stage. William was pushed up reluctantly. His time for awards was long gone; it was time for others. Richardson was holding a bag in his hands. He placed William directly across from him. He handed him the bag. William reached into the bag and pulled out a plaque covered with wrapping paper. Richardson urged him to remove the paper.

William looked at the plaque and smiled to himself. He held the plaque up for all of them to see. The plaque said "The World's Greatest College Professor."

Katherine came over to see the plaque and congratulate her sweet William. She was never so proud of him. Two college professors in the family. She went to hug him. He grabbed her and kissed her passionately on the lips. He had never been able so show affection in public before; he felt released to finally be who he wanted to be. He said softly to her, "Thank you. I'll always love you."

On their way out leaving the back room, Angelo placed a note in William's hand. William assumed it was another congratulatory note from someone at the restaurant who knew him. When he looked at the note he was quite surprised. It was a note from Richard Sprague, his former CEO at Consolidated Unlimited. He had hoped to never see him again in his life. His note said that he would like to see William for a few minutes. William's first reaction was to write on the note something like "go fuck yourself" and give it to Angelo to return. But he thought to himself that if it weren't for Sprague, he wouldn't be having the life he had always wanted. Why not go talk to him? William could afford to be charitable and generous.

William showed the note to Katherine and told her he would see Sprague for a few minutes. She understood quite fully. It was really something that William had to do.

Many thoughts and visions came to William as he thought about how to handle Richard Sprague. He had been gone from Consolidated Unlimited for over seven years now, but he still felt resentment, not that he was let go, but the inhumane way in which it was done. Those bastards owed more to their employees. It was only now that William saw that.

As William followed Angelo to where Sprague was sitting, he remembered something about Sprague being eased out as CEO. Something about Sprague letting too many employees go to cut costs and raise short term stock prices. Then the bottom fell out. Consolidated couldn't compete any more; they had let go of their competencies with their employees. Ultimately, as earnings plummeted, so did Sprague. The Board of Directors let him go. William had gloated when he read about it, but only a little as he had his own life to be concerned about. Those who live by the saw, die by the saw.

Sprague was sitting alone at a small table in the back of the main restaurant. He looked the same as William had remembered him, still with a CEO's arrogant aura about him but now with some worry lines. He motioned for William to sit down in the chair across from him. Once a CEO giving orders, always a CEO giving orders. William sat down next to him so that Sprague could see clearly that William was doing well, physically and emotionally. William said nothing as he had nothing to say to this man. At this point in William's life, this man represented the enemy.

Sprague held out his hand for William to shake and said, "Hello, William. It's good to see you." Sprague would say nothing about how he treated William, and neither would William. Sprague would see nothing wrong in what he had done; it was for the good of the company. He knew that William understood that. William didn't.

William ignored his hand and said nothing. It wasn't that William wanted to be rude; he just didn't want to encourage a relationship with this man. Sprague's face automatically flinched with a facial tic. The years of pressure had not been kind to him. He had never liked William; he thought of him as a rich socialite prick. Even now when he knew differently, he couldn't change his opinion. He wouldn't have thought, however, that William could feel the same way, or worse, about him. After all he had been William's CEO and superior.

"I guess you've heard about my troubles at Consolidated." Sprague waited for a response, William gave him none. "I don't understand it. I did what I could to save the company. I gave them my life, and they did that to me." Sprague would assume no blame. William gave him and others like him all the blame.

"William, Sprague continued, "I'd like to become part of The Life Light. I hear you are doing wonderful things there."

William knew what he wanted. Sprague wanted to buy respectability after his years of being hated by his employees, his vendors, his customers, and his competitors but not his stockholders. When his stockholders turned on him he realized he was all alone. Now he wanted to make amends to society through William's center. William thought to himself, "The hell he will."

Sprague waited for William's answer. Neither one said anything. There was just an uncomfortable silence. William wanted to just get up and walk away from him. But something nagged at him. The man should pay something back.

"Richard," William said. "Would you consider an anonymous gift as a sign of good faith? I'll see what I can do to get you involved." Even if William was sincere, he knew that the others, John and Brad, would stop him. He felt safe in making the offer.

Sprague thought about this. He had plenty of money, money that he had made as a result of thousands of people losing their jobs and self respect. "How much were you thinking of?" Sprague asked William.

William thought for a moment. He knew this man had multi-millions, maybe even billions.

"Let's say two to three million." William had nothing to lose. He would rather not take this man's money, the center would survive without it, but the corporate Nazi should make some sort of reparations to his victims. He wouldn't do it without coercion, William knew that.

Sprague said nothing. He sat staring into his empty glass. This was a man who had determined the destiny of thousands. He now had his own in his hands. He took a check book out of his right jacket pocket and wrote out a check to The Life Light. He looked it over before handing it over to William. William looked at it. It was a check for five million dollars. This was an awful guilty man. William put the check in his pocket and walked away.

William found Katherine talking to Jameson and Rita, most likely about the upcoming grandchild. When Katherine saw William returning, she went over to him and held him. He looked like he used to when he worked for those damn devils. Seeing Sprague again was not good for his health, physically and mentally.

"So," Katherine asked, "how was it?" She kissed William softly on the lips, her tongue licked his lips.

"Okay, I let him ease his conscience. It was a cheap price for him to pay." William thought it was only a start. He would pay more. Society would demand it. He showed her the check.

"Oh my God! William, that's an awful lot of money. What does he want for it?"

"Involvement with The Life Light, to buy back his respectability."

"Any chance of that?" Katherine asked.

"Not by the world's greatest college professor."

"Oh, William, I'm so proud of you."

"You should be. I just made five million dollars for The Life Light for three minutes' work. That's more than I make as a college professor."

"Yes, it is, but not as rewarding," Katherine said.

" No, it isn't. Let's get out of here. I feel a need to clean up."

"And happy hour awaits."

"Yes, it does. Shall we?"

He walked out with Katherine planning to enjoy the rest of their lives happily together. His conscience was clear. He had found what he was looking for, his humanity and compassion. He had turned his anger into kindness, resentment into forgiveness, hatred into friendliness, and disgust into love. What he thought had been prejudice had become understanding. As he understood his own story, he was willing to understand others' stories. He had found that power and hostility were for cowards, and that sensitivity and fairness were for heroes. He had turned himself from a corporate Nazi into a worldly mensch. Ruth Selzer would be proud. Katherine was proud, and so was he.

They left the restaurant and went outside. They breathed in the polluted Manhattan air. It filled their lungs with the taste of freedom. It was a splendidly beautiful early evening. They decided to walk back to their apartment, taking the long way there through the park. As they walked up Fifth Avenue, hand in hand close together, the eyes of passersbys would turn to look at them. Some would look back at Katherine's walk, others at her beauty and grace; some would look at William's physique, but all would look at the lovely couple encircled in love.

They arrived home in time for their customary evening happy hour. They watched the sunset from the patio sipping their vodka tinis. Tonight, they sat at the very edge of the patio overlooking the skyline of Manhattan. They held hands, sipped on their martinis, and thought of their lives and their love. Tonight, Katherine would make slow love to the "world's greatest college professor." They smiled at each other as the sun went down on the horizon. Another day gone. They looked forward to tomorrow and the rest of their lives together. They had so much more to do and so much more to learn.

They stood up to watch the sun set behind the Manhattan skyline. They drank their normal toast to the end of another wonderful day. "To Life and

Love!" they said in unison as they clinked their glasses together. They stood and watched the sun descend behind the buildings. As the sun went down, Katherine's hand went down toward William's ass. Her hand rested across his buttocks. She looked at him and winked. His hand went over and cupped her right buttock; his hand fit perfectly, it was meant to be. He winked back. Life was indeed wonderful. He had found his way back home.